Praise for the holiday novels of Debbie Macomber

"A sweet holiday treat from Macomber has become an annual staple for many readers."

—*RT Book Reviews*

"Familiar townspeople, three impulsive brothers on the hunt, and a pair of appealing protagonists bring to life this sweet, humorous romance that, with its many obvious parallels, is a satisfying, almost tongue-in-cheek retelling of the Christmas story."

—*Library Journal* on *A Cedar Cove Christmas*

"A lighthearted, decidedly modern retelling of the Christmas story, this is vintage Macomber. Its charm and humor are balanced by the emotional impact of heroine Mary Jo's situation, and many readers will find it irresistible."

—*RT Book Reviews* on *A Cedar Cove Christmas*

"Macomber's latest charming contemporary Christmas romance is a sweetly satisfying, gently humorous story that celebrates the joy and love of the holiday season."

—*Booklist* on *Christmas Letters*

"It's just not Christmas without a Debbie Macomber story."

—*Armchair Interviews*

"No one pens a Christmas story like Macomber."

—*RT Book Reviews*

DEBBIE MACOMBER

Season of Love

mira

mira

ISBN-13: 978-0-7783-0783-9

Season of Love

Copyright © 2019 by Harlequin Books S.A.

The publisher acknowledges the copyright holder of the individual works as follows:

Thanksgiving Prayer
Copyright © 1984 by Debbie Macomber

Christmas Masquerade
Copyright © 1985 by Debbie Macomber

Recycling programs for this product may not exist in your area.

For questions and comments about the quality of this book, please contact us at CustomerService@Harlequin.com.

Harlequin.com

Printed in U.S.A.

Also available from Debbie Macomber and MIRA Books

CONTENTS

THANKSGIVING PRAYER

In memory of Marie Macomber,
mother-in-law extraordinaire.

One

The radiant blue heavens drew Claudia Masters's eyes as she boarded the jet for Nome, Alaska. Her heart rate accelerated with excitement. In less than two hours she would be with Seth—manly, self-assured, masterful Seth. She made herself comfortable and secured the seat belt, anticipating the rumble of the engines that would thrust the plane into the air.

She had felt some uncertainty when she boarded the plane that morning in Seattle. But she'd hastily placed a phone call during her layover in Anchorage and been assured by Seth's assistant that yes, he had received her message, and yes, he would meet her at the airport. Confident now, Claudia relaxed and idly flipped through a magazine.

A warmth, a feeling of contentment, filled her. Cooper's doubts and last-ditch effort to change her mind were behind her now, and she was free to make her life with Seth.

Cooper had been furious with her decision to leave medical school. But he was only her uncle. He hadn't understood her love for her Alaskan oilman, just as he couldn't understand her faith in the Lord.

A smile briefly curved her soft mouth upward. Cooper had shown more emotion in that brief twenty-minute visit to his office than she'd seen in all her twenty-five years.

"Quitting med school is the dumbest idea I've ever heard," he'd growled, his keen brown eyes challenging the serene blue of hers.

"Sometimes loving someone calls for unusual behavior," she had countered, knowing anything impractical was foreign to her uncle.

For a moment all Cooper could do was stare at her. She could sense the anger drain from him as he lowered himself into the desk chair.

"Contrary to what you may believe, I have your best interests at heart. I see you throwing away years of study for some ignorant lumberjack. Can you blame me for doubting your sanity?"

"Seth's an oilman, not a lumberjack. There aren't any native trees in Nome." It was easier to correct Cooper than to answer the questions that had plagued her, filling her with doubts. The choice hadn't been easy; indecision had tormented her for months. Now that she'd decided to marry Seth and share his life in the Alaskan wilderness, a sense of joy and release had come over her.

"It's taken me two miserable months to realize that my future isn't in any hospital," she continued. "I'd be a rotten doctor if I couldn't be a woman first. I love Seth. Someday I'll finish medical school, but if a decision has to be made, I'll choose Seth Lessinger every time."

But Cooper had never been easily won over. The tense atmosphere became suddenly quiet as he digested the thought. He expelled his breath, but it was several seconds before he spoke. "I'm not thinking of myself, Claudia. I want you to be absolutely sure you know what you're doing."

"I am," she replied with complete confidence.

Now, flying high above the lonely, barren Alaska tundra, Claudia continued to be confident she was doing the right thing. God had confirmed the decision. Seth had known from the beginning, but it had taken her much longer to realize the truth.

Gazing out the plane window, she viewed miles upon miles of the frozen, snow-covered ground. It was just as Seth had described: a treeless plain of crystalline purity. There would be a summer, he'd promised, days that ran into each other when the sun never set. Flowers would blossom, and for a short time the tundra would explode into a grassy pasture. Seth had explained many things about life in the North. At first she'd resented his letters, full of enticements to lure her to Nome. If he really loved her, she felt, he should be willing to relocate in Seattle until she'd completed her studies. It wasn't so much to ask. But as she came to know and love Seth, it became evident that Nome was more than the location of his business. It was a way of life, Seth's life. Crowded cities, traffic jams and shopping malls would suffocate him.

She should have known that the minute she pushed the cleaning cart into the motel room. Her being a housekeeper at the Wilderness Motel had been something of a miracle in itself.

Leaning back, Claudia slowly lowered her lashes as the memories washed over her.

Ashley Robbins, her lifetime friend and roommate, had been ill—far too sick to spend the day cleaning rooms. By the time Ashley admitted as much, it was too late to call the motel and tell them she wouldn't be coming to work, so Claudia had volunteered to go in her place.

Claudia had known from the moment she slid the pass key into the lock that there was something different, something special, about this room.

Her hands rested on her slender hips as she looked around. A single man slept here. She smiled as she realized how accurate she was becoming at describing the occupants of each room, and after just one day. She was having fun speculating. Whoever was staying in here had slept uneasily. The sheet and blankets were pulled free of the mattress and rumpled haphazardly at the foot of the king-size bed.

As she put on the clean sheets, she couldn't help wondering what Cooper would think if he could see her now. He would be aghast to know she was doing what he would call "menial work."

As she lifted the corner of the mattress to tuck in the blanket, she noticed an open Bible on the nightstand, followed by the sudden feeling that she wasn't alone. As she turned around, a smile lit up her sky-blue eyes. But her welcome died: no one was there.

After finishing the bed, she plugged in the vacuum. With the flip of the switch the motor roared to life. A minute later she had that same sensation of being watched, and she turned off the machine. But when she turned, she once again discovered she was alone.

Pausing, she studied the room. There was something about this place: not the room itself, but the occupant. She could sense it, feel it: a sadness that seemed to reach out and touch her, wrapping itself around her. She wondered why she was receiving these strange sensations. Nothing like this had ever happened to her before.

A prayer came to her lips as she silently petitioned God on behalf of whoever occupied this room. When she finished she released a soft sigh. Once, a long time ago, she remembered reading that no one could come to the Lord unless someone prayed for them first. She wasn't sure how scriptural that was, but the thought had stuck with her. Often she found herself offering silent prayers for virtual strangers.

After cleaning the bathroom and placing fresh towels on the rack, she began to wheel the cleaning cart into the hallway. Again she paused, brushing wisps of copper-colored hair from her forehead as she examined the room. She hadn't forgotten anything, had she? Everything looked right. But again that terrible sadness seemed to reach out to her.

Leaving the cart, she moved to the desk and took out a postcard and a pen from the drawer. In large, bold letters she printed one of her favorite verses from Psalms. It read: "May the Lord give you the desire of your heart and make all your plans succeed." Psalm 20:4. She didn't question why that particular verse had come to mind. It didn't offer solace, even though she had felt unhappiness here. Perplexed and a little unsure, she tucked the card into the corner of the dresser mirror.

Back in the hall, she checked to be sure the door had locked automatically. Her back ached. Ashley hadn't been kidding when she said this was hard work. It was that and more. She was so glad that had been her final room for the day. A thin sheen of perspiration covered Claudia's brow, and she pushed her thick, naturally curly hair from her face. Her attention was still focused on the door when she began wheeling the cart toward the elevator. She hadn't gone more than a few feet when she struck something. A quick glance upward told her that she'd run into a man.

"I'm so sorry," she apologized immediately. "I wasn't watching where I was going." Her first impression was that this was the largest, most imposing man she'd ever seen. He loomed above her, easily a foot taller than her five-foot-five frame. His shoulders were wide, his waist and hips lean, and he was so muscular that the material of his shirt was pulled taut across his broad chest. He was handsome in a reckless-looking way, his hair magnificently dark. His well-trimmed beard was a shade lighter.

"No problem." The stranger smiled, his mouth sensuous and appealing, his eyes warm.

Claudia liked that. He might be big, but one look told her he was a gentle giant.

Not until she was in her car did she realize she hadn't watched to see if the giant had entered the room where she'd gotten such a strange feeling.

By the time Claudia got back to the apartment, Ashley looked better. She was propped against the arm of the sofa, her back cushioned by several pillows. A hand-knit afghan covered her, and a box of tissues sat on the coffee table, the crumpled ones littering the polished surface.

"How'd it go?" she asked, her voice scratchy and unnatural. "Were you able to figure out one end of the vacuum from the other?"

"Of course." Claudia laughed. "I had fun playing house, but next time warn me—I broke my longest nail."

"That's the price you pay for being so stubborn," Ashley scolded as she grabbed a tissue, anticipating a sneeze. "I told you it was a crazy idea. Did old Burns say anything?"

"No, she was too grateful. Finding a replacement this late in the day would have been difficult."

Fall classes at the University of Washington had resumed that Monday, and Ashley had been working at the motel for only a couple of weeks, one of the two part-time jobs she had taken to earn enough to stay in school.

Claudia knew Ashley had been worried about losing the job, so she'd been happy to step in and help. Her own tuition and expenses were paid by a trust fund her father had established before his death. She had offered to lend Ashley money on numerous occasions, but her friend had stubbornly refused. Ashley believed that if God wanted her to have a degree in education, then He would provide the necessary money. Apparently He did want that for her, because the funds were always there when she needed them.

Ashley's unshakable faith had taught Claudia valuable lessons. She had been blessed with material wealth, while Ashley struggled from one month to the next.

But of the two of them, Claudia considered Ashley the richer.

Claudia often marveled at her friend's faith. Everything had been taken care of in her own life. Decisions had been made for her. As for her career, she'd known from the time she was in grade school that she would be a doctor, a dream shared by her father. The last Christmas before his death he'd given her a stethoscope. Later she realized that he must have known he wouldn't be alive to see their dream fulfilled. Now there was only Cooper, her pompous, dignified uncle.

"How are you feeling?"

Ashley sneezed into a tissue, which did little to muffle the sound. "Better," she murmured, her eyes red and watery. "I should be fine by tomorrow. I don't want you to have to fill in for me again."

"We'll see," Claudia said, hands on her hips. Ashley was so stubborn, she mused—she seemed to be surrounded by strong-willed people.

Later that night she lay in bed, unable to sleep. She hadn't told Ashley about what had happened in the last room she'd cleaned. She didn't know how she could explain it to anyone. Now she wished she'd waited to see if the stranger outside had been the one occupying that room. The day had been unusual in more ways than one. With a yawn, she rolled over and forced herself to relax and go to sleep.

The clouds were gray and thick the next morning. Claudia was up and reading over some material from one of her classes when Ashley strolled into the living room, looking just as miserable as she had the day before.

"Don't you ever let up?" she complained with a long yawn. "I swear, all you do is study. Take a break. You've got all quarter to hit the books."

With deliberate slowness Claudia closed the textbook. "Do you always wake up so cheerful?"

"Yes," Ashley snapped. "Especially when I feel I could be dying. You're going to be a doctor—do something!"

Claudia brandished the thick book, which happened to be on psychology. "All right," she said. "Take two aspirin, drink lots of liquids and stay in bed. I'll check on you later."

"Wonderful," Ashley murmured sarcastically as she stumbled back into her bedroom. "And for this she goes to medical school."

A half hour later Claudia tapped lightly before letting herself into Ashley's bedroom. "Feel any better?"

"A little." Ashley spoke in a tight voice. She was curled into a ball as if every bone ached.

"You probably have a touch of the flu to go along with that rotten cold."

"This isn't a touch," Ashley insisted vehemently. "This is a full-scale beating. Why did this have to happen to me now?"

"Don't ask me," Claudia said, as she set a tray of tea and toast on the nightstand. "But have you ever stopped to think that maybe your body has decided it needs a rest? You're going to kill yourself working at the motel and the bookstore, plus doing all your course-

work. Something's got to give, and in this instance it's
your health. I think you should take warning."

"Uh-oh, here it comes." Ashley groaned and rolled
over, placing the back of her hand to her forehead. "I
wondered how long it would take to pull your corny
doctor routine on me."

"It's not corny." Claudia's blue eyes flashed. "Don't
you recognize good advice when you hear it?"

Ashley gestured weakly with her hand. "That's the
problem, I guess. I don't."

"Well, trust me. This advice is good," Claudia said
and fluffed up a pillow so Ashley could sit up comfortably.

"I'm better, honest," Ashley said and coughed.
"Good enough to work. I hate the thought of you breaking another fingernail."

"Sure you do, Ash, sure you do."

Claudia wheeled the cleaning cart from one room to
the next without incident. The small of her back ached,
and she paused to rub it. She hadn't exactly done much
housecleaning in her life.

Her fingers trembled when she inserted the pass key
into the final room—the same one she had finished
with yesterday. Would she feel the same sensations as
before? Or had it all been her imagination? The room
looked almost identical to the way it had yesterday. The
sheets and blankets were rumpled at the foot of the bed,
as if the man had once again slept restlessly.

Her attention flew to the mirror, and she was pleased
to note that the card was gone. Slowly she walked
around the room, waiting to feel the sensations she'd

had yesterday, but whatever she had felt then was gone. Maybe she had conjured up the whole thing in her mind. The brain could do things like that. She should know. She'd studied enough about the human mind these past couple of years.

She was placing the fresh white towels in the bathroom when a clicking noise was followed by the sound of the door opening.

She stiffened, her fingers nervously toying with the towel as she pretended to straighten it.

"Hello." The male voice came from behind her, rich and deep.

"Hello," she mumbled and managed a smile as she turned. The man she had bumped into yesterday was framed in the doorway. Somehow she had known this was his room. "I'll be out of your way in a minute."

"No," he insisted. "Don't go. I want to talk to you."

Turning away from him, she moistened her suddenly parched lips.

"Do I frighten you?" he asked.

Claudia realized that his size probably intimidated a lot of people. "No," she answered honestly. This man could probably lift a refrigerator by himself, yet he wouldn't hurt an ant. She wasn't sure how she knew that, but she did.

"Are you the one who left this?" He pulled the card she'd placed in the mirror from his shirt pocket.

Numbly she nodded. She didn't know anything about motel policy. What if she'd gotten Ashley into trouble?

His thick brows lifted, as if he'd expected more than a simple movement of her head. "Why?" The single word seemed to be hurled at her.

"I...I don't really know," she began weakly, surprised at how feeble her voice sounded. "If it offended you, then please accept my apology."

"I wasn't displeased," he assured her. "But I was a little curious about your reasons." He released her gaze as he put the card back into his shirt pocket. "Do you do this often?"

Claudia looked away uneasily. "No. Never before."

His dark eyes narrowed on her. "Do you think we could have a cup of coffee somewhere when you're through? I really would like to talk to you."

"I..." She looked down at the uniform skirt the motel had provided and noticed a couple of smudges.

"You look fine."

No doubt he assumed she did this full-time, which made his invitation into an interesting opportunity. So many times she had wished she could meet someone without the fear of intimidating him with her brains and financial situation. Although she wasn't an heir to millions, she would receive a large sum of cash at age thirty or the day she married—whichever came first.

"I'd like that." Obviously this stranger needed to speak to someone. The open Bible on his nightstand had convinced her that he was a Christian. Was it because he was lonely that she had felt that terrible sadness in the room? No, she was sure it was more than loneliness—a lot more.

"Can we meet someplace?" he suggested. "There's a coffee shop around the corner."

"Fine," she said, and nodded, knowing Cooper would have a fit if he knew what she was doing. "I can be ready in about twenty minutes."

"I'll see you there." He stepped aside, and she could feel him studying her as she moved back toward her cart. What was the matter with her? She had never done anything as impulsive as agreeing to meet a stranger for coffee.

Finished for the day, Claudia returned the cart to Mrs. Burns, who thanked her for helping out again. Next she made a stop in the ladies' room. One glance in the mirror made her groan at her reflection. Her hair was an unruly auburn mass. She took the brush from her purse and ran it through her long curls until they practically sparked with electricity. Her thick, naturally curly hair had always been a problem. For several years now she had kept it long and tied away from her face with a ribbon at the base of her neck. When she first applied and was accepted into medical school, she'd been determined to play down her femininity. Women weren't the rarity they once were, but she didn't want her gender, combined with her money, to prejudice any of her classmates against her. There had been some tension her first year, but she had long since proved herself.

The coffee shop was crowded, but her searching gaze instantly located the stranger, who towered head and shoulders above everyone else. Even when he was sitting down, his large, imposing build couldn't be disguised. Weaving her way between chairs, she sauntered toward him.

The welcome in his smile warmed her. He stood and pulled out a chair for her. She noticed that he chose the one beside him, as if he wanted her as close as possible. The thought didn't disturb her, but her reaction to him did. She wanted to be close to him.

"I suddenly realized I don't know your name," she said after sitting down.

"Seth Lessinger." He lifted a thick eyebrow in silent inquiry. "And yours?"

"Claudia Masters."

"I'm surprised they don't call you Red with that hair."

In any other family she might well have been tagged with the nickname, but not in hers. "No, no one ever has." Her voice sounded strangely husky. To hide her discomfort, she lifted the menu and began studying it, although she didn't want anything more than coffee.

The waitress arrived, and Claudia placed her order, adding an English muffin at Seth's urging. He asked for a club sandwich.

"What brings you to Seattle?" Claudia asked once the waitress was gone. She found herself absently smoothing a wrinkle from the skirt.

"A conference."

"Are you enjoying the Emerald City?" She was making small talk to cover up her nervousness. Maybe meeting a strange man like this wasn't such a good idea after all.

"Very much. It's my first visit to the Northwest, and I'll admit, it's nicer than I expected. Big cities tend to intimidate me. I never have understood how anyone can live like this, surrounded by so many people."

Claudia didn't mean to smile, but amusement played at the edges of her mouth. "Where are you from? Alaska?" She'd meant it as a joke and was surprised when he nodded in confirmation.

"Nome," he supplied. "Where the air is pure and the skies are blue."

"You make it sound lovely."

"It's not," he told her with a half-smile. "It can be dingy and gray and miserable, but it's home."

Her coffee arrived, and she cupped the mug, grateful to have something to do with her hands.

He seemed to be studying her, and when their gazes clashed, a lazy smile flickered from the dark depths of his eyes.

"What do you do in Nome?" she asked to distract herself from the fact that his look was disturbingly like a gentle caress. Not that it made her uncomfortable; the effect was quite the opposite. He touched a softness in her, a longing to be the woman she had denied for so long.

"I'm a commissioning agent for a major oil company."

"That sounds interesting." She knew the words came out stiff and stilted.

"It's definitely the right job for me. What about you?"

"Student at the University of Washington." She didn't elaborate.

A frown creased the wide brow. "You look older than a college student."

She ignored that and focused her gaze on the black coffee. "How long will you be in Seattle?"

If he noticed she was disinclined to talk about herself, he didn't say anything. "I'll be flying back in a few days. I'd like to be home by the end of the week."

A few days, her mind echoed. She would remember to pray for him. She believed that God brought everyone into her life for a specific reason. The purpose of her meeting Seth might be for her to remember to pray for him. He certainly had made an impression on her.

"How long have you been a Christian?" he inquired.

"Five years." That was another thing Cooper had never understood. He found this "religious interest" of hers amusing. "And you?" Again she directed the conversation away from herself.

"Six months. I'm still an infant in the Lord, although my size disputes that!" He smiled, and Claudia felt mesmerized by the warmth in his eyes.

She returned his smile, suddenly aware that he was as defensive about his size as she was about her money and her brains.

"So why *did* you leave that Bible verse on the mirror?"

This was the crux of his wanting to talk to her. How could she explain? "Listen, I've already apologized for that. I realize it's probably against the motel policy."

A hand twice the size of her own reached over the table and trapped hers. "Claudia." The sound of her name was low-pitched and reassuring. "Don't apologize. Your message meant more to me than you can possibly realize. My intention is to thank you for it."

His dark, mysterious eyes studied hers. Again Claudia sensed more than saw a sadness, a loneliness, in him. She made a show of glancing at her watch. "I...I really should be going."

"Can I see you again? Tomorrow?"

She'd been afraid he was going to ask her that. And also afraid that he wouldn't.

"I was planning on doing some grocery shopping at the Pike Place Market tomorrow," she said without accepting or refusing.

"We could meet somewhere." His tone held a faint challenge. At the same time, he sounded almost unsure.

Claudia had the impression there wasn't much that unsettled this man. She wondered what it was about her that made him uncertain.

"All right," she found herself agreeing. "But I feel I'd better warn you, if you find large cities stifling, downtown Seattle at that time of the day may be an experience you'd rather avoid."

"Not this time," he said with a chuckle.

They set a time and place as Seth walked her back to the motel lot, where she'd left her car. She drove a silver compact, even though Cooper had generously given her a fancy sports car when she was accepted into medical school. She'd never driven it around campus and kept it in one of Cooper's garages. Not that she didn't appreciate the gift. The car was beautiful, and a dream to drive, but she already had her compact and couldn't see the need for two cars. Not when one of them would make her stand out and draw unnecessary and unwanted attention. Never had she been more grateful for the decision she'd made than she was now, though. At least she wouldn't have to explain to Seth why a hotel housekeeper was driving a car that cost as much as she made in a year.

"Hi," Claudia said later as she floated into the apartment, a Cheshire Cat grin on her face.

"Wow!" Ashley exclaimed from the sofa. "You look like you've just met Prince Charming."

"I have." Claudia dropped her purse on the end table and sat on the sofa arm opposite the end where Ashley was resting. "He's about this tall." She held her hand high above her head. "With shoulders this wide." She held her hands out ridiculously wide to demonstrate. "And he has the most incredible dark eyes."

"Oh, honestly, Claudia, that's not Prince Charming. That's the Incredible Hulk," Ashley admonished.

Claudia tilted her head to one side, a slow smile spreading over her mouth. "'Incredible' is the word, all right."

Not until the following morning, when Claudia dressed in her best designer jeans and cashmere sweater, with knee-high leather boots, did Ashley take her seriously.

"You really did meet someone yesterday, didn't you?"

Claudia nodded, pouring steaming cocoa into a mug. "Want some?"

"Sure," Ashley said, then hesitated. "When did you have the chance? The only place you've been is school and—" she paused, her blue eyes widening "—the Wilderness and back. Claudia," she gasped, "it isn't someone from the motel, is it?"

Two pieces of toast blasted from the toaster with the force of a skyrocket. Deftly Claudia caught them in the air. "Yup."

For the first time in recent history, Ashley was speechless. "But, Claudia, you can't...I mean...all kinds of people stay there. He could be *anyone*..."

"Seth isn't just anyone. He *is* a big guy, but he's gentle and kind. And I like him."

"I can tell," Ashley murmured with a worried look pinching her face.

"Don't look so shocked. Women have met men in stranger ways. I'm seeing him this afternoon. I told him I have some grocery shopping to do." When she saw the glare Ashley was giving her, Claudia felt obliged to add, "Well, I do. I wanted to pick up some fresh vegetables. I was just reading an article on the importance of fiber in the diet."

"We bought a whole month's worth of food last Saturday," Ashley mumbled under her breath.

"True." Claudia shrugged, then picked up a light jacket. "But I think we could use some fresh produce. I'll be sure and pick up some prunes for you."

Seth was standing on the library steps waiting when Claudia arrived. Again she noted his compelling male virility. She waited at the bottom of the stairs for him to join her. The balmy September breeze coming off Puget Sound teased her hair, blowing auburn curls across her cheek. He paused, standing in front of her, his eyes smiling deeply into hers.

The mesmerizing quality of his gaze held her motionless. Her hand was halfway to her face to remove the lock of maverick hair, but it, too, was frozen by the warmth in his look, which seemed to reach out and caress her. She had neither the will nor the desire to glance away.

The rough feel of his callused hand removing the hair brought her out of the trance. "Hello, Claudia."

"Seth."

"You're beautiful." The words appeared to come involuntarily.

"So are you," she joked. The musky scent of his aftershave drifted pleasantly toward her, and an unwilling sigh broke from between her slightly parted lips.

Someone on the busy sidewalk bumped into Claudia, throwing her off balance. Immediately Seth reached out protectively and pulled her close. The iron band of his arm continued to hold her against him far longer than necessary. His touch warmed her through the thin jacket. No man had ever been able to awaken this kind of feeling in her. This was uncanny, unreal.

Two

"Are you ready to call it quits?" Claudia asked. Seth had placed a guiding hand on her shoulder, and she wondered how long his touch would continue to produce the warm, glowing sensation spreading down her spine.

"More than ready," he confirmed.

The Pike Place Market in the heart of downtown Seattle had always been a hub of activity as tourists and everyday shoppers vied for the attention of the vendors displaying their wares. The two of them had strolled through the market, their hands entwined. Vegetables that had been hand-picked that morning were displayed on long tables, while the farmers shouted their virtues, enticing customers to their booths. The odd but pleasant smell of tangy spices and fresh fish had drifted agreeably around them.

"I did warn you," she said with a small laugh. "What's the life expectancy of someone from Nome, Alaska, in a crowd like this?"

Seth glanced at his watch. "About two hours," he

said. "And we've been at it nearly that. Let's take a break."

"I agree."

"Lunch?"

Claudia nodded. She hadn't eaten after her last class, hurrying instead to meet Seth. Now she realized she was hungry. "Sounds good."

"Chinese okay?"

For once it was a pleasure to have someone take her out and not try to impress her with the best restaurant in town, or how much money he could spend. "Yes, that's fine."

He paused. "You sure?"

She squeezed his hand. "Very sure. And I know just the place."

They rode the city bus to Seattle's International District and stepped off into another world. Seth looked around in surprise. "I didn't know Seattle had a Chinatown."

"Chinatown, Little Italy, Mexico, all within a few blocks. Interesting, isn't it?"

"Very."

They lingered over their tea, delaying as long as possible their return to the hectic pace of the world outside.

"Why do you have a beard?" Claudia asked curiously. She didn't mean to be abrupt, but his beard fascinated her—it looked so soft—and the question slipped out before she could stop herself.

Seth looked surprised by the question, rubbing the dark hair in question with one hand as he spoke. "Does it bother you? I can always shave it off."

"Oh, no," she protested instantly. "I like it. Very much. But I've always been curious why some men choose to grow their beards."

"I can't speak for anyone else, but my beard offers some protection to my face during the long winter months," he explained.

His quick offer to shave it off had shocked Claudia with the implication that he would do it for her. She couldn't understand his eagerness.

"I've about finished my shopping. What about you?" She hated to torture him further.

The tiny teacup was dwarfed by his massive hands. "I was finished a long time ago."

"Want to take a walk along the waterfront and ride the trolley?" she suggested, looking for reasons to prolong their time together.

"I'd like that."

While Seth paid for their meal she excused herself to reapply her lipstick and comb her hair. Then, hand in hand, they walked the short distance back to the heart of downtown Seattle. They paused in front of a department store to study a window display in autumn colors.

Her eyes were laughing into his when he placed a possessive hand around her waist, drawing her close to his side. Then they stepped away from the window and started down the street toward the waterfront.

It was then that Claudia spotted Cooper walking on the opposite side of the street. Even from this distance she could see his disapproving scowl, and she felt the blood drain from her face. The differences between these two men were so striking that to make a comparison struck her as ludicrous.

"I'll get us a taxi," Seth suggested, his eyes showing concern. "I've been walking your legs off." Apparently he thought her pale face was the result of the
brisk pace he'd set.

"No, I'd rather walk," she insisted, and reached for
his hand. "If we hurry, we can make this light."

Their hands were still linked when she began to run
toward the corner. There had never been any chance of
their reaching the crosswalk before the light changed,
but even so, she hurried between the busy shoppers.

"Claudia." Seth stopped, placing his arm over her
shoulders, his wide brow creased with concern. "What's
the matter?"

"Nothing," she said hesitantly, looking around. She
was certain Cooper had seen them, and she didn't want
him to ruin things. "Really, let's go." Her voice was
raised and anxious.

"Claudia."

Cooper's voice coming from behind her stopped her
heart.

"Introduce me to your friend," he said in a crisp,
businesslike tone.

Frustration washed over her. Cooper would take one
look at Seth and condemn him as one of the fortune
hunters he was always warning her about.

"Cooper Masters, this is Seth Lessinger." She made
the introduction grudgingly.

The two men eyed each other shrewdly while exchanging handshakes.

"Masters," Seth repeated. "Are you related to Claudia?"

Cooper ignored the question, instead turning toward

Claudia. "I'll pick you up for dinner Sunday at about two. If that's convenient?"

"It was fine last week and the week before, so why should it be any different this week?"

Her uncle flashed her an impatient glance.

"Who is this man?" Seth asked, the look in his eyes almost frightening. Anger darkened his face. He dropped his hand to his side, and she noted how his fist was clenched until his knuckles turned white.

Claudia watched, stunned. *He thinks I'm Cooper's wife.* Placing a hand on his forearm, she implored, "Seth, let me explain."

He shook his arm free. "You don't need to say anything more. I understand. Do you do this kind of thing often? Is this how you get your thrills?"

For a moment she was speechless, the muscles of her throat paralyzed with anger. "You don't understand. Cooper's my uncle."

"And I believe in Santa Claus," Seth returned sarcastically.

"I've warned you about men like this," Cooper said at the same time.

"Will you please be quiet!" she shouted at him.

"There's no excuse for you to talk to me in such a tone," Cooper countered in a huff.

People were beginning to stare, but she didn't care. "He really is my uncle." Desperately her eyes pleaded with Seth, asking for understanding and the chance to explain. *His* eyes were dark, clouded and unreasonable.

"You don't want to hear, do you?" she asked him.

"We definitely need to have a discussion, Claudia," Cooper interrupted again.

"You're right, I don't." Seth took a step away from her.

Claudia breathed in sharply, the rush of oxygen making her lungs hurt. She bit her lip as Seth turned and walked away. His stride was filled with purpose, as if he couldn't get away from her fast enough.

"You've really done it this time," she flared at her uncle.

"Really, Claudia," he said with a relieved look. "That type of man is most undesirable."

"That man—" she pointed at Seth's retreating figure "—is one of the most desirable men I've ever known." Without waiting for his response, she turned and stalked away.

An hour later, Claudia was banging pans around in the kitchen. Ashley came through the front door and paused, watching her for a moment. "What's wrong?"

"Nothing," Claudia responded tersely.

"Oh, come on. I always know when you're upset, because you bake something."

"That's so I can eat it."

Ashley scanned the ingredients that lined the counter. "Chocolate chip cookies," she murmured. "This must really be bad. I'm guessing you had another run-in with Cooper?"

"Right again," Claudia snapped.

"You don't want to talk about it?"

"That's a brilliant deduction." With unnecessary force, she cracked two eggs against the mixing bowl.

"You want me to quit interrogating you, huh?"

Claudia paused, closing her eyes as the waves of impatience rippled over her. "Yes, please."

"All right, all right. I'm leaving."

Soon the aroma of freshly baked cookies filled the apartment, though Claudia didn't notice. Almost automatically she lifted the cookies from the baking sheet and placed them on a wire rack to cool.

"I can't stand it anymore." Ashley stumbled into the kitchen dramatically. "If you don't want to talk, fine, but at least let me have a cookie."

Claudia sighed, placed four on a plate and set it on the kitchen table.

Ashley poured herself a tall glass of milk and sat down, her eyes following Claudia's movements. "Feel like talking now?" she asked several minutes later. There was a sympathetic tone in her voice that came from many years of friendship.

Ashley had been Claudia's only friend as a child. Ashley's mother had been Claude Masters's cook and housekeeper, and she had brought her daughter with her to keep the lonely Claudia company. The two of them had been best friends ever since.

"It's Seth," Claudia admitted and sighed, taking a chair opposite Ashley.

"Seth? Oh, the guy you met at the motel. What happened?"

"We ran into Cooper, and he had a fit of righteous indignation over seeing me with someone who wasn't wearing a business suit and a silk tie. To complicate matters, Seth apparently thought Cooper and I were married, or at least used to be. He didn't wait for an explanation."

Ashley's look was thoughtful. "You really like him, don't you?"

Claudia worried the soft flesh of her bottom lip. "Yes," she said simply. "I like him very much."

"If he's so arrogant that he wouldn't wait for you to explain, then I'd say it was his loss," Ashley said, attempting to comfort her.

"No." Claudia shook her head and lowered her gaze to the tabletop. "In this case, I think I'm the one who lost."

"I don't think I've ever heard you talk this way about a man. What makes him so special?"

Claudia's brow furrowed in concentration. "I'm not really sure. He's more attractive than any man I can remember, but it's not his looks. Or not only his looks, anyway." She smiled. "He's a rare man." She paused to formulate her thoughts. "Strong and intelligent."

"You know all this and you've only seen him twice?" Ashley sounded shocked.

"No." Claudia hung her head, and her long auburn curls fell forward to hide her expression. "I sensed more than I saw, and even then, I'm only skimming the surface. This man is deep."

"If he's so willing to jump to conclusions, I'd say it's his own fault—"

"Ashley, please," Claudia interrupted. "Don't. I know you're trying to make me feel better, but I'd appreciate it if you didn't."

"All right." Ashley was quiet for a long time. After a while she took a chocolate chip cookie and handed it to Claudia.

With a weak smile, Claudia accepted the cookie. "Now, that's what I need."

They talked for a while, but it wasn't until they headed into the living room that Claudia noticed Ashley's suitcase in front of the door.

"You're going away?"

"Oh, I almost forgot. I talked to Mom this morning, and she wants me home for a few days. Jeff and John have the flu, and she needs someone there so she can go to work. I shouldn't be any more than a couple of days, and luckily I'm not on the schedule to work until the weekend. You don't mind, do you?"

"Not at all," Claudia said with a smile. Although Ashley's family lived in the nearby suburb of Kent, Ashley shared the apartment with Claudia because it was easier for her to commute to school. But she occasionally moved back home for a few days when her family needed her.

"You're sure you'll be all right?"

"Are you kidding?" Claudia joked. "The kitchen's full of cookies!"

Ashley laughed, but her large blue eyes contained a knowing look. "Don't be too hard on Cooper," she said, and gave Claudia a small hug before she left.

What good would it do to be angry with her uncle? Claudia thought. He had reacted the only way he knew how. Anger wouldn't help the situation.

The apartment felt large and lonely with Ashley gone. Claudia turned on the television and flipped through the channels, hoping to find something interesting, feeling guilty because she was ignoring her schoolwork. Nothing interesting on. Good, she decided, and forced herself to hit the books. This quarter wasn't going to be easy, and the sooner she sharpened her study habits, the better.

Two hours later she took a leisurely bath, dressed in a long purple velour robe, curled up on the sofa and lost herself in a good book. Long ago she'd recognized that reading was her escape. When things were really bothering her, she would plow through one mystery after another, not really caring about the characters or the plot so long as the book was complicated enough to distract her from her troubles.

The alarm rang at six, and she stumbled out of bed, then stepped into the shower. As she stood under the hot spray, her thoughts drifted to Seth Lessinger. She felt definitely regretful at the way things had ended. She would have liked to get to know him better. On Sunday she would definitely have a talk with Cooper. She was old enough to choose who she wanted to date without his interference. It was bad enough being forced to endure a stilted dinner with him every Sunday afternoon.

She dressed in jeans, a long-sleeved blouse and a red sweater vest. As she poured herself a cup of coffee, she wondered how long she would have to force thoughts of Seth from her mind. The mystery novel had diverted her attention last night, but she couldn't live her life with her nose in a book. Today and tomorrow she would be busy with school, but this was Thursday, and she wasn't looking forward to spending the evenings and weekend alone. She decided to ask a friend in her psych class if she wanted to go to a movie tonight.

She sat sipping from her mug at the kitchen table, her

feet propped on the opposite chair, and read the morning paper. A quick look at her watch and she placed the cup in the sink and hurried out the door for school.

Claudia pulled into the apartment parking lot early that afternoon. It seemed everyone had already made plans for this evening, so she was on her own. Several of her friends were attending the Seahawks game. She loved football, and decided to microwave popcorn and watch the game on television. She had no sooner let herself into the apartment and hung up her jacket when the doorbell rang.

The peephole in the door showed an empty hall. Odd, but it could be her neighbor's son collecting for the jogathon. Claudia had sponsored the ten-year-old, who was trying to earn enough money for a soccer uniform. Todd had probably seen her pull into the parking lot. She opened the door and looked out into the hallway.

"Claudia?" There was surprise in his tone as he stepped away from the wall he'd been leaning on.

"Seth." Her heart tripped over itself.

"What are you doing here?" they both asked at the same time.

Claudia smiled. It was so good to see him, it didn't matter what had brought him here.

"I was looking for Ashley Robbins, the motel maid," he told her.

"Ashley?" Her curiosity was evident in her voice. "Come in," she said, then closed the door after him. "Ashley's gone home for a few days to help out her parents. Do you know her?"

"No." He stroked the side of his beard. "But I was hoping she could tell me how to find you."

"We're roommates," she explained, no doubt unnecessarily. "So…you were looking for me? Why?"

He looked slightly ill at ease. "I wanted to apologize for yesterday. I could at least have stayed and listened to your explanation."

"Cooper really is my uncle."

"I should have known you wouldn't lie. It wasn't until later that I realized I'd behaved like an idiot," he said, his face tight and drawn. "If I hadn't reacted like a jealous fool, I would have realized you would never lead anyone on like that."

"I know what you thought." She paused and glanced away. "And I know how it looked—how Cooper wanted it to look."

Seth ran a hand over his face. "Your uncle." He chuckled. Wrapping his arms around her, he lifted her off the ground and swung her around. Hands resting on the hard muscles of his shoulders, she threw back her head and laughed.

Soon the amusement died as their gazes met and held. Slowly he released her until her feet had securely settled on the carpet. With infinite gentleness, his hand brushed her face, caressing her smooth skin. It was so beautiful, so sweet, that she closed her eyes to the sensuous assault. Her fingers clung to his arms as he drew her into his embrace, and her lips trembled, anticipating his kiss.

Seth didn't disappoint either of them as his mouth settled firmly over hers. His hand slid down her back, molding her against him, arching her upward to meet the demand of his kiss.

Claudia felt her limbs grow weak as she surrendered to the sensations swirling inside her. Her hands spread over his chest, feeling she belonged there in his arms.

When he freed her mouth, his lips caressed the sensitive cord along the side of her neck.

"Does this mean you'll give me another chance?" he murmured, his voice faintly husky from the effects of the kiss.

"I'd say the prognosis is excellent," she replied, her breathing still affected. "But I'd like to explain a few things."

She led the way into the kitchen, poured mugs of coffee and added sugar to his the way she'd seen him do.

When she set his cup on the table, Seth reached for her hand and kissed her fingers. "Your family has money?" he asked.

"Yes, but I don't," she explained. "At least not yet. Cooper controls the purse strings for a little while longer. My father was Claude Masters. You may or may not have heard of him. He established a business supply corporation that has branch offices in five states. Dad died when I was in high school. Cooper is president of the company now, and my legal guardian." Her soft mouth quirked to one side. "He takes his responsibility seriously. I apologize if he offended you yesterday."

Humor glinted briefly in his expression. "The only thing that could possibly offend me is if you were married." He laughed, and she stared at him curiously. "I'll never wear five-hundred-dollar business suits. You understand that?"

Nodding, she smiled. "I can't imagine you in a suit at all."

"Oh, I've been known to wear one, but I hate it."

Again she smiled.

"Do you hate having money?" He was regarding her steadily, his wide brow creased.

"No," she replied honestly. "I like having money when I need it. What I hate is being different from others, like Ashley and you. I have a hard time trusting people. I'm never really sure whether they like *me*. I find myself looking at any relationship with a jaundiced eye, wondering what the other person is expecting to receive from my friendship." She lowered her gaze, her fingers circling the top of the mug. "My father was the same way, and it made him close himself off from the world. I was brought up in a protected environment. I fought tooth and nail to convince Cooper I should attend the University of Washington. He wanted to send me to study at a private university in Switzerland."

"I'm glad you're here."

Claudia watched as Seth clenched and unclenched his hands.

"Do you think the reason I came back is because I figured out you have money?" he finally asked.

Something in his voice conveyed the seriousness of the question. "No, I don't think you're the type of person to be impressed by wealth. Just knowing you this little while, I believe if you wanted money, you'd have it. You're that type of man." Having stated her feelings, she fell silent.

"God gives the very best." The throaty whisper was

barely discernible, and she glanced up, her blue eyes questioning.

"Pardon?"

Seth took her hand and carried it to his lips. The coarse hairs of his beard prickled her fingertips. "Nothing," he murmured. "I'll explain it to you later."

"I skipped lunch and I'm hungry, so I was going to fix myself a sandwich. Would you like one?" she offered.

"I would. In fact, you don't even need to ask. I'm always hungry. Let me help," he volunteered. "Believe it or not, I'm a darn good cook."

"You can slice the cheese if you like." She flashed him a happy smile.

"I hope you don't have any plans for the evening," he said, easing a knife through the slab of cheese. "I've got tickets for the game. The Seahawks are playing tonight, and I..." He paused, his look brooding, disconcerted.

"What's wrong?"

He sighed, walked to the other side of the small kitchen and stuck his huge hands inside his pants pockets. "Football isn't much of a woman's sport, is it?"

"What makes you say that?"

"I mean..." He looked around uneasily. "You don't have to go. It's not that important. I know that someone like you isn't—"

She didn't give him the chance to finish. "Someone like me," she repeated, "would love going to that game." Her eyes were smiling into his.

Amusement dominated his face as he slid his arms around her waist. One hand toyed with a strand of her hair. "We'll eat a sandwich now, then grab something for dinner after the game. All right, Red?" He said the name as if it were an endearment. "You don't mind if I call you that, do you?"

"Only you," she murmured just before his mouth claimed hers. "Only you."

The day was wonderful. They spent two hours talking almost nonstop. Claudia, who normally didn't drink more than a cup or two of coffee, shared two pots with Seth. She told him things she had never shared with anyone: her feelings during her father's short illness and after his death; the ache, the void in her life, afterward; and how the loss and the sadness had led her to Christ. She told him about her lifelong friendship with Ashley, the mother she had never known, medical school and her struggle for acceptance. There didn't seem to be anything she couldn't discuss with him.

In return he talked about his oil business, life in Nome and his own faith.

Before they knew it, it was time to get going. Claudia hurried to freshen up, but took the time to spray a light perfume at her pulse points. After running a comb through the unruly curls that framed her face, she tied them back at the base of her neck with a silk scarf. Seth was waiting for her in the living room. Checking her appearance one last time, she noted the happy sparkle in her eyes and paused to murmur a special thank-you that God had sent Seth back into her life.

Seth helped her into her jacket. Then he lovingly ran a rough hand up and down her arm as he brought her even closer to his side.

"I don't know when I've enjoyed an afternoon more," he told her. "Thank you."

"I should be the one to thank you, Seth." She avoided eye contact, afraid how much her look would reveal.

"I knew the minute I saw you that you were someone very special. I didn't realize until today how right my hunch was." He looked down at her gently. "It wasn't so long ago that I believed Christians were a bunch of do-gooders. Not long ago that I thought religion was for the weak-minded. But I didn't know people like you. Now I wonder how I managed to live my life without Christ."

Claudia tugged at Seth's hand as she excitedly walked up the cement ramp of the Kingdome. "The game's about to start." They'd parked on the street, then walked the few blocks to the stadium, hurrying up First Avenue. The traffic was so heavy that they were a few minutes later than planned.

"I love football," she said, her voice high with enthusiasm.

"Look at all these people." Seth stopped and looked around in amazement.

"Seth," she groaned. "I don't want to miss the kick-off."

Because the game was being televised nationwide, the kickoff was slated for five o'clock Pacific time. More than sixty thousand fans filled the Kingdome to capacity. Seahawk fever ran high, and the entire stadium was on its feet for the kickoff. In the beginning she only applauded politely so she wouldn't embarrass Seth with her enthusiasm. But when it came to her favorite sport, no one could accuse her of being unemotional. Within minutes she was totally involved with the action on the field. She cheered wildly when the Seahawks made a good play, then shouted at the officials in protest of any call she thought was unfair.

Seth's behavior was much more subdued, and several times when she complained to him about a call, she found that he seemed to be watching her more closely than the game.

There was something about football that allowed her to be herself, something that broke down her natural reserve. With her class schedule, she couldn't often afford the time to attend a game. But if at all possible she watched on TV, jumping on the furniture in exaltation, pounding the couch cushions in despair. Most of her classmates wouldn't have believed it was her. At school she was serious, all about the work, since she still felt the need to prove herself to her classmates. Although she had won respect from most of the other students, a few still believed her name and money were the only reasons she had been accepted.

"Touchdown!" Her arms flew into the air, and she leaped to her feet.

For the first time since the game had started, Seth showed as much emotion as she did. Lifting her high, he held her tight against him. Her hands framed his face, and it seemed the most natural thing in the world, as she stared into his dark, hungry eyes, to press her lips to his. Immediately he deepened the kiss, wrapping his arms around her, lifting her higher off the ground.

The cheering died to an excited chatter before either of them was aware of the crowd.

"We have an audience," he murmured huskily in her ear.

"It's just as well, don't you think?" Her face was flushed lightly. She had known almost from the beginning that the attraction between them was stronger than anything she had experienced with another man. Seth seemed to have recognized that, as well. The effect they had on each other was strong and disturbing. He had kissed her only three times, and already they were aware of how easy it would be to let their attraction rage out of control. It was exciting, but it was also frightening.

After the game—which the Seahawks won—they stopped for hamburgers. When Seth had finished his meal, he returned to the counter and bought them each an ice cream sundae.

"When you come to Alaska, I'll have my Inuit friends make you some of their ice cream," he said. His eyes flashed her a look of amusement.

Claudia's stomach tightened. *When* she came to Alaska? She hadn't stopped to think about visiting America's last frontier. From the beginning she had known that Seth would be in Seattle for only a few days. She had known and accepted that as best she could.

Deciding it was best to ignore the comment, she cocked her head to one side. "Okay, I'll play your little game. What's Inuit ice cream?"

"Berries, snow and rancid seal oil."

"Well, at least it's organic."

Seth chuckled. "It's that, all right."

Claudia twisted the red plastic spoon, making circles in the soft ice cream. She avoided Seth's gaze, just as she had been eluding facing the inevitable.

Gathering her resolve, hoping maybe his plans had changed, she raised her face, her eyes meeting his. "When will you be returning to Nome?"

He pushed his dessert aside, his hand reaching for hers. "My flight's booked for tomorrow afternoon."

Three

The muscles of Claudia's throat constricted. "Tomorrow," she repeated, knowing she sounded like a parrot. Lowering her gaze, she continued, "That doesn't leave us much time, does it?" She'd thought she was prepared. After all, she reminded herself yet again, she'd known from the beginning that Seth would only be in Seattle for a few days.

Lifting her eyes to his watchful gaze, she offered Seth a weak smile. "I know this sounds selfish, but I don't want you to go."

"Then I won't," he announced casually.

Her head shot up. "What do you mean?"

The full force of his magnetic gaze was resting on her. "I mean I'll stay a few more days."

Her heart seemed to burst into song. "Over the weekend?" Eyes as blue as the Caribbean implored him. "My only obligation is dinner Sunday with Cooper, but you could come. In fact, I'd like it if you did. My uncle will probably bore you to tears, but I'd like you to get to know each other. Will you stay that long?" She tilted her head questioningly, hopefully.

Seth chuckled. She loved his laugh. The loud, robust sound seemed to roll from deep within his chest. She'd watched him during the football game and couldn't help laughing with him.

"Will you?" she repeated.

"I have the feeling your uncle isn't going to welcome me with open arms."

"No." She smiled beguilingly. "But I will."

The restaurant seemed to go still. Seth's gaze was penetrating, his voice slightly husky. "Then I'll stay, but no longer than Monday."

"Okay." She was more than glad, she was jubilant. There hadn't been time to question this magnetic attraction that had captured them, and deep down she didn't want to investigate her feelings, even though she knew this was all happening too fast.

Seth's slipped his arm around her waist as they walked to the car. He held open the door for her and waited until she was seated. Unconsciously she smoothed the leather seat cushion, the texture smooth against the tips of her fingers. The vehicle had surprised her. Seth didn't fit the luxury-car image, but she hadn't mentioned it earlier, before the game.

"This thing *is* a bit much, isn't it?" His gaze briefly scanned the interior. The high-end sedan was fitted with every convenience, from the automatic sunroof to a satellite sound system to built-in Bluetooth technology.

"So why did you rent it?" she felt obliged to ask.

"Why did I—heavens, no! This is all part of the sisters' efforts to get me to sign the contract."

"The sisters?"

"That's a slang expression for the major oil conglomerates. They seem to feel the need to impress me. They originally had me staying at one of those big downtown hotels, in a suite that was over seven hundred dollars a night. I didn't feel comfortable with that and found my own place. But I couldn't refuse the car without offending some important people."

"We all get caught in that trap sometimes."

Seth agreed with a short, preoccupied nod. Although the game had finished over an hour earlier, the downtown traffic was at a standstill. Cautiously he eased the car into the heavy flow of bumper-to-bumper traffic.

While they were caught in the snarl of impatient drivers, Claudia studied his strong profile. Several times his mouth tightened, and he shook his head in disgust.

"I'm sorry, Seth," she said solemnly, and smiled lamely when he glanced at her.

He arched his thick brows. "You're sorry? Why?"

"The traffic. I should have known to wait another hour, until things had thinned out a bit more."

"It's not your fault." His enormous hand squeezed hers reassuringly.

"Don't you have traffic jams in Nome?" she asked, partly to keep the conversation flowing, and partly to counteract the crazy reaction her heart seemed to have every time he touched her.

"Traffic jams in Nome?" He smiled. "Red, Nome's population is under four thousand. Some days my car is the only one on the road."

Her eyes narrowed suspiciously. "You're teasing? I thought Nome was a major city."

He laughed as he returned both hands to the wheel, and her heartbeat relaxed. "The population of the entire state is only 700,000, a fraction of Washington's nearly seven million." A smile softened his rugged features. "Anchorage is the largest city in Alaska, with under 300,000 residents."

An impatient motorist honked, and Seth pulled forward onto the freeway entrance ramp. The traffic remained heavy but finally it was at least moving at a steady pace.

"I couldn't live like this," he said and expelled his breath forcefully. "Too many people, too many buildings and," he added with a wry grin, "too many cars."

"Don't worry. You won't have to put up with it much longer," she countered with a smile that she hoped didn't look as forced as it felt.

Seth scowled thoughtfully and didn't reply.

He parked the car in the lot outside her apartment building and refused her invitation to come in for coffee. "I have a meeting in the morning, but it shouldn't go any longer than noon. Can I see you then?"

She nodded, pleased. "Of course." She would treasure every minute she had left with him. "Shall I phone Cooper and tell him you're coming for dinner Sunday?"

"He won't mind?"

"Oh, I'm sure he will, but if he objects too strongly, we'll have our own dinner."

He reached out to caress the delicate curve of her cheek and entwined his fingers with the auburn curls along the nape of her neck. "Would it be considered bad manners to hope he objects strenuously?" he asked.

"Cooper's not so bad." She felt as if she should at

least make the effort to explain her uncle. "I don't think he means to come off so pompous, he just doesn't know how else to act. What he needs is a woman to love." She smiled inwardly. "I can just hear him cough and sputter if I were to tell him that."

"*I* need a woman to love," Seth whispered as his mouth found hers. The kiss was deep and intense, as if to convince her of the truth of his words.

Claudia wound her arms around his neck, surrendering to the mastery of his kiss. *He's serious*, her mind repeated. *Dead serious.* The whole world seemed right when he was holding her like this. He covered her neck and the hollow of her throat with light, tiny kisses. She tilted her head to give him better access, reveling in the warm feel of his lips against the creamy smoothness of her skin. A shudder of desire ran through her, and she bit into her bottom lip to conceal the effect he had on her senses.

Taking a deep breath, he straightened. "Let's get you inside before this gets out of hand." His voice sounded raw and slightly uneven.

He kissed her again outside her apartment door, but this kiss lacked the ardor of a few minutes earlier. "I'll see you about noon tomorrow."

With a trembling smile she nodded.

"Don't look at me like that," he groaned. His strong hands stroked the length of her arms as he edged her body closer. "It's difficult enough to say good night."

Standing on tiptoe, she lightly brushed her mouth over his.

"Claudia," he growled in warning.

She placed her fingertips over her moist lips, then over his, to share the mock kiss with him.

He closed his eyes as if waging some deep inner battle, then covered her fingers with his own.

"Good night," she whispered, glorying in the way he reacted to her.

"I'll see you tomorrow."

"Tomorrow," she repeated dreamily.

Dressed in her pajamas and bathrobe, Claudia sat on top of her bed an hour later, reading her Bible. Her concentration drifted to the events of the past week and all the foreign emotions she had encountered. This thing with Seth was happening too fast, far too fast. No man had ever evoked such an intensity of emotion within her. No man had made her feel the things he did. Love, real love, didn't happen like this. The timing was all wrong. She couldn't fall in love—not now. Not with a man who was only going to be in Seattle for a few more days. But why had God sent Seth into her life when it would be so easy to fall in love with him? Was it a test? A lesson in faith? She was going to be a doctor. The Lord had led her to that decision, and there wasn't anything in her life she was more sure of. Falling in love with Seth Lessinger could ruin that. Still troubled, she turned off the light and attempted to sleep.

Claudia was ready at noon, but for what she wasn't sure. Dressed casually in jeans and a sweater, she thought she might suggest a drive to Snoqualmie Falls. And if Seth felt ambitious, maybe a hike around Mount Si. She didn't have the time to do much hiking herself, but she enjoyed the outdoors whenever possible. The mental picture of idly strolling with Seth, appreciating the beautiful world God had provided, was an appealing one. Of course, doing anything with Seth was appealing.

When he hadn't shown up or called by one, she started to get worried. Every minute seemed interminable, and she glanced at her watch repeatedly. When the phone rang at one-thirty, she grabbed the receiver before it had a chance to ring again.

"Hello?" she said anxiously.

"Red?" Seth asked.

"Yes, it's me." He didn't sound right; he seemed tired, impatient.

"I've been held up here. There's not much chance of my getting out of this meeting until late afternoon."

"Oh." She tried to hide the disappointment in her voice.

"I know, honey, I feel the same way." The depth of his tone relayed his own frustration. "I'll make it up to you tonight. Can you be ready around seven for dinner? Wear something fancy."

"Sure." She forced a cheerful note into her voice. "I'll see you then. Take care."

"I've got to get back inside. If you happen to think of me, say a prayer. I want this business over so we can enjoy what's left of our time."

If she thought of him? She nearly laughed out loud. "I will," she promised, knowing it was a promise she would have no trouble keeping.

Cooper phoned about ten minutes later. "You left a message for me to call?" he began.

Claudia half suspected that he expected her to apologize for the little scene downtown with Seth. "Yes," she replied evenly. "I'm inviting a guest for dinner Sunday."

"Who?" he asked, and she could almost picture him bracing himself because he knew the answer.

"Seth Lessinger. You already met him once this week."

The line seemed to crackle with a lengthy silence. "As you wish," he said tightly.

A mental picture formed of Cooper writing down Seth's name. Undoubtedly, before Sunday, her uncle would know everything there was to know about Seth, from his birth weight to his high school grade point average.

"We'll see you then."

"Claudia," Cooper said, then hesitated. Her uncle didn't often hesitate. Usually he knew his mind and wasn't afraid to speak it. "You're not serious about this—" he searched for the right word "—man, are you?"

"Why?" It felt good to turn the tables, answering her cagey uncle with a question of her own. Why should he be so concerned? She was old enough to do anything she pleased.

He allowed an unprecedented second pause. "No reason. I'll see you Sunday."

Thoughtfully she replaced the receiver and released her breath in a slow sigh. Cooper had sounded different, on edge, not like his normal self at all. Her mouth quivered with a suppressed smile. He was worried; she'd heard it in his voice. For the first time since he'd been appointed her guardian, he had showed some actual feelings toward her. The smile grew. Maybe he wasn't such a bad guy after all.

Scanning the contents of her closet later that afternoon, Claudia chose a black lace dress she had bought on impulse the winter before. It wasn't the type of dress she would wear to church, although it wasn't low-cut or revealing. It was made of Cluny lace and had a three-tiered skirt. She had seen it displayed in an exclusive boutique and hadn't been able to resist, though she was angry with herself afterward for buying something so extravagant. She was unlikely to find a reason to wear such an elegant dress, but she loved it anyway. Even Ashley had been surprised when Claudia had showed it to her. No one could deny that it was a beautiful, romantic dress.

She arranged her auburn curls into a loose chignon at the top of her head, with tiny ringlets falling at the sides of her face. The diamond earrings she popped in had been her mother's, and Claudia had worn them only a couple of times. Seth had said fancy, though, so he was going to get fancy!

He arrived promptly at seven. One look at her and his eyes showed surprise, then something else she couldn't decipher.

Slowly his gaze traveled over her face and figure, openly admiring the curves of her hips and her slender legs.

"Wow."

"Wow yourself," she returned, equally impressed. She'd seen him as a virile and intriguing man even without the rich dark wool suit. But now he was compelling, so attractive she could hardly take her eyes off him.

"Turn around. I want to look at you," he requested,

his attention centered on her. His voice sounded ragged, as if seeing her had stolen away his breath.

Claudia did as he asked, slowly twirling around. "Now you."

"Me?" He looked stunned.

"You." She laughed, her hands directing his movements. Self-consciously he turned, his movements abrupt and awkward. "Where are we going?" she asked while she admired.

"The Space Needle." He took her coat out of her hands and held it open for her. She turned and slid her arms into the satin-lined sleeves. He guided it over her shoulders, and his hands lingered there as he brought her back against him. She heard him inhale sharply before kissing the gentle slope of her neck.

"Let's go," he murmured, "while I'm still able to resist other temptations."

Seth parked outside the Seattle Center, and they walked hand in hand toward the city's most famous landmark.

"Next summer we'll go to the Food Circus," she mentioned casually. If he could say things about her visiting Alaska, she could talk the same way to him.

Seth didn't miss a step, but his hand tightened over hers. "Why next summer? Why not now?"

"Because you've promised me dinner on top of the city, and I'm not about to let you out of that. But no one visiting Seattle should miss the Food Circus. I don't even know how many booths there are, all serving exotic dishes from all over the world. The worst part is having to make a decision. When Ashley and I go there, we each buy something different and divide it. That way we each get to taste more new things." She stopped talking and smiled. "I'm chattering, aren't I?"

"A little." She could hear the amusement in his voice.

The outside elevators whisked them up the Space Needle to the observation deck six-hundred-and-seven feet above the ground. The night was glorious, and brilliant lights illuminated the world below. Seth stood behind her, his arms looped over her shoulders, pulling her close.

"I think my favorite time to see this view is at night," she said. "I love watching all the lights. I've never stopped to wonder why the night lights enthrall me the way they do. But I think it's probably because Jesus told us we were the light of the world, and from up here I can see how much even one tiny light can illuminate."

"I hadn't thought of it like that," he murmured close to her ear. "But you have to remember I'm a new Christian. There are a lot of things I haven't discovered yet."

"That's wonderful, too."

"How do you mean?"

She shrugged lightly. "God doesn't throw all this knowledge and insight at us at once. He lets us digest it little by little, as we're able."

"Just as any loving father would do," Seth said quietly.

They stood for several minutes until a chill ran over Claudia's arms.

"Cold?" he questioned.

"Only a little. It's so lovely out here, I don't want to leave."

"It's beautiful, all right, but it's more the woman I'm with than the scenery."

"Thank you," she murmured, pleased by his words.

"You're blushing," he said as he turned her around to face him. "I don't believe it—you're blushing."

Embarrassed, she looked away. "Men don't usually say such romantic things to me."

"Why not? You're a beautiful woman. By now you must have heard those words a thousand times over."

"Not really." The color was creeping up her neck. "That's the floating bridge over there." She pointed into the distance, attempting to change the subject. "It's the largest concrete pontoon bridge in the world. It connects Mercer Island and Seattle."

"Claudia," Seth murmured, his voice dipping slightly, "you are a delight. If we weren't out here with the whole city looking on, I'd take you in my arms and kiss you senseless."

"Promises, promises," she teased and hurried inside before he could make good on his words.

They ate a leisurely meal and talked over coffee for so long that she looked around guiltily. Friday night was one of the busiest nights for the restaurant business, and they were taking up a table another couple could be using.

"I'll make us another cup at my place," she volunteered.

Seth didn't argue.

The aroma of fresh-brewed coffee filled the apartment. Claudia poured two cups and carried them into the living room.

Seth was sitting on the long green couch, flipping through the pages of one of the medical journals she had stacked on the end table.

"Are you planning on specializing?"

She nodded. "Yes, pediatrics."

His dark brown eyes became intent. "Do you enjoy children that much, Red?"

"Oh, yes," she said fervently. "Maybe it's because I was an only child and never had enough other kids around. I can remember lining up my dolls and playing house."

"I thought every little girl did that?"

"At sixteen?" she teased, then laughed at the expression on his face. "The last two summers I've worked part-time in a day care center, and the experience convinced me to go into pediatrics. But that's a long way down the road. I'm only a second-year med student."

When they'd finished their coffee, she carried the cups to the kitchen sink. He followed her, slipping his hands around her waist. All her senses reacted to his touch.

"Can I see you in the morning?" he asked.

She nodded, afraid her voice would tremble if she spoke. His finger traced the line of her cheek, and she held her breath, bracing herself as his touch trailed over her soft lips. Instinctively she reached for him, her hands gliding up his chest and over the corded muscles of his shoulders, which flexed beneath her exploring fingers.

He rasped out her name before his mouth hungrily descended on hers. A heady excitement engulfed her. Never had there been a time in her life when she was more gloriously happy. The kiss was searing, turbulent, wrenching her heart and touching her soul.

"Red?" His hold relaxed, and with infinite care he studied her soft, yielding eyes, filled with the depth of her emotions. "Oh, Red." He inhaled several sharp breaths and pressed his forehead to hers. "Don't tempt me like this." The words were a plea that seemed to come deep from within him.

"You're doing the same thing to me," she whispered softly, having trouble with her own breathing.

"We should stop now."

"I know," she agreed, but neither of them pulled away.

How could she think reasonable thoughts when he was so close? A violent eruption of Mount St. Helens couldn't compare with the ferocity of her emotions.

Slowly she pulled back, easing herself from his arms.

He dropped his hands to his sides. "We have to be careful, Red. My desire for you is strong, but I want us to be good. I don't think I could ever forgive myself if I were to lead us into temptation."

"Oh, Seth," she whispered, her blue eyes shimmering with tears. "It's not all you. I'm feeling these things just as strongly. Maybe it's not such a good idea for us to be alone anymore."

"No." His husky voice rumbled with turmoil. A tortured silence followed. He paced the floor, raking his fingers through his thick brown hair. "It's selfish, I know, but there's so little time left. We'll be careful and help one another. It won't be much longer that we'll be able…" He let the rest of the sentence fade.

Not much longer, her mind repeated.

He picked up the jacket he'd discarded over the back of a chair and held out a hand to her. "Walk me to the door."

Linking her fingers with his, she did as he asked. He paused at the door, his hand on the knob. "Good night."

"Good night," she responded with a weak smile.

He bent downward and gently brushed her lips. Although the contact was light, almost teasing, Claudia's response was immediate. She yearned for the feel of his arms again, and felt painfully empty when he turned away and closed the door behind him.

They spent almost every minute of Saturday together. In the morning Seth drove them to Snoqualmie Falls, where they ate a picnic lunch, then took a leisurely stroll along the trails leading to the water. Later in the day they visited the Seattle Aquarium on the waterfront, and ate a dinner of fresh fish and crusty, deep-fried potatoes.

When she got home that night, there was a message from Cooper. When she called back, he said he just wanted to tell her that he was looking forward to getting to know Seth over Sunday dinner, a gesture that surprised her.

"He's a good man," her uncle announced. "I've been hearing quite a few impressive things about your friend. I'll apologize to him for my behavior the other day," he continued.

"I'm sure Seth understands," she assured him.

She hadn't known Seth for even a week, and yet it felt like a lifetime. Her feelings for him were clear now. She had never experienced the deep womanly yearnings Seth aroused within her. The attraction was sometimes so strong that it shocked her—and she could tell that it shocked him, too. Aware of their vulnerability, they'd carefully avoided situations that would tempt them. Even though Seth touched her often and made excuses to caress her, he was cautious, and their kisses were never allowed to deepen into the passion they'd shared the night they dined at the Space Needle.

On Sunday morning Claudia woke early, with an eagerness that reminded her of her childhood. The past week had been her happiest since before her father's death.

She and Seth attended the early morning church service together, and she introduced him to her Christian family. Her heart filled with emotion as he sat beside her in the wooden pew. There was nothing more she would ask of a man than a deep, committed faith in the Lord.

Afterward they went back to her apartment. The table was set with her best dishes and linen. Now she set out fresh-squeezed orange juice and delicate butter croissants on china plates. A single candle and dried-flower centerpiece decorated the table.

She had chosen a pink dress and piled her hair high on her head again, with tiny curls falling free to frame her face. Although Seth would be leaving tomorrow, she didn't want to deal with that now, and she quickly dismissed the thought. Today was special, their last day together, and she refused to let the reality of a long separation trouble her.

"I hope you're up to my cooking," she said to him as she took her special egg casserole from the oven.

He stood framed in the doorway, handsome and vital. He still wore his dark wool suit, but he held his tie in one hand as if he didn't want that silken noose around his neck any longer than absolutely necessary.

Just having him this close made all her senses pulsate with happiness, and a warm glow stole over her.

"You don't need to worry. My stomach can handle just about anything," he teased gently. He studied her for a moment. "I can't call you Red in a dress like that." He came to her and kissed her lightly. Claudia sighed at the sweetness of his caress.

"I hope I don't have to wait much longer. I'm starved."

"You really *are* always hungry," she teased. "But how can you think about food when I'm here to tempt you?"

"It's more difficult than you know," he said with a smile. "Can I do anything?"

Claudia answered him with a short shake of her head.

"Then are you going to feed me or not?" His roguish smile only highlighted his irresistible masculinity.

The special baked egg recipe was one Ashley's mother had given her. Claudia was pleased when Seth asked for seconds.

When he finished eating, he took a small package from his coat pocket. "This thing has been burning a hole in my pocket all morning. Open it now."

Claudia took the package and shook it, holding it close to her ear. "For me?" she asked, her eyes sparkling with excitement.

"I brought it with me from Nome."

From Nome? That was certainly intriguing. Carefully she untied the bow and removed the red foil paper, revealing a black velvet jeweler's box.

"Before you open it, I want to explain something." He leaned forward, resting his elbows on the table. "For a long time I've been married to my job, building my company. It wasn't until…" He hesitated. "I won't go into the reason, but I decided I wanted a wife. Whenever I needed anything in the past, I simply went out and bought it, but I knew finding a good woman wouldn't work like that. She had to be someone special, someone I could love and respect, someone who shared my faith. The more I thought about the complexities of finding that special woman, the more I realized how difficult it would be to find her."

"Seth—"

"No, let me explain," he continued, reaching for her hand. He gripped it hard, his eyes studying her intently. "I was reading my Bible one night and came across the story of Abraham sending a servant to find a wife for Isaac. Do you remember the story?"

She nodded, color draining from her features. "Seth, please—"

"There's more. Bear with me." He raised her hand to his lips and very gently kissed her fingers. "If you remember, the servant did as Abraham bade and traveled to the land of his master's family. But he was uncertain. The weight of his responsibility bore heavily upon him. So the servant prayed, asking God to give him a sign. God answered that prayer and showed the servant that Rebekah was the right woman for Isaac. Scripture says how much Isaac loved his wife, and how she comforted him after the death of his mother, Sarah."

"Seth, please, I know what you're going to say—"

"Be patient, my love," he interrupted her again.

"After reading that account, I decided to trust the Lord to give me a wife. I was also traveling to the land of my family. Both my mother and father originally came from Washington State. I prayed about it. I also purchased the engagement ring before I left Nome. And like Abraham's servant, I, too, asked God for a sign. I was beginning to lose hope. I'd already been here several days before you placed that card with the verse in the mirror. You can't imagine how excited I was when I found it."

Claudia swallowed tightly, recalling his telling her that the message had meant more to him than she would ever know. She wanted to stop him, but the lump in her throat had grown so large that speaking was impossible.

"I want you to come back to Nome with me tomorrow, Red. We can be married in a few days."

Four

Claudia's eyes widened with incredulous disbelief. "Married in a few days?" she repeated. "But, Seth, we've only been together less than a week! We can't—"

"Sure we can," he countered, his eyes serious. "I knew even before I found the Bible verse in the mirror that it was you. Do you remember how you bumped into me that first day in the outside corridor?" Although he asked the question, he didn't wait for the answer. "I was stunned. Didn't you notice how my eyes followed you? Something came over me right then. I had to force myself not to run and stop you. At the time I assumed I was simply physically reacting to a beautiful woman. But once I found the Bible verse on the mirror, I knew."

"What about school?" Somehow the words made it past the large knot constricting her throat.

A troubled look tightened his mouth. "I've done a lot of thinking about that. It's weighed heavily on me. I know how much becoming a doctor means to you." He caught her hand and gently kissed the palm. "Someday,

Red, we'll be able to move to Anchorage and you can finish med school. I promise you that."

Taking her hand from his, Claudia closed the jeweler's box. The clicking sound seemed to be magnified a thousand times, a cacophony of sound echoing around the room.

"Seth, we've only known each other a short time. So much more goes into building the foundation for a relationship that will support a marriage. It takes more than a few days."

"Rebekah didn't even meet Isaac. She responded in faith, going with the servant to a faraway land to join a man she had never seen. Yet she went," he argued.

"You're being unfair," she said as she stood and walked to the other side of the room. Her heart was pounding so hard she could feel the blood pulsating through her veins. "We live in the twentieth century, not biblical times. How do we know what Rebekah was feeling? Her father was probably the one who said she would go. More than likely, Rebekah didn't have any choice in the matter."

"You don't know that," he said.

"You don't, either," she shot back. "We hardly know each other."

"You keep saying that! What more do you need to know?"

She gestured weakly with her hands. "Everything."

"Come on, Red. You're overreacting. You know more about me than any other woman ever has. We've done nothing but talk every day. I'm thirty-six, own and operate the Arctic Barge Company, wear size thirteen shoes, like ketchup on my fried eggs and peanut butter on my pancakes. My tastes are simple, my needs few. I tend to be impatient, but God and I are working on that. Usually I don't anger quickly, but when I do, stay clear. After we're married, there will undoubtedly be things we'll need to discuss, but nothing we shouldn't be able to settle."

"Seth, I—"

"Let me see," he continued undaunted. "Did I leave anything out?" He paused again. "Oh yes. The most important part is that I love you, Claudia Masters."

The sincerity with which he said the words trapped the oxygen in her lungs, leaving her speechless.

"This is the point where you're supposed to say, 'And I love you, Seth.'" He rose, coming to stand directly in front of her. His hands cupped her shoulders as his gaze fell lovingly upon her. "Now, repeat after me: *I... love...you.*"

Claudia couldn't. She tried to say something, but nothing would come. "I can't." She had to choke out the words. "It's unfair to ask me to give up everything I've worked so hard for. I'm sorry, Seth, really sorry."

"Claudia!" His mouth was strained and tight; there was no disguising the bitter disappointment in his voice. "Don't say no, not yet. Think about it. I'm not leaving until tomorrow morning."

"Tomorrow morning." She closed her eyes. "I'm supposed to know by then?"

"You should know now," he whispered.

"But I don't," she snapped. "You say that God gave you a sign that I was to be the wife He had chosen for you. Don't you find it the least bit suspicious that God would say something to you and *nothing* to me?"

"Rebekah didn't receive a sign," he explained rationally. "Abraham's servant did. She followed in faith."

"You're comparing two entirely different times and situations."

"What about the verse you stuck in the mirror? Haven't you ever wondered about that? You told me you'd never done anything like that before."

"But…"

"You have no argument, Red."

"I most certainly do."

"Can you honestly say you don't feel the electricity between us?"

How could she? "I can't deny it, but it doesn't change anything."

Seth smoothed a coppery curl from her forehead, his touch gentle, his eyes imploring. "Of course it does. I think that once you come to Nome you'll understand."

"I'm not going to Nome," she reiterated forcefully. "If you want to marry me, then you'll have to move to Seattle. I won't give up my dreams because of a six-day courtship and your feeling that you received a sign from God."

Seth looked shocked for a moment but recovered quickly. "I can't move to Seattle. My business, my home and my whole life are in Nome."

"But don't you understand? That's exactly what you're asking *me* to do. My education, my home and my friends are all here in Seattle."

Seth glanced uncomfortably around the room, then directed his gaze back to her. His dark eyes were filled with such deep emotion that it nearly took Claudia's breath away. Tears shimmered in her eyes, and his tall, masculine figure blurred as the moisture welled.

Gently Seth took her in his arms, holding her head to his shoulder. His jacket felt smooth and comforting against her cheek.

Tenderly he caressed her neck, and she could feel his breath against her hair. "Red, I'm sorry," he whispered with such love that fresh tears followed a crooked course down her wan cheeks. "I've known all this from the first day. It's unfair to spring it on you at the last minute. I know it must sound crazy to you now. But think about what I've said. And remember that I love you. Nothing's going to change that. Now dry your eyes and we'll visit your uncle. I promise not to mention this again today." He kissed the top of her head and gently pulled away.

"Here." She handed him the jeweler's box.

"No." He shook his head. "I want you to keep the ring. You may not feel like you want it now, but you will soon. I have to believe that, Red."

Her face twisted with pain. "I don't know that I should."

"Yes, you should." Brief anger flared in his eyes. "Please."

Because she couldn't refuse without hurting him even more, Claudia agreed with an abrupt nod.

Since she certainly couldn't wear the ring, she placed the velvet box in a drawer. Her hand trembled when she pushed the drawer back into place, but she put on a brave smile when she turned toward Seth.

To her dismay, his returning smile was just as sad as hers.

* * *

Cooper knew something was wrong almost immediately. That surprised Claudia, who had never found her uncle to be sensitive to her moods. But when he asked what was troubling her, she quickly denied that anything was. She couldn't expect him to understand what was happening.

The two men eyed each other like wary dogs that had crossed paths unexpectedly. Cooper, for his part, was welcoming, but Seth was brooding and distant.

When they sat down to dinner, Seth smiled ruefully.

"What's wrong?" Claudia asked.

"Nothing," he said, shaking his head. "It's just this is the first time I've needed three spoons to eat one meal."

Cooper arched his thick brows expressively, as if to say he didn't know how anyone could possibly do without three spoons for anything.

Claudia looked from one man to the other, noting the differences. They came from separate worlds. Although she found Cooper's attitudes and demeanor boring and confining, she was, after all, his own flesh and blood. If she were to marry Seth, give up everything that was important to her and move to Alaska, could she adjust to his way of life?

During the remainder of the afternoon she often found her gaze drawn to Seth. He and Cooper played a quiet game of chess in the den, while she sat nearby, studying them.

In the few days they had spent together, she had been witness to the underlying thread of tenderness that ran through Seth's heart. At the same time, he was self-assured, and although she had never seen the ruthless side of his nature, she didn't doubt that it existed. He was the kind of man to thrive on challenges; he wasn't afraid of hardships. But would she?

Resting her head against the back of the velvet swivel rocker, she slowly lowered her gaze. The problem was that she also knew Seth was the type of man who loved intensely. His love hadn't been offered lightly; he wanted her forever. But most of all, he wanted her now—today. At thirty-six he had waited a long time to find a wife. His commitment was complete. He had looked almost disbelieving when she hadn't felt the same way.

Or did she? She couldn't deny that the attraction between them was powerful, almost overwhelming. But that was physical, and there was so much more to love than the physical aspect. Spiritually they shared the same faith. To Claudia, that was vital; she wouldn't share her life with a man who didn't believe as she did. But mentally they were miles apart. Each of them had goals and dreams that the other would never share. Seth seemed almost to believe medical school was a pastime, a hobby, for her. He had no comprehension of the years of hard work and study that had gotten her this far. The dream had been ingrained in her too long for her to relinquish it on the basis of a six-day courtship. And it wasn't only her dream, but one her beloved father had shared.

Seth hadn't understood any of that. Otherwise he wouldn't have asked her to give it all up without a question or thought. He believed that God had shown him that she was to be his wife, and that was all that mattered. If only life were that simple! Seth was a new

Christian, eager, enthusiastic, but also unseasoned—not that she was a tower of wisdom and discernment. But she would never have prayed for anything so crazy. She was too down to earth—like Cooper. She hated to compare herself to her uncle, but in this instance it was justified.

Cooper's smile turned faintly smug, and Claudia realized he was close to putting Seth in check, if not checkmate. She didn't need to be told that Seth's mind was preoccupied with their conversation this morning and not on the game. Several times in the last hour he had lifted his gaze to hers. One look could reveal so much, although until that day she had never been aware just how *much* his eyes could say. He wanted her so much, more than he would ever tell her. Guiltily her lashes fluttered downward; watching him was hurting them both too much.

Not long afterwards he kissed her good night outside her apartment, thanking her for the day. The lump that had become her constant companion blocked her throat, keeping her from thanking him for the beautiful solitaire diamond she would probably never wear.

"My flight's due to take off at seven-thirty," he said without looking at her.

"I'll be there," she whispered.

He held her then, so tightly that for a moment she found it impossible to breathe. She felt him shudder, and tears prickled her eyes as he whispered, "I love you, Red."

She couldn't say it, couldn't repeat the words he desperately longed to hear. She bit her tongue to keep from sobbing. She longed to tell him how she felt, but the

words wouldn't come. They stuck in her throat until it
constricted painfully and felt raw. Why had God given
her a man who could love her so completely when she
was so wary?

Claudia set the alarm for five. If Seth's flight took
off at seven-thirty, then she should meet him at the airport at six. That early, he would be able to clear security
quickly. On the ride back from Cooper's she'd volunteered to drive him, but he'd declined the invitation and
said he would take a taxi.

Sleep didn't come easily, and when it did, her dreams
were filled with questions. Although she searched ev-
erywhere, she couldn't find the answers.

Claudia's blue eyes looked haunted and slightly red
when she woke up, though she tried to camouflage the
effects of her restless night with cosmetics.

The morning was dark and drizzly as she climbed
inside her car and started the engine. The heater soon
took the bite out of early morning, and she pulled onto
the street. With every mile her heart grew heavier. A
prayer came automatically to her lips. She desperately
wanted to do the right thing: right for Seth, right for
her. She prayed that if her heavenly Father wanted her
to marry Seth, then He would make the signs as clear
for her as He'd apparently done for Seth. Did she lack
faith? Was that the problem.

"No," she answered her own question aloud. But
her heart seemed to respond with a distant "yes" that
echoed through her mind.

She parked in the garage, pulled her purse strap over
her shoulder and hurried along the concourse. *I'm doing*

the right thing, she mentally repeated with each step. Her heels clicked against the marble floor, seeming to pound out the message—right thing, right thing, right thing.

She paused when she saw Seth waiting for her, as promised, in the coffee shop. The only word for the way he looked was "dejected." She whispered a prayer, seeking strength and wisdom.

"Morning, Seth," she greeted him, forcing herself to smile.

His expression remained blank as he purposely looked away from her.

This was going to be more difficult than she'd imagined. The atmosphere was so tense and strained, she could hardly tolerate it. "You're angry, aren't you?"

"No," he responded dryly. "I've gone beyond the anger stage. Disillusioned, perhaps. You must think I'm a crazy man, showing up with an engagement ring and the belief that God had given me this wonderful message that we were to marry."

"Seth, no." She placed a hand on his arm.

He looked down at it and moved his arm, breaking her light hold. It was almost as if he couldn't tolerate her touch.

"The funny thing is," he continued, his expression stoic, "until this minute I didn't accept that I'd be returning to Alaska alone. Even when I woke up this morning, I believed that something would happen and you'd decide to come with me." He took a deep breath, his gaze avoiding hers. "I've behaved like a fool."

"Don't say that," she pleaded.

He glanced at her then, with regret, doubt and a deep

sadness crossing his face. "We would have had beautiful children, Red." He lightly caressed her cheek.

"Will you stop talking like that?" she demanded, becoming angry. "You're being unfair."

He tilted his head and shrugged his massive shoulders. "I know. You love me, Red. You haven't admitted it to yourself yet. The time will come when you can, but I doubt that even then it will make much difference. Because, although you love me, you don't love me enough to leave the luxury of your life behind."

She wanted to argue with him, but she couldn't. Unbidden tears welled in the blue depths of her eyes, and she lowered her head, blinking frantically to still their fall.

She held her head high and glared at him with all her anguish in her eyes for him to see. "I'm going to forgive you for that, because I know you don't mean it. You're hurting, and because of that you want me to suffer, too." Tugging the leather purse strap over her shoulder, she stood and took a step back. "I can't see that my being here is doing either of us any good. I wish you well, and I thank you for six of the most wonderful days of my life. God bless you, Seth." She turned and stalked away down the corridor. For several moments she was lost in a painful void. Somehow she managed to make it to a ladies' room.

Avoiding the curious stares of others, she wiped the tears from her face and blew her nose. Seth had been cold and cruel, offering neither comfort nor understanding. Earlier she had recognized that his capacity for ruthlessness was as strong as his capability for tenderness, but she'd never been exposed to the former. Now she had. How sad that they had to part like this. There had been so much she'd longed to say, but maybe it was better left unsaid.

When she felt composed enough to face the outside world, she moved with quick, purposeful steps toward the parking garage.

She had gone only a few feet when a hand gripped her shoulder and whirled her around. Her cry of alarm was muffled as she was dragged against Seth's muscular chest.

"I thought you'd gone," he whispered into her hair, a desperate edge to his voice. "I'm sorry, Red. You're right. I didn't mean that—not any of it."

He squeezed her so tightly that her ribs ached. Then he raised his head and looked around at the attention they were receiving. He quickly pulled her into a secluded nook behind a pillar. The minute he was assured they were alone, his mouth sought hers, fusing them together with a fiery kiss filled with such emotion that she was left weak and light-headed.

"I need you," he whispered hoarsely against the delicate hollow of her throat. He lifted his face and smoothed a curl from her forehead, his eyes pleading with her.

Claudia was deluged with fresh pain. She needed him, too, but here in Seattle. She couldn't leave everything behind, not now, when she was so close to making her dream come true.

"No, don't say it." He placed a finger over her mouth to prevent the words of regret from spilling out. "I understand, Red. Or at least I'm trying to understand."

He sighed heavily and gently kissed her again. "I have to go or I'll never make it through security in time."

He sounded so final, as if everything between them was over. She blinked away the tears that were burning her eyes. No sound came from her parched throat as he gently eased her out of his embrace. Her heart hammered furiously as she walked with him to the security line.

A feeling of panic overcame her when she heard the announcement that Seth's plane was already being boarded. The time was fast approaching when he would be gone.

Once again he gently caressed her face, his dark eyes burning into hers. "Goodbye, Red." His lips covered hers very gently.

In the next instant, Seth Lessinger turned and strolled out of her world.

Part of her screamed silently in tortured protest as she watched him go and longed to race after him. The other part, the more level-headed, sensible part, recognized that there was nothing she could do to change his leaving. But every part of her was suffering. Her brain told her that she'd done the right thing, but her heart found very little solace in her decision.

The days passed slowly and painfully. Claudia knew Ashley had grown worried over her loss of appetite and the dark shadows beneath her eyes. She spent as much time as she could in her room alone, blocking out the world, but closing the door on reality didn't keep the memories of Seth at bay. He was in her thoughts continually, haunting her dreams, obsessing her during the days, preying on her mind.

She threw herself into her studies with a ferocity that surprised even Ashley, and that helped her handle the days, but nothing could help the nights. Often she lay awake for hours, wide-eyed and frustrated, afraid that once she did sleep her dreams would be haunted by Seth. She prayed every minute, it seemed—prayed harder than she had about anything in her life. But no answer came. No flash of lightning, no writing on the wall, not even a Bible verse stuck to a mirror. Nothing. Wasn't God listening? Didn't He know that this situation was tormenting her?

Two weeks after Seth's departure she still hadn't heard from him. She was hollow-eyed, and her cheeks were beginning to look gaunt. She saw Ashley glance at her with concern more than once, but she put on a weak smile and dismissed her friend's worries. *No*, she insisted, *she was fine. Really.*

The next Saturday Ashley was getting ready to go to work at the University Book Store near the U. of W. campus when one of the girls she worked with, Sandy Hoover, waltzed into the apartment.

"Look." She proudly beamed and held out her hand, displaying a small diamond.

"You're engaged!" Ashley squealed with delight.

"Jon asked me last night," Sandy burst out. "I was so excited I could hardly talk. First, like an idiot, I started to cry, and Jon didn't know what to think. But I was so happy, I couldn't help it, and then I wasn't even able to talk, and Jon finally asked me if I wanted to marry him or not and all I could do was nod."

"Oh, Sandy, I'm so happy for you." Ashley threw her arms around her friend and hugged her. "You've been in love with Jon for so long."

Sandy's happy smile lit her eyes. "I didn't ever think he'd ask me to marry him. I've known so much longer than Jon how I felt, and it was so hard to wait for him to feel the same way." She sighed, and a dreamy look stole over the pert face. "I love him so much it almost frightens me. He's with me even when he isn't with me." She giggled. "I know that sounds crazy."

It didn't sound so crazy to Claudia. Seth was thousands of miles away, but in some ways he had never left. If anything was crazy, it was the way she could close her eyes and feel the taste of his mouth over hers. It was the memory of that last gentle caress and the sweet kiss that was supposed to say goodbye.

She was so caught up in her thoughts she didn't even notice that Sandy had left until Ashley's voice broke into her reverie.

"I wish you could see yourself," Ashley said impatiently, her expression thoughtful. "You look so miserable that I'm beginning to think you should see a doctor."

"A doctor isn't going to be able to help me," Claudia mumbled.

"You've got to do something. You can't just sit around here moping like this. It isn't like you. Either you settle whatever's wrong between you and Seth or I'll contact him myself."

"You wouldn't," Claudia insisted.

"Don't count on it. Cooper's as worried about you as I am. If I don't do something, *he* might."

"It isn't going to do any good." Claudia tucked her

chin into her neck. "I simply can't do what Seth wants. Not now."

"And what *does* he want? Don't you think it's time you told me? I'm your best friend, after all."

"He wants me to marry him and move to Nome," Claudia whispered weakly. "But I can't give up my dream of a medical degree and move to some no-man's-land. And he just as adamantly refuses to move to Seattle. As far as I can see, there's no solution."

"You idiot!" Ashley flared incredulously. "The pair of you! You're both behaving like spoiled children, each wanting your own way. For heaven's sake, does it have to be so intense? You've only known each other a few days. It would be absurd to make such a drastic change in your life on such a short acquaintance. And the same thing goes for Seth. The first thing to do is be sure of your feelings—both of you. Get to know each other better and establish a friendship, then you'll know what you want."

"Good idea. But Seth's three thousand miles away, in case you'd forgotten, and forming a relationship when we're thousands of miles apart isn't going to be easy."

"How did you ever make the dean's list, girl?" Ashley asked in a scathing tone. "Ever hear of letters? And I'm not talking e-mail, either. I mean the real thing, pen on paper, to prove you put a little time and thought into what you're saying. Some people have been known to faithfully deliver those white envelopes as they fill their appointed rounds—through snow, through rain—"

"I get the picture," Claudia interrupted.

She had thought about writing to Seth, but she didn't have his address and, more importantly, didn't know what she could say. One thing was certain, the next move would have to come from her. Seth was a proud man. He had made his position clear. It was up to her now.

Ashley left for work a few minutes later, and Claudia once again mentally toyed with the idea of writing to Seth. She didn't need to say anything about his proposal. As usual, her level-headed friend had put things into perspective. Ashley was right. She couldn't make such a major decision without more of a basis for their relationship than six days. They could write, phone and even visit each other until she was sure of her feelings. Because, she realized, she couldn't go on living like this.

The letter wasn't easy. Crumpled pieces of paper littered the living room floor. When it got to the point that the carpet had all but disappeared under her discarded efforts, she paused and decided it would go better if she ate something. She stood, stretched and was making herself a sandwich when she realized that, for the first time since Seth had left, she was actually hungry. A pleased smile spread slowly across her face.

Once she'd eaten, the letter flowed smoothly. She wrote about the weather and her classes, a couple of idiosyncrasies of her professors. She asked him questions about Nome and his business. Finally she had two sheets of neat, orderly handwriting, and she signed the letter simply "Claudia." Reading it over, she realized she'd left so much unsaid. Chewing on the end of her pen, she scribbled a postscript that said she missed him. Would he understand?

She had the letter almost memorized by the time she dropped it into a mailbox an hour later. She'd walked it there as soon as she'd finished writing it, afraid she would change her mind if she let it lie around all weekend. She hadn't even tried to find his address, even though she was sure she could track him down on the internet. She simply wrote his name and Nome, Alaska. If it arrived, then it would be God's doing. This whole relationship was God's doing.

Calculating that the letter would arrive on Wednesday or Thursday, she guessed that, if he wrote back right away, she could have something from him by the following week. Until then, she was determined to let it go and try to think of anything else. That night she crawled into bed and, for the first time in two and a half desolate weeks, slept peacefully.

All day Thursday, Claudia was fidgety. Seth would get her letter today if he hadn't already. How would he react to it? Would he be glad, or had he given up on her completely? How much longer would it be before she knew? How long before she could expect an answer? She smiled as she let herself into the apartment; it was as if she expected something monumental to happen. By ten she'd finished her studies, and, after a leisurely bath she read her Bible and went to bed, unreasonably disappointed.

Nothing happened Friday, either. Steve Kali, another medical student, asked her out for coffee after anatomy lab, and she accepted, pleased by the invitation. Steve was nice. He wasn't Seth, but he was nice.

The phone rang Saturday afternoon. She was bringing in the groceries and dropped a bag of oranges as she rushed across the carpet to answer it.

"Hello." She sounded out of breath.

"Hello, Red," Seth's deep, rich voice returned.

Her hand tightened on the receiver, and her heartbeat accelerated wildly. "You got my letter?" Her voice was still breathless, but this time it had nothing to do with hurrying to answer the phone.

"About time. I didn't know if I'd ever hear from you."

Claudia suddenly felt so weak that she had to sit down. "How are you?"

"Miserable," he admitted. "Your letter sounded so bright and newsy. If you hadn't added that note at the bottom, I don't know what I would have thought."

"Oh, Seth," she breathed into the phone. "I've been wretched. I really do miss you."

"It's about time you admitted as much. I had no idea it would take you this long to realize I was right. Do you want me to fly down there so we can do the blood tests?"

"Blood tests?"

"Yes, silly woman. Alaska requires blood tests for a marriage license."

Five

"Marriage license? I didn't write because I was ready to change my mind," Claudia said, shocked. Did Seth believe this separation was a battle of wills and she'd been the first to surrender? "I'm staying here in Seattle. I thought you understood that."

Her announcement was followed by a lengthy pause. She could practically hear his anger and the effort he made to control his breathing. "Then why did you write the letter?" he asked at last.

"You still don't understand, do you?" She threw the words at him. "Someday, Seth Lessinger, I'm going to be a fabulous doctor. That's been my dream from the time I was a little girl." She forced herself to stop and take a calming breath; she didn't want to argue with him. "Seth, I wrote you because I've been miserable. I've missed you more than I believed possible. I thought it might work if you and I got to know one another better. We can write and—"

"I'm not interested in a pen pal." His laugh was harsh and bitter.

"Neither am I," she returned sharply. "You're being unfair again. Can't we compromise? Do we have to do everything your way? Give me time, that's all I'm asking."

Her words were met with another long silence, and for an apprehensive second she thought he might have hung up on her. "Seth," she whispered, "all I'm asking is for you to give me more time. Is that so unreasonable?"

"All right, Red, we'll do this your way," he conceded. "But I'm not much for letter writing, and this is a busy time of the year for me, so don't expect much."

She let out the breath she hadn't realized she'd been holding and smiled. "I won't." It was a beginning.

Seth's first letter arrived four days later. Home from her classes before Ashley, Claudia stopped to pick up the mail in the vestibule. There was only one letter, the address written in large, bold handwriting. She stared at it with the instant knowledge that it was from Seth. Clutching the envelope tightly, she rushed up the stairs, fumbled with the apartment lock and barged in the front door. She tossed her coat and books haphazardly on the couch before tearing open the letter. Like hers, his was newsy, full of tidbits of information about his job and what this new contract would do for his business, Arctic Barge Company. He talked a little about the city of Nome and what she should expect when she came.

Claudia couldn't prevent the smile that trembled across her lips. When she came, indeed! He also explained that when she packed her things she would have to ship everything she couldn't fit in her suitcases. Arrangements would need to be made to have her belong-ings transported on a barge headed north. The only way into Nome was either by air or by sea, and access by sea was limited to a few short weeks in the summer before the water froze again. The pressure for her to make her decision soon was subtle. He concluded by saying that he missed her and, just in case she'd forgotten, he loved her. She read the words and closed her eyes to the flood of emotions that swirled through her.

She answered the letter that night and sent off another two days later. A week passed, but finally she received another long response from Seth, with an added postscript that there was a possibility he would be in Seattle toward the end of October for a conference. He didn't know how much unscheduled time he would have, but he was hoping to come a day early. That, he said, would be the time for them to sit down and talk, because letters only made him miss her more. He gave her the dates and promised to contact her when he knew more. Again he told her that he loved her and needed her.

Claudia savored both letters, reading them so many times she knew each one by heart. In some ways, their correspondence was building a more solid relationship than having him in Seattle would have. If he'd been here, she would have been more easily swayed by her physical response to him. This way she could carefully weigh each aspect of her decision, and give Seth and the move to Nome prayerful consideration. And she *did* pray, fervently, every day. But after so many weeks she was beginning to believe God was never going to answer.

One afternoon Ashley saw her reading one of Seth's

letters for the tenth time and laughingly tossed a throw pillow at her.

"Hey," Claudia snapped, "what did you do that for?"

"Because I couldn't stand to see you looking so miserable!"

"I'm not miserable," Claudia denied. "I'm happy. Seth wrote about how much he wants me to marry him and…and…" Her voice cracked, and she swallowed back tears that burned for release. "I…didn't know I would cry about it."

"You still don't know what you want, do you?"

Claudia shook her head. "I pray and pray and pray, but God doesn't seem to hear me. He gave Seth a sign, but there's nothing for me. It's unfair!"

"What kind of confirmation are you looking for?" Ashley sat beside Claudia and handed her a tissue.

Claudia sniffled and waved her hand dramatically. "I don't know. Just something—anything! When I made my commitment to Christ, I told Him my life was no longer my own but His. If He wants me digging ditches, then I'll dig ditches. If He wants me to give up medical school and marry Seth, then I'll do it in a minute. Seth seems so positive that it's the right thing, and I'm so unsure."

Ashley pinched her lips together for a moment, then went into her bedroom. She returned a minute later with her Bible. "Do you remember the story of Elijah?"

"Of course. I would never forget the Old Testament prophets."

Ashley nodded as she flipped through the worn pages of her Bible. "Here it is. Elijah was hiding from the wicked Jezebel. God sent the angel of the Lord, who led Elijah into a cave. He told him to stay there and wait, because God was coming to speak to him. Elijah waited and waited. When a strong wind came, he rushed from the cave and cried out, but the wind wasn't God. An earthquake followed, and again Elijah hurried outside, certain this time that the earthquake was God speaking to him. But it wasn't the earthquake. Next came a fire, and again Elijah was positive that the fire was God speaking to him. But it wasn't. Finally, when everything was quiet, Elijah heard a soft, gentle whisper. That was the Lord." Ashley transferred the open Bible to Claudia's lap. "Here, read the story yourself."

Thoughtfully Claudia read over the chapter before looking up. "You're telling me I should stop looking for that bolt of lightning in the sky that spells out *Marry Seth*?"

"Or the handwriting on the wall," Ashley added with a laugh.

"So God is answering my prayers, and all I need to do is listen?"

"I think so."

"It sounds too simple," Claudia said with a sigh.

"I don't know that it is. But you've got to quit looking for the strong wind, the earthquake and the fire, and listen instead to your heart."

"I'm not even a hundred percent sure I love him. I don't think I know him well enough yet." The magnetic physical attraction between them was overwhelming, but there was so much more to love and a lifetime commitment.

"You'll know," Ashley assured her confidently. "I

don't doubt that for a second. When the time is right, you'll know."

Claudia felt as if a weight had been lifted from her, and she sighed deeply before forcefully expelling her breath. "Hey, do you know what today is?" she asked, then answered before Ashley had the opportunity. "Columbus Day. A day worthy of celebrating with something special." Carefully she tucked Seth's letter back inside the envelope. "Let's bring home Chinese food and drown our doubts in pork fried rice."

"And egg rolls," Ashley added. "Lots of egg rolls."

By the time they returned to the apartment, Claudia and Ashley had collected more than dinner. They had bumped into Steve Kali and a friend of his at the restaurant, and after quick introductions, the four of them realized they could get two extra items for free if they combined their orders. From there it was a quick step to inviting the guys over to eat at their place.

They sat on the floor in a large circle, laughing and eating with chopsticks directly from the white carry-out boxes, passing them around so everyone could try everything.

Steve's friend, Dave Kimball, was a law student, and he immediately showed a keen interest in Ashley. Claudia watched with an amused smile as her friend responded with some flirtatious moves of her own.

The chopsticks were soon abandoned in favor of forks, but the laughter continued.

"You know what we're celebrating, don't you?" Ashley asked between bites of ginger-spiced beef and tomato.

"No." Both men shook their heads, glancing from one girl to the other.

"Columbus Day," Claudia supplied.

"As in 'Columbus sailed the ocean blue'?" Steve jumped up and danced around the room singing.

Everyone laughed.

The phone rang, and since Steve was right near it, he picked up the cordless. "I'll get that for you," he volunteered, then promptly dropped the receiver. "Oops, sorry," he apologized into the receiver.

Claudia couldn't help smiling as she realized she was having a good time. It felt good to laugh again. Ashley was right, this whole thing with Seth was too intense. She needed to relax. Her decision had to be based on the quiet knowledge that marriage to Seth was what God had ordained.

"I'm sorry, would you mind repeating that?" Steve said into the phone. "Claudia? Yeah, she's here." He covered the receiver with the palm of his hand. "Are you here, Claudia?" he asked with a silly grin.

"You nut. Give me that." She stood and took the phone. "Hello." With her luck, it would be Cooper, who would no doubt demand to know what a man was doing in her apartment and answering her phone, no less. "This is Claudia."

"What's going on?"

The color drained from her flushed cheeks. "Seth? Is that you?" she asked incredulously. Breathlessly, she repeated herself. "Seth, it is really you?"

"It's me," he confirmed, his tone brittle. "Who's the guy who answered the phone."

"Oh." She swallowed, and turned her back to the others. "He's a classmate of mine. We have a few friends over," she explained, stretching the truth. She didn't want Seth to get the wrong impression. "We're celebrating Columbus Day…you know, Columbus, the man who sailed across the Atlantic looking for India and discovered America instead. Do you celebrate Columbus Day in Alaska?" she asked, embarrassingly aware that she was babbling.

"I know what day it is. You sound like you've been drinking."

"Not unless the Chinese tea's got something in it I don't know about."

"Does the guy who answered the phone mean anything to you?"

The last thing Claudia wanted to do was make explanations to Seth with everyone listening. On the other hand, carrying the phone into her bedroom so they could talk privately would only invite all kinds of questions she didn't want to answer. "It would be better if we…if we talked later," she said, stammering slightly.

"Everyone's there listening, right?" Seth guessed.

"Right," she confirmed with a soft sigh. "Do you mind?"

"No, but before you hang up, answer me one thing. Have you been thinking about how much I love you and want you here with me?"

"Oh, Seth," she murmured miserably. "Yes, I've hardly thought of anything else."

"And you still don't know what you want to do?" he asked, his voice heavy with exasperation.

"Not yet."

"All right, Red. I'll call back in an hour."

* * *

In the end it was almost two hours before the phone rang again. Steve and Dave had left an hour earlier, and Ashley had made a flimsy excuse about needing to do some research at the library. Claudia didn't question her and appreciated the privacy.

She answered the phone on the first ring. "Hello."

"Now tell me who that guy was who picked up the phone before," Seth demanded without even a greeting.

Claudia couldn't help it. She laughed. "Seth Lessinger, you sound almost jealous."

"Almost?" he shot back.

"His name's Steve Kali, and we have several classes together, that's all," she explained, pleased at his concern. "I didn't know you were the jealous sort," she said gently.

"I never have been before. And I don't like the way it feels, if that makes you any happier."

"I'd feel the same way," she admitted. "I wish you were here, Seth. Ashley and I walked by a skating rink tonight and stopped to watch some couples skating together. Do you realize that you and I have never skated? If I close my eyes, I can almost feel your arm around me."

Seth sucked in his breath. "Why do you say things like that when we're separated by thousands of miles? Your sense of timing is really off. Besides, we don't need skating as an excuse for me to be near you," he murmured, his voice low. "Listen, honey, I'll be in Seattle a week from Saturday."

"Saturday? Oh, Seth!" She was too happy to express her thoughts coherently. "It'll be so good to see you!"

"My plane arrives early that morning. I couldn't manage the extra day, but I'll phone you as soon as I can review the conference schedule and figure out when I'll be able to see you."

"I won't plan a thing. No," she said, laughing, "I'll plan everything. Can you stay over through Monday? I'll skip classes and we can have a whole extra day alone."

"I can't." He sounded as disappointed as she felt.

They talked for an hour, and Claudia felt guilty at the thought of his phone bill, but the conversation had been wonderful.

Did she love him? The question kept repeating itself for the next two weeks. If she could truthfully answer that one question, then everything else would take care of itself. Just talking to him over the phone had lifted her spirits dramatically. But could she leave school and everything, everyone, she had ever known and follow him to a place where she knew no one but him and would have no way to follow her dream?

Her last class on the day before he arrived was a disaster. Her attention span was no longer than a four-year-old's. Time and time again she was forced to bring herself back into reality. So many conflicting emotions and milestones seemed to be coming at her. The first big tests of the quarter, Seth's visit. She felt pounded from every side, tormented by her own indecision.

Steve walked out of the building with her.

"Why so glum?" he asked. "If anyone's got complaints, it should be me." They continued down the stairs, and Claudia cast him a sidelong glance.

"What have you got to complain about?"

"Plenty," he began in an irritated tone. "You remember Dave Kimball?"

She nodded, recalling Steve's tall, sandy-haired friend who had flirted so outrageously with Ashley. "Sure, I remember Dave."

"We got picked up by the police a couple of nights ago."

She glanced apprehensively at him. "What happened?"

"Nothing, really. We'd been out having a good time and decided to walk home after a few beers. About halfway to the dorm, Dave starts with the crazies. He was climbing up the streetlights, jumping on parked cars. I wasn't doing any of that, but we were both brought into the police station for disorderly conduct."

Claudia's blue eyes widened incredulously. Steve was one of the straightest, most clean-cut men she had met. This was so unlike anything she would have expected from him that she didn't know how to react.

"That's not the half of it," he continued. "Once we were at the police station, Dave kept insisting that he was a law student and knew his rights. He demanded his one phone call."

"Well, it's probably a good thing he did know what to do," she said.

"Dave made his one call, all right." Steve inhaled a shaky breath. "And twenty minutes later the desk sergeant came in to ask which one of us had ordered the pizza."

Claudia couldn't stop herself from bursting into giggles, and it wasn't long before Steve joined her. He placed a friendly arm around her shoulders as their laughter faded. Together they strolled toward the parking lot.

"I do feel bad about the police thing…" she said. Before she could complete her thought, she caught sight of a broad-shouldered man walking toward her with crisp strides. She knew immediately it was Seth.

His look of contempt was aimed directly at her, his rough features darkened by a fierce frown. Even across the narrowing distance she recognized the tight set of his mouth as he glared at her.

Steve's arm resting lightly across her shoulders felt as if it weighed a thousand pounds.

Six

Claudia's mouth was dry as she quickened her pace and rushed forward to meet Seth. If his look hadn't been so angry and forbidding, she would have walked directly into his arms. "When—how did you get here? I thought you couldn't come until tomorrow?" Only now was she recovering from the shock of seeing him.

An unwilling smile broke his stern expression as he pulled her to him and crushed her in his embrace.

Half lifted from the sidewalk, Claudia linked her hands behind his neck and felt his warm breath in her hair. "Oh, Seth," she mumbled, close to tears. "You idiot, why didn't you say something?"

So many emotions were filling her at once. She felt crushed yet protected, jubilant yet tearful, excited but afraid. Ignoring the negatives, she began spreading eager kisses over his face.

Slowly he released her, and the two men eyed each other skeptically.

Seth extended his hand. "I'm Seth Lessinger, Claudia's fiancé."

She had to bite her lip to keep from correcting him, but she wouldn't say anything that could destroy the happiness of seeing him again.

Steve's eyes were surprised, but he managed to mumble a greeting and exchange handshakes. Then he made some excuse about catching a ride and was gone.

"Who was that?"

"Steve," she replied, too happy to see him to question the way he had introduced himself to her friend. "He answered the phone the other night when you called. He's just a friend, don't worry."

"Then why did he have his arm around you?" Seth demanded with growing impatience.

Claudia ignored the question, instead standing on the tips of her toes and lightly brushing her mouth over his. His whiskers tickled her face, and she lifted both hands to his dark beard, framing his lips so she could kiss him soundly.

His response was immediate as he pulled her into his arms. "I've missed you. I won't be able to wait much longer. Who would believe such a little slip of nothing could bring this giant to his knees? Literally," he added. "Because I'll propose again right here on the sidewalk if you think it will make a difference."

Claudia's eyes widened with feigned offense. "Little slip of nothing? Come on, you make me sound like some anorexic supermodel."

He laughed, the robust, deep laugh that she loved. "Compared to me, you're pint-size." Looping his arm around her waist, he walked beside her. She felt protected and loved beyond anything she had ever known. She smiled up at him, and his eyes drank deeply from hers as a slow grin spread over his face, crinkling tiny lines at his eyes. "You may be small, but you hold a power over me I don't think I'll ever understand."

Leaning her head against his arm, Claudia relaxed. "Why didn't you say anything about coming today?"

"I didn't know that I was going to make the flight until the last minute. As it was, I hired a pilot out of Nome to make the connection in Fairbanks."

"You could have called when you landed."

"I tried, but no one answered at the apartment and your cell went straight to voicemail."

She pulled the phone out of her purse and checked. "Oops. I turned it off during class, and I guess I forgot to turn it on again." She remedied that as she asked, "So how'd you know where to find me?"

"I went to your apartment to wait for you and ran into Ashley just getting home. She drew me a map of the campus and told me where you'd be. You don't mind?"

"Of course not," she assured him with a smile and a shake of her head. "I just wish I'd known. I could have ducked out of class and met you at the airport."

By then they had reached her car. Seth asked to drive, so she gave him her keys. It wasn't until they were stuck in heavy afternoon traffic that she noticed Seth was heading in the opposite direction from her apartment.

"Where are we going?" She looked down at her jeans and Irish cable-knit sweater. She wasn't dressed for anything but a casual outing.

"My hotel," he answered without looking at her, focusing his attention on the freeway. "I wanted to talk to you privately, and from the look of things at your place, Ashley is going to be around for a while."

Claudia knew just what he was talking about. Ashley was deep into a project that she'd been working on for two nights. Magazines, newspapers and pages of scribbled notes were scattered over the living room floor.

"I know what you mean about the apartment." She laughed softly in understanding.

He slowed the car as he pulled off the freeway and onto Mercer Avenue. "She's a nice girl. I like her. Those blue eyes of hers are almost as enchanting as yours."

Something twitched in Claudia's stomach. Jealousy? Over Ashley? She was her best friend! Quickly she tossed the thought aside.

Seth reached for her hand. Linking their fingers, he carried her hand to his mouth and gently kissed her knuckles. Shivers tingled up her arm, and she smiled contentedly.

The hotel lobby was bristling with activity. In contrast, Seth's room in the conference hotel was quiet and serene. Situated high above the city, it offered a sweeping view of Puget Sound and the landmarks Seattle was famous for: the Pacific Science Center, the Space Needle and the Kingdome.

The king-size bed was bordered on each side by oak nightstands with white ceramic lamps. Two easy chairs were set obliquely in front of a hi-def television and state-of-the-art gaming system. Claudia glanced over the room, feeling slightly uneasy.

The door had no sooner closed than Seth placed a hand on her shoulder and turned her around to face him. Their eyes met, hers uncertain and a little afraid, his warm and reassuring. When he slipped his arms around her, she went willingly, fitting herself against the hard contours of his solid body. Relaxing, she savored the fiery warmth of his kiss. She slipped her hands behind his neck and yielded with the knowledge that she wanted him to kiss her, needed his kisses. Nothing on earth came so close to heaven as being cradled in his arms.

Arms of corded steel locked around her, held her close. Yet he was gentle, as if she were the most precious thing in the world. With a muted groan, he dragged his mouth from hers and showered the side of her neck with urgent kisses.

"I shouldn't be doing this," he moaned hoarsely. "Not when I don't know if I have the will to stop." One hand continued down her back, arching her upward while the fingers of the other hand played havoc with her hair.

Claudia's mind was caught in a whirl of desire and need. This shouldn't be happening, but it felt so right. For a moment she wanted to stop him, tell him they should wait until they were married—*if* they married. But she couldn't speak.

Seth pulled away and paused, his eyes searching hers. His breath came in uneven gasps.

She knew this was the time to stop, to back away, but she couldn't. The long weeks of separation, the doubts, the uncertainties that had plagued her night and day, the restless dreams, all exploded in her mind as she lifted her arms to him. It had been like this between them almost from the beginning, this magnetic, overpowering attraction.

Slowly Seth lowered his mouth to hers until their breaths merged, and the kiss that followed sent her world into a crazy spin.

"I can't do it," he whispered hoarsely into her ear, the bitter words barely distinct. "I can't," he repeated, and broke the embrace.

His voice filtered through her consciousness, and she forced her eyes open. Seth was standing away from her. He wasn't smiling now, and his troubled, almost tormented, expression puzzled her.

"Seth," she asked softly, "what is it?"

"I'm sorry." He crossed his arms and turned his back, as if offering her the chance to escape.

Her arms felt as if they'd been weighed down with lead, and her heart felt numb, as if she'd been exposed to the Arctic cold without the proper protective gear.

"Forgive me, Red." Seth covered his eyes with a weary hand and walked across the room to stand by the window. "I brought you here with the worst of intentions," he began. "I thought if we were to make love, then all your doubts would be gone." He paused to take in a labored breath. "I knew you'd marry me then without question."

Understanding burned like a laser beam searing through her mind, and she half moaned, half cried. Her arms cradled her stomach as the pain washed over her. Color blazed in her cheeks at how close she had come to letting their passion rage out of control. It had been a trick, a trap, in order for him to exert his will over her.

Several long moments passed in silence. Claudia turned to Seth, whose profile was outlined by the dim light of dusk. He seemed to be struggling for control of his emotions.

"I wouldn't blame you if you hated me after this," he said at last.

"I...I don't hate you." Her voice was unsteady, soft and trembling.

"You don't love me, either, do you?" He hurled the words at her accusingly and turned to face her.

The muscles in her throat constricted painfully. "I don't know. I just don't know."

"Will you ever be completely sure?" he asked with obvious impatience.

Claudia buried her face in her hands, defeated and miserable.

"Red, please don't cry. I'm sorry." The anger was gone, and he spoke softly, reassuringly.

She shivered with reaction. "If...if we did get married, could I stay here until I finished med school?"

"No," he returned adamantly. "I want a wife and children. Look at me, Red. I'm thirty-six. I can't wait another five or six years for a family. And I work too hard to divide my life between Nome and Seattle."

Wasn't there any compromise? Did everything have to be his way? "You're asking for so much," she cried.

"But I'm offering even more," he countered.

"You don't understand," she told him. "If I quit med school now, I'll probably never be able to finish. Especially if I won't be able to come back for several years."

"There isn't any compromise," he said with a note of finality. "If God wants you to be a doctor, He'll provide the way later. We both have to trust Him for that."

"I can't give up my entire life. It's not that easy," she whispered.

"Then there's nothing left to say, is there?" Dark shadows clouded his face, and he turned sharply and resumed his position in front of the window.

There didn't seem to be anything left to do but to leave quietly. She forced herself to open the door, but she knew she couldn't let it end like this. She let the door click softly shut.

At the sound Seth slammed his fist against the window ledge. Claudia gave a small cry of alarm, and he spun to face her. His rugged features were contorted with anger as he stared at her. But one look told her that the anger was directed at himself and not her.

"I thought you'd gone." His gaze held hers.

"I couldn't," she whispered.

He stared deeply into her liquid blue eyes and paused as if he wanted to say something, but finally he just shook his head in defeat and turned his back to her again.

Her eyes were haunted as she covered the distance between them. She slid her hands around his waist, hugging him while she rested a tearstained cheek against his back.

"We have something very special, Red, but it's not going to work." The dejected tone of his voice stabbed at her heart.

"It *will* work. I know it will. But I want to be sure, very sure, before I make such a drastic change in my life. Give me time, that's all I'm asking."

"You've had almost six weeks."

"It's not enough."

He tried to remove her hands, but she squeezed tighter. "We're both hurt and angry tonight, but that doesn't mean things between us won't work."

"I could almost believe you," he murmured and turned, wrapping her securely in his arms.

She met his penetrating gaze and answered in a soft, throbbing voice, "Believe me, Seth. Please believe me."

His gaze slid to her lips before his mouth claimed hers in a fierce and flaming kiss that was almost savage, as if to punish her for the torment she had caused him. But it didn't matter how he kissed her as long as she hadn't lost him.

They had dinner at the hotel but didn't return to Seth's room. They discussed his conference schedule, which would take up pretty much all of Saturday. His plane left Sunday afternoon. They made plans to attend the Sunday morning church service together, and for her to drive him to the airport afterward.

Her heart was heavy all the next day. Several times she wished she could talk to him and clear away the ghosts of yesterday. For those long, miserable weeks she had missed him so much that she could hardly function. Then, at the first chance to see each other again, they had ended up fighting. Why didn't she know what to do? Was this torment her heart was suffering proof of love?

The question remained unanswered as they sat together in church Sunday morning. It felt so right to have him by her side. Claudia closed her eyes to pray, fervently asking God to guide her. She paused, recalling the verses she had found in the Gospel of Matthew just the other night, verses all about asking, seeking, knocking. God had promised that anyone who asked would receive, and anyone who sought would find. It had all sounded so simple and straightforward when she read it, but it wasn't—not for her.

When she finished her prayer and opened her eyes,

she felt Seth's gaze burn over her, searching her face. She longed to reassure him but could find no words. Gently she reached for his hand and squeezed it.

They rode to the airport in an uneasy silence. Their time had been bittersweet for the most part. What she had hoped would be a time to settle doubts had only raised more.

"You don't need to come inside with me," he said as they neared the airport. His words sliced into her troubled thoughts.

"What?" she asked, confused and hurt. "But I'd like to be with you as long as possible."

He didn't look pleased with her decision. "Fine, if that's what you want."

The set of his mouth was angry and impatient, but she didn't know why. "You don't want me there, do you?" She tried to hide the hurt in her voice.

His cool eyes met her look of defiance. "Oh, for goodness sake, settle down, Red. I take it all back. Come in if you want. I didn't mean to make a federal case out of this."

Claudia didn't want to argue again, not during this last chance to spend time together. Seth continued to look withdrawn as they parked in the cement garage and walked into the main terminal.

She reached out tentatively and rested her hand on his arm. "Friends?" she asked and offered him a smile.

He returned the gesture and tenderly squeezed her delicate hand. "Friends."

The tension between them eased, and she waited while Seth hit the check-in kiosk. He returned with a wry grin. "My flight's been delayed an hour. How about some lunch?"

She couldn't prevent the smile that softly curved her mouth. Her eyes reflected her pleasure at the unexpected time together.

Claudia noted that Seth barely touched his meal. Her appetite wasn't up to par, either. Another separation loomed before them.

"How long will it be before you'll be back?" she asked as they walked toward the security line.

There was a moment of grim hesitation before Seth answered. "I don't know. Months, probably. This conference wasn't necessary. If it hadn't been for you, I wouldn't have attended, but I can't afford to keep taking time away from my business like this."

Claudia swallowed past the lump forming in her throat. "Thanksgiving break is coming soon. Maybe I could fly up and visit you. I'd like to see the beauty of Alaska for myself. You've told me so much about it already." Just for a moment, for a fleeting second, she was tempted to drop everything and leave with him now. Quickly she buried the impulsive thought and clenched her fists inside the pockets of her wool coat.

Seth didn't respond either way to her suggestion.

"What do you think?" she prompted.

He inclined his head and nodded faintly. "If that's what you'd like."

Claudia had the feeling he didn't really understand any of what she'd been trying to explain about her dreams and what it would mean to her to move, or how big a step it was for her to offer to visit.

When he couldn't delay any longer and had to get in

line to pass through the security screening process, her
façade of composure began to slip. It was difficult not to
cry, and she blinked several times, not wanting Seth to
remember her with tears shimmering in her eyes. With
a proud lift of her chin, she offered him a brave smile.

He studied her unhappy face. "Goodbye, Red." His
eyes continued to hold hers.

Her hesitation before her answer only emphasized
her inner turmoil. "Goodbye, Seth," she whispered
softly, a slight catch in her voice.

He cupped her face with the palm of his hand, and his
thumb gently wiped away the single tear that was weaving a slow course down her pale cheek. Claudia buried
her chin in his hand and gently kissed his callused palm.

Gathering her into his embrace, Seth wrapped his
arms around her as he buried his face in her neck and
breathed deeply. When his mouth found hers, the kiss
was gentle and sweet, and so full of love that fresh tears
misted her eyes.

His hold relaxed, and he began to pull away, but
she wouldn't let him. "Seth." She murmured his name
urgently. She had meant to let him go, relinquish him
without a word, but somehow she couldn't.

He scooped her in his arms again, crushing her
against him with a fierceness that stole her breath away.
"I'm a man," he bit out in an impatient tone, "and I can't
take much more of this." He released her far enough to
study her face. His dark eyes clearly revealed his needs.
"I'm asking you again, Claudia. Marry me and come to
Nome. I promise you a good life. I need you."

Claudia felt raw. The soft, womanly core of her cried
out a resounding yes, but she couldn't let herself base

such a life-changing decision on the emotion of the moment. She didn't want to decide something so important to both of them on the basis of feelings. Indecision and uncertainty raced through her mind, and she could neither reject nor accept his offer. Unable to formulate words, she found a low, protesting groan slipping from her throat. Her brimming blue eyes pleaded with him for understanding.

Seth's gaze sliced into her as a hardness stole over his features, narrowing his mouth. Forcefully he turned and, with quick, impatient steps, joined the line of passengers waiting to pass security and head to their gates.

Unable to do anything more, she watched him until he was out of sight, and then she turned and headed dejectedly back to the garage. At least she'd canceled her regular Sunday dinner with Cooper, so she wouldn't have to put on a happy face for him, and could just go home and give in to her depression.

The following week was wretched. At times Claudia thought it would have been easier not to have seen Seth again than endure the misery of another parting. To complicate her life further, it was the week of midterm exams. Never had she felt less like studying. Each night she wrote Seth long, flowing letters. School had always come first, but suddenly writing to him was more important. When she did study, her concentration waned and her mind wandered to the hurt look on Seth's face when they'd said goodbye. That look haunted her.

She did poorly on the first test, so, determined to do better on the next, she forced herself to study. With her textbooks lying open on top of the kitchen table, she propped her chin on both hands as she stared into space. Despite her best intentions, her thoughts weren't on school but on Seth. The illogical meanderings of her mind continued to torment her with the burning question of her future. Was being a pediatrician so important if it meant losing Seth?

"You look miserable," Ashley commented as she strolled into the kitchen to pour herself a glass of milk.

"That's because I feel miserable," Claudia returned, trying—and failing—to smile.

"There's been something different about you since Seth went back to Alaska again."

"No there hasn't," Claudia denied. "It's just the stress of midterms." Why did she feel the need to make excuses? She'd always been able to talk to Ashley about anything.

Her roommate gave her a funny look but didn't say anything as she turned and went back to the living room.

Angry with herself and the world, Claudia studied half the night, finally staggering into her bedroom at about three. That was another thing. She hadn't been sleeping well since Seth had gone.

Ashley was cooking dinner when Claudia got home the next afternoon. After her exam, she'd gone to the library to study, hoping a change of scenery would help keep her mind off Seth and let her concentrate on her studies.

"You had company," Ashley announced casually, but she looked a bit flushed and slightly uneasy.

Claudia's heart stopped. Seth. He had come back

for her. She needed so desperately to see him again, to talk to him.

"Seth?" she asked breathlessly.

"No, Cooper. I didn't know what time you were going to get home, so instead of waiting here, he decided to run an errand and come back later," Ashley explained.

"Oh." Claudia didn't even try to disguise the disappointment in her voice. "I can do without another unpleasant confrontation with my uncle. I wonder how he found out about how badly I did on that test already."

"Why do you always assume the worst with Cooper?" Ashley demanded with a sharp edge of impatience. "I, for one, happen to think he's nice. I don't think I've ever seen him treat anyone unfairly. It seems to me that you're the one who—" She stopped abruptly and turned back toward the stove, stirring the browning hamburger with unnecessary vigor. "I hope spaghetti sounds good."

"Sure," Claudia responded. "Anything."

Cooper didn't return until they had eaten and were clearing off the table. Claudia made a pot of coffee and brought him a cup in the living room. She could feel him studying her.

"You don't look very good," he commented, taking the cup and saucer out of her hand. Most men would have preferred a mug, but not Cooper.

"So Ashley keeps telling me." She sat opposite him. "Don't do the dishes, Ash," she called into the kitchen. "Wait until later and I'll help."

"No need." Ashley stuck her head around the kitchen

door. "You go ahead and visit. Shout if you need anything."

"No, Ashley," Cooper stood as he spoke. "I think that
it might be beneficial if you were here, too."

Ashley looked from one of them to the other, dried
her hands on a towel and came into the room.

"I don't mean to embarrass you, Ashley, but in all
fairness I think Claudia should know that you were the
one to contact me."

Claudia's gaze shot accusingly across the room to
her friend. "What does he mean?"

Ashley shrugged. "I've been so worried about you
lately. You're hardly yourself anymore. I thought if you
talked to Cooper, it might help you make up your mind.
You can't go on like this, Claudia." Her voice was gentle
and stern all at the same time.

"What do you mean?" Claudia vaulted to her feet.
"This is unfair, both of you against me."

"Against you?" Cooper echoed. "Come on now, Claudia, you seem to have misjudged everything."

"No I haven't." Tears welled in her eyes, burning
for release.

"I think it would probably be best if I left the two of
you alone." Ashley stood and excused herself, returning to the kitchen.

Claudia shot her an angry glare as she stepped past.
Some friend!

"I hope you'll talk honestly with me, Claudia," Cooper began. "I'd like to know what's got you so upset that
you're a stranger to your own best friend."

"Nothing," she denied adamantly, but her voice

cracked and the first tears began spilling down her cheeks.

She was sure Cooper had never seen her cry. He looked at a loss as he stood and searched hurriedly through his suit jacket for a handkerchief. Just watching him made her want to laugh, and she hiccuped in an attempt to restrain both tears and laughter.

"Here." He handed her a white linen square, crisply pressed. Claudia didn't care; she wiped her eyes and blew her nose. "I'm fine, really," she declared in a wavering voice.

"It's about Seth, isn't it?" her uncle prompted.

She nodded, blowing her nose again. "He wants me to marry him and move to Alaska."

The room suddenly became still as he digested the information. "Are you going to do it?" he asked in a quiet voice she had long ago learned to recognize as a warning.

"If I knew that, I wouldn't be here blubbering like an idiot," she returned defensively.

"I can't help but believe it would be a mistake," he continued. "Lessinger's a good man, don't misunderstand me, but I don't think you'd be happy in Alaska. Where did you say he was from again?" he asked.

"Nome."

"I don't suppose there's a med school in Nome where you could continue your studies?"

"No." The word was clipped, impatient.

Cooper nodded. "You were meant to be a doctor," he said confidently as he rose to his feet. "You'll get over Seth. There's a fine young man out there somewhere who will make you very happy when you finally meet."

"Sure," she agreed without enthusiasm.

Cooper left a few minutes later, and at the sound of the door closing, Ashley stepped out of the kitchen. "You aren't mad, are you?"

At first Claudia had been, but not anymore. Ashley had only been thinking of her welfare, after all. And thanks to her friend's interference, now she knew where Cooper stood on the subject and what she would face if she did decide to marry Seth.

"Oh, Seth," she whispered that night, sitting up in bed. He hadn't contacted her since his return to Nome, not even answering her long letters, though she had eagerly checked the mail every day. Once again, she understood that the next move would have to be from her. Her Bible rested on her knees, and she opened it for her devotional reading in Hebrews. She read Chapter 11 twice, the famous chapter on faith. Had Rebekah acted in faith when the servant had come to her family, claiming God had given him a sign? Flipping through the pages of her Bible, she turned to Genesis to reread the story Seth had quoted when he had given her the engagement ring and they had argued. She had said that Rebekah probably didn't have any choice in the matter, but reading the story now, she realized that the Bible said she had. Rebekah's family had asked her if she was willing to go with Abraham's servant, and she'd replied that she would.

Rebekah had gone willingly!

Claudia reread the verses as a sense of release came over her. Her hands trembled with excitement as she closed the Bible and stopped to pray. The prayer was so familiar. She asked God's guidance and stated her willingness to do as He wished. But there was a difference this time. This time the peace she had so desperately sought was there, and she knew that at last she could answer Seth in faith, and that her answer would be yes.

Slipping out of the sheets, she opened the drawer that contained the jeweler's box holding the engagement ring. With a happy sigh she hugged it to her breast. The temptation to slip the ring on her finger now was strong, but she would wait until Seth could do it.

Claudia slept peacefully that night for the first time since Seth had left. And the next morning she stayed in her pajamas, with no intention of going to school.

Ashley, who was dressed and ready to go out the door, looked at her in surprise. "Did you oversleep? I'm sorry I didn't wake you, but I thought I heard you moving around in your room."

"You did," Claudia answered cheerfully, but her eyes grew serious as her gaze met Ashley's. "I've decided what to do," she announced solemnly. "I love Seth. I'm going to him as soon as I can make the arrangements."

Ashley's blue eyes widened with joy as she laughed and hugged her friend. "It's about time! I knew all along that the two of you belonged together. I'm so happy for you."

Once the decision was made, there seemed to be a hundred things to be dealt with all at once. Claudia searched the internet for the number she needed, then phoned Seth's company, her fingers trembling, and reached his assistant, who told her that he had flown to Kotzebue on an emergency. She didn't know when he would be returning, but she would give him the message as soon as he walked in the door. Releasing a sigh of disappointment, Claudia replaced the headset in the charger.

Undaunted by the uncertainties of the situation, she drove to the university and officially withdrew from school. Next she purchased the clothes she would be needing to face an Arctic winter, along with a beautiful wedding dress. Finally, focusing on her luck in finding an available dress that was a perfect fit and not on the difficult conversation to come, she drove to Cooper's office.

He rose and smiled broadly when she entered. "You look in better spirits today," he said. "I knew our little talk would help."

"You'd better sit down, Cooper," she said, smiling back at him. "I've made my decision. I love Seth. I've withdrawn from school, and I've made arrangements for my things to be shipped north as soon as possible. I'm marrying Seth Lessinger."

Cooper stiffened, his eyes raking over her. "That's what you think."

Seven

It was dark and stormy when the plane made a jerky landing on the Nome runway, jolting her back to the present, away from the memories of the difficult emotional journey that had brought her to this point. Claudia shifted to relieve her muscles, tired and stiff from the uncomfortable trip. The aircraft had hit turbulent weather shortly after takeoff from Anchorage, and the remainder of the flight had been far too much like a roller-coaster ride for her taste. More than once she had felt the pricklings of fear, but none of the other passengers had showed any concern, so she had accepted the jarring ride as a normal part of flying in Alaska.

Her blue eyes glinted with excitement as she stood and gathered the small bag stored in the compartment above the seat. There wasn't a jetway to usher her into a dry, warm airport. When she stepped from the cozy interior of the plane, she was greeted by a solid blast of Arctic wind. The bitter iciness stole her breath, and she groped for the handrail to maintain her balance. Half-way down the stairs, she was nearly knocked over by a fresh gust of wind. Her hair flew into her face, blinding her. Momentarily unable to move either up or down, she stood stationary until the force of the wind decreased.

Unexpectedly the small bag was wrenched from her numb fingers and she was pulled protectively against a solid male form.

Her rescuer shouted something at her, but the wind carried his voice into the night and there was no distinguishing the message.

She tried to speak but soon realized the uselessness of talking. She was half carried, half dragged the rest of the way down. Once on solid ground, they both struggled against the ferocity of the wind as it whipped and lashed against them. If he hadn't taken the brunt of its force, Claudia had a feeling she might not have made it inside.

As they neared the terminal, the door was opened by someone who'd been standing by, watching. The welcoming warmth immediately stirred life into her frozen body. Nothing could have prepared her for the intensity of the Arctic cold. Before she could turn and thank her rescuer, she was pulled into his arms and crushed in a smothering embrace.

"Seth?" Her arms slid around his waist as she returned the urgency of his hug.

He buried his face in her neck and breathed her name. His hold was almost desperate, and when he spoke, his voice was tight and worried.

"Are you all right?" Gently his hands framed her face, pushing back the strands of hair that had been whipped free by the wind. He searched her features as if looking for any sign of harm.

"I'm fine," she assured him and, wrapping her arms around him a second time, pressed her face into his parka. "I'm so glad to be here."

"I've been sick with worry," he ground out hoarsely. "The storm hit here several hours ago, and there wasn't any way your flight could avoid the worst of it."

"I'm fine, really." Her voice wobbled, not because she was shaky from the flight but from the effect of being in Seth's arms.

"If anything had happened to you, I don't know…" He let the rest fade and tightened his already secure hold.

"I'm glad we won't have to find out," she said and lightly touched her lips to the corner of his mouth.

He released her. The worried look in his eyes had diminished now that he knew she was safe. "Let's get out of here," he said abruptly, and left her standing alone as he secured her luggage. Everything she could possibly get into the three large suitcases—along with whatever she could buy locally—would have to see her through until the freight barge arrived in the spring.

They rode to the hotel she'd booked herself into in his four-wheel-drive SUV. They didn't speak, because Seth needed to give his full attention to maneuvering safely through the storm. Claudia looked out the windshield in awe. The barren land was covered with snow. The buildings were a dingy gray. In her dreams she had conjured up a romantic vision of Seth's life in Nome. Reality shattered the vision as the winds buffeted the large car.

The hotel room was neat and clean—not elegant, but she'd hoped for a certain homey, welcoming appeal. It was not to be. It contained a bed with a plain white bed-spread, a small nightstand, a lamp, a phone, a TV and one chair. Seth followed her in, managing the suitcases.

"You packed enough," he said with a sarcastic un-dertone. She ignored the comment, and busied herself by removing her coat and hanging it in the bare closet. She gave him a puzzled look. Something was wrong. He had hardly spoken to her since they'd left the air-port. At first she'd assumed the tight set of his mouth was a result of the storm, but not now, when she was safe and ready for his love. Her heart ached for him to hold her. Every part of her longed to have him slip the engagement ring onto the third finger of her left hand.

"How's everything in Seattle?" Again that strange inflection in his voice.

"Fine."

He remained on the far side of the room, his hands clenched at his sides.

"Let me take your coat," she offered. As she studied him, the gnawing sensation that something wasn't right increased.

He unzipped his thick parka, but he didn't remove it. He sat at the end of the bed, his face tight and drawn. Resting his elbows on his knees, he leaned forward and buried his face in his hands.

"Seth, what's wrong?" she asked calmly, although she was far from feeling self-possessed.

"I've only had eight hours' sleep in the last four days. A tanker caught fire in port at Kotzebue, and I've been there doing what I could for the past week. You cer-tainly couldn't have chosen a worse time for a visit. Isn't it a little early for Thanksgiving break?"

She wanted to scream that this wasn't a visit, that she'd come to stay, to be his wife and share his world. But she remained quiet, guided by the same inner sense that she had to take this carefully.

Quietly Seth stood and stalked to the far side of the small room. She noticed that he seemed to be limping slightly. He paused and glanced over his shoulder, then turned away from her.

Uncertainty clouded her deep blue eyes, and her mind raced with a thousand questions that she didn't get a chance to ask, because he spoke again.

"I'm flying back to Kotzebue as soon as possible. I shouldn't have taken the time away as it is." He turned around, and his eyes burned her with the intensity of his glare. His mouth was drawn, hard and inflexible. "I'll have one of my men drive you back to the airport for the first available flight to Anchorage." There was no apology, no explanation, no regrets.

Claudia stared back at him in shocked disbelief. Even if he had assumed she was here for a short visit, he was treating her as he would unwanted baggage.

Belying the hurt, she smiled lamely. "I can't see why I have to leave. Even if you aren't here, this would be a good opportunity for me to see Nome. I'd like to—"

"Can't you do as I ask just once?" he shouted.

She lowered her gaze to fight the anger building within her. Squaring her shoulders, she prepared for the worst. "There's something I don't know, isn't there?" she asked in quiet challenge. She wanted to hear the truth, even at the risk of being hurt.

Her question was followed by a moment of grim silence. "I don't want you here."

"I believe you've made that obvious." Her fingers trembled, and she willed them to hold still.

"I tried to reach you before you left."

She didn't comment, only continued to stare at him with questioning eyes.

"It's not going to work between us, Claudia," he announced solemnly. "I think I realized as much when you didn't return with me when I gave you the ring. You must think I was a fool to propose to you the way I did."

"You know I didn't. I—"

He interrupted her again. "I want a wife, Claudia, not some virtuous doctor out to heal the world. I need a woman, someone who knows what she wants in life."

White-lipped, she stiffened her back and fought her building rage with forced control. "Do you want me to hate you, Seth?" she asked softly as her fingers picked an imaginary piece of lint from the sleeve of her thick sweater.

He released a bitter sigh. "Yes. It would make things between us a lot easier if you hated me," he replied flatly. He walked as far away as the small room would allow, as if he couldn't bear to see the pain he was causing her. "Even if you were to change your mind and relinquish your lofty dreams to marry me, I doubt that we could make a marriage work. You've been tossing on a wave of indecision for so long, I don't think you'll ever decide what you really want."

She studied the pattern of the worn carpet, biting her tongue to keep from crying out that she knew what she wanted now. What would be the point? He had witnessed her struggle in the sea of uncertainty. He would assume that her decision was as fickle as the turning tide.

"If we married, what's to say you wouldn't regret it later?" he went on. "You've wanted to be a doctor for so many years that, frankly, I don't know if my love could satisfy you. Someday you might have been able to return to medical school—I would have wanted that for you—but my life, my business, everything I need, is here in Nome. It's where I belong. But not you, Red." The affectionate endearment rolled easily from his lips, seemingly without thought. "We live in two different worlds. And my world will never satisfy you."

"What about everything you told me about the sign from God? You were the one who was so sure. You were the one who claimed to feel a deep, undying love." She hurled the words at him bitterly, intent on hurting him as much as he was hurting her.

"I was wrong. I don't know how I could have been so stupid."

She had to restrain herself from crying out that it had never been absurd, it was wonderful. The Bible verse in the mirror had meant so much to them both. But she refused to plead, and the dull ache in her heart took on a throbbing intensity.

"That's not all," he added with a cruel twist. "There's someone else now."

Nothing could have shocked her more. "Don't lie to me, Seth. Anything but that!"

"Believe it, because it's true. My situation hasn't changed. I need a wife, someone to share my life. There's—" he hesitated "—someone I was seeing before I met you. I was going to ask her to marry me as soon as I got the engagement ring back from you."

"You're lucky I brought it with me, then!" she

shouted as she tore open her purse and dumped the contents out on the bedspread. Carelessly she sorted through her things. It took only a couple of seconds to locate the velvet box, turn around and viciously hurl it at him.

Instinctively he brought his hands up and caught it. Their eyes met for a moment; then, without another word, he tucked it in his pocket.

A searing pain burned through her heart.

Seth seemed to hesitate. He hovered for a moment by the door. "I didn't mean to hurt you." Slowly he lowered his gaze to meet hers.

She avoided his look. Nothing would be worse than to have him offer her sympathy. "I'm sure you didn't," she whispered on a bitter note, and her voice cracked. "Please leave," she requested urgently.

Without another word, he opened the door and walked away.

Numb with shock, Claudia couldn't cry, couldn't move. Holding up her head became an impossible task. A low, protesting cry came from deep within her throat, and she covered her mouth with the palm of one hand. Somehow she made it to the bed, collapsing on the mattress.

When Claudia woke the next morning the familiar lump of pain formed in her throat at the memory of her encounter with Seth. For a while she tried to force herself to return to the black cloud of mindless sleep, but to no avail.

She dressed and stared miserably out the window. The winds were blustery, but nothing compared to yesterday's gales. Seth would have returned to Kotzebue. Her world had died, but Nome lived. The city appeared calm; people were walking, laughing and talking. She wondered if she would ever laugh again. What had gone wrong? Hadn't she trusted God, trusted in Seth's love? How could her world dissolve like this? The tightness in her throat grew and grew.

The small room became her prison. She waited an impatient hour, wondering what she should do, until further lingering became intolerable. Since she was here, she might as well explore the city Seth loved.

The people were friendly, everyone offering an easy smile and a cheery good morning as she passed. There weren't any large stores, nothing to compare with Seattle. She strolled down the sidewalk, not caring where her feet took her. Suddenly she saw a sign proclaiming ARCTIC BARGE COMPANY—Seth's business. A wave of fresh pain swamped her, destroying her fragile composure, and she turned and briskly walked in the opposite direction. Ahead, she spotted a picturesque white church with a bell in its steeple. She was hopeful that she would find peace inside.

The interior was dark as she slipped quietly into the back pew. Thanksgiving would be here at the end of the month—a time for sharing God's goodness with family and friends. She was trapped in Nome with neither. When she'd left Seattle, her heart had nearly burst with praise for God. Now it was ready to burst with the pain of Seth's rejection.

She didn't mean to cry, but there was something so peaceful and restful about the quiet church. A tear slipped from the corner of her eye, and she wiped it aside. She'd left Seattle so sure of Seth's love, filled with the joy of her newfound discovery that she loved him, too, and was ready to be his wife. She'd come in faith. And this was where faith had led her. To an empty church, with a heart burdened by bitter memories.

She'd painted herself into a dark corner. She'd lost her apartment. In the few days between her decision and her flight, Ashley had already found herself a cheaper place and a new roommate. If she did return to school, she would be forced to repeat the courses she'd already taken—not that there was any guarantee she would even be admitted back into the program. Every possession she owned that wasn't in her suitcases had been carefully packed and loaded onto a barge that wouldn't arrive in Nome for months.

She poured out her feelings in silent prayer. She still couldn't believe that she had come here following what she thought was God's plan, and now it seemed she had made a terrible mistake. Lifting the Bible from the pew, she sat and read, desperately seeking guidance, until she caught a movement from the corner of her eye. A stocky middle-aged man was approaching.

"Can I help you?" he asked her softly.

She looked up blankly.

He must have read the confusion in her eyes. "I'm Paul Reeder, the pastor," he said, and sat beside her.

She held out her hand and smiled weakly. "Claudia Masters."

"Your first visit to Nome?" His voice was gentle and inquiring.

"Yes, how'd you know?" she couldn't help but wonder aloud.

He grinned, and his brown eyes sparkled. "Easy. I know everyone in town, so either you're a visitor or I've fallen down in my duties."

She nodded and hung her head at the thought of why she had come to Nome.

"Is there something I can do for you, child?" he asked kindly.

"I don't think there's much anyone can do for me anymore." Her voice shook slightly, and she lowered her lashes in an effort to conceal the desperation in her eyes.

"Things are rarely as difficult as they seem. Remember, God doesn't close a door without opening a window."

She attempted a smile. "I guess I need someone to point to the window."

"Would you feel better if you confided in someone?" he urged gently.

She didn't feel up to explanations but knew she should say something. "I quit school and moved to Alaska expecting…a job." The pastor was sure to know Seth, and she didn't want to involve this caring man in the mess of her relationship. "I…I assumed wrong… and now…"

"You need a job and place to live," he concluded for her. A light gleamed in the clear depths of his eyes. "There's an apartment for rent near here. Since it belongs to the church, the rent is reasonable. As for your other problem…" He paused thoughtfully. "Do you have any specific skills?"

"No, not really." Her tone was despairing. "I'm in medical school, but other than that—"

"My dear girl!" Pastor Reeder beamed in excitement.

"You are the answer to our prayers. Nome desperately needs medical assistants. We've advertised for months for another doctor—"

"Oh, no, please understand," Claudia said, "I'm not a doctor. All I have is the book knowledge so far."

Disregarding her objections, Pastor Reeder stood and anxiously moved into the wide aisle. "There's someone you must meet."

A worried frown marred Claudia's smooth brow. She licked her dry lips and followed the pastor as he pulled on his coat and strode briskly from the church and out to the street.

They stopped a block or two later. "While we're here, I'll show you the apartment." He unlocked the door to a small house, and Claudia stepped inside.

"Tiny" wasn't the word for the apartment. It was the most compact space Claudia had ever seen: living room with a sleeper sofa, miniature kitchen and a very small bathroom.

"It's perfect," she stated positively. Perfect if she didn't have to return to Seattle and face Cooper. Perfect if she could show Seth she wasn't like a wave tossed to and fro by the sea. She had made her decision and was here to stay, with or without him. She had responded in faith; God was her guide.

"The apartment isn't on the sewer," the pastor added. "I hope that won't inconvenience you."

"Of course not." She smiled. It didn't matter to her if she had a septic tank.

He nodded approvingly. "I'll arrange for water delivery, then."

She didn't understand but let the comment pass as he showed her out and locked the door behind them.

He led her down the street. "I'm taking you to meet a friend of mine, Dr. Jim Coleman. I'm sure Jim will share my enthusiasm when I tell him about your medical background."

"Shouldn't I sign something and make a deposit on the apartment first?"

Pastor Reeder's eyes twinkled. "We'll settle that later. Thanksgiving has arrived early in Nome. I can't see going through the rigmarole of deposits when God Himself has sent you to us." He handed her the key and smiled contentedly.

The doctor's waiting room was crowded with people when Claudia and Pastor Reeder entered. Every chair was taken, and small children played on the floor.

The receptionist greeted them warmly. "Good morning, Pastor. What can I do for you? Not another emergency, I hope."

"Quite the opposite. Tell Jim I'd like to see him, right away, if possible. I promise to take only a few minutes of his time."

They were ushered into a private office and sat down to wait. The large desk was covered with correspondence, magazines and medical journals. A pair of glasses had been carelessly tossed on top of the pile.

The young doctor who entered the room fifteen minutes later eyed Claudia skeptically, his dark eyes narrowing.

Eagerly Paul Reeder stood and beamed a smile toward Claudia. "Jim, I'd like to introduce you to God's Thanksgiving present to you. This is Claudia Masters."

She stood and extended her hand. The smile on her face died as she noted the frown that flitted across the doctor's face.

His handshake was barely civil. "Listen, Paul, I don't have the time for your matchmaking efforts today. There are fifteen people in my waiting room and the hospital just phoned. Mary Fulton's in labor."

Her eyes snapped with blue sparks at his assumption and his dismissive tone. "Let me assure you, Dr. Coleman, that you are the last man I'd care to be matched with!"

A wild light flashed in Jim's eyes and it looked as if he would have snapped out a reply if Pastor Reeder hadn't scrambled to his feet to intervene.

"I'll not have you insulting the woman the good Lord sent to help you. And you, Claudia—" he turned to her, waving his finger "—don't be offended. Jim made an honest mistake. He's simply overworked and stressed."

Confusion and embarrassment played rapidly over the physician's face. "The Lord sent her?" he repeated. "You're a nurse?"

Sadly Claudia shook her head. "Medical student. Ex-medical student," she corrected. "I don't know if I'll be much help. I don't have much practical experience."

"If you work with me, you'll gain that fast enough." He looked at her as if she had suddenly descended from heaven. "I've been urgently looking for someone to work on an emergency medical team. With your background and a few months of on-the-job training, you can take the paramedic test and easily qualify. What do you say, Claudia? Can we start again?" His boyish grin offered reassurance.

She smiled reluctantly, not knowing what to say. Only minutes before she'd claimed to be following God, responding to faith. Did He always move so quickly? "Why not?" she said with a laugh.

"Can you start tomorrow?"

"Sure," she confirmed, grateful that she would be kept so busy she wouldn't have time to remember that the reason she had come to Nome had nothing to do with paramedic training.

A message was waiting for her when she returned to the hotel. It gave a phone number and name, with information for upcoming flights leaving Nome for Anchorage. Crumpling the paper, Claudia checked out of the hotel.

She spent the rest of the afternoon unpacking and settling into the tiny apartment. If only Cooper could see her now!

Hunger pangs interrupted her work, and she realized she hadn't eaten all day. Just as she was beginning to wonder about dinner, there was a knock on the door. Her immediate thought was that Seth had somehow learned she hadn't returned to Seattle. Though that was unlikely, she realized, since Seth was no doubt back in Kotzebue by now.

Opening the door, she found a petite blonde with warm blue eyes and a friendly smile. "Welcome to Nome! I'm Barbara Reeder," she said, and handed Claudia a warm plate covered with aluminum foil. "Dad's been talking about his miracle ever since I walked in the door this afternoon, and I decided to meet this Joan of Arc myself." Her laugh was free and easy.

Claudia liked her immediately. Barbara's personality was similar to Ashley's, and she soon fell into easy conversation with the pastor's daughter. She let Barbara do most of the talking. She learned that the woman was close to her own age, worked as a legal assistant and was engaged to a man named Teddy. Claudia felt she needed a friend, someone bright and cheerful to lift her spirits from a tangled web of self-pity, and Barbara seemed like the answer to a prayer.

"Barbara, while you're here, would you mind explaining about the bathroom?" She had been shocked to discover the room was missing the most important fixture.

Barbara's eyes widened. "You mean Dad didn't explain that you aren't on the sewer?"

"Yes, but—"

"Only houses on the sewers have flush toilets, plumbing and the rest. You, my newfound friend, have your very own 'honey bucket.' It's like having an indoor outhouse. When you need to use it, just open the door in the wall, pull it inside and—*voilà*."

Claudia looked up shocked. "Yes, but—"

"You'll need to get yourself a fuzzy cover, because the seat is freezing. When you're through, open the door, push it back outside and it'll freeze almost immediately."

"Yes, but—"

"Oh, and the water is delivered on Monday, Wednesday and Friday. Garbage is picked up once a week, but be sure and keep it inside the house, because feral dogs will get into it if it's outside."

"Yes, but—"

"And I don't suppose Dad explained about ordering

food, either. Don't worry, I'll get you the catalog, and you'll have plenty of time to decide what you need. Grocery prices are sometimes as much as four times higher than Seattle, so we order the nonperishables once a year. The barge from Seattle arrives before winter."

Claudia breathed in deeply. The concepts of honey buckets, no plumbing and feral dogs were almost too much to grasp in one lump. This lifestyle was primitive compared to the way things were in Seattle. But she would grow stronger from the challenges, grow— or falter and break.

Concern clouded Barbara's countenance. "Have I discouraged you?"

Pride and inner strength shimmered in Claudia's eyes. "No, Nome is where I belong," she stated firmly.

Jim Coleman proved to be an excellent teacher. Her admiration for him grew with every day and every patient. At the end of her first week, Claudia was exhausted. Together they had examined and treated a steady flow of the sick and injured, eating quick lunches when they got a few free minutes between patients. At the end of the ten-to-twelve-hour days, he was sometimes due to report to the hospital. She spent her evenings studying the huge pile of material he had given her to prepare for the paramedic exam that spring. She marveled at how hard he drove himself, but he explained that his work load wasn't by choice. Few medical professionals were willing to set up practice in the frozen North.

Barbara stopped by the apartment during Claudia's second week with an invitation for Thanksgiving din-

ner. Jim had also been invited, along with Barbara's
fiancé and another couple. Claudia thanked her and
accepted, but she must have appeared preoccupied, because Barbara left soon afterward.

Claudia closed the door after her, leaning against the
wood frame and swallowing back the bitter hurt. When
she'd left Seattle, she'd told Ashley that she was hoping the wedding would be around Thanksgiving. Now
she would be spending the day with virtual strangers.

"Good morning, Jim," Claudia said cheerfully the next
day as she entered the office. "And you, too, Mrs. Lucy."

The receptionist glanced up, grinning sheepishly
to herself.

"Something funny?" Jim demanded brusquely.

"Did either of you get a chance to read Pastor Reeder's sign in front of the church this morning?" Mrs.
Lucy asked.

Claudia shook her head and waited.

"What did he say this time?" Jim asked, his interest piqued.

"The sign reads 'God Wants Spiritual Fruit, Not Religious Nuts.'"

Jim tipped his head back and chuckled, but his face
soon grew serious. "I suggest we get moving," he said.
"We've got a full schedule."

He was right. The pace at which he drove himself
and his staff left little time for chatting. With so many
people in need of medical attention and only two doctors dividing the load, they had to work as efficiently as
possible. By six Claudia had barely had time to grab a

sandwich. She was bandaging a badly cut hand after Jim had stitched it when he stuck his head around the corner.

"I want you to check the man in the first room. Let me know what you think. I've got a phone call waiting for me. I'll take it in my office and join you in a few minutes."

A stray curl of rich auburn hair fell haphazardly across her face as she stopped outside the exam room a few minutes later, and she paused long enough to tuck it around her ear and straighten her white smock.

Tapping lightly, her smile warm and automatic, she entered the room. "Good afternoon, my name's—"

Stopping short, she felt her stomach pitch wildly. Seth. His eyes were cold and hard, and his mouth tightened ominously as he asked, "What are *you* doing here?"

Eight

"I work here," Claudia returned, outwardly calm, although her heartbeat was racing frantically. She had realized it would be only a matter of time before she ran into Seth, and had in fact been mildly surprised it hadn't happened before now. But nothing could have prepared her for the impact of seeing him again.

His mouth tightened grimly. "Why aren't you in Seattle?" he demanded in a low growl.

"Because I'm here," she countered logically. "Why should you care if I'm in Seattle or Timbuktu? As I recall, you've washed your hands of me."

Her answer didn't please him, and he propelled himself from the examination table in one angry movement. But he couldn't conceal a wince of pain.

Clearly he was really hurting. "Jim asked me to look at you—now get back on the table."

"Jim?" Seth said derisively. "You seem to have arrived at a first-name basis pretty quickly."

Pinching her lips tightly together, she ignored the implication. "I'm going to examine you whether you like it or not," she said with an authority few patients would dare to question.

His dark eyes narrowed mutinously at her demand.

Winning any kind of verbal contest with him had been impossible to date. She wouldn't have been surprised if he'd limped out of the office rather than obey her demand. He might well have done exactly that if Jim Coleman hadn't entered at that precise minute.

"I've been talking to the hospital," he remarked, handing Claudia Seth's medical chart. Sheer reflex prevented the folder from falling as it slipped through her fingers. She caught it and glanced up guiltily.

Jim seemed oblivious to the tense atmosphere in the room. "Have you examined the wound?" he asked her, and motioned for Seth to return to the table.

Seth hesitated for a moment before giving in. With another flick of his hand, Jim directed Seth to lie down. Again he paused before lying back on the red vinyl cushion. He lay with his eyes closed, and Claudia thought her heart would burst. She loved this man, even though he had cast her out of his life, tossing out cruel words in an attempt to make her hate him. He had failed. And surely he had lied, as well. He couldn't possibly have decided to marry someone else so quickly.

Jim lifted the large bandage on Seth's leg, allowing Claudia her first look at the angry wound. Festering with yellow pus, the cut must have been the source of constant, throbbing pain. When Jim gently tested the skin around the infection Seth's face took on a deathly pallor, but he didn't make a sound as he battled to disguise the intense pain. A faint but nonetheless distinct red line extended from the wound, reaching halfway up his thigh.

"Blood poisoning," Claudia murmured gravely. She could almost feel his agony and paled slightly. Anxiously she glanced at Jim.

"Blood poisoning or not, just give me some medicine and let me out of here. I've got a business to run. I can't be held up here all day while you two ooh and ah over a minor cut." He spoke sharply and impatiently as he struggled to sit upright.

"You seem to think you can work with that wound," Jim shot back angrily. "Go ahead, if you don't mind walking on a prosthetic leg for the rest of your life. You need to be in the hospital."

"So *you* say," Seth retorted.

Stiff with concern, Claudia stepped forward when Seth let out a low moan and lay back down.

"Do whatever you have to," he said in a resigned tone.

"I'd like to talk to you in my office for a minute, Claudia," Jim said. "Go ahead and wait for me there."

The request surprised her, but she did as he asked, pacing the small room as she waited for him. He joined her a few minutes later, a frown of concern twisting his features.

"I've already spoken to the hospital," he announced as he slumped defeatedly into his chair. "There aren't any beds available." He ran a hand over his face and looked up at her with unseeing eyes. "It's times like these that make me wonder why I chose to work in Nome. Inadequate facilities, no private nurses, overworked staff…I don't know how much more of the stress my health will take."

She hadn't known Jim long, but she had never seen him more frustrated or angry.

"I've contacted the airport to have him flown out by charter plane, but there's a storm coming. Flying for the next twelve hours would be suicidal," he continued. "His leg can't wait that long. Something's got to be done before that infection spreads any farther." He straightened and released a bitter sigh. "I don't have any choice but to send you home with him, Claudia. He's going to need constant care or he could lose that leg. I can't do it myself, and there's no one else I can trust."

She leaned against the door, needing its support as the weight of what he was asking pressed heavily on her shoulders—and her heart. Despite the emotional cost to herself, she couldn't refuse.

Patiently Jim outlined what Seth's treatment would entail. He studied Claudia for any sign of confusion or misunderstanding, then gave her the supplies she would need and reminded her of the seriousness of the infection.

An hour later, with Seth strongly protesting, Claudia managed to get him into his house and into his bed. After propping his leg up with a pillow, she removed the bandage to view the open wound again. She cringed at the sight, thinking of how much pain he had to be in.

Her eyes clouded with worry as she worked gently and efficiently to make him as comfortable as possible. She intentionally avoided his gaze in an attempt to mask her concern.

He appeared somewhat more comfortable as he

lay back and rested his head against a pillow. A tight clenching of his jaw was the only sign of pain he allowed to show on his ruggedly carved features. She didn't need to see his agony to know he was in intense pain, though.

"Why are you here?" he asked, his eyes closed as he echoed the question he'd asked when she walked into the exam room.

"I'm taking care of your leg," she replied gently. "Don't talk now, try to sleep if you can." Deftly she opened the bag of supplies and laid them out on the dresser. Then, standing above him, she rested her cool hand against his forehead. She could feel how feverish he was.

At the tender touch of her fingers, he raised his hand and gripped her wrist. "Don't play games with me, Red." He opened his eyes to hold her gaze. "Why are you in Nome?" The words were weak; there wasn't any fight left in him. Protesting Jim's arrangements had depleted him of strength. Now it took all his effort to disguise his pain. "Did you come back just to torment me?"

"I never left," she answered, and touched a finger to his lips to prevent his questions. "Not now," she whispered. "We'll talk later, and I'll explain then."

He nodded almost imperceptibly and rolled his head to the side.

Examining the cut brought a liquid sheen to her eyes. "How could you have let this go so long?" she protested. Jim had explained to her that Seth had fallen against a cargo crate while in Kotzebue. Claudia recalled that he'd had a slight limp the day he picked her up from the airport. Had he let the injury go untreated all that time? Was he crazy?

He didn't respond to her question, only exhaled a sharp breath as she gently began carefully swabbing the wound. She bit into her lip when he winced again, but it was important to clean the cut thoroughly. Jim had given Seth antibiotics and painkillers before leaving the office, but the antibiotics needed time to kick in, and as for the painkillers, their effect had been minor.

When she'd finished, she heated hot water in the kitchen, then steeped strips of cloth in the clean water. After allowing them to cool slightly, she placed them over his thigh, using heat to draw infection from the wound. His body jerked taut and his mouth tightened with the renewed effort to conceal his torment. She repeated the process until the wound was thoroughly cleansed, then returned to the kitchen.

"I'm going to lose this leg," Seth mumbled as she walked into the bedroom.

"Not if I can help it," she said with a determination that produced a weak smile from him.

"I'm glad you're here," he said, his voice fading.

She gently squeezed his hand. "I'm glad I'm here, too." Even if she did eventually return to Seattle, she would always cherish the satisfaction of having been able to help Seth.

He rested fitfully. Some time later, she again heated water, adding the medicine Jim had given her to it as it steamed. A pungent odor filled the room. As quietly as possible, so not to disturb him, she steeped new strips of fabric. Cautiously she draped them around the swollen leg, securing them with a large plastic bag to keep them moist and warm as long as possible. When the second stage of Jim's instructions had been completed, she slumped wearily into a chair at Seth's bedside.

Two hours later she repeated the process, and again after another two-hour interval. She didn't know what time it was when Jim arrived. But Seth was still asleep, and there didn't seem to be any noticeable improvement in his condition.

"How's the fever?" Jim asked as he checked Seth's pulse.

"High," she replied, unable to conceal her worry.

"Give him time," Jim cautioned. He gave Seth another injection and glanced at his watch. "I'm due at the hospital. I'll see what I can do to find someone to replace you."

"No!" she said abruptly. Too abruptly. "I'll stay."

Jim eyed her curiously, his gaze searching. "You've been at this for hours now. The next few could be crucial, and I don't want you working yourself sick."

"I'm going to see him through this," she said with determination. Avoiding the question in his eyes, she busied herself neatening up the room. She would explain later if she had to, but right now all that mattered was Seth and getting him well.

Jim left a few minutes later, and she paused to fix herself a meal. She would need her strength, but although she tried to force herself to eat, her fears mounted, dispelling her appetite.

The small of her back throbbed as she continued to labor through the night. Again and again she applied the hot cloths to draw out the infection.

Claudia fidgeted anxiously when she took his temperature and discovered that his fever continued to rage, despite her efforts. She gently tested the flesh surrounding the wound and frowned heavily.

Waves of panic mounted again a few minutes later when he stirred restlessly. He rolled his head slowly from side to side as the pain disturbed his sleep.

"Jesus, please help us," Claudia prayed as she grew more dismayed. Nothing she did seemed to be able to control Seth's fever.

She'd repeatedly heard about the importance of remaining calm and clearheaded when treating a patient. But her heart was filled with dread as the hours passed, each one interminable, and still his fever raged. If she couldn't get his fever down, he might lose his leg.

His Bible lay on the nightstand, and she picked it up, holding it in both hands. She brought the leather-bound book to her breast and lifted her eyes to heaven, murmuring a fervent prayer.

Another hour passed, and he began to moan and mumble incoherently as he slipped into a feverish delirium. He tossed his head, and she was forced to hold him down as he struggled, flinging out his arms.

He quieted, and she tenderly stroked his face while whispering soothing words of comfort.

Unexpectedly, with an amazing strength, Seth jerked upright and cried out in anguish, "John…watch out… no…no…"

Gently but firmly she laid him back against the pillow, murmuring softly in an effort to calm him. Absently she wondered who John was. She couldn't remember Seth ever mentioning anyone by that name.

He kept mumbling about John. Once he even

laughed, the laugh she loved so much. But only seconds later he cried out in anguish again.

Tears that had been lingering so close to the surface quickly welled. Loving someone as she loved Seth meant that his torment became one's own. Never had she loved this completely, this strongly.

"Hush, my darling," she murmured softly.

She was afraid to leave him, even for a moment, so she pulled a chair as close as she could to his bedside and sank wearily into it. Exhaustion claimed her mind, wiping it clean of everything but prayer.

Toward daylight Seth seemed to be resting more comfortably, and Claudia slipped into a light sleep.

Someone spoke her name, and Claudia shifted from her uncomfortable position to find Seth, eyes open, regarding her steadily.

"Good morning," he whispered weakly. His forehead and face were beaded with sweat, his shirt damp with perspiration. The fever had broken at last.

A wave of happiness washed through her, and she offered an immediate prayer of thanksgiving.

"Good morning," she returned, her voice light as relief lightened her heart. She beamed with joy as she tested his forehead. It felt moist but cool, and she stood to wipe the sweat from his face with a fresh washcloth.

He reached out and stopped her, closing his hand over her fingers, as if touching her would prove she was real. "I'm not dreaming. It *is* you."

She laughed softly. "The one and only." Suddenly conscious of her disheveled appearance, she ran her fingers through her tangled hair and straightened her blouse.

His gaze was warm as he watched her, and she felt unexpectedly shy.

"You told me you never left Nome?" The inflection in his voice made the statement a question.

"I didn't come here to turn around and go back home," she said and smiled, allowing all the pent-up love to burn in her eyes.

His eyes questioned her as she examined his leg. The improvement was remarkable. She smiled, remembering her frantic prayers during the night. Only the Great Physician could have worked this quickly.

She helped Seth sit up and removed his damp shirt. They worked together silently as she wiped him down and slipped a fresh shirt over his head. Taking the bowl of dirty water and tucking his shirt under her arm, she smiled at him and walked toward the door.

"Red, don't go," he called urgently.

"I'll be right back," she assured him. "I'm just going to take these into the kitchen and fix you something to eat."

"Not now." He extended his hand to her, his look intense. "We need to talk."

She walked back to the dresser to deposit the bowl before moving to the bed. Their eyes locked as they studied each other. The radiant glow of love seemed to reach out to her from his gaze. She took his hand in her own and, raising it to her face, rested it against her cheek and closed her eyes. She didn't resist as the pressure of his arm pulled her downward. She knelt on the carpet beside the bed and let herself be wrapped in his embrace.

His breathing was heavy and labored as he buried his face in the gentle slope of her neck. This was what she'd needed, what she'd yearned for from the minute she stepped off the plane—Seth and the assurance of his love.

"I've been a fool," he muttered thickly.

"We both have. But I'm here now, and it's going to take a lot more than some angry words to pry me out of your arms." She pulled away slightly, so she would be able to look at him as she spoke. "I need to take some responsibility here," she murmured, and brushed the hair from the sides of his face. He captured her hand and pressed a kiss against her palm. "I'd never once told you I loved you."

His hand tightened around hers punishingly. "You love me?"

"Very much." She confirmed her words with a nod and a smile. "You told me so many times that you needed me, but I discovered I'm the one who needs you."

"Why didn't you tell me when you arrived that you intended to stay?" He met her eyes, and she watched as his filled with regret.

"I'm a little slow sometimes," she said, ignoring his question in favor of explaining how she'd come to realize she loved him. She sat in the chair but continued to hold his hand in hers. "I couldn't seem to understand why God would give you a sign and not say anything to me. I was miserable—the indecision was disrupting my whole life. Then one day I decided to read the passage in Genesis that you'd talked about. I read about Abraham's servant and learned that Rebekah had been given a choice and had made the decision to accompany the servant. I felt as if God was offering me the same decision and asking that I respond in faith. It didn't take me long to recognize how much I loved you. I can't understand why I fought it so long. Once I admitted it to myself, quitting school and leaving Seattle were easy."

"You quit school?"

"Without hesitation." She laughed with sudden amusement. "I'd make a rotten doctor. Haven't you noticed that I become emotionally involved with my patients?"

"What about your uncle?"

"He's accepted my decision. He's not happy about it, but I think he understands more than he lets on."

"We'll make him godfather to our first son," Seth said, and slipped a large hand around her nape, pulling her close so her soft mouth could meet his. The kiss was so gentle that tears misted her eyes. His hands framed the sides of her face as his mouth slanted across hers, the contact deepening until he seemed capable of drawing out her soul.

Jim Coleman stopped by later, but only long enough to quickly check Seth's leg and give him another injection of antibiotic. He was thrilled that the fever had broken, but he spoke frankly with Seth and warned him that it would take weeks to regain the full use of the leg.

He hesitated once, and Claudia was sure he'd noticed the silent communication and emotional connection that flashed between her and Seth. Jim's eyes narrowed, and the corner of his mouth twitched. For a fleeting moment she thought the look held contempt. She dismissed the idea as an illusion based on a long night and an overactive imagination. Jim left shortly afterward, promising to return that evening.

She heated a lunch for the two of them and waited until Seth had eaten. He fell asleep while she washed the dishes. When she checked on him later, her heart swelled with the wonder and joy of their love. How many other married couples had received such a profound confirmation of their commitment as they had? He had spoken of a son, and she realized how much she wanted this man's child.

Smiling, she rested her hands lightly on her flat stomach and started to daydream. They would have tall lean sons with thick dark hair, and perhaps a daughter. A glorious happiness stole through her.

Content that Seth would sleep, she opened the other bedroom door, crawled into the bed and drifted into a deep sleep. Her dreams were happy, confident of the many years she would share with Seth.

When she awoke later she rolled over and glanced at the clock. Seven. She had slept for almost five hours. Sitting up, she stretched, lifting her arms high above her head, then rotated her neck to ease the tired muscles.

The house was quiet as she threw back the covers and walked back to Seth's room. He was awake, his face turned toward the wall. Something prevented her from speaking and drawing attention to herself. His posture said that he was troubled, worried. What she could see of his face was tight. Was he in pain? Was something about his business causing him concern?

As if feeling her regard, he turned his head and their eyes met. His worried look was gone immediately, replaced by a loving glance that sent waves of happiness through her.

"Hello. Have you been awake long?" she asked softly.

"About an hour. What about you?"

"Just a few minutes." She moved deeper into the room. "Is something troubling you, Seth? You had a strange look just now. I don't exactly know how to describe it…sadness, maybe?"

His hand reached for hers. "It's nothing, my love."

She felt his forehead, checking for fever, but it was cool, and she smiled contentedly. "I don't know about you, but I'm starved. I think I'll see what I can dig up in the kitchen."

He nodded absently.

As she left the room, she couldn't help glancing over her shoulder. Her instincts told her that something wasn't right. But what?

A freshly baked pie was sitting in the middle of the kitchen table, and she glanced at it curiously. When had that appeared? She shrugged and opened the refrigerator. Maybe Seth had some eggs and she could make an omelette. There weren't any eggs, but a gelatin salad sat prominently on the top shelf. Something was definitely going on here. When she turned around, she noticed that the oven light was on, and a quick look through the glass door showed a casserole dish warming. Someone had been to the house when she'd been asleep and brought an entire meal. How thoughtful.

"You didn't tell me you had company," she said a

little while later as she carried a tray into the bedroom for him.

He was sitting on the edge of the mattress, and she could see him clench his teeth as he attempted to stand.

"Seth, don't!" she cried and quickly set the tray down to hurry to his side. "You shouldn't be out of bed."

He sank back onto the mattress and closed his eyes to mask a resurgence of pain. "You know, I think you're right about that."

"Here, let me help you." With an arm around his shoulders, she gently lifted the injured leg and propped it on top of a thick pillow. When she'd finished, she turned to him and smiled. She couldn't hide the soft glow that warmed her eyes as she looked at this man she loved.

Sitting up, his back supported by pillows, he held his arms out to her and drew her into his embrace. His mouth sought hers, and the kisses spoke more of passion than gentleness. But she didn't care. She returned his kisses, linking her hands around his neck, her fingers exploring the black hair at the base of his head. His hands moved intimately over her back as if he couldn't get enough of her.

"I think your recovery will impress Dr. Coleman, especially if he could see us now," she teased and tried to laugh. But her husky tone betrayed the extent of her arousal. When Seth kissed her again, hard and long, she offered no resistance.

Crushed in his embrace, held immobile by the steel band of his arm encircling her waist, she submitted happily to the mastery of his kisses.

When they took a break to breathe, she smiled happily into his gleaming eyes. "There are only a few more days before Thanksgiving," she murmured, and kissed him. "I have so much to thank God for this year—more happiness than one woman was ever meant to have. I had hoped when I first came that we might be married Thanksgiving week. It seemed fitting somehow." She relaxed as she realized that she truly had no more doubts. She was utterly his.

Although Seth continued to hold her, she felt again the stirring sense of something amiss. When she leaned her head back to glance at him, she saw that his look was distant, preoccupied.

"Seth, is something wrong?" she asked, worried.

A smile of reassurance curved his lips, but she noticed that it didn't reach his eyes. "Everything's fine."

"Are you hungry?"

He nodded and straightened so that she could bring him the tray. "You know me. I'm always hungry."

But he hardly touched his meal.

She brought him a cup of coffee after taking away the dinner tray, then sat in the chair beside the bed, her hands cupping her own hot mug.

"If you don't object, I'd like Pastor Reeder to marry us," she said, and took a sip of coffee.

"You know Paul Reeder?" He looked over at her curiously.

She nodded. "I'm very grateful for his friendship. He's the one who introduced me to Jim Coleman. He also rented me an apartment the church owns—honey bucket and all," she said with a smile. "I'm going to like Nome. There are some wonderful people here, and that very definitely includes Pastor Reeder."

"Paul's the one who talked to me about Christ and salvation. I respect him greatly."

"I suspected as much." She recalled Seth telling her about the pastor who had led him to Christ. From the first day she had suspected it was Pastor Reeder. "Jim needed help with an emergency, so I didn't get to church last Sunday to hear him preach, but I bet he packs a powerful sermon."

"He does," Seth said, and looked away.

Claudia's gaze followed his, and she realized that Jim Coleman had let himself into the house. The two men eyed each other, and an icy stillness seemed to fill the room. She looked from one man to the other and lightly shook her head, sure she was imagining things.

"I think you'll be impressed with how well Seth is doing," she said, and moved aside so Jim could examine the wound himself.

Neither man spoke, and the tension in the room was so thick that she found herself stiffening. Something was wrong between these two, *very* wrong.

Claudia walked Jim to the front door when he was done with the exam. Again he praised her efforts. "He might have lost that leg if it hadn't been for you."

"I was glad to help," she said, studying him. "But I feel God had more to do with the improvement than I did."

"That could be." He shrugged and expelled a long, tired sigh. "He should be okay by himself tonight if you want to go home and get a good night's sleep."

"I might," she responded noncommittally.

He nodded and turned to leave. She stopped him with

a hand on his arm. "Jim, something's going on between you and Seth, isn't it?"

"Did he tell you that?"

"No."

"Then ask *him*," he said, casting a wary glance in the direction of Seth's bedroom.

"I will," she replied, determined to do just that.

Seth's eyes were closed when she returned to his room, but she wasn't fooled. "Don't you like Jim Coleman?" she asked right out.

"He's a fine Christian man. There aren't many doctors as dedicated as he is."

"But you don't like him, do you?"

Seth closed his eyes again and let out a sharp breath. "I don't think it's a question of how I feel. Jim doesn't like me, and at the moment I can't blame him," he responded cryptically.

She didn't know what to say. It was obvious Seth didn't want to talk about it, and she didn't feel she should pry. It hurt a little, though, that he wouldn't confide in her. There wasn't anything she would ever keep from him. But she couldn't and wouldn't force him to talk, not if he wasn't ready. She left him to rest and went into the kitchen to clean up.

An hour later she checked on him and saw that he appeared to be asleep. Leaning down, she kissed his brow. She was undecided about spending another night. A hot shower and a fresh change of clothes sounded tempting.

"Seth," she whispered, and he stirred. "I'm going home for the night. I'll see you early tomorrow morning."

"No." He sat up and winced, apparently having forgotten about his leg in his eagerness to stop her. "Don't go, Red. Stay tonight. You can leave in the morning if you want." He reached for her, holding her so tight she ached.

"Okay, my love," she whispered tenderly. "Just call if you need me."

"I'll need you all my life. Don't ever forget that, Red."

He sounded so worried that she frowned, drawing her delicate brows together. "I won't forget."

Claudia woke before Seth the next morning. She was in the kitchen putting on a pot of coffee when she heard a car pull up outside the kitchen door.

Barbara Reeder slammed the car door closed and waved. Claudia returned the wave and opened the door for her friend.

"You're out bright and early this morning," she said cheerfully. "I just put on coffee."

"Morning." Barbara returned the smile. "How's the patient?"

"Great. It's amazing how much better he is after just two days."

"I was sorry to miss you yesterday." Barbara pulled out a chair and set her purse on the table while she unbuttoned her parka.

"Miss me?" Claudia quizzed.

"Yes, I brought dinner by, but you were in the bedroom sound asleep. From what I understand, you were up all night. You must have been exhausted. I didn't want to wake you, so I just waved at your patient, left the meal and headed out."

"Funny Seth didn't say anything," Claudia said, speaking her thoughts out loud.

Barbara's look showed mild surprise. "Honestly, that man! You'd think it was top secret or something." Happiness gleamed in her eyes, and she held out her left hand so Claudia could admire the sparkling diamond. "Teddy and I are going to be married next month."

Nine

"Teddy?" Claudia repeated. She felt as if someone had kicked her in the stomach. Seth hadn't been lying after all. There really was another woman. Somehow she managed to conceal her shock.

"It's confusing, I know," Barbara responded with a happy laugh. "But Seth has always reminded me of a teddy bear. He's so big and cuddly, it seemed natural to call him Teddy."

Claudia's hand shook as she poured coffee into two mugs. Barbara continued to chat excitedly about her wedding plans, explaining that they hoped to have the wedding before Christmas.

Strangely, after that first shock Claudia felt no emotion. She sipped her coffee, adding little to the conversation.

Barbara didn't seem to notice. "Teddy changed after John's death," she said, and blew on her coffee to cool it.

"John," Claudia repeated. Seth had called out that name several times while his fever was raging.

"John was his younger brother, his partner in Arctic

Barge. There was some kind of accident on a barge—
I'm not sure I ever got the story straight. Seth was with
him when it happened. Something fell on top of him and
ruptured his heart. He died in Seth's arms."

Claudia stared into her coffee. From that first day
when she'd walked into his room at the Wilderness
Motel, she'd known there was a terrible sadness in
Seth's life. She'd felt it even then. But he had never
shared his grief with her. As much as he professed to
love her and want her for his wife, he hadn't shared the
deepest part of himself. Knowing this hurt as much as
his engagement to Barbara.

"Could I ask a favor of you?" Claudia said and stood,
placing her mug in the kitchen sink. "Would you mind
dropping me off at my apartment? I don't want to take
Seth's car, since I don't know when I'll be back. It
should only take a minute."

"Of course. Then I'll come back and surprise Seth
with breakfast."

He would be amazed all right, Claudia couldn't help
musing.

She managed to maintain a fragile poise until Barbara dropped her off. Waving her thanks, she entered
her tiny home. She looked around the room that had so
quickly become her own and bit the inside of her cheek.
With purposeful strides she opened the lone closet and
pulled out her suitcases. She folded each garment with
unhurried care and placed it neatly inside the luggage.

Someone knocked at the door, but she obstinately
ignored the repeated rapping.

"Open up, Claudia, I know you're in there. I saw
Barbara drop you off." It was Jim Coleman.

"Go away!" she called, and her voice cracked. A tear squeezed free, despite her determination not to cry, and she angrily wiped it away with the back of her hand.

Ignoring her lack of an invitation, Jim pushed open the door and stepped inside the room.

"I like the way people respect my privacy around here," she bit out sarcastically, wondering how she could have been foolish enough to leave her door unlocked. "I don't feel up to company at the moment, Jim. Another time, maybe." She turned away and continued packing.

"I want you to listen to me for a minute." Clearly he was angry.

"No, I won't listen. Not to anyone. Go away, just go away." She pulled a drawer from the dresser and flipped it over, emptying the contents into the last suitcase.

"Will you stop acting like a lunatic and listen? You can't leave now."

She whirled around and placed both hands challengingly on her hips. "Can't leave? You just watch me. I don't care where the next plane's going, I'll be on it," she shot back, then choked on a sob.

He took her in his arms. She struggled at first, but he deflected her hands and held her gently. "Let it out," he whispered soothingly.

Again she tried to jerk away, but, undeterred, he held her fast, murmuring comforting words.

"You knew all along, didn't you?" she asked accusingly, raising hurt, questioning eyes to search his face.

He arched one brow and shrugged his shoulders. "About Barbara and Seth? Of course. But about *you* and Seth? How could I? But then I saw the two of you, and no one could look at you without knowing you're in love. I was on my way to his house this morning when I saw Barbara with you. Something about your expression told me you must have found out the truth. Did you say anything to her?"

Claudia shook her head. "No. I couldn't. But why does it have to be Barbara?" she asked unreasonably. "Why couldn't it be some anonymous woman I could feel free to hate? But she's bright and cheerful, fun to be around. She's my friend. And she's so in love with him. You should have heard her talk about the wedding."

"I have," he stated, and rammed his hands into his pockets. He walked to the other side of the couch that served as her bed.

"I'm not going to burst that bubble of happiness. I don't think Seth knows what he wants. He's confused and unsure. The only thing I can do is leave."

Jim turned and regarded her steadily. "You can't go now. You don't seem to understand what having you in Nome means to me, to all of us. When Pastor Reeder said you were God's Thanksgiving gift to us, he wasn't kidding. I've been praying for someone like you for months." He heaved a sigh, his eyes pleading with her. "For the first time in weeks I've been able to do some of the paperwork that's cluttering my desk. And I was planning to take a day off next week, the first one in three months."

"But you don't know what you're asking."

"I do. Listen, if it will make things easier, I could marry you."

The proposal was issued sincerely, and his gaze didn't waver as he waited for her reaction.

She smiled "Now you're being ridiculous."

His taut features relaxed, and she laughed outright at how relieved he looked.

"Will you stay a bit longer, at least until someone answers our advertisement in the medical journals? Two or three months at the most."

Gesturing weakly with one hand, Claudia nodded. She was in an impossible position. She couldn't stay, and she couldn't leave. And there was still Seth to face.

Jim sighed gratefully. "Thank you. I promise you won't regret it." He glanced at his watch. "I'm going to talk to Seth. Something's got to be done."

She walked him to the door, then asked the question his proposal had raised in her mind. "Why haven't you ever married?"

"Too busy in med school," he explained. "And since I've been here, there hasn't been time to date the woman I wanted." He pulled his car keys from his pocket.

There was something strange about the way he spoke, or maybe it was the look in his eyes. Suddenly it all came together for her. She stopped him by placing a hand on his arm. "You're in love with Barbara, aren't you?" If she hadn't been caught up in her own problems, she would have realized it long ago. Whenever Jim talked about Barbara there was a softness in his voice that spoke volumes.

He began to deny his feelings, then seemed to notice the knowing look in Claudia's blue eyes. "A lot of good it's done me." His shoulders slumped forward in defeat. "I'm nothing more than a family friend to her. Barbara's been in love with Seth for so long, she doesn't even know I'm around. And with the hours I'm forced to work, there hasn't been time to let her know how I feel."

"Does Seth love her?" Pride demanded that she hold her chin high.

"I don't know. But he must feel genuine affection for her or he wouldn't have proposed."

Both of them turned suddenly introspective, unable to find the words to comfort each other. He left a minute later, and she stood at the window watching him go.

She walked over to her suitcases and began to unpack. As she replaced each item in the closet or the drawers, she tried to pray. God had brought her to Nome. She had come believing she would marry Seth. Did He have other plans for her now that she was here? How could she bear to live in the same city as Seth when she loved him so completely? How could she bear seeing him married to another?

No sooner had the last suitcase been tucked away than there was another knock at the door.

Barbara's cheerful smile greeted her as she stuck her head in the front door. "Are you busy?"

Claudia was grateful that she had her back turned as she felt tears come into her eyes. Barbara was the last person she wanted to see. It would almost be preferable to face Seth. Inwardly she groaned as she turned, forcing a smile onto her frozen lips.

"Sure, come in."

Barbara let herself in and held out a large gift-wrapped box. "I know you're probably exhausted and this is a bad time, but I wanted to give this to you, and then I'll get back to Teddy's."

Numbly Claudia took the gift, unable to look higher than the bright pink bow that decorated the box. Words seemed to knot in her throat.

"I'll only stay a minute," Barbara added. "Jim Coleman came by. It looked like he wanted to see Teddy alone for a few minutes, so I thought it was the perfect time to run this over."

"What is it?" The words sounded strange even to herself.

"Just a little something to show my appreciation for all you've done for Teddy. All along, Dad's said that God sent you to us. You've only been here a short time, but already you've affected all our lives. Teddy could have lost his leg if it hadn't been for you. And Dad said your being here will save Jim from exhausting himself with work. All that aside, I see you as a very special sister the Lord sent to me. I can't remember a time when I've felt closer to anyone more quickly." She ended with a shaky laugh. "Look at me," she mumbled, wiping a tear from the corner of her eye. "I'm going to start crying in a minute, and that's all we both need. Now go ahead and open it."

Claudia sat and rested the large box on her knees. Carefully she tore away the ribbon and paper. The ever-growing lump in her throat constricted painfully. Lifting the lid, she discovered a beautiful hand-crocheted afghan in bold autumn colors of gold, orange, yellow and brown. She couldn't restrain her gasp of pleasure. "Oh, Barbara!" She lifted it from the box and marveled at the weeks of work that had gone into its creation. "I can't accept this—it's too much." She blinked rapidly in an effort to forestall her tears.

"It's hardly enough," Barbara contradicted. "God sent you to Nome as a helper to Jim, a friend to me and a nurse for my Teddy."

A low moan of protest and guilt escaped Claudia's parched throat. She couldn't refuse the gift, just as she couldn't explain why she'd come to Nome.

"How…how long have you been engaged?" she asked in a choked whisper.

"Not very long. In fact, Teddy didn't give me the ring until a few days ago."

Claudia's gaze dropped to rest on the sparkling diamond. She felt a sense of relief that at least it wasn't the same ring he'd offered *her*.

"His proposal had to be about the most unromantic thing you can imagine," she said with a girlish smile. "I didn't need a fortune-teller to realize he's in love with someone else."

Claudia's breathing grew shallow. "Why would you marry someone when he…?" She couldn't finish the sentence and, unable to meet Barbara's gaze, she fingered the afghan on her lap.

"It sounds strange, doesn't it?" Barbara answered with a question. "But I love him. I have for years. We've talked about this other girl. She's someone he met on a business trip. She wasn't willing to leave everything behind for Teddy and Nome. Whoever she is, she's a fool. The affection Teddy has for me will grow, and together we'll build a good marriage. He wants children right away."

With a determined effort Claudia was able to smile. "You'll make him a wonderful wife. And you're right, the other girl *was* a terrible fool." Her mouth ached with the effort of maintaining a smile.

Luckily Barbara seemed to misread the look of strain on Claudia's pale face as fatigue. Standing, she slipped her arms into her thick coat. "I imagine Jim's done by now. I'd better go, but we'll get together soon. And don't forget Thanksgiving dinner. You're our guest of honor."

Claudia felt sick to her stomach and stood unsteadily. The guest of honor? This was too much.

Together they walked to the door.

"Thank you again for the beautiful gift," Claudia murmured in a wavering voice.

"No, Claudia, *I* need to thank *you*. And for so much—you saved the leg and maybe the life of the man I love."

"You should thank God for that, not me."

"Believe me, I do."

Barbara was halfway out the door when Claudia blurted out, "What do you think of Jim Coleman?" She hadn't meant to be so abrupt and quickly averted her face.

To her surprise, Barbara stepped back inside and laughed softly. "I told Dad a romance would soon be brewing between the two of you. It's inevitable, I suppose, working together every day. The attraction between you must be a natural thing. I think Jim's a great guy, though he's a bit too arrogant for my taste. But you two are exactly right for one another. Jim needs someone like you to mellow him." A smile twinkled in her eyes. "We'll talk more about Jim later. I've got to get back. Teddy will be wondering what's going on. He was asleep when Jim arrived, so I haven't had a chance to tell him where I was going."

That afternoon Jim phoned and asked if Claudia could meet him at the office. An outbreak of flu had hit town, and several families had been affected. He needed her help immediately.

Several hours later, she was exhausted. She came home and cooked a meal, then didn't eat. She washed the already clean dishes and listened to a radio broadcast for ten minutes before she realized it wasn't in English.

The water in her bathtub was steaming when there was yet another knock at her door. The temptation to let it pass and pretend she hadn't heard was strong. She didn't feel up to another chat with either Barbara or Jim. Again the knock came, this time more insistent.

Impatiently she stalked across the floor and jerked open the door. Her irritation died the minute she saw that it was Seth. He was leaning heavily on a cane, his leg causing him obvious pain.

"What are you doing here?" she demanded. "You shouldn't be walking on that leg."

Lines of strain were etched beside his mouth. "Then invite me inside so I can sit down." He spoke tightly, and she moved aside, then put a hand on his elbow as she helped him to the couch.

Relief was evident when he lowered himself onto it. "We have to talk, Red," he whispered, his eyes seeking hers.

Fearing the powerful pull of his gaze, she turned away. The control he had over her senses was frightening. "No, I think I understand everything."

"You couldn't possibly understand," he countered.

"Talk all you like, but it isn't going to change things." She moved to the tiny kitchen and poured water into the kettle to heat. He stood and followed her, unable to hide a grimace of pain as he moved.

"Where are you going?" he demanded.

"Sit down," she snapped. The evidence of his pain upset her more than she cared to reveal. "I'm making us coffee. It looks like we can both use it." She moved across the room and gestured toward the bathroom door. "Now I'm going to get a pair of slippers. I was about to take a bath, and now my feet are cold." She'd taken off her shoes, and the floor was chilly against her bare feet. "Any objections?"

"Plenty, but I doubt they'll do any good."

She was glad for the respite as she found her slippers and slid her feet inside. She felt defenseless and naked, even though she was fully clothed. Seth knew her too well. The bathroom was quiet and still, and she paused to pray. Her mind was crowded with a thousand questions.

"Are you coming out of there, or do I have to knock that door down?" he demanded in a harsh tone.

"I'm coming." A few seconds later she left the bathroom and entered the kitchen to pour their coffee.

"I can't take this. Yell, scream, rant, rave, call me names, but for goodness sake, don't treat me like this. As if you didn't care, as if you weren't dying on the inside, when I know you must be."

She licked her dry lips and handed him the steaming cup. "I don't need to yell or scream. I admit I might have wanted to this morning, when I talked to Barbara, but not now. I have a fairly good understanding of the situation. I don't blame you. There was no way for you to know I was coming to Nome to stay." She made a point of sitting in the lone chair across the room from him, her composure stilted as she clutched the hot mug.

"Look at me, Red," he ordered softly.

She raised unsure eyes to meet his and time came to a halt. The unquestionable love that glowed in his dark eyes was her undoing. She vaulted to her feet and turned away from him before the anguish of her own eyes became obvious.

"No," she murmured brokenly.

He reached for her, but she easily sidestepped his arm.

"Don't touch me, Seth."

"I love you, Claudia Masters." His words were coaxing and low.

"Don't say that!" she burst out in a half-sob.

"Don't look! Don't touch! Don't love!" His voice was sharp "You're mine. I'm not going to let you go."

"I'm *not* yours," she cut in swiftly. "You don't own me. What about Barbara? I won't see you hurt her like this. She loves you, she'll make you a good wife. You were right about me. I don't belong here. I should be in Seattle with my family, back in medical school. I never should have come."

"That's not true and you know it," he said harshly, the blood draining from his face.

"Answer me something, Seth." She paused, and her lips trembled. For a moment she found it difficult to continue. "Why didn't you tell me about your brother?"

If possible, he paled even more. "How do you know about John? Did Barbara tell you?"

Claudia shook her head. "You called out to him that first night when your fever was so high. Then Barbara said something later, and I asked her to explain."

He covered his face with his hands. "I don't like to talk about it, Red. It's something I want to forget. That feeling of utter helplessness, watching the life flow out of John. I would have told you in time. To be frank, it hasn't been a year yet, and I still have trouble talking about it." He straightened and wiped a hand across his face. "John's death has been one of the most influential events of my life. I could find no reason why I should live and my brother should die. It didn't make sense. Other than the business, my life lacked purpose. I was completely focused on personal gain and satisfaction. That was when I talked to Pastor Reeder, seeking answers, and that led to my accepting Jesus Christ. And both John's death and my acceptance of the Lord led to my decision that it was time for me to get married and have a family."

Unable to speak, Claudia nodded. She had been with him the other night as he relived the torment of his brother's death. She had witnessed just a little of the effect it had had on his life.

"I'll be leaving Nome in a couple of months," she said. "Once Jim finds someone to help at the clinic. I want—"

"No," Seth objected strenuously.

"I'm going back to Seattle," she continued. "And someday, with God's help, I'll be one of Washington's finest pediatricians."

"Red, I admit I've made a terrible mess of this thing. When I told you God and I were working on the patience part of me, I wasn't kidding." His voice was low and tense. "But I can't let you go, not when I love you. Not when…"

"Not when Barbara's wearing your ring," she finished for him.

"Barbara…" he began heatedly, then stopped, defeated. "I have to talk to her. She's a wonderful woman, and I don't want to hurt her."

Claudia laughed softly. "We're both fools, aren't we? I think that at the end of three months we'd be at each other's throats." She marveled at how calm she sounded.

"You're going to marry me." Hard resolve flashed in his eyes.

"No, Seth, I'm not. There's nothing anyone can say that will prevent me from leaving."

He met her look, and for the first time she noticed the red stain on his pant leg. Her composure flew out the window. "Your wound has opened. It was crazy for you to have come here," she said, her voice rising. "I've got to get you home and back into bed."

"You enjoy giving orders, don't you?" he bit out savagely. "Marry Barbara. Go home. Stay in bed." He sounded suddenly weary, as if the effort of trying to talk to her had become too much. "I'll leave, but you can be sure that we're not through discussing the subject."

"As far as I'm concerned, we are." She ripped her coat off the hanger and got her purse.

"What are you doing now?"

"Taking you home and, if necessary, putting you back in bed."

Carefully Seth forced himself off the couch. The pain the movement caused him was clear in his eyes. Standing, he leaned heavily on the cane and dragged his leg as he walked.

"Let me help." She hastened to his side.

"I'm perfectly fine without you," he insisted.

Claudia paused and stepped back. "Isn't that the point I've been making?"

The next days were exhausting. The flu reached epidemic proportions. Both Jim and Claudia were on their feet eighteen hours a day. She traveled from house to house with him, often out to the surrounding villages, because the sick were often too ill to come into the city.

When the alarm sounded early the morning of the fifth day, she rolled over and groaned. Every muscle ached, her head throbbed, and it hurt to breathe. As she stirred from the bed, her stomach twisted into tight cramps. She forced herself to sit up, but her head swam and waves of nausea gripped her. A low moan escaped her parted lips, and she laid her head back on the pillow. She groped for the telephone, which sat on the end table beside the bed, and sluggishly dialed Jim's number to tell him she was the latest flu victim.

He promised to check on her later, but she assured him that she would be fine, that she just needed more sleep.

After struggling into the bathroom and downing some aspirin, she went back to bed and floated naturally into a blissful sleep.

Suddenly she was chilled to the bone and shivering uncontrollably, unconsciously incorporating the iciness into her dreams. She was lost on the tundra in a heavy snowstorm, searching frantically for Seth. He was lost, and now she was, too. Then it was warm, the snowflakes ceased, and the warmest summer sun stole through her until she was comfortable once again.

"Red?" A voice sliced into her consciousness.

Gasping, Claudia opened her eyes, and her gaze flew to the one chair in the room. Seth was sitting there, his leg propped on the coffee table. A worried frown furrowed his brow. As she struggled to a sitting position, she pulled the covers against her breast and flashed him a chilling glare. "How did you get in here?" The words emerged in a hoarse whisper, the lingering tightness in her chest still painful.

"Jim Coleman got a key from Paul Reeder and let me in. He was concerned about you. I thought it was only right that I volunteer to watch over you. I owe you one."

"You don't owe me anything, Seth Lessinger, except the right to leave here when the time comes."

He responded with a gentle smile. "We'll talk about that later. I'm not going to argue with you now, not when you're sick. How are you feeling?"

"Like someone ran over me with a two-ton truck." She leaned against the pillow. The pain in her chest continued, but it hurt a bit less to breathe if she was propped up against something solid. Her stomach felt better, and the desperate fatigue had fled.

"I haven't had a chance to talk to Barbara," he said as his gaze searched her face. "She's been helping Jim and her father the last couple of days. But I'm going to explain things. We're having dinner tonight."

"Seth, please." She looked away. "Barbara loves you, while I…"

"You love me, too."

"I'm going back to Seattle. I was wrong to have ever come north."

"Don't say that, Red. Please."

She slid down into the bed and pulled the covers over her shoulders. Closing her eyes, she hoped to convince him she was going back to sleep.

Imitation became reality, and when she opened her eyes again, the room was dark and Seth was gone. A tray had been placed on the table, and she saw that it held a light meal he had apparently fixed for her.

Although she tried to eat, she couldn't force anything down. The world outside her door was dark. There was very little sunlight during the days now, making it almost impossible to predict time accurately. The sun did rise, but only for a few short hours, and it was never any brighter than the light of dusk or dawn.

She was still awake when Seth returned. His limp was less pronounced as he let himself into her apartment.

"What are you doing here?" She was shocked at how weak her voice sounded.

"Barbara's got the flu," he murmured defeatedly. "I only got to see her for a couple of minutes." He sighed heavily as he lowered himself into the chair.

Instantly Claudia was angry. "You beast! You don't have any business being here! You should be with her, not me. She's the one who needs you, not me."

"Barbara's got her father. You've only got me," he countered gently.

"Don't you have any concern for her at all? What if she found out you were here taking care of me? How do you think she'd feel? You can't do this to her." A tight cough convulsed her lungs, and she shook violently with the spasm. The exertion drained her of what little strength she possessed. Wearily she slumped back and closed her eyes, trying to ignore the throbbing pain in her chest.

Cool fingers rested on her forehead. "Would you like something to drink?"

She looked up and nodded, though the effort was almost more than she could manage. The feeble attempt brought a light of concern to Seth's eyes.

The tea he offered hurt to swallow, and she shook her head after the first few sips.

"I'm phoning Jim. You've got something more than the flu." A scowl darkened his face.

"Don't," she whispered. "I'm all right, and Jim's so busy. He said he'd stop by later. Don't bother him. He's overworked enough as it is." Her heavy eyelids drooped, and she fell into a fitful slumber.

Again the rays of the sun appeared in her dream, but this time with an uncomfortably fiery intensity. She thrashed, kicking away the blankets, fighting off imaginary foes who wanted to take her captive.

Faintly she could hear Jim's voice, as if he were speaking from a great distance.

"I'm glad you phoned." His tone was anxious.

Gently she was rolled to her side and an icy-cold stethoscope was placed against her bare back. "Do you hear me, Claudia?" Jim asked.

"Of course I hear you." Her voice was shockingly weak and strained.

"I want you to take deep breaths."

Every inhalation burned like fire, searing a path

through her lungs. Moaning, she tried to speak again and found the effort too much.

"What is it, man?" She opened her eyes to see that Seth was standing above her, his face twisted in grim concern.

Jim was standing at his side, and now he sighed heavily. "Pneumonia."

Ten

"Am I dying?" Claudia whispered weakly. Cooper and Ashley stood looking down at her by the side of her hospital bed.

Cooper's mouth tightened into a hard line as his gaze traveled over her, and the oxygen tubes and intravenous drip that were attached to her.

"You'll live," Ashley said, and responded to Claudia's weak smile with one of her own.

"You fool. Why didn't you let me know things hadn't worked out here?" Cooper demanded. "Are you so full of pride that you couldn't come to me and admit I was right?"

Sparks of irritation flashed from Claudia's blue eyes. "Don't you ever give up? I'm practically on my deathbed and you're preaching at me!"

"I am not preaching," he denied quickly. "I'm only stating the facts."

Jim Coleman chuckled, and for the first time Claudia noticed that he had entered the room. "It's beginning to sound like you're back among the living, and sooner than we expected." Standing at the foot of her bed, he read her chart and smiled wryly. "You're looking better all the time. But save your strength to talk some sense into these folks. They seem to think they're going to take you back to Seattle."

Claudia rolled her head away so that she faced the wall and wouldn't need to look at Jim. "I *am* going back," she mumbled in a low voice, though she felt guilty, knowing how desperately Jim wanted her to stay.

A short silence followed. Claudia could feel Cooper's eyes boring holes into her back, but to his credit he didn't say anything.

"You've got to do what you think is right," Jim said at last.

"All I want is to go home. And the sooner the better." She would return to Seattle and rebuild her life.

"I don't think it's such a good idea to rush out of here," Jim said, and she could tell by the tone of his voice that he'd accepted her decision. "I want you to gain back some of your strength before you go."

"Pastor Reeder introduced himself to us when we arrived. He's offered to have you stay and recuperate at his home until you feel up to traveling," Ashley added.

"No." Claudia's response was adamant. "I want to go back to Seattle as soon as possible. Cooper was right, I don't belong in Nome. I shouldn't have come in the first place." The words produced a strained silence around the small room. "How soon can I be discharged, Jim?" Her questioning eyes sought his troubled ones.

"Tomorrow, if you like," he said solemnly.

"I would."

"Thanksgiving Day," Ashley announced.

Claudia's eyes met her friend's. Ashley knew the special significance the holiday held for her. The day she'd left Seattle, Claudia had told Ashley to expect the wedding around Thanksgiving. And Ashley had teased her, saying Claudia was making sure no one would ever forget their anniversary. Recalling the conversation brought a physical ache to her heart. No, she'd said, she wanted to be married around Thanksgiving because she wanted to praise God for giving her such a wonderful man as Seth. Now there would be no wedding. She would never have Seth.

"If you feel she needs more time, Doctor," Cooper began, "Ashley and I could stay a few days."

"No," Claudia interrupted abruptly. "I don't want to stay any longer than necessary." Remaining even one extra day was intolerable.

She closed her eyes, blotting out the world. Maybe she could fool the others, but not Ashley, who gently squeezed her hand. Shortly afterward Claudia heard the sound of hushed voices and retreating footsteps.

The stay in the hospital had been a nightmare from the beginning. Seth had insisted on flying in another doctor from Anchorage. As weak as she'd been, she had refused to have anyone but Jim Coleman treat her. Jim and Seth had faced each other, their eyes filled with bitter anger. Claudia was sure they'd argued later when she wasn't there to watch.

She had seen Seth only once since that scene, and only to say goodbye. The relationship was over, she'd said, finished, and he had finally accepted the futility of trying to change her mind.

Pastor Reeder had been a regular visitor. He tried to

talk to her about the situation between Seth, Barbara
and herself, but she had made it clear that she didn't
want to talk about it. He hadn't brought up the subject again.

Barbara had come once, but Claudia had pretended
she was asleep, unable to imagine facing the woman
who would share Seth's life, or making explanations
that would only embarrass both of them.

Now she relaxed against the pillows, weak after the
short visit. Without meaning to, she slipped into a restful slumber.

When she awoke an hour later, Seth was sitting at her
bedside. She had hoped not to see him again, but she felt
no surprise as she lifted her lashes and their eyes met.

"Hello, Seth," she whispered. She longed to reach out
and touch his haggard face. He looked as if he hadn't
slept in days.

"Hello, Red." He paused and looked away. "Claudia," he corrected. "Cooper and Ashley arrived okay?"

She nodded. "They were here this morning."

"I thought you might want someone with you." She
could tell from his tone that he knew he would never
be the one she relied on.

"Thank you. They said you were the one who
phoned." She didn't know how she could be so calm.
She felt the way she had in the dream, lost and wander-
ing aimlessly on the frozen tundra.

He shrugged, dismissing her gratitude.

"You'll marry Barbara, won't you?"

His hesitation was only slight. "If she'll have me."

She put on a brave smile. "I'm sure she will. She
loves you. You'll have a good life together."

He neither agreed with nor denied the statement. "And you?"

"I'm going back to school." The smile on her face died, and she took a quivering breath.

He stood and walked across the room to stare out the window, his back to her. He seemed to be gathering his resolve. "I couldn't let you go without telling you how desperately sorry I am," he began before returning to the chair at her side. "It was never my intention to hurt you. I can only beg your forgiveness."

"Don't, please." Her voice wobbled with the effort of suppressing tears. Seeing Seth humble himself this way was her undoing. "It's not your fault. Really, there's no one to blame. We've both learned a valuable lesson from this. We never should have sought a supernatural confirmation from God. Faith comes from walking daily with our Lord until we're so close to Him that we don't need anything more to know His will."

Until then Seth had avoided touching her, but now he took her hand and gently held it between his large ones. "When do you leave?"

Even that slight touch caused shivers to shoot up her arm. She struggled not to withdraw her hand. "Tomorrow."

He nodded, accepting her decision. "I won't see you again," he said. Then he took a deep breath and, very gently, lifted her fingers to his lips and kissed the back of her hand. "God go with you, Red, and may your life be full and rewarding." His eyes were haunted as he stood, looked down on her one last time, turned around and walked from the room.

"Goodbye, Seth." Her voice was wavering, and she closed her eyes unable to watch him leave.

"Honestly, Cooper, I don't need that." She was dressed and ready to leave the hospital when Cooper came into her room pushing a wheelchair. "I'm not an invalid."

Jim Coleman rounded the corner into her room. "No backtalk, Claudia. You have to let us wheel you out for insurance purposes."

"That's a likely story," she returned irritably. Cooper gave her a hand and helped her off the bed. "Oh, all right, I don't care what you use, just get me to the plane on time." It should have been the church, she reminded herself bitterly.

Jim drove the three of them to the airport. Ashley sat in the back seat with Claudia.

"This place is something." Cooper looked around curiously as they drove.

"It really is," Jim answered as he drove. Although it was almost noon, he used the car headlights.

"I wish I'd seen the tundra in springtime. From what everyone says, it's magnificent," Claudia murmured to no one in particular. "The northern lights are fantastic. I was up half one night watching them. Some people claim they can hear the northern lights. The stars here are breathtaking. Millions and millions, like I've never seen before. I…I guess I'd never noticed them in Seattle."

"The city obliterates their light," Jim explained.

Cooper turned around to look at Claudia. She met his worried look and gave a poor replica of a smile.

"Is the government ever planning to build a road into Nome?" Ashley asked. "I was surprised to learn we could only come by plane."

"Rumors float around all the time. The last thing I heard was the possibility of a highway system that would eventually reach us here."

No one spoke again until the airport was in sight. "You love it here, don't you?" Ashley asked Claudia, looking at her with renewed concern.

Claudia glanced out the side window, afraid of what her eyes would reveal if she met her friend's eyes. "It's okay," she said, doubting that she'd fooled anyone.

As soon as they parked, Cooper got out of the car and removed the suitcases from the trunk. Ashley helped him carry the luggage inside.

Jim opened the back door and gave Claudia a hand, quickly ushering her inside the warm terminal. His fingers held hers longer than necessary. "I've got to get back to the office."

"I know. Thank you, Jim. I'll always remember you," she said in a shaky voice. "You're the kind of doctor I hope to be: dedicated, gentle, compassionate. I deeply regret letting you down."

He hugged her fiercely. "No, don't say that. You're doing what you have to do. Goodbye. I'm sorry things didn't work out for you here. Maybe we'll meet again someday." He returned to the car, pausing to wave before he climbed inside and started the engine.

"Goodbye, Jim." The ache in her throat was almost unbearable.

Ashley was at her side immediately. "You made some

good friends in the short time you were here, didn't you?"

Claudia nodded rather than attempt an explanation that would destroy her fragile control over her composure.

A few minutes later, she watched as the incoming aircraft circled the airstrip. She was so intent that she didn't notice Barbara open the terminal door and walk inside.

"Claudia," she called softly, and hurried forward to meet her.

Claudia turned around, shock draining the color from her face.

"I know about you and Seth, and...don't leave," Barbara said breathlessly, her hands clenched at her sides.

"Please don't say that," Claudia pleaded. "Seth's yours. This whole thing is a terrible misunderstanding that everyone regrets."

"Seth will never be mine," Barbara countered swiftly. "It's you he loves. It will always be you."

"I didn't mean for you ever to know."

"If I hadn't been so blind, so stupid, I would have guessed right away. I thank God I found out."

"Did...Seth tell you?" Claudia asked.

Barbara shook her head. "He didn't need to. From the moment Jim brought you into the hospital, Seth was like a madman. He wouldn't leave, and when Jim literally escorted him out of your room, Seth stood in the hallway grilling anyone who went in or out."

For a moment Claudia couldn't speak. Then she put on a false smile and gently shook her head. "Good heavens, you're more upset about my leaving than I am.

Things will work out between you and Seth once I'm gone."

"Are you crazy? Do you think I could marry him now? He loves you so much it's almost killing him. How can you be so calm? Don't you care?" Barbara argued desperately. "I can't understand either one of you. Seth is tearing himself apart, but he wouldn't ask you to stay if his life depended on it." She stalked a few feet away, then spun sharply. "This is Thanksgiving!" she cried. "You should be thanking God that someone like Seth loves you."

Claudia closed her eyes to the shooting pain that pierced her heart.

"I once said, without knowing it was you, that the girl in Seattle was a fool. If you fly out of here, you're an even bigger fool than I thought."

Paralyzed by indecision, Claudia turned and realized that Cooper and Ashley had walked over and had clearly heard the conversation. Her eyes filled with doubt, she turned to her uncle.

"Don't look at me," he told her. "This has to be your own choice."

"Do you love him, honestly love him?" Ashley asked her gently.

"Yes, oh yes."

Ashley smiled and inclined her head toward the door. "Then what are you doing standing around here?"

Claudia turned to face Barbara again. "What about you?" she asked softly.

"I'll be all right. Seth was never mine, I'm only returning what is rightfully yours. Hurry, Claudia, go to him. He's at the office—on Thanksgiving! He needs you." She handed Claudia her car keys and smiled broadly through her tears. "Take my car. I'll catch a cab."

Claudia took a step backward. "Ashley...Cooper, thank you. I love you both."

"I'd better be godmother to your first child," Ashley called after her as Claudia rushed out the door.

Seth's building looked deserted when Claudia entered. The door leading to his office was tightly shut. She tapped lightly, then turned the handle and stepped inside.

He was standing with his back to her, his attention centered on an airplane making its way into the darkening sky.

"If you don't mind, Barbara, I'd rather be alone right now." His voice was filled with stark pain.

"It isn't Barbara," she whispered softly.

He spun around, his eyes wide with disbelief. "What are you doing here?"

Instead of answering him with words, she moved slowly across the room until she was standing directly in front of him. Gently she glided her fingers over the stiff muscles of his chest. He continued to hold himself rigid with pride. "I love you, Seth Lessinger. I'm yours now and for all our lives."

Groaning, he hauled her fiercely into his arms. "You'd better not change your mind, Red. I don't have the strength to let you go a second time." His mouth burned a trail of kisses down her neck and throat. Claudia surrendered willingly to each caress, savoring each kiss, reveling in the protective warmth of his embrace.

Epilogue

"Honey, what are you doing up?" Seth asked as he wandered sleepily from the master bedroom. Claudia watched her husband with a translucent happiness, her heart swelling with pride and love. They'd been married almost a year now: the happiest twelve months of her life.

He stepped up beside her, his hand sliding around the full swell of her stomach. "Is the baby keeping you awake?"

She relaxed against him, savoring the gentle feel of his touch. "No, I was just thinking how good God has been to us. A verse I read in the Psalms the other day kept running through my mind." She reached for her Bible. "It's Psalm 16:11.

"'Thou wilt make known to me the path of life; in Thy presence is fullness of joy; in Thy right hand there are pleasures forever.'"

Seth tenderly kissed the side of her creamy, smooth neck. "God has done that for us, hasn't He? He made known to us that our paths in life were linked, and together we've known His joy."

She nodded happily, rested the back of her head against his shoulder and sighed softly. "You know what tomorrow is, don't you?"

He gave an exaggerated sigh. "It couldn't be our anniversary. That isn't until the end of the month."

"No, silly, it's Thanksgiving."

"Barbara and Jim are coming, aren't they?"

"Yes, but she insisted on bringing the turkey. You'd think just because I was going to have a baby I was helpless."

"Those two are getting pretty serious, aren't they?"

"I think it's more than serious. It wouldn't surprise me if they got married before Christmas."

"It may be sooner than that. Jim's already asked me to be his best man," Seth murmured, and he nibbled at her earlobe, dropping little kisses along the way.

The two men had long ago settled their differences and had become good friends, which pleased her no end. Claudia had worked for Jim until two additional doctors had set up practice in Nome. The timing had been perfect. She had just learned she was pregnant, and she was ready to settle into the role of homemaker and mother.

"I don't know how you can love me in this condition." She turned and slipped her arms around his waist.

"You're not so bad-looking from the neck up," he teased affectionately, and kissed the tip of her nose. "Has it really been a year, Red?" His gaze grew serious.

She nodded happily, and her eyes were bright with

love. "There's no better time to thank God for each other, and for His love."

"No better time," he agreed, cradling her close to his side. "When I thought I had lost you forever, God gave you back to me."

"It was fitting that it was on Thanksgiving Day, wasn't it?"

"Very fitting," he murmured huskily in her ear, leading her back into their room.

* * * * *

CHRISTMAS MASQUERADE

Prologue

The blast of a jazz saxophone that pierced the night was immediately followed by the jubilant sounds of a dixieland band. A shrieking whistle reverberated through the confusion. Singing, dancing, hooting and laughter surrounded Jo Marie Early as she painstakingly made her way down Tulane Avenue. Attracted by the parade, she'd arrived just in time to watch the flambeaux carriers light a golden arc of bouncing flames from one side of the street to the other. Now she was trapped in the milling mass of humanity when she had every intention of going in the opposite direction. The heavy Mardi Gras crowds hampered her progress to a slow crawl. The observation of the "Fat Tuesday" had commenced two weeks earlier with a series of parades and festive balls. Tonight the celebrating culminated in a frenzy of singing, lively dancing and masqueraders who roamed the brilliant streets.

New Orleans went crazy at this time of year, throwing a city-wide party that attracted a million guests. After twenty-three years, Jo Marie thought she would be accustomed to the maniacal behavior in the city she loved. But how could she criticize when she was a participant herself? Tonight, if she ever made it out of this crowd, she was attending a private party dressed as Florence Nightingale. Not her most original costume idea, but the best she could do on such short notice. Just this morning she'd been in a snowstorm in Minnesota and had arrived back this afternoon to hear the news that her roommate, Kelly Beaumont, was in the hospital for a tonsillectomy. Concerned, Joe Marie had quickly donned one of Kelly's nurse's uniforms so she could go directly to the party after visiting Kelly in the hospital.

With a sigh of abject frustration, Jo Marie realized she was being pushed in the direction opposite the hospital.

"Please, let me through," she called, struggling against the swift current of the merrymaking crowd.

"Which way?" a gravelly, male voice asked in her ear. "Do you want to go this way?" He pointed away from the crowd.

"Yes…please."

The voice turned out to be one of three young men who cleared a path for Jo Marie and helped her onto a side street.

Laughing, she turned to find all three were dressed as cavaliers of old. They bowed in gentlemanly fashion, tucking their arms at their waists and sweeping their plumed hats before them.

"The Three Musketeers at your disposal, fair lady."

"Your rescue is most welcome, kind sirs," Jo Marie shouted to be heard above the sound of the boisterous celebration.

"Your destination?"

Rather than try to be heard, Jo Marie pointed toward the hospital.

"Then allow us to escort you," the second offered gallantly.

Jo Marie wasn't sure she should trust three young men wearing red tights. But after all, it was Mardi Gras and the tale was sure to cause Kelly to smile. And that was something her roommate hadn't been doing much of lately.

The three young men formed a protective circle around Jo Marie and led the way down a less crowded side street, weaving in and out of the throng when necessary.

Glancing above to the cast iron balcony railing that marked the outer limits of the French Quarter, Jo Marie realized her heroes were heading for the heart of the partying, apparently more interested in capturing her for themselves than in delivering her to the hospital. "We're headed the wrong way," she shouted.

"This is a short cut," the tallest of the trio explained humorously. "We know of several people this way in need of nursing."

Unwilling to be trapped in their game, Jo Marie broke away from her gallant cavaliers and walked as quickly as her starched white uniform would allow. Dark tendrils of her hair escaped the carefully coiled chignon and framed her small face. Her fingers pushed them aside, uncaring for the moment.

Heavy footsteps behind her assured Jo Marie that the Three Musketeers weren't giving up on her so easily. Increasing her pace, she ran across the street and was within a half block of the hospital parking lot when she collided full speed into a solid object.

Stunned, it took Jo Marie a minute to recover and recognize that whatever she'd hit was warm and lean. Jo Marie raised startled brown eyes to meet the intense gray eyes of the most striking man she had ever seen. His hands reached for her shoulder to steady her.

"Are you hurt?" he asked in a deep voice that was low and resonant, oddly sensuous.

Jo Marie shook her head. "Are you?" There was some quality so mesmerizing about this man that she couldn't move her eyes. Although she was self-consciously staring, Jo Marie was powerless to break eye contact. He wasn't tall—under six feet so that she had only to tip her head back slightly to meet his look. Nor dark. His hair was brown, but a shade no deeper than her own soft chestnut curls. And he wasn't handsome. Not in the urbane sense. Although his look and his clothes spoke of wealth and breeding, Jo Marie knew intuitively that this man worked, played and loved hard. His brow was creased in what looked like a permanent frown and his mouth was a fraction too full.

Not tall, not dark, not handsome, but the embodiment of every fantasy Jo Marie had ever dreamed.

Neither of them moved for a long, drawn-out moment. Jo Marie felt as if she'd turned to stone. All those silly, schoolgirl dreams she'd shelved in the back of her mind as products of a whimsical imagination stood before her. He was the swashbuckling pirate to her captured maiden, Rhett Butler to her Scarlett O'Hara, Heathcliff to her Catherine...

"Are you hurt?" He broke into her thoughts. Eyes as gray as a winter sea narrowed with concern.

"No." She assured him with a shake of her head and forced her attention over her shoulder. Her three gallant heroes had discovered another female attraction and had directed their attention elsewhere, no longer interested in following her.

His hands continued to hold her shoulder. "You're a nurse?" he asked softly.

"Florence Nightingale," she corrected with a soft smile.

His finger was under her chin. Lifting her eyes, she saw his softly quizzical gaze. "Have we met?"

"No." It was on the tip of her tongue to tell him that yes they had met once, a long time ago in her romantic daydreams. But he'd probably laugh. Who wouldn't? Jo Marie wasn't a star-struck teenager, but a woman who had long since abandoned the practice of reading fairy tales.

His eyes were intent as they roamed her face, memorizing every detail, seeking something he couldn't define. He seemed as caught up in this moment as she.

"You remind me of a painting I once saw," he said, then blinked, apparently surprised that he'd spoken out loud.

"No one's ever done my portrait," Jo Marie murmured, frozen into immobility by the breathless bewilderment that lingered between them.

His eyes skidded past her briefly to rest on the fun-seeking Musketeers. "You were running from them?"

The spellbinding moment continued.

"Yes."

"Then I rescued you."

Jo Marie confirmed his statement as a large group of merrymakers crossed the street toward them. But she barely noticed. What captured her attention was the way in which this dream man was studying her.

"Every hero deserves a reward," he said.

Jo Marie watched him with uncertainty. "What do you mean?"

"This." The bright light of the streetlamp dimmed as he lowered his head, blocking out the golden rays. His warm mouth settled over hers, holding her prisoner, kissing her with a hunger as deep as the sea.

In the dark recesses of her mind, Jo Marie realized she should pull away. A man she didn't know was kissing her deeply, passionately. And the sensations he aroused were far beyond anything she'd ever felt. A dream that had become reality.

Singing voices surrounded her and before she could recognize the source the kiss was abruptly broken.

The Three Musketeers and a long line of others were doing a gay rendition of the rumba. Before she could protest, before she was even aware of what was happening, Jo Marie was grabbed from behind by the waist and forced to join in the rambunctious song and dance.

Her dark eyes sought the dream man only to discover that he was frantically searching the crowd for her, pushing people aside. Desperately, Jo Marie fought to break free, but couldn't. She called out, but to no avail, her voice drowned out by the song of the others. The long line of singing pranksters turned the corner, forcing Jo Marie to go with them. Her last sight of the dream man was of him pushing his way through the crowd to find her, but by then it was too late. She, too, had lost him.

One

"You've got that look in your eye again," pixie-faced Kelly Beaumont complained. "I swear every time you pick me up at the hospital something strange comes over you."

Jo Marie forced a smile, but her soft mouth trembled with the effort. "You're imagining things."

Kelly's narrowed look denied that, but she said nothing.

If Jo Marie had felt like being honest, she would have recognized the truth of what her friend was saying. Every visit to the hospital produced a deluge of memories. In the months that had passed, she was certain that the meeting with the dream man had blossomed and grown out of proportion in her memory. Every word, every action had been relived a thousand times until her mind had memorized the smallest detail, down to the musky, spicy scent of him. Jo Marie had never told anyone about that night of the Mardi Gras. A couple of times she'd wanted to confide in Kelly, but the words wouldn't come. Late in the evenings after she'd prepared for bed, it was the dream man's face that drifted into her consciousness as she fell asleep. Jo Marie couldn't understand why this man who had invaded her life so briefly would have such an over-whelming effect. And yet those few minutes had lin-gered all these months. Maybe in every woman's life there was a man who was meant to fulfill her dreams. And, in that brief five-minute interlude during Mardi Gras, Jo Marie had found hers.

"…Thanksgiving's tomorrow and Christmas is just around the corner." Kelly interrupted Jo Marie's thoughts. The blaring horn of an irritated motorist caused them both to grimace. Whenever possible, they preferred taking the bus, but both wanted an early start on the holiday weekend.

"Where has the year gone?" Jo Marie commented absently. She was paying close attention to the heavy traffic as she merged with the late evening flow that led Interstate 10 through the downtown district. The freeway would deliver them to the two-bedroom apart-ment they shared.

"I saw Mark today," Kelly said casually.

Something about the way Kelly spoke caused Jo Marie to turn her head. "Oh." It wasn't unnatural that her brother, a resident doctor at Tulane, would run into Kelly. After all, they both worked in the same hospital. "Did World War Three break out?" Jo Marie had never known any two people who could find more things to argue about. After three years, she'd given up trying to figure out why Mark and Kelly couldn't get along. Say-ing that they rubbed each other the wrong way seemed too trite an explanation. Antagonistic behavior wasn't characteristic of either of them. Kelly was a dedicated nurse and Mark a struggling resident doctor. But when the two were together, the lightning arced between them like a turbulent electrical storm. At one time Jo Marie had thought Kelly and Mark might be interested in each other. But after months of constant bickering she was forced to believe that the only thing between them was her overactive imagination.

"What did Mark have to say?"

Pointedly, Kelly turned her head away and stared out the window. "Oh, the usual."

The low, forced cheerfulness in her roommate's voice didn't fool Jo Marie. Where Kelly was concerned, Mark was merciless. He didn't mean to be cruel or insulting, but he loved to tease Kelly about her family's wealth. Not that money or position was that important to Kelly. "You mean he was kidding you about playing at being a nurse again." That was Mark's favorite crack.

One delicate shoulder jerked in response. "Sometimes I think he must hate me," she whispered, pretending a keen interest in the view outside the car window.

The soft catch in Kelly's voice brought Jo Marie's attention from the freeway to her friend. "Don't mind Mark. He doesn't mean anything by it. He loves to tease. You should hear some of the things he says about my job—you'd think a travel agent did nothing but hand out brochures for the tropics."

Kelly's abrupt nod was unconvincing.

Mentally, Jo Marie decided to have a talk with her big brother. He shouldn't tease Kelly as if she were his sister. Kelly didn't know how to react to it. As the youngest daughter of a large southern candy manufacturer, Kelly had been sheltered and pampered most of her life. Her only brother was years older and apparently the age difference didn't allow for many sibling conflicts. With four brothers, Jo Marie was no stranger to family squabbles and could stand her own against any one of them.

The apartment was a welcome sight after the twenty-minute freeway drive. Jo Marie and Kelly thought of it as their port in the storm. The two-floor apartment building resembled the historic mansion from *Gone With the Wind.* It maintained the flavor of the Old South without the problem of constant repairs typical of many older buildings.

The minute they were in the door, Kelly headed for her room. "If you don't mind I think I'll pack."

"Sure. Go ahead." Carelessly, Jo Marie kicked off her low-heeled shoes. Slouching on the love seat, she leaned her head back and closed her eyes. The strain of the hectic rush hour traffic and the tension of a busy day ebbed away with every relaxing breath.

The sound of running bathwater didn't surprise Jo Marie. Kelly wanted to get an early start. Her family lived in an ultramodern home along Lakeshore Drive. The house bordered Lake Pontchartrain. Jo Marie had been inside the Beaumont home only once. That had been enough for her to realize just how good the candy business was.

Jo Marie was sure that Charles Beaumont may have disapproved of his only daughter moving into an apartment with a "nobody" like her, but once he'd learned that she was the great-great granddaughter of Jubal Anderson Early, a Confederate Army colonel, he'd sanctioned the move. Sometime during the Civil War, Colonel Early had been instrumental in saving the life of a young Beaumont. Hence, a-hundred-and-some-odd years later, Early was a name to respect.

Humming Christmas music softly to herself, Jo Marie wandered into the kitchen and pulled the orange juice from the refrigerator shelf.

"Want a glass?" She held up the pitcher to Kelly who stepped from the bathroom, dressed in a short terry-cloth robe, with a thick towel securing her bouncy blond curls. One look at her friend and Jo Marie set the ceramic container on the kitchen counter.

"You've been crying." They'd lived together for three years, and apart from one sad, sentimental movie, Jo Marie had never seen Kelly cry.

"No, something's in my eye," she said and sniffled.

"Then why's your nose so red?"

"Maybe I'm catching a cold." She offered the weak explanation and turned sharply toward her room.

Jo Marie's smooth brow narrowed. This was Mark's doing. She was convinced he was the cause of Kelly's uncharacteristic display of emotion.

Something rang untrue about the whole situation between Kelly and Mark. Kelly wasn't a soft, southern belle who fainted at the least provocation. That was another teasing comment Mark enjoyed hurling at her. Kelly was a lady, but no shrinking violet. Jo Marie had witnessed Kelly in action, fighting for her patients and several political causes. The girl didn't back down often. After Thanksgiving, Jo Marie would help Kelly fine-tune a few witty comebacks. As Mark's sister, Jo Marie was well acquainted with her brother's weak spots. The only way to fight fire was with fire she mused humorously. Together, Jo Marie and Kelly would teach Mark a lesson.

"You want me to fix something to eat before you head for your parents?" Jo Marie shouted from the kitchen. She was standing in front of the cupboard, scanning its meager contents. "How does soup and a sandwich sound?"

"Boring," Kelly returned. "I'm not really hungry."

"Eight hours of back-breaking work on the surgical ward and you're not interested in food? Are you having problems with your tonsils again?"

"I had them out, remember?"

Slowly, Jo Marie straightened. Yes, she remembered. All too well. It had been outside the hospital that she'd literally run into the dream man. Unbidden thoughts of him crowded her mind and forcefully she shook her head to free herself of his image.

Jo Marie had fixed herself dinner and was sitting in front of the television watching the evening news by the time Kelly reappeared.

"I'm leaving now."

"Okay." Jo Marie didn't take her eyes off the television. "Have a happy Thanksgiving; don't eat too much turkey and trimmings."

"Don't throw any wild parties while I'm away." That was a small joke between them. Jo Marie rarely dated these days. Not since—Mardi Gras. Kelly couldn't understand this change in her friend and affectionately teased Jo Marie about her sudden lack of an interesting social life.

"Oh, Kelly, before I forget—" Jo Marie gave her a

wicked smile "—bring back some pralines, would you? After all, it's the holidays, so we can splurge."

At any other time Kelly would rant that she'd grown up with candy all her life and detested the sugary sweet concoction. Pralines were Jo Marie's weakness, but the candy would rot before Kelly would eat any of it.

"Sure, I'll be happy to," she agreed lifelessly and was gone before Jo Marie realized her friend had slipped away. Returning her attention to the news, Jo Marie was more determined than ever to have a talk with her brother.

The doorbell chimed at seven. Jo Marie was spreading a bright red polish on her toenails. She grumbled under her breath and screwed on the top of the bottle. But before she could answer the door, her brother strolled into the apartment and flopped down on the sofa that sat at right angles to the matching love seat.

"Come in and make yourself at home," Jo Marie commented dryly.

"I don't suppose you've got anything to eat around here." Dark brown eyes glanced expectantly into the kitchen. All five of the Early children shared the same dusty, dark eyes.

"This isn't a restaurant, you know."

"I know. By the way, where's money bags?"

"Who?" Confused, Jo Marie glanced up from her toes.

"Kelly."

Jo Marie didn't like the reference to Kelly's family wealth, but decided now wasn't the time to comment. Her brother worked long hours and had been out of sorts lately. "She's left for her parents' home already."

A soft snicker followed Jo Marie's announcement.

"Damn it, Mark, I wish you'd lay off Kelly. She's not used to being teased. It really bothers her."

"I'm only joking," Mark defended himself. "Kell knows that."

"I don't think she does. She was crying tonight and I'm sure it's your fault."

"Kelly crying?" He straightened and leaned forward, linking his hands. "But I was only kidding."

"That's the problem. You can't seem to let up on her. You're always putting her down one way or another."

Mark reached for a magazine, but not before Jo Marie saw that his mouth was pinched and hard. "She asks for it."

Rolling her eyes, Jo Marie continued adding the fire-engine-red color to her toes. It wouldn't do any good for her to argue with Mark. Kelly and Mark had to come to an agreement on their own. But that didn't mean Jo Marie couldn't hand Kelly ammunition now and again. Her brother had his vulnerable points, and Jo Marie would just make certain Kelly was aware of them. Then she could sit back and watch the sparks fly.

Busy with her polish, Jo Marie didn't notice for several minutes how quiet her brother had become. When she lifted her gaze to him, she saw that he had a pained, troubled look. His brow was furrowed in thought.

"I lost a child today," he announced tightly. "I couldn't understand it either. Not medically, I don't mean that. Anything can happen. She'd been brought in last week with a ruptured appendix. We knew from the beginning it was going to be touch and go." He paused and breathed in sharply. "But you know, deep down inside I believed she'd make it. She was their only daughter. The apple of her parents' eye. If all the love in that mother's heart couldn't hold back death's hand, then what good is medical science? What good am I?"

Mark had raised these questions before and Jo Marie had no answers. "I don't know," she admitted solemnly and reached out to touch his hand in reassurance. Mark didn't want to hear the pat answers. He couldn't see that now. Not when he felt like he'd failed this little girl and her parents in some obscure way. At times like these, she'd look at her brother who was a strong, committed doctor and see the doubt in his eyes. She had no answers. Sometimes she wasn't even sure she completely understood his questions.

After wiping his hand across his tired face, Mark stood. "I'm on duty tomorrow morning so I probably won't be at the folks' place until late afternoon. Tell Mom I'll try to make it on time. If I can't, the least you can do is to be sure and save a plate for me."

Knowing Mark, he was likely to go without eating until tomorrow if left to his own devices. "Let me fix you something now," Jo Marie offered. From his unnatural pallor, Jo Marie surmised that Mark couldn't even remember when he'd eaten his last decent meal, coffee and a doughnut on the run excluded.

He glanced at his watch. "I haven't got time. Thanks anyway." Before she could object, he was at the door.

Why had he come? Jo Marie wondered absently. He'd done a lot of that lately—stopping in for a few minutes without notice. And it wasn't as if her apartment were close to the hospital. Mark had to go out of his way to visit her. With a bemused shrug, she followed him to the front door and watched as he sped away in that run-down old car he was so fond of driving. As he left, Jo Marie mentally questioned if her instincts had been on target all along and Kelly and Mark did hold some deep affection for each other. Mark hadn't come tonight for any specific reason. His first question had been about Kelly. Only later had he mentioned losing the child.

"Jo Marie," her mother called from the kitchen. "Would you mind mashing the potatoes?"

The large family kitchen was bustling with activity. The long white counter top was filled with serving bowls ready to be placed on the linen-covered dining room table. Sweet potato and pecan pies were cooling on the smaller kitchen table and the aroma of spice and turkey filled the house.

"Smells mighty good in here," Franklin Early proclaimed, sniffing appreciatively as he strolled into the kitchen and placed a loving arm around his wife's waist.

"Scat," Jo Marie's mother cried with a dismissive wave of her hand. "I won't have you in here sticking your fingers in the pies and blaming it on the boys. Dinner will be ready in ten minutes."

Mark arrived, red faced and slightly breathless. He kissed his mother on the cheek and when she wasn't looking, popped a sweet pickle into his mouth. "I hope I'm not too late."

"I'd say you had perfect timing," Jo Marie teased and handed him the electric mixer. "Here, mash these potatoes while I finish setting the table."

"No way, little sister." His mouth was twisted mockingly as he gave her back the appliance. "I'll set the table. No one wants lumpy potatoes."

The three younger boys, all in their teens, sat in front of the television watching a football game. The Early family enjoyed sports, especially football. Jo Marie's mother had despaired long ago that her only daughter would ever grow up properly. Instead of playing with dolls, her toys had been cowboy boots and little green army men. Touch football was as much a part of her life as ballet was for some girls.

With Mark out of the kitchen, Jo Marie's mother turned to her. "Have you been feeling all right lately?"

"Me?" The question caught her off guard. "I'm feeling fine. Why shouldn't I be?"

Ruth Early lifted one shoulder in a delicate shrug. "You've had a look in your eye lately." She turned and leaned her hip against the counter, her head tilted at a thoughtful angle. "The last time I saw that look was in your Aunt Bessie's eye before she was married. Tell me, Jo Marie, are you in love?"

Jo Marie hesitated, not knowing how to explain her feelings for a man she had met so briefly. He was more illusion than reality. Her own private fantasy. Those few moments with the dream man were beyond explaining, even to her own mother.

"No," she answered finally, making busy work by placing the serving spoons in the bowls.

"Is he married? Is that it? Save yourself a lot of grief, Jo Marie, and stay away from him if he is. You understand?"

"Yes," she murmured, her eyes avoiding her mother's. For all she knew he could well be married.

Not until late that night did Jo Marie let herself into her apartment. The day had been full. After the huge family dinner, they'd played cards until Mark trapped Jo Marie into playing a game of touch football for old times' sake. Jo Marie agreed and proved that she hadn't lost her "touch."

The apartment looked large and empty. Kelly stayed with her parents over any major holidays. Kelly's family seemed to feel that Kelly still belonged at home and always would, no matter what her age. Although Kelly was twenty-four, the apartment she shared with Jo Marie was more for convenience sake than any need to separate herself from her family.

With her mother's words echoing in her ear, Jo Marie sauntered into her bedroom and dressed for bed. Friday was a work day for her as it was for both Mark and Kelly. The downtown area of New Orleans would be hectic with Christmas shoppers hoping to pick up their gifts from the multitude of sales.

As a travel agent, Jo Marie didn't have many walk-in customers to deal with, but her phone rang continuously. Several people wanted to book holiday vacations, but there was little available that she could offer. The most popular vacation spots had been booked months in advance. Several times her information was accepted with an irritated grumble as if she were to blame. By the time she stepped off the bus outside her apartment, Jo Marie wasn't in any mood for company.

No sooner had the thought formed than she caught sight of her brother. He was parked in the lot outside the apartment building. Hungry and probably looking for a hot meal, she guessed. He knew that their mother had sent a good portion of the turkey and stuffing home with Jo Marie so Mark's appearance wasn't any real surprise.

"Hi," she said and knocked on his car window. The faraway look in his eyes convinced her that after all these years Mark had finally learned to sleep with his eyes open. He was so engrossed in his thoughts that Jo Marie was forced to tap on his window a second time.

"Paging Dr. Early," she mimicked in a high-pitched hospital voice. "Paging Dr. Mark Early."

Mark turned and stared at her blankly. "Oh, hi." He sat up and climbed out of the car.

"I suppose you want something to eat." Her greeting wasn't the least bit cordial, but she was tired and irritable.

The edge of Mark's mouth curled into a sheepish grin. "If it isn't too much trouble."

"No," she offered him an apologetic smile. "It's just been a rough day and my feet hurt."

"My sister sits in an office all day, files her nails, reads books and then complains that her feet hurt."

Jo Marie was too weary to rise to the bait. "Not even your acid tongue is going to get a rise out of me tonight."

"I know something that will," Mark returned smugly.

"Ha." From force of habit, Jo Marie kicked off her shoes and strolled into the kitchen.

"Wanna bet?"

"I'm not a betting person, especially after playing cards with you yesterday, but if you care to impress me, fire away." Crossing her arms, she leaned against the refrigerator door and waited.

"Kelly's engaged."

Jo Marie slowly shook her head in disbelief. "I didn't think you'd stoop to fabrications."

That familiar angry, hurt look stole into Mark's eyes. "It's true, I heard it from the horse's own mouth."

Lightly shaking her head from side to side to clear her thoughts, Jo Marie still came up with a blank. "But who?" Kelly wasn't going out with anyone seriously.

"Some cousin. Rich, no doubt," Mark said and straddled a kitchen chair. "She's got a diamond as big as a baseball. Must be hard for her to work with a rock that size weighing down her hand."

"A cousin?" New Orleans was full of Beaumonts, but none that Kelly had mentioned in particular. "I can't believe it," Jo Marie gasped. "She'd have said something to me."

"From what I understand, she tried to phone last night, but we were still at the folks' house. Just as well," Mark mumbled under his breath. "I'm not about to toast this engagement. First she plays at being nurse and now she wants to play at being a wife."

Mark's bitterness didn't register past the jolt of surprise that Jo Marie felt. "Kelly engaged," she repeated.

"You don't need to keep saying it," Mark snapped.

"Saying what?" A jubilant Kelly walked in the front door.

"Never mind," Mark said and slowly stood. "It's time for me to be going, I'll talk to you later."

"What about dinner?"

"There's someone I'd like you both to meet," Kelly announced.

Ignoring her, Mark turned to Jo Marie. "I've suddenly lost my appetite."

"Jo Marie, I'd like to introduce you to my fiancé, Andrew Beaumont."

Jo Marie's gaze swung from the frustrated look on her brother's face to an intense pair of gray eyes. There was only one man on earth with eyes the shade of a winter sea. The dream man.

Two

Stunned into speechlessness, Jo Marie struggled to maintain her composure. She took in a deep breath to calm her frantic heartbeat and forced a look of pleasant surprise. Andrew Beaumont apparently didn't even remember her. Jo Marie couldn't see so much as a flicker of recognition in the depth of his eyes. In the last nine months it was unlikely that he had given her more than a passing thought, if she'd been worthy of even that. And yet, she vividly remembered every detail of him, down to the crisp dark hair, the broad, muscular shoulders and faint twist of his mouth.

With an effort that was just short of superhuman, Jo Marie smiled. "Congratulations, you two. But what a surprise."

Kelly hurried across the room and hugged her tightly. "It was to us, too. Look." She held out her hand for Jo Marie to admire the flashing diamond. Mark hadn't been exaggerating. The flawless gem mounted in an antique setting was the largest Jo Marie had ever seen.

"What did I tell you," Mark whispered in her ear.

Confused, Kelly glanced from sister to brother. "Drew and I are celebrating tonight. We'd love it if you came. Both of you."

"No," Jo Marie and Mark declared in unison.

"I'm bushed," Jo Marie begged off.

"...and tired," Mark finished lamely.

For the first time, Andrew spoke. "We insist." The deep, resonant voice was exactly as Jo Marie remembered. But tonight there was something faintly arrogant in the way he spoke that dared Jo Marie and Mark to put up an argument.

Brother and sister exchanged questioning glances, neither willing to be drawn into the celebration. Each for their own reasons, Jo Marie mused.

"Well—" Mark cleared his throat, clearly ill at ease with the formidable fiancé "—perhaps another time."

"You're Jo Marie's brother?" Andrew asked with a mocking note.

"How'd you know?"

Kelly stuck her arm through Andrew's. "Family resemblance, silly. No one can look at the two of you and not know you're related."

"I can't say the same thing about you two. I thought it was against the law to marry a cousin." Mark didn't bother to disguise his contempt.

"We're distant cousins," Kelly explained brightly. Her eyes looked adoringly into Andrew's and Jo Marie felt her stomach tighten. Jealousy. This sickening feeling in the pit of her stomach was the green-eyed monster. Jo Marie had only experienced brief tastes of the emotion; now it filled her mouth until she thought she would choke on it.

"I...had a horribly busy day." Jo Marie sought frantically for an excuse to stay home.

"And I'd have to go home and change," Mark added, looking down over his pale gray cords and sport shirt.

"No, you wouldn't," Kelly contradicted with a provocative smile. "We're going to K-Paul's."

"Sure, and wait in line half the night." A muscle twitched in Mark's jaw.

K-Paul's was a renowned restaurant that was ranked sixth in the world. Famous, but not elegant. The small establishment served creole cooking at its best.

"No," Kelly supplied, and the dip in her voice revealed how much she wanted to share this night with her friends. "Andrew's a friend of Paul's."

Mark looked at Jo Marie and rolled his eyes. "I should have known," he muttered sarcastically.

"What time did you say we'd be there, darling?"

Jo Marie closed her eyes to the sharp flash of pain at the affectionate term Kelly used so freely. These jealous sensations were crazy. She had no right to feel this way. This man... Andrew Beaumont, was a blown-up figment of her imagination. The brief moments they shared should have been forgotten long ago. Kelly was her friend. Her best friend. And Kelly deserved every happiness.

With a determined jut to her chin, Jo Marie flashed her roommate a warm smile. "Mark and I would be honored to join you tonight."

"We would?" Mark didn't sound pleased. Irritation rounded his dark eyes and he flashed Jo Marie a look that openly contradicted her agreement. Jo Marie wanted to tell him that he owed Kelly this much for all the teasing he'd given her. In addition, her look pleaded with him to understand how much she needed his support tonight. Saying as much was impossible, but she hoped her eyes conveyed the message.

Jo Marie turned slightly so that she faced the tall figure standing only a few inches from her. "It's generous of you to include us," she murmured, but discovered that she was incapable of meeting Andrew's penetrating gaze.

"Give us a minute to freshen up and we'll be on our way," Kelly's effervescent enthusiasm filled the room. "Come on, Jo Marie."

The two men remained in the compact living room. Jo Marie glanced back to note that Mark looked like a jaguar trapped in an iron cage. When he wasn't pacing, he stood restlessly shifting his weight repeatedly from one foot to the other. His look was weary and there was an uncharacteristic tightness to his mouth that narrowed his eyes.

"What do you think," Kelly whispered, and gave a long sigh. "Isn't he fantastic? I think I'm the luckiest girl in the world. Of course, we'll have to wait until after the holidays to make our announcement official. But isn't Drew wonderful?"

Jo Marie forced a noncommittal nod. The raw disappointment left an aching void in her heart. Andrew should have been hers. "He's wonderful." The words came out sounding more like a tortured whisper than a compliment.

Kelly paused, lowering the brush. "Jo, are you all right? You sound like you're going to cry."

"Maybe I am." Tears burned for release, but not for

the reason Kelly assumed. "It's not every day I lose my best friend."

"But you're not losing me."

Jo Marie's fingers curved around the cold bathroom sink. "But you are planning to get married?"

"Oh yes, we'll make an official announcement in January, but we haven't set a definite date for the wedding."

That surprised Jo Marie. Andrew didn't look like the kind of man who would encourage a long engagement. She would have thought that once he'd made a decision, he'd move on it. But then, she didn't know Andrew Beaumont. Not really.

A glance in the mirror confirmed that her cheeks were pale, her dark eyes haunted with a wounded, perplexed look. A quick application of blush added color to her bloodless face, but there was little she could do to disguise the troubled look in her eyes. She could only pray that no one would notice.

"Ready?" Kelly stood just outside the open door.

Jo Marie's returning smile was frail as she mentally braced herself for the coming ordeal. She paused long enough to dab perfume to the pulse points at the hollow of her neck and at her wrists.

"I, for one, am starved," Kelly announced as they returned to the living room. "And from what I remember of K-Paul's, eating is an experience we won't forget."

Jo Marie was confident that every part of this evening would be indelibly marked in her memory, but not for the reasons Kelly assumed.

Andrew's deep blue Mercedes was parked beside

Mark's old clunker. The differences between the two men were as obvious as the vehicles they drove.

Clearly ill at ease, Mark stood on the sidewalk in front of his car. "Why don't Jo Marie and I follow you?"

"Nonsense," Kelly returned, "there's plenty of room in Drew's car for everyone. You know what the traffic is like. We could get separated. I wouldn't want that to happen."

Mark's twisted mouth said that he would have given a weeks' pay to suddenly disappear. Jo Marie studied her brother carefully from her position in the back seat. His displeasure at being included in this evening's celebration was confusing. There was far more than reluctance in his attitude. He might not get along with Kelly, but she would have thought that Mark would wish Kelly every happiness. But he didn't. Not by the stiff, unnatural behavior she'd witnessed from him tonight.

Mark's attitude didn't change any at the restaurant. Paul, the robust chef, came out from the kitchen and greeted the party himself.

After they'd ordered, the small party sat facing one another in stony silence. Kelly made a couple of attempts to start up the conversation, but her efforts were to no avail. The two men eyed each other, looking as if they were ready to do battle at the slightest provocation.

Several times while they ate their succulent Shrimp Remoulade, Jo Marie found her gaze drawn to Andrew. In many ways he was exactly as she remembered. In others, he was completely different. His voice was low pitched and had a faint drawl. And he wasn't a talker. His expression was sober almost to the point of being somber, which was unusual for a man celebrating his

engagement. Another word that her mind tossed out
was disillusioned. Andrew Beaumont looked as though
he was disenchanted with life. From everything she'd
learned he was wealthy and successful. He owned a land
development firm. Delta Development, Inc. had been
in the Beaumont family for three generations. Accord-
ing to Kelly, the firm had expanded extensively under
Andrew's direction.

But if Jo Marie was paying attention to Andrew, he
was nothing more than polite to her. He didn't acknowl-
edge her with anything more than an occasional look.
And since she hadn't directed any questions to him, he
hadn't spoken either. At least not to her.

Paul's special touch for creole cooking made the meal
memorable. And although her thoughts were troubled
and her heart perplexed, when the waitress took Jo Marie's plate away she had done justice to the meal. Even
Mark, who had sat uncommunicative and sullen through
most of the dinner, had left little on his plate.

After K-Paul's, Kelly insisted they visit the French
Quarter. The others were not as enthusiastic. After an
hour of walking around and sampling some of the best
jazz sounds New Orleans had to offer, they returned
to the apartment.

"I'll make the coffee," Kelly proposed as they
climbed from the luxury car.

Mark made a show of glancing at his watch. "I think
I'll skip the chicory," he remarked in a flippant tone.
"Tomorrow's a busy day."

"Come on, Mark—" Kelly pouted prettily "—don't
be a spoil sport."

Mark's face darkened with a scowl. "If you insist."

"It isn't every day I celebrate my engagement. And, Mark, have you noticed that we haven't fought once all night? That must be some kind of a record."

A poor facsimile of a smile lifted one corner of his mouth. "It must be," he agreed wryly. He lagged behind as they climbed the stairs to the second-story apartment.

Jo Marie knew her brother well enough to know he'd have the coffee and leave as soon as it was polite to do so.

They sat in stilted silence, drinking their coffee.

"Do you two work together?" Andrew directed his question to Jo Marie.

Flustered she raised her palm to her breast. "Me?"

"Yes. Did you and Kelly meet at Tulane Hospital?"

"No, I'm a travel agent. Mark's the one in the family with the brains." She heard the breathlessness in her voice and hoped that he hadn't.

"Don't put yourself down," Kelly objected. "You're no dummy. Did you know that Jo Marie is actively involved in saving our wetlands? She volunteers her time as an office worker for the Land For The Future organization."

"That doesn't require intelligence, only time," Jo Marie murmured self-consciously and congratulated herself for keeping her voice even.

For the first time that evening, Andrew directed his attention to her and smiled. The effect it had on Jo Marie's pulse was devastating. To disguise her reaction, she raised the delicate china cup to her lips and took a tentative sip of the steaming coffee.

"And all these years I thought the LFTF was for little old ladies."

"No." Jo Marie was able to manage only the one word.

"At one time Jo Marie wanted to be a biologist," Kelly supplied.

Andrew arched two thick brows. "What stopped you?"

"Me," Mark cut in defensively. "The schooling she required was extensive and our parents couldn't afford to pay for us both to attend university at the same time. Jo Marie decided to drop out."

"That's not altogether true." Mark was making her sound noble and self-sacrificing. "It wasn't like that. If I'd wanted to continue my schooling there were lots of ways I could have done so."

"And you didn't?" Again Andrew's attention was focused on her.

She moistened her dry lips before continuing. "No. I plan to go back to school someday. Until then I'm staying active in the causes that mean the most to me and to the future of New Orleans."

"Jo Marie's our neighborhood scientist," Kelly added proudly. "She has a science club for children every other Saturday morning. I swear she's a natural with those kids. She's always taking them on hikes and planning field trips for them."

"You must like children." Again Andrew's gaze slid to Jo Marie.

"Yes," she answered self-consciously and lowered her eyes. She was grateful when the topic of conversation drifted to other subjects. When she chanced a look at Andrew, she discovered that his gaze centered on her lips. It took a great deal of restraint not to moisten them. And even more to force the memory of his kiss from her mind.

Once again, Mark made a show of looking at his watch and standing. "The evening's been—" he faltered looking for an adequate description "—interesting. Nice meeting you, Beaumont. Best wishes to you and Florence Nightingale."

The sip of coffee stuck in Jo Marie's throat, causing a moment of intense pain until her muscles relaxed enough to allow her to swallow. Grateful that no one had noticed, Jo Marie set her cup aside and walked with her brother to the front door. "I'll talk to you later," she said in farewell.

Mark wiped a hand across his eyes. He looked more tired than Jo Marie could remember seeing him in a long time. "I've been dying to ask you all night. Isn't Kelly's rich friend the one who filled in the swampland for that housing development you fought so hard against?"

"And lost." Jo Marie groaned inwardly. She had been a staunch supporter of the environmentalists and had helped gather signatures against the project. But to no avail. "Then he's also the one who bought out Rose's," she murmured thoughtfully as a feeling of dread washed over her. Rose's Hotel was in the French Quarter and was one of the landmarks of Louisiana. In addition to being a part of New Orleans' history, the hotel was used to house transients. It was true that Rose's was badly in need of repairs, but Jo Marie hated to see the wonderful old building destroyed in the name of progress. If annihilating the breeding habitat of a hundred different species of birds hadn't troubled Andrew Beaumont, then she doubted that an old hotel in ill-repair would matter to him either.

Rubbing her temple to relieve an unexpected and throbbing headache, Jo Marie nodded. "I remember Kelly saying something about a cousin being responsible for Rose's. But I hadn't put the two together."

"He has," Mark countered disdainfully. "And come up with megabucks. Our little Kelly has reeled in quite a catch, if you like the cold, heartless sort."

Jo Marie's mind immediately rejected that thought. Andrew Beaumont may be the man responsible for several controversial land acquisitions, but he wasn't heartless. Five minutes with him at the Mardi Gras had proven otherwise.

Mark's amused chuckle carried into the living room. "You've got that battle look in your eye. What are you thinking?"

"Nothing," she returned absently. But already her mind was racing furiously. "I'll talk to you tomorrow."

"I'll give you a call," Mark promised and was gone.

When Jo Marie returned to the living room, she found Kelly and Andrew chatting companionably. They paused and glanced at her as she rejoined them.

"You've known each other for a long time, haven't you?" Jo Marie lifted the half-full china cup, making an excuse to linger. She sat on the arm of the love seat, unable to decide if she should stay and speak her mind or repress her tongue.

"We've known each other since childhood." Kelly answered for the pair.

"And Andrew is the distant cousin you said had bought Rose's."

Kelly's sigh was uncomfortable. "I was hoping you wouldn't put two and two together."

"To be honest, I didn't. Mark figured it out."

A frustrated look tightened Kelly's once happy features.

"Will someone kindly tell me what you two are talking about?" Andrew asked.

"Rose's," they chimed in unison.

"Rose's," he repeated slowly and a frown appeared between his gray eyes.

Apparently Andrew Beaumont had so much land one small hotel didn't matter.

"The hotel."

The unexpected sharpness in his voice caused Jo Marie to square her shoulders. "It may seem like a little thing to you."

"Not for what that piece of land cost me," he countered in a hard voice.

"I don't think Drew likes to mix business with pleasure," Kelly warned, but Jo Marie disregarded the well-intended advice.

"But the men living in Rose's will have nowhere to go."

"They're bums."

A sadness filled her at the insensitive way he referred to these men. "Rose's had housed homeless men for twenty years. These men need someplace where they can get a hot meal and can sleep."

"It's a prime location for luxury condominiums," he said cynically.

"But what about the transients? What will become of them?"

"That, Miss Early, is no concern of mine."

Unbelievably Jo Marie felt tears burn behind her eyes. She blinked them back. Andrew Beaumont wasn't the dream man she'd fantasized over all these months. He was cold and cynical. The only love he had in his life was profit. A sadness settled over her with a weight she thought would be crippling.

"I feel very sorry for you, Mr. Beaumont," she said smoothly, belying her turbulent emotions. "You may be very rich, but there's no man poorer than one who has no tolerance for the weakness of others."

Kelly gasped softly and groaned. "I knew this was going to happen."

"Are you always so opinionated, Miss Early?" There was no disguising the icy tones.

"No, but there are times when things are so wrong that I can't remain silent." She turned to Kelly. "I apologize if I've ruined your evening. If you'll excuse me now, I think I'll go to bed. Good night, Mr. Beaumont. May you and Kelly have many years of happiness together." The words nearly stuck in her throat but she managed to get them out before walking from the room.

"If this offends you in any way I won't do it." Jo Marie studied her roommate carefully. The demonstration in front of Rose's had been planned weeks ago. Jo Marie's wooden picket sign felt heavy in her hand. For the first time in her life, her convictions conflicted with her feelings. She didn't want to march against Andrew. It didn't matter what he'd done, but she couldn't stand by and see those poor men turned into the streets, either. Not in the name of progress. Not when progress was at the cost of the less fortunate and the fate of a once lovely hotel.

"This picket line was arranged long before you met Drew."

"That hasn't got anything to do with this. Drew is important to you. I wouldn't want to do something that will place your relationship with him in jeopardy."

"It won't."

Kelly sounded far more confident than Jo Marie felt.

"In fact," she continued, "I doubt that Drew even knows anything about the demonstration. Those things usually do nothing to sway his decision. In fact, I'd say they do more harm than good as far as he's concerned."

Jo Marie had figured that much out herself, but she couldn't stand by doing nothing. Rose's was scheduled to be shut down the following week…a short month before Christmas. Jo Marie didn't know how anyone could be so heartless. The hotel was to be torn down a week later and new construction was scheduled to begin right after the first of the year.

Kelly paused at the front door while Jo Marie picked up her picket sign and tossed the long strap of her purse over her shoulder.

"You do understand why I can't join you?" she asked hesitatingly.

"Of course," Jo Marie said and exhaled softly. She'd never expected Kelly to participate. This fight couldn't include her friend without causing bitter feelings.

"Be careful." Her arms wrapped around her waist to chase away a chill, Kelly walked down to the parking lot with Jo Marie.

"Don't worry. This is a peaceful demonstration. The

only wounds I intend to get are from carrying this sign. It's heavy."

Cocking her head sideways, Kelly read the sign for the tenth time. Save Rose's Hotel. A Piece Of New Orleans History. Kelly chuckled and slowly shook her head. "I should get a picture of you. Drew would get a real kick out of that."

The offer of a picture was a subtle reminder that Drew wouldn't so much as see the sign. He probably wasn't even aware of the protest rally.

Friends of Rose's and several others from the Land For The Future headquarters were gathered outside the hotel when Jo Marie arrived. Several people who knew Jo Marie raised their hands in welcome.

"Have the television and radio stations been notified?" the organizer asked a tall man Jo Marie didn't recognize.

"I notified them, but most weren't all that interested. I doubt that we'll be given air time."

A feeling of gloom settled over the group. An unexpected cloudburst did little to brighten their mood. Jo Marie hadn't brought her umbrella and was drenched in minutes. A chill caused her teeth to chatter and no matter how hard she tried, she couldn't stop shivering. Uncaring, the rain fell indiscriminately over the small group of protesters.

"You little fool," Mark said when he found her an hour later. "Are you crazy, walking around wet and cold like that?" His voice was a mixture of exasperation and pride.

"I'm making a statement," Jo Marie argued.

"You're right. You're telling the world what a fool you are. Don't you have any better sense than this?"

Jo Marie ignored him, placing one foot in front of the other as she circled the sidewalk in front of Rose's Hotel.

"Do you think Beaumont cares?"

Jo Marie refused to be drawn into his argument. "Instead of arguing with me, why don't you go inside and see what's holding up the coffee?"

"You're going to need more than a hot drink to prevent you from getting pneumonia. Listen to reason for once in your life."

"No!" Emphatically Jo Marie stamped her foot. "This is too important."

"And your health isn't?"

"Not now." The protest group had dwindled down to less than ten. "I'll be all right." She shifted the sign from one shoulder to the other and flexed her stiff fingers. Her back ached from the burden of her message. And with every step the rain water in her shoes squished noisily. "I'm sure we'll be finished in another hour."

"If you aren't, I'm carting you off myself," Mark shouted angrily and returned to his car. He shook his finger at her in warning as he drove past.

True to his word, Mark returned an hour later and followed her back to the apartment.

Jo Marie could hardly drive she was shivering so violently. Her long chestnut hair fell in limp tendrils over her face. Rivulets of cold water ran down her neck and she bit into her bottom lip at the pain caused by gripping the steering wheel. Carrying the sign had formed painful blisters in the palms of her hands. This was one protest rally she wouldn't soon forget.

Mark seemed to blame Andrew Beaumont for the fact that she was cold, wet and miserable. But it wasn't Andrew's fault that it had rained. Not a single forecaster had predicted it would. She'd lived in New Orleans long enough to know she should carry an umbrella with her. Mark was looking for an excuse to dislike Andrew. Any excuse. In her heart, Jo Marie couldn't. No matter what he'd done, there was something deep within her that wouldn't allow any bitterness inside. In some ways she was disillusioned and hurt that her dream man wasn't all she'd thought. But that was as deep as her resentments went.

"Little fool," Mark repeated tenderly as he helped her out of the car. "Let's get you upstairs and into a hot bath."

"As long as I don't have to listen to you lecture all night," she said, her teeth chattering as she climbed the stairs to the second-story apartment. Although she was thoroughly miserable, there was a spark of humor in her eyes as she opened the door and stepped inside the apartment.

"Jo Marie," Kelly cried in alarm. "Good grief, what happened?"

A light laugh couldn't disguise her shivering. "Haven't you looked out the window lately? It's raining cats and dogs."

"This is your fault, Beaumont," Mark accused harshly and Jo Marie sucked in a surprised breath. In her misery, she hadn't noticed Andrew, who was casually sitting on the love seat.

He rose to a standing position and glared at Mark as if her brother were a mad man. "Explain yourself," he demanded curtly.

Kelly intervened, crossing the room and placing a hand on Andrew's arm. "Jo Marie was marching in that rally I was telling you about."

"In front of Rose's Hotel," Mark added, his fists tightly clenched at his side. He looked as if he wanted to get physical. Consciously, Jo Marie moved closer to her brother's side. Fist fighting was so unlike Mark. He was a healer, not a boxer. One look told Jo Marie that in a physical exchange, Mark would lose.

Andrew's mouth twisted scornfully. "You, my dear Miss Early, are a fool."

Jo Marie dipped her head mockingly. "And you, Mr. Beaumont, are heartless."

"But rich," Mark intervened. "And money goes a long way in making a man attractive. Isn't that right, Kelly?"

Kelly went visibly pale, her blue eyes filling with tears. "That's not true," she cried, her words jerky as she struggled for control.

"You will apologize for that remark, Early." Andrew's low voice held a threat that was undeniable.

Mark knotted and unknotted his fists. "I won't apologize for the truth. If you want to step outside, maybe you'd like to make something of it."

"Mark!" Both Jo Marie and Kelly gasped in shocked disbelief.

Jo Marie moved first. "Get out of here before you cause trouble." Roughly she opened the door and shoved him outside.

"You heard what I said," Mark growled on his way out the door.

"I've never seen Mark behave like that," Jo Marie murmured, her eyes lowered to the carpet where a small pool of water had formed. "I can only apologize." She paused and inhaled deeply. "And, Kelly, I'm sure you know he didn't mean what he said to you. He's upset because of the rally." Her voice was deep with emotion as she excused herself and headed for the bathroom.

A hot bath went a long way toward making her more comfortable. Mercifully, Andrew was gone by the time she had finished. She didn't feel up to another confrontation with him.

"Call on line three."

Automatically Jo Marie punched in the button and reached for her phone. "Jo Marie Early, may I help you?"

"You won."

"Mark?" He seldom phoned her at work.

"Did you hear me?" he asked excitedly.

"What did I win?" she asked humoring him.

"Beaumont."

Jo Marie's hand tightened around the receiver. "What do you mean?"

"It just came over the radio. Delta Development, Inc. is donating Rose's Hotel to the city," Mark announced with a short laugh. "Can you believe it?"

"Yes," Jo Marie closed her eyes to the onrush of emotion. Her dream man hadn't let her down. "I can believe it."

Three

"But you must come," Kelly insisted, sitting across from Jo Marie. "It'll be miserable without you."

"Kell, I don't know." Jo Marie looked up from the magazine she was reading and nibbled on her lower lip.

"It's just a Christmas party with a bunch of stuffy people I don't know. You know how uncomfortable I am meeting new people. I hate parties."

"Then why attend?"

"Drew says we must. I'm sure he doesn't enjoy the party scene any more than I do, but he's got to go or offend a lot of business acquaintances."

"But I wasn't included in the invitation," Jo Marie argued. She'd always liked people and usually did well at social functions.

"Of course you were included. Both you and Mark," Kelly insisted. "Drew saw to that."

Thoughtfully, Jo Marie considered her roommate's request. As much as she objected, she really would like to go, if for no more reason than to thank Andrew for his generosity regarding Rose's. Although she'd seen him briefly a couple of times since, the opportunity hadn't presented itself to express her appreciation. The party was one way she could do that. New Orleans was famous for its festive balls and holiday parties. Without Kelly's invitation, Jo Marie doubted that there would ever be the chance for her to attend such an elaborate affair.

"All right," she conceded, "but I doubt that Mark will come." Mark and Andrew hadn't spoken since the last confrontation in the girls' living room. The air had hung heavy between them then and Jo Marie doubted that Andrew's decision regarding Rose's Hotel would change her brother's attitude.

"Leave Mark to me," Kelly said confidently. "Just promise me that you'll be there."

"I'll need a dress." Mentally Jo Marie scanned the contents of her closet and came up with zero. Nothing she owned would be suitable for such an elaborate affair.

"Don't worry, you can borrow something of mine," Kelly offered with a generosity that was innate to her personality.

Jo Marie nearly choked on her laughter. "I'm three inches taller than you." And several pounds heavier, but she preferred not to mention that. Only once before had Jo Marie worn Kelly's clothes. The night she'd met Andrew.

Kelly giggled and the bubbly sound was pleasant to the ears. "I heard miniskirts were coming back into style."

"Perhaps, but I doubt that the fashion will arrive in time for Christmas. Don't worry about me, I'll go out this afternoon and pick up some material for a dress."

"But will you have enough time between now and the party to sew it?" Kelly's blue eyes rounded with doubt.

"I'll make time." Jo Marie was an excellent seamstress. She had her mother to thank for that. Ruth Early had insisted that her only daughter learn to sew. Jo Marie had balked in the beginning. Her interests were anything but domestic. But now, as she had been several times in the past, she was grateful for the skill.

She found a pattern of a three-quarter-length dress with a matching jacket. The simplicity of the design made the outfit all the more appealing. Jo Marie could dress it either up or down, depending on the occasion. The silky, midnight blue material she purchased was perfect for the holiday, and Jo Marie knew that shade to be one of her better colors.

When she returned to the apartment, Kelly was gone. A note propped on the kitchen table explained that she wouldn't be back until dinner time.

After washing, drying, and carefully pressing the material, Jo Marie laid it out on the table for cutting. Intent on her task, she had pulled her hair away from her face and had tied it at the base of her neck with a rubber band. Straight pins were pressed between her lips when the doorbell chimed. The neighborhood children often stopped in for a visit. Usually Jo Marie welcomed their company, but she was busy now and interruptions could result in an irreparable mistake. She toyed with the idea of not answering.

The impatient buzz told her that her company was irritated at being kept waiting.

"Damn, damn, damn," she grumbled beneath her breath as she made her way across the room. Extracting the straight pins from her mouth, she stuck them in the small cushion she wore around her wrist.

"Andrew!" Secretly she thanked God the pins were out of her mouth or she would have swallowed them in her surprise.

"Is Kelly here?"

"No, but come in." Her heart was racing madly as he walked into the room. Nervous fingers tugged the rubber band from her chestnut hair in a futile attempt to look more presentable. She shook her hair free, then wished she'd kept it neatly in place. For days Jo Marie would have welcomed the opportunity to thank Andrew, but she discovered as she followed him into the living room that her tongue was tied and her mouth felt gritty and dry. "I'm glad you're here… I wanted to thank you for your decision about Rose's…the hotel."

He interrupted her curtly. "My dear Miss Early, don't be misled. My decision wasn't—"

Her hand stopped him. "I know," she said softly. He didn't need to tell her his reasoning. She was already aware it wasn't because of the rally or anything that she'd done or said. "I just wanted to thank you for whatever may have been your reason."

Their eyes met and held from across the room. Countless moments passed in which neither spoke. The air was electric between them and the urge to reach out and touch Andrew was almost overwhelming. The same breathlessness that had attacked her the night of the Mardi Gras returned. Andrew had to remember, he had to. Yet he gave no indication that he did.

Jo Marie broke eye contact first, lowering her gaze to the wool carpet. "I'm not sure where Kelly is, but she said she'd be back by dinner time." Her hand shook as she handed him the note off the kitchen counter.

"Kelly mentioned the party?"

Jo Marie nodded.

"You'll come?"

She nodded her head in agreement. "If I finish sewing this dress in time." She spoke so he wouldn't think she'd suddenly lost the ability to talk. Never had she been more aware of a man. Her heart was hammering at his nearness. He was so close all she had to do was reach out and touch him. But insurmountable barriers stood between them. At last, after all these months she was alone with her dream man. So many times a similar scene had played in her mind. But Andrew didn't remember her. The realization produced an indescribable ache in her heart. What had been the most profound moment in her life had been nothing to him.

"Would you like to sit down?" she offered, remembering her manners. "There's coffee on if you'd like a cup."

He shook his head. "No, thanks." He ran his hand along the top of the blue cloth that was stretched across the kitchen table. His eyes narrowed and he looked as if his thoughts were a thousand miles away.

"Why don't you buy a dress?"

A smile trembled at the edge of her mouth. To a man who had always had money, buying something as simple as a dress would seem the most logical solution.

"I sew most of my own things," she explained softly, rather than enlightening him with a lecture on economics.

"Did you make this?" His fingers touched the short

sleeve of her cotton blouse and brushed against the sensitive skin of her upper arm.

Immediately a warmth spread where his fingers had come into contact with her flesh. Jo Marie's pale cheeks instantly flushed with a crimson flood of color. "Yes," she admitted hoarsely, hating the way her body, her voice, everything about her, was affected by this man.

"You do beautiful work."

She kept her eyes lowered and drew in a steadying breath. "Thank you."

"Next weekend I'll be having a Christmas party at my home for the employees of my company. I would be honored if both you and your brother attended."

Already her heart was racing with excitement; she'd love to visit his home. But seeing where he lived was only an excuse. She'd do anything to see more of him. "I can't speak for Mark," she answered after several moments, feeling guilty for her thoughts.

"But you'll come?"

"I'd be happy to. Thank you." Her only concern was that no one from Delta Development would recognize her as the same woman who was active in the protest against the housing development and in saving Rose's Hotel.

"Good," he said gruffly.

The curve of her mouth softened into a smile. "I'll tell Kelly that you were by. Would you like her to phone you?"

"No, I'll be seeing her later. Goodbye, Jo Marie."

She walked with him to the door, holding onto the knob longer than necessary. "Goodbye, Andrew," she murmured.

Jo Marie leaned against the door and covered her face with both hands. She shouldn't be feeling this eager excitement, this breathless bewilderment, this softness inside at the mere thought of him. Andrew Beaumont was her roommate's fiancé. She had to remember that. But somehow, Jo Marie recognized that her conscience could repeat the information all day, but it would have little effect on her restless heart.

The sewing machine was set up at the table when Kelly walked into the apartment a couple of hours later.

"I'm back," Kelly murmured happily as she hung her sweater in the closet.

"Where'd you go?"

"To see a friend."

Jo Marie thought she detected a note of hesitancy in her roommate's voice and glanced up momentarily from her task. She paused herself, then said, "Andrew was by."

A look of surprise worked its way across Kelly's pixie face. "Really? Did he say what he wanted?"

"Not really. He didn't leave a message." Jo Marie strove for nonchalance, but her fingers shook slightly and she hoped that her friend didn't notice the telltale mannerism.

"You like Drew, don't you?"

For some reason, Jo Marie's mind had always referred to him as Andrew. "Yes." She continued with the mechanics of sewing, but she could feel Kelly's eyes roam over her face as she studied her. Immediately a guilty flush reddened her cheeks. Somehow, some way, Kelly had detected how strongly Jo Marie felt about Andrew.

"I'm glad," Kelly said at last. "I'd like it if you two would fall in…" She hesitated before concluding with, "Never mind."

The two words were repeated in her mind like the dwindling sounds of an echo off canyon walls.

The following afternoon, Jo Marie arrived home from work and took a crisp apple from the bottom shelf of the refrigerator. She wanted a snack before pulling out her sewing machine again. Kelly was working late and had phoned her at the office so Jo Marie wouldn't worry. Holding the apple between her teeth, she lugged the heavy sewing machine out of the bedroom. No sooner had she set the case on top of the table than the doorbell chimed.

Releasing a frustrated sigh, she swallowed the bite of apple.

"Sign here, please." A clipboard was shoved under her nose.

"I beg your pardon," Jo Marie asked.

"I'm making a delivery, lady. Sign here."

"Oh." Maybe Kelly had ordered something without telling her. Quickly, she penned her name along the bottom line.

"Wait here," was the next abrupt instruction.

Shrugging her shoulder, Jo Marie leaned against the door jamb as the brusque man returned to the brown truck parked below and brought up two large boxes.

"Merry Christmas, Miss Early," he said with a sheepish grin as he handed her the delivery.

"Thank you." The silver box was the trademark of New Orleans' most expensive boutique. Gilded lettering wrote out the name of the proprietor, Madame Renaux Marceau, across the top. Funny, Jo Marie couldn't recall Kelly saying she'd bought something there. But with the party coming, Kelly had apparently opted for the expensive boutique.

Dutifully Jo Marie carried the boxes into Kelly's room and set them on the bed. As she did so the shipping order attached to the smaller box, caught her eye. The statement was addressed to her, not Kelly.

Inhaling a jagged breath, Jo Marie searched the order blank to find out who would be sending her anything. Her parents could never have afforded something from Madame Renaux Marceau.

The air was sucked from her lungs as Jo Marie discovered Andrew Beaumont's name. She fumbled with the lids, peeled back sheer paper and gasped at the beauty of what lay before her. The full-length blue dress was the same midnight shade as the one she was sewing. But this gown was unlike anything Jo Marie had ever seen. A picture of Christmas, a picture of elegance. She held it up and felt tears prickle the back of her eyes. The bodice was layered with intricate rows of tiny pearls that formed a V at the waist. The gown was breathtakingly beautiful. Never had Jo Marie thought to own anything so perfect or so lovely. The second box contained a matching cape with an ornate display of tiny pearls.

Very carefully, Jo Marie folded the dress and cape and placed them back into the boxes. An ache inside her heart erupted into a broken sob. She wasn't a charity case. Did Andrew assume that because she sewed her own clothes that what she was making for the party would be unpresentable?

The telephone book revealed the information she needed. Following her instincts, Jo Marie grabbed a sweater and rushed out the door. She didn't stop until she pulled up in front of the large brick building with the gold plaque in the front that announced that this was the headquarters for Delta Development, Inc.

A listing of offices in the foyer told her where Andrew's was located. Jo Marie rode the elevator to the third floor. Most of the building was deserted, only a few employees remained. Those that did gave her curious stares, but no one questioned her presence.

The office door that had Andrew's name lettered on it was closed, but that didn't dissuade Jo Marie. His receptionist was placing the cover over her typewriter when Jo Marie barged inside.

"I'd like to see Mr. Beaumont," she demanded in a breathless voice.

The gray-haired receptionist glanced at the boxes under Jo Marie's arms and shook her head. "I'm sorry, but the office is closed for the day."

Jo Marie caught the subtle difference. "I didn't ask about the office. I said I wanted to see Mr. Beaumont." Her voice rose with her frustration.

A connecting door between two rooms opened. "Is there a problem, Mrs. Stewart?"

"I was just telling…"

"Jo Marie." Andrew's voice was an odd mixture of surprise and gruffness, yet gentle. His narrowed look centered on the boxes clasped under each arm. "Is there a problem?"

"As a matter of fact there is," she said, fighting to

disguise the anger that was building within her to volcanic proportions.

Andrew stepped aside to admit her into his office.

"Will you be needing me further?" Jo Marie heard his secretary ask.

"No, thank you, Mrs. Stewart. I'll see you in the morning."

No sooner had Andrew stepped in the door than Jo Marie whirled on him. The silver boxes from the boutique sat squarely in the middle of Andrew's huge oak desk.

"I think you should understand something right now, Mr. Beaumont," she began heatedly, not bothering to hold back her annoyance. "I am not Cinderella and you most definitely are not my fairy godfather."

"Would I be amiss to guess that my gift displeases you?"

Jo Marie wanted to scream at him for being so calm. She cut her long nails into her palms in an effort to disguise her irritation. "If I am an embarrassment to you wearing a dress I've sewn myself, then I'll simply not attend your precious party."

He looked shocked.

"And furthermore, I am no one's poor relation."

An angry frown deepened three lines across his wide forehead. "What makes you suggest such stupidity?"

"I may be many things, but stupid isn't one of them."

"A lot of things?" He stood behind his desk and leaned forward, pressing his weight on his palms. "You mean like opinionated, headstrong, and impatient."

"Yes," she cried and shot her index finger into the air. "But not stupid."

The tight grip Andrew held on his temper was visible by the way his mouth was pinched until the grooves stood out tense and white. "Maybe not stupid, but incredibly inane."

Her mouth was trembling and Jo Marie knew that if she didn't get away soon, she'd cry. "Let's not argue over definitions. Stated simply, the gesture of buying me a presentable dress was not appreciated. Not in the least."

"I gathered that much, Miss Early. Now if you'll excuse me, I have a dinner engagement."

"Gladly." She pivoted and stormed across the floor ready to jerk open the office door. To her dismay, the door stuck and wouldn't open, ruining her haughty exit.

"Allow me," Andrew offered bitterly.

The damn door! It would have to ruin her proud retreat.

By the time she was in the parking lot, most of her anger had dissipated. Second thoughts crowded her mind on the drive back to the apartment. She could have at least been more gracious about it. Second thoughts quickly evolved into constant recriminations so that by the time she walked through the doorway of the apartment, Jo Marie was thoroughly miserable.

"Hi." Kelly was mixing raw hamburger for meatloaf with her hands. "Did the dress arrive?"

Kelly knew! "Dress?"

"Yes. Andrew and I went shopping for you yesterday afternoon and found the most incredibly lovely party dress. It was perfect for you."

Involuntarily, Jo Marie stiffened. "What made you think I needed a dress?"

Kelly's smile was filled with humor. "You were sewing one, weren't you? Drew said that you were really attending this function as a favor to me. And since this is such a busy time of year he didn't want you spending your nights slaving over a sewing machine."

"Oh." A sickening feeling attacked the pit of her stomach.

"Drew can be the most thoughtful person," Kelly commented as she continued to blend the ground meat. Her attention was more on her task than on Jo Marie. "You can understand why it's so easy to love him."

A strangled sound made its way past the tightness in Jo Marie's throat.

"I'm surprised the dress hasn't arrived. Drew gave specific instructions that it was to be delivered today in case any alterations were needed."

"It did come," Jo Marie announced, more miserable than she could ever remember being.

"It did?" Excitement elevated Kelly's voice. "Why didn't you say something? Isn't it the most beautiful dress you've ever seen? You're going to be gorgeous." Kelly's enthusiasm waned as she turned around. "Jo, what's wrong? You look like you're ready to burst into tears."

"That's…that's because I am," she managed and covering her face with her hands, she sat on the edge of the sofa and wept.

Kelly's soft laugh only made everything seem worse. "I expected gratitude," Kelly said with a sigh and handed Jo Marie a tissue. "But certainly not tears. You don't cry that often."

Noisily Jo Marie blew her nose. "I… I thought I was

an embarrassment…to you two…that…you didn't want me…at the party…because I didn't have…the proper clothes…and…"

"You thought what?" Kelly interrupted, a shocked, hurt look crowding her face. "I can't believe you'd even think anything so crazy."

"That's not all. I…" She swallowed. "I took the dress to… Andrew's office and practically…threw it in his face."

"Oh, Jo Marie." Kelly lowered herself onto the sofa beside her friend. "How could you?"

"I don't know. Maybe it sounds ridiculous, but I really believed that you and Andrew would be ashamed to be seen with me in an outfit I'd made myself."

"How could you come up with something so dumb? Especially since I've always complimented you on the things you've sewn."

Miserably, Jo Marie bowed her head. "I know."

"You've really done it, but good, my friend. I can just imagine Drew's reaction to your visit." At the thought Kelly's face grew tight. "Now what are you going to do?"

"Nothing. From this moment on I'll be conveniently tucked in my room when he comes for you…"

"What about the party?" Kelly's blue eyes were rounded with childlike fright and Jo Marie could only speculate whether it was feigned or real. "It's only two days away."

"I can't go, certainly you can understand that."

"But you've got to come," Kelly returned adamantly. "Mark said he'd go if you were there and I need you both. Everything will be ruined if you back out now."

"Mark's coming?" Jo Marie had a difficult time believing her brother would agree to this party idea. She'd have thought Mark would do anything to avoid another confrontation with Andrew.

"Yes. And it wasn't easy to get him to agree."

"I can imagine," Jo Marie returned dryly.

"Jo Marie, please. Your being there means so much to me. More than you'll ever know. Do this one thing and I promise I won't ask another thing of you as long as I live."

Kelly was serious. Something about this party was terribly important to her. Jo Marie couldn't understand what. In order to attend the party she would need to apologize to Andrew. If it had been her choice she would have waited a week or two before approaching him, giving him the necessary time to cool off. As it was, she'd be forced to do it before the party while tempers continued to run hot. Damn! She should have waited until Kelly was home tonight before jumping to conclusions about the dress. Any half-wit would have known her roommate was involved.

"Well?" Kelly regarded her hopefully.

"I'll go, but first I've got to talk to Andrew and explain."

Kelly released a rush of air, obviously relieved. "Take my advice, don't explain a thing. Just tell him you're sorry."

Jo Marie brushed her dark curls from her forehead. She was in no position to argue. Kelly obviously knew Andrew far better than she. The realization produced a rush of painful regrets. "I'll go to his office first thing tomorrow morning," she said with far more conviction in her voice than what she was feeling.

"You won't regret it," Kelly breathed and squeezed Jo Marie's numb fingers. "I promise you won't."

If that was the case, Jo Marie wanted to know why she regretted it already.

To say that she slept restlessly would be an understatement. By morning, dark shadows had formed under her eyes that even cosmetics couldn't completely disguise. The silky blue dress was finished and hanging from a hook on her closet door. Compared to the lovely creation Andrew had purchased, her simple gown looked drab. Plain. Unsophisticated. Swallowing her pride had always left a bitter aftertaste, and she didn't expect it to be any different today.

"Good luck," Kelly murmured her condolences to Jo Marie on her way out the door.

"Thanks, I'll need that and more." The knot in her stomach grew tighter every minute. Jo Marie didn't know what she was going to say or even where to begin.

Mrs. Stewart, the gray-haired guardian, was at her station when Jo Marie stepped inside Andrew's office.

"Good morning."

The secretary was too well trained to reveal any surprise.

"Would it be possible to talk to Mr. Beaumont for a few minutes?"

"Do you have an appointment?" The older woman flipped through the calendar pages.

"No," Jo Marie tightened her fists. "I'm afraid I don't."

"Mr. Beaumont will be out of the office until this afternoon."

"Oh." Discouragement nearly defeated her. "Could I make an appointment to see him then?"

The paragon of virtue studied the appointment calendar. "I'm afraid not. Mr. Beaumont has meetings scheduled all week. But if you'd like, I could give him a message."

"Yes, please," she returned and scribbled out a note that said she needed to talk to him as soon as it was convenient. Handing the note back to Mrs. Stewart, Jo Marie offered the woman a feeble smile. "Thank you."

"I'll see to it that Mr. Beaumont gets your message," the efficient woman promised.

Jo Marie didn't doubt that the woman would. What she did question was whether Andrew would respond.

By the time Jo Marie readied for bed that evening, she realized that he wouldn't. Now she'd be faced with attending the party with the tension between them so thick it would resemble an English fog.

Mark was the first one to arrive the following evening. Dressed in a pin-stripe suit and a silk tie he looked exceptionally handsome. And Jo Marie didn't mind telling him so.

"Wow." She took a step in retreat and studied him thoughtfully. "Wow," she repeated.

"I could say the same thing. You look terrific."

Self-consciously, Jo Marie smoothed out an imaginary wrinkle from the skirt of her dress. "You're sure?"

"Of course, I am. And I like your hair like that."

Automatically a hand investigated the rhinestone

combs that held the bouncy curls away from her face and gave an air of sophistication to her appearance.

"When will money bags be out?" Mark's gaze drifted toward Kelly's bedroom as he took a seat.

"Any minute."

Mark stuck a finger in the collar of his shirt and ran it around his neck. "I can't believe I agreed to this fiasco."

Jo Marie couldn't believe it either. "Why did you?"

Her brother's shrug was filled with self-derision. "I don't know. It seemed to mean so much to Kelly. And to be honest, I guess I owe it to her for all the times I've teased her."

"How do you feel about Beaumont?"

Mark's eyes narrowed fractionally. "I'm trying not to feel anything."

The door opened and Kelly appeared in a red frothy creation that reminded Jo Marie of Christmas and Santa and happy elves. She had seen the dress, but on Kelly the full-length gown came to life. With a lissome grace Jo Marie envied, Kelly sauntered into the room. Mark couldn't take his eyes off her as he slowly rose to a standing position.

"Kelly." He seemed to have difficulty speaking. "You…you're lovely."

Kelly's delighted laughter was filled with pleasure. "Don't sound so shocked. You've just never seen me dressed up is all."

For a fleeting moment Jo Marie wondered if Mark had ever really seen her roommate.

The doorbell chimed and three pairs of eyes glared at the front door accusingly. Jo Marie felt her stomach tighten with nervous apprehension. For two days she'd dreaded this moment. Andrew Beaumont had arrived.

Kelly broke away from the small group and answered the door. Jo Marie watched her brother's eyes narrow as Kelly stood on her tiptoes and lightly brushed her lips across Andrew's cheek. The involuntary reaction stirred a multitude of questions in Jo Marie about Mark's attitude toward Kelly. And her own toward Andrew.

When her gaze drifted from her brother, Jo Marie discovered that Andrew had centered his attention on her.

"You look exceedingly lovely, Miss Early."

"Thank you. I'm afraid the dress I should have worn was mistakenly returned." She prayed he understood her message.

"Let's have a drink before we leave," Kelly suggested. She'd been in the kitchen earlier mixing a concoction of coconut milk, rum, pineapple and several spices.

The cool drink helped relieve some of the tightness in Jo Marie's throat. She sat beside her brother, across from Andrew. The silence in the room was interrupted only by Kelly, who seemed oblivious to the terrible tension. She chattered all the way out to the car.

Again Mark and Jo Marie were relegated to the back seat of Andrew's plush sedan. Jo Marie knew that Mark hated this, but he submitted to the suggestion without comment. Only the stiff way he held himself revealed his discontent. The party was being given by an associate of Andrew's, a builder. The minute Jo Marie heard the name of the firm she recognized it as the one that had worked on the wetlands project.

Mark cast Jo Marie a curious glance and she shook her head indicating that she wouldn't say a word. In some ways, Jo Marie felt that she was fraternizing with the enemy.

Introductions were made and a flurry of names and faces blurred themselves in her mind. Jo Marie recognized several prominent people, and spoke to a few. Mark stayed close by her side and she knew without asking that this whole party scene made him uncomfortable.

In spite of being so adamant about needing her, Kelly was now nowhere to be seen. A half hour later, Jo Marie noticed that Kelly was sitting in a chair against the wall, looking hopelessly lost. She watched amazed as Mark delivered a glass of punch to her and claimed the chair beside her roommate. Kelly brightened immediately and soon the two were smiling and chatting.

Scanning the crowded room, Jo Marie noticed that Andrew was busy talking to a group of men. The room suddenly felt stuffy. An open glass door that led to a balcony invited her outside and into the cool evening air.

Standing with her gloved hands against the railing, Jo Marie glanced up at the starlit heavens. The night was clear and the black sky was adorned with a thousand glittering stars.

"I received a message that you wanted to speak to me." The husky male voice spoke from behind her.

Jo Marie's heart leaped to her throat and she struggled not to reveal her discomfort. "Yes," she said with a relaxing breath.

Andrew joined her at the wrought-iron railing. His nearness was so overwhelming that Jo Marie closed her eyes to the powerful attraction. Her long fingers tightened their grip.

"I owe you an apology. I sincerely regret jumping to conclusions about the dress. You were only being kind."

An eternity passed before Andrew spoke. "Were you afraid I was going to demand a reward, Florence Nightingale?"

Four

Jo Marie's heart went still as she turned to Andrew with wide, astonished eyes. "You do remember." They'd spent a single, golden moment together so many months ago. Not once since Kelly had introduced Andrew as her fiancé had he given her the slightest inkling that he remembered.

"Did you imagine I could forget?" he asked quietly.

Tightly squeezing her eyes shut, Jo Marie turned back to the railing, her fingers gripping the wrought iron with a strength she didn't know she possessed.

"I came back every day for a month," he continued in a deep, troubled voice. "I thought you were a nurse."

The color ebbed from Jo Marie's face, leaving her pale. She'd looked for him, too. In all the months since the Mardi Gras she'd never stopped looking. Every time she'd left her apartment, she had silently searched through a sea of faces. Although she'd never known his name, she had included him in her thoughts every day since their meeting. He was her dream man, the stranger who had shared those enchanted moments of magic with her.

"It was Mardi Gras," she explained in a quavering voice. "I'd borrowed Kelly's uniform for a party."

Andrew stood beside her and his wintry eyes narrowed. "I should have recognized you then," he said with faint self-derision.

"Recognized me?" Jo Marie didn't understand. In the short time before they were separated, Andrew had said she reminded him of a painting he'd once seen.

"I should have known you from your picture in the newspaper. You were the girl who so strongly protested the housing development for the wetlands."

"I… I didn't know it was your company. I had no idea." A stray tendril of soft chestnut hair fell forward as she bowed her head. "But I can't apologize for demonstrating against something which I believe is very wrong."

"To thine own self be true, Jo Marie Early." He spoke without malice and when their eyes met, she discovered to her amazement that he was smiling.

Jo Marie responded with a smile of her own. "And you were there that night because of Kelly."

"I'd just left her."

"And I was on my way in." Another few minutes and they could have passed each other in the hospital corridor without ever knowing. In some ways Jo Marie wished they had. If she hadn't met Andrew that night, then she could have shared in her friend's joy at the coming marriage. As it was now, Jo Marie was forced to fight back emotions she had no right to feel. Andrew belonged to Kelly and the diamond ring on her finger declared as much.

"And...and now you've found Kelly," she stammered, backing away. "I want to wish you both a life filled with much happiness." Afraid of what her expressive eyes would reveal, Jo Marie lowered her lashes which were dark against her pale cheek. "I should be going inside."

"Jo Marie."

He said her name so softly that for a moment she wasn't sure he'd spoken. "Yes?"

Andrew arched both brows and lightly shook his head. His finger lightly touched her smooth cheek, following the line of her delicate jaw. Briefly his gaze darkened as if this was torture in the purest sense. "Nothing. Enjoy yourself tonight." With that he turned back to the railing.

Jo Marie entered the huge reception room and mingled with those attending the lavish affair. Not once did she allow herself to look over her shoulder toward the balcony. Toward Andrew, her dream man, because he wasn't hers, would never be hers. Her mouth ached with the effort to appear happy. By the time she made it to the punch bowl her smile felt brittle and was decidedly forced. All these months she'd hoped to find the dream man because her heart couldn't forget him. And now that she had, nothing had ever been more difficult. If she didn't learn to curb the strong sensual pull she felt toward him, she could ruin his and Kelly's happiness.

Soft Christmas music filled the room as Jo Marie found a plush velvet chair against the wall and sat down, a friendly observer to the party around her. Forcing herself to relax, her toe tapped lightly against the floor with an innate rhythm. Christmas was her favorite time of year—no, she amended, Mardi Gras was. Her smile became less forced.

"You look like you're having the time of your life," Mark announced casually as he took the seat beside her.

"It is a nice party."

"So you enjoy observing the life-style of the rich and famous." The sarcastic edge to Mark's voice was less sharp than normal.

Taking a sip of punch, Jo Marie nodded. "Who wouldn't?"

"To be honest I'm surprised at how friendly everyone's been," Mark commented sheepishly. "Obviously no one suspects that you and I are two of the less privileged."

"Mark," she admonished sharply. "That's a rotten thing to say."

Her brother had the good grace to look ashamed. "To be truthful, Kelly introduced me to several of her friends and I must admit I couldn't find anything to dislike about them."

"Surprise, surprise." Jo Marie hummed the Christmas music softly to herself. "I suppose the next thing I know, you'll be playing golf with Kelly's father."

Mark snorted derisively. "Hardly."

"What have you got against the Beaumonts anyway? Kelly's a wonderful girl."

"Kelly's the exception," Mark argued and stiffened.

"But you just finished telling me that you liked several of her friends that you were introduced to tonight."

"Yes. Well, that was on short acquaintance."

Standing, Jo Marie set her empty punch glass aside. "I think you've got a problem, brother dearest."

A dark look crowded Mark's face, and his brow was furrowed with a curious frown. "You're right, I do." With an agitated movement he stood and made his way across the room.

Jo Marie mingled, talking with a few women who were planning a charity benefit after the first of the year. When they asked her opinion on an important point, Jo Marie was both surprised and pleased. Although she spent a good portion of the next hour with these older ladies, she drifted away as they moved toward the heart of the party. If Andrew had recognized her as the girl involved in the protest against the wetlands development, others might too. And she didn't want to do anything that would cause him and Kelly embarrassment.

Kelly, with her blue eyes sparkling like sapphires, rushed up to Jo Marie. "Here you are!" she exclaimed. "Drew and I have been looking for you."

"Is it time to leave?" Jo Marie was more than ready, uncomfortably aware that she could be recognized at any moment.

"No…no, we just wanted to be certain some handsome young man didn't cart you away."

"Me?" Jo Marie's soft laugh was filled with incredulity. Few men would pay much attention to her, especially since she'd gone out of her way to remain unobtrusively in the background.

"It's more of a possibility than you realize," Andrew spoke from behind her, his voice a gentle rasp against her ear. "You're very beautiful tonight."

"Don't blush, Jo Marie," Kelly teased. "You really

are lovely and if you'd given anyone half a chance, they'd have told you so."

Mark joined them and murmured something to Kelly. As he did so, Andrew turned his head toward Jo Marie and spoke so that the other two couldn't hear him. "Only Florence Nightingale could be more beautiful."

A tingling sensation raced down Jo Marie's spine and she turned so their eyes could meet, surprised that he would say something like that to her with Kelly present. Silently, she pleaded with him not to make this any more difficult for her. Those enchanted moments they had shared were long past and best forgotten for both their sakes.

Jo Marie woke to the buzz of the alarm early the next morning. She sat on the side of the bed and raised her arms high above her head and yawned. The day promised to be a busy one. She was scheduled to work in the office that Saturday morning and then catch a bus to LFTF headquarters on the other side of the French Quarter. She was hoping to talk to Jim Rowden, the director and manager of the conservationists' group. Jim had asked for additional volunteers during the Christmas season. And after thoughtful consideration, Jo Marie decided to accept the challenge. Christmas was such a busy time of year that many of the other volunteers wanted time off.

The events of the previous night filled her mind. Lowering her arms, Jo Marie beat back the unexpected rush of sadness that threatened to overcome her. Andrew hadn't understood any of the things she'd tried to tell him last night. Several times she found him watching her, his look brooding and thoughtful as if she'd displeased him. No matter where she went during the course of the evening, when she looked up she found Andrew studying her. Once their eyes had met and held and everyone between them had seemed to disappear. The music had faded and it was as if only the two of them existed in the party-filled crowd. Jo Marie had lowered her gaze first, frightened and angry with them both.

Andrew and Mark had been sullen on the drive home. Mark had left the apartment almost immediately and Jo Marie had fled to the privacy of her room, unwilling to witness Andrew kissing Kelly goodnight. She couldn't have borne it.

Now, in the light of the new day, she discovered that her feelings for Andrew were growing stronger. She wanted to banish him to a special area of her life, long past. But he wouldn't allow that. It had been in his eyes last night as he studied her. Those moments at the Mardi Gras were not to be forgotten by either of them.

At least when she was at the office, she didn't have to think about Andrew or Kelly or Mark. The phone buzzed continually. And because they were short-staffed on the weekends, Jo Marie hardly had time to think about anything but airline fares, bus routes and train schedules the entire morning.

She replaced the telephone receiver after talking with the Costa Lines about booking a spring Caribbean cruise for a retired couple. Her head was bowed as she filled out the necessary forms. Jo Marie didn't hear Paula Shriver, the only other girl in the office on Saturday, move to her desk.

"Mr. Beaumont's been waiting to talk to you," Paula announced. "Lucky you," she added under her breath as Andrew took the seat beside Jo Marie's desk.

"Hello, Jo Marie."

"Andrew." Her hand clenched the ballpoint pen she was holding. "What can I do for you?"

He crossed his legs and draped an arm over the back of the chair giving the picture of a man completely at ease. "I was hoping you could give me some suggestions for an ideal honeymoon."

"Of course. What did you have in mind?" Inwardly she wanted to shout at him not to do this to her, but she forced herself to smile and look attentive.

"What would you suggest?"

She lowered her gaze. "Kelly's mentioned Hawaii several times. I know that's the only place she'd enjoy visiting."

He dismissed her suggestion with a short shake of his head. "I've been there several times. I was hoping for something less touristy."

"Maybe a cruise then. There are several excellent lines operating in the Caribbean, the Mediterranean or perhaps the inside passage to Alaska along the Canadian west coast."

"No." Again he shook his head. "Where would *you* choose to go on a honeymoon?"

Jo Marie ignored his question, not wanting to answer him. "I have several brochures I can give you that could spark an idea. I'm confident that any one of these places would thrill Kelly." As she pulled out her bottom desk drawer, Jo Marie was acutely conscious of Andrew studying her. She'd tried to come across with a strict business attitude, but her defenses were crumbling.

Reluctantly, he accepted the brochures she gave him. "You didn't answer my question. Shall I ask it again?"

Slowly, Jo Marie shook her head. "I'm not sure I'd want to go anywhere," she explained simply. "Not on my honeymoon. Not when the most beautiful city in the world is at my doorstep. I'd want to spend that time alone with my husband. We could travel later." Briefly their eyes met and held for a long, breathless moment. "But I'm not Kelly, and she's the one you should consider while planning this trip."

Paula stood and turned the sign in the glass door, indicating that the office was no longer open. Andrew's gaze followed her movements. "You're closing."

Jo Marie's nod was filled with relief. She was uncomfortable with Andrew. Being this close to him was a test of her friendship to Kelly. And at this moment, Kelly was losing…they both were. "Yes. We're only open during the morning on Saturdays."

He stood and placed the pamphlets on the corner of her desk. "Then let's continue our discussion over lunch."

"Oh, no, really that isn't necessary. We'll be finished in a few minutes and Paula doesn't mind waiting."

"But I have several ideas I want to discuss with you and it could well be an hour or so."

"Perhaps you could return another day."

"Now is the more convenient time for me," he countered smoothly.

Everything within Jo Marie wanted to refuse. Surely

he realized how difficult this was for her. He was well aware of her feelings and was deliberately ignoring them.

"Is it so difficult to accept anything from me, Jo Marie?" he asked softly. "Even lunch?"

"All right," she agreed ungraciously, angry with him and angrier with herself. "But only an hour. I've got things to do."

A half smile turned up one corner of his mouth. "As you wish," he said as he escorted her to his Mercedes.

Jo Marie was stiff and uncommunicative as Andrew drove through the thick traffic. He parked on a narrow street outside the French Quarter and came around to her side of the car to open the door for her.

"I have reservations at Chez Lorraine's."

"Chez Lorraine's?" Jo Marie's surprised gaze flew to him. The elegant French restaurant was one of New Orlean's most famous. The food was rumored to be exquisite, and expensive. Jo Marie had always dreamed of dining there, but never had.

"Is it as good as everyone says?" she asked, unable to disguise the excitement in her voice.

"You'll have to judge for yourself," he answered, smiling down on her.

Once inside, they were seated almost immediately and handed huge oblong menus featuring a wide variety of French cuisine. Not having sampled several of the more traditional French dishes, Jo Marie toyed with the idea of ordering the calf's sweetbread.

"What would you like?" Andrew prompted after several minutes.

"I don't know. It all sounds so good." Closing the menu she set it aside and lightly shook her head. "I think you may regret having brought me here when I'm so hungry." She'd skipped breakfast, and discovered now that she was famished.

Andrew didn't look up from his menu. "Where you're concerned, there's very little I regret." As if he'd made a casual comment about the weather, he continued. "Have you decided?"

"Yes...yes," she managed, fighting down the dizzying effect of his words. "I think I'll try the salmon, but I don't think I should try the French pronunciation."

"Don't worry, I'll order for you."

As if by intuition, the waiter reappeared when they were ready to place their order. "The lady would like *les mouilles à la creme de saumon fumé,* and I'll have the *le canard de rouen braise.*"

With a nod of approval the red-jacketed waiter departed.

Self-consciously, Jo Marie smoothed out the linen napkin on her lap. "I'm impressed," she murmured, studying the old world French provincial decor of the room. "It's everything I thought it would be."

The meal was fabulous. After a few awkward moments Jo Marie was amazed that she could talk as freely to Andrew. She discovered he was a good listener and she enjoyed telling him about her family.

"So you were the only girl."

"It had its advantages. I play a mean game of touch football."

"I hope you'll play with me someday. I've always enjoyed a rousing game of touch football."

The fork was raised halfway to her mouth and Jo

Marie paused, her heart beating double time. "I... I only play with my brothers."

Andrew chuckled. "Speaking of your family, I find it difficult to tell that you and Mark are related. Oh, I can see the family resemblance, but Mark's a serious young man. Does he ever laugh?"

Not lately, Jo Marie mused, but she didn't admit as much. "He works hard, long hours. Mark's come a long way through medical school." She hated making excuses for her brother. "He doesn't mean to be rude."

Andrew accepted the apology with a wry grin. "The chip on his shoulder's as big as a California redwood. What's he got against wealth and position?"

"I don't know," she answered honestly. "He teases Kelly unmercifully about her family. I think Kelly's money makes him feel insecure. There's no reason for it; Kelly's never done anything to give him that attitude. I never have understood it."

Pushing her clean plate aside, Jo Marie couldn't recall when she'd enjoyed a meal more—except the dinner they'd shared at K-Paul's the night Kelly and Andrew had announced their engagement. Some of the contentment faded from her eyes. Numbly, she folded her hands in her lap. Being here with Andrew, sharing this meal, laughing and talking with him wasn't right. Kelly should be the one sitting across the table from him. Jo Marie had no right to enjoy his company this way. Not when he was engaged to her best friend. Pointedly, she glanced at her watch.

"What's wrong?"

"Nothing." She shook her head slightly, avoiding

his eyes, knowing his look had the ability to penetrate her soul.

"Would you care for some dessert?"

Placing her hand on her stomach, she declined with a smile. "I couldn't," she declared, but her gaze fell with regret on the large table display of delicate French pastries.

The waiter reappeared and a flurry of French flew over her head. Like everything else Andrew did, his French was flawless.

Almost immediately the waiter returned with a plate covered with samples of several desserts which he set in front of Jo Marie.

"Andrew," she objected, sighing his name, "I'll get fat."

"I saw you eyeing those goodies. Indulge. You deserve it."

"But I don't. I can't possibly eat all that."

"You can afford to put on a few pounds." His voice deepened as his gaze skimmed her lithe form.

"Are you suggesting I'm skinny?"

"My, my," he said, slowly shaking his head from side to side. "You do like to argue. Here, give me the plate. I'll be the one to indulge."

"Not on your life," she countered laughingly, and dipped her fork into the thin slice of chocolate cheesecake. After sampling three of the scrumptious desserts, Jo Marie pushed her plate aside. "Thank you, Andrew," she murmured as her fingers toyed with the starched, linen napkin. "I enjoyed the meal and…and the company, but we can't do this again." Her eyes were riveted to the tabletop.

"Jo Marie—"

"No. Let me finish," she interrupted on a rushed breath. "It…it would be so easy…to hurt Kelly and I won't do that. I can't. Please, don't make this so difficult for me." With every word her voice grew weaker and shakier. It shouldn't be this hard, her heart cried, but it was. Every womanly instinct was reaching out to him until she wanted to cry with it.

"Indulge me, Jo Marie," he said tenderly. "It's my birthday and there's no one else I'd rather share it with."

No one else…his words reverberated through her mind. They were on treacherous ground and Jo Marie felt herself sinking fast.

"Happy birthday," she whispered.

"Thank you."

They stood and Andrew cupped her elbow, leading her to the street.

"Would you like me to drop you off at the apartment?" Andrew asked several minutes later as they walked toward his parked car.

"No. I'm on my way to the LFTF headquarters." She stuck both hands deep within her sweater pockets.

"Land For The Future?"

She nodded. "They need extra volunteers during the Christmas season."

His wide brow knitted with a deep frown. "As I recall, that building is in a bad part of town. Is it safe for you to—"

"Perfectly safe." She took a step in retreat. "Thank you again for lunch. I hope you have a wonderful birthday," she called just before turning and hurrying along the narrow sidewalk.

Jo Marie's pace was brisk as she kept one eye on the

darkening sky. Angry gray thunderclouds were rolling in and a cloud burst was imminent. Everything looked as if it was against her. With the sky the color of Andrew's eyes, it seemed as though he was watching her every move. Fleetingly she wondered if she'd ever escape him…and worse, if she'd ever want to.

The LFTF headquarters were near the docks. Andrew's apprehensions were well founded. This was a high crime area. Jo Marie planned her arrival and departure times in daylight.

"Can I help you?" The stocky man with crisp ebony hair spoke from behind the desk. There was a speculative arch to his bushy brows as he regarded her.

"Hello." She extended her hand. "I'm Jo Marie Early. You're Jim Rowden, aren't you?" Jim had recently arrived from the Boston area and was taking over the manager's position of the nonprofit organization.

Jim stepped around the large oak desk. "Yes, I remember now. You marched in the demonstration, didn't you?"

"Yes, I was there."

"One of the few who stuck it out in the rain, as I recall."

"My brother insisted that it wasn't out of any sense of purpose, but from a pure streak of stubbornness." Laughter riddled her voice. "I'm back because you mentioned needing extra volunteers this month."

"Do you type?"

"Reasonably well. I'm a travel agent."

"Don't worry I won't give you a time test."

Jo Marie laughed. "I appreciate that more than you know."

The majority of the afternoon was spent typing personal replies to letters the group had received after the demonstration in front of Rose's. In addition, the group had been spurred on by their success, and was planning other campaigns for future projects. At four-thirty, Jo Marie slipped the cover over the typewriter and placed the letters on Jim's desk for his signature.

"If you could come three times a week," Jim asked, "it would be greatly appreciated."

She left forty minutes later feeling assured that she was doing the right thing by offering her time. Lending a hand at Christmas seemed such a small thing to do. Admittedly, her motives weren't pure. If she could keep herself occupied, she wouldn't have to deal with her feelings for Andrew.

A lot of her major Christmas shopping was completed, but on her way to the bus stop, Jo Marie stopped in at a used-book store. Although she fought it all afternoon, her thoughts had been continually on Andrew. Today was his special day and she desperately wanted to give him something that would relay her feelings. Her heart was filled with gratitude. Without him, she may never have known that sometimes dreams can come true and that fairy tales aren't always for the young.

She found the book she was seeking. A large leather-bound volume of the history of New Orleans. Few cities had a more romantic background. Included in the book were hundreds of rare photographs of the city's architecture, courtyards, patios, ironwork and cemeteries. He'd love the book as much as she. Jo Marie had come by for weeks, paying a little bit each pay day. Not only was this book rare, but extremely expensive. Because the proprietor knew Jo Marie, he had made special arrangements for her to have this volume. But Jo Marie couldn't think of anything else Andrew would cherish more. She wrote out a check for the balance and realized that she would probably be short on cash by the end of the month, but that seemed a small sacrifice.

Clenching the book to her breast, Jo Marie hurried home. She had no right to be giving Andrew gifts, but this was more for her sake than his. It was her thank you for all that he'd given her.

The torrential downpour assaulted the pavement just as Jo Marie stepped off the bus. Breathlessly, while holding the paper-wrapped leather volume to her stomach, she ran to the apartment and inserted her key into the dead bolt. Once again she had barely escaped a thorough drenching.

Hanging her Irish knit cardigan in the hall closet, Jo Marie kicked off her shoes and slid her feet into fuzzy, worn slippers.

Kelly should arrive any minute and Jo Marie rehearsed what she was going to say to Kelly. She had to have some kind of explanation to be giving her friend's fiancé a birthday present. Her thoughts came back empty as she paced the floor, wringing her hands. It was important that Kelly understand, but finding a plausible reason without revealing herself was difficult. Jo Marie didn't want any ill feelings between them.

When her roommate hadn't returned from the hospital by six, Jo Marie made herself a light meal and turned on the evening news. Kelly usually phoned if she

was going to be late. Not having heard from her friend
caused Jo Marie to wonder. Maybe Andrew had picked
her up after work and had taken her out to dinner. It
was, after all, his birthday; celebrating with his fiancé
would only be natural. Unbidden, a surge of resentment
rose within her and caused a lump of painful hoarse-
ness to tighten her throat. Mentally she gave herself a
hard shake. *Stop it,* her mind shouted. *You have no right
to feel these things. Andrew belongs to Kelly, not you.*

A mixture of pain and confusion moved across her
smooth brow when the doorbell chimed. It was probably
Mark, but for the first time in recent memory, Jo Marie
wasn't up to a sparring match with her older brother.
Tonight she wanted to be left to her own thoughts.

But it wasn't Mark.

"Andrew." Quickly she lowered her gaze, praying he
couldn't read her startled expression.

"Is Kelly ready?" he asked as he stepped inside the
entryway. "We're having dinner with my mother."

"She isn't home from work yet. If you'd like I could
call the hospital and see what's holding her up." So they
were going out tonight. Jo Marie successfully managed to rein in her feelings of jealousy, having dealt
with them earlier.

"No need, I'm early. If you don't mind, I'll just wait."

"Please, sit down." Self-consciously she gestured
toward the love seat. "I'm sure Kelly will be here any
minute."

Impeccably dressed in a charcoal-gray suit that emphasized the width of his muscular shoulders, Andrew
took a seat.

With her hands linked in front of her, Jo Marie fought

for control of her hammering heart. "Would you like a cup of coffee?"

"Please."

Relieved to be out of the living room, Jo Marie hurried into the kitchen and brought down a cup and saucer. Spending part of the afternoon with Andrew was difficult enough. But being alone in the apartment with him was impossible. The tension between them was unbearable as it was. But to be separated by only a thin wall was much worse. She yearned to touch him. To hold him in her arms. To feel again, just this once, his mouth over hers. She had to know if what had happened all those months ago was real.

"Jo Marie," Andrew spoke softly from behind her.

Her pounding heart leaped to her throat. Had he read her thoughts and come to her? Her fingers dug unmercifully into the kitchen counter top. Nothing would induce her to turn around.

"What's this?" he questioned softly.

A glance over her shoulder revealed Andrew holding the book she'd purchased earlier. Her hand shook as she poured the coffee. "It's a book about the early history of New Orleans. I found it in a used-book store and…" Her voice wobbled as badly as her hand.

"There was a card on top of it that was addressed to me."

Jo Marie set the glass coffeepot down. "Yes… I knew you'd love it and I wanted you to have it as a birthday present." She stopped just before admitting that she wanted him to remember her. "I also heard on the news tonight that…that Rose's Hotel is undergoing some expensive and badly needed repairs, thanks to

you." Slowly she turned, keeping her hands behind her.
"I realize there isn't anything that I could ever buy for
you that you couldn't purchase a hundred times over.
But I thought this book might be the one thing I could
give you…" She let her voice fade in midsentence.

A slow faint smile touched his mouth as he opened
the card and read her inscription. "To Andrew, in appreciation for everything." Respectfully he opened the
book, then laid it aside. "Everything, Jo Marie?"

"For your generosity toward the hotel, and your
thoughtfulness in giving me the party dress and…"

"The Mardi Gras?" He inched his way toward her.

Jo Marie could feel the color seep up her neck and
tinge her cheeks. "Yes, that too." She wouldn't deny how
speical those few moments had been to her. Nor could
she deny the hunger in his hard gaze as he concentrated
on her lips. Amazed, Jo Marie watched as Andrew's
gray eyes darkened to the shade of a stormy Arctic sea.

No pretense existed between them now, only a shared
hunger that could no longer be repressed. A surge of
intense longing seared through her so that when Andrew drew her into his embrace she gave a small cry
and went willingly.

"Haven't you ever wondered if what we shared that
night was real?" he breathed the question into her hair.

"Yes, a thousand times since, I've wondered." She
gloried in the feel of his muscular body pressing against
the length of hers. Freely her hands roamed his back.
His index finger under her chin lifted her face and her
heart soared at the look in his eyes.

"Jo Marie," he whispered achingly and his thumb
leisurely caressed the full curve of her mouth.

Her soft lips trembled in anticipation. Slowly, deliberately, Andrew lowered his head as his mouth sought hers. Her eyelids drifted closed and her arms reached up and clung to him. The kiss was one of hunger and demand as his mouth feasted on hers.

The feel of him, the touch, the taste of his lips filled her senses until Jo Marie felt his muscles strain as he brought her to him, riveting her soft form to him so tightly that she could no longer breathe. Not that she cared.

Gradually the kiss mellowed and the intensity eased until he buried his face in the gentle slope of her neck. "It was real," he whispered huskily. "Oh, my sweet Florence Nightingale, it was even better than I remembered."

"I was afraid it would be." Tears burned her eyes and she gave a sad little laugh. Life was filled with ironies and finding Andrew now was the most painful.

Tenderly he reached up and wiped the moisture from her face. "I shouldn't have let this happen."

"It wasn't your fault." Jo Marie felt she had to accept part of the blame. She'd wanted him to kiss her so badly. "I... I won't let it happen again." If one of them had to be strong, then it would be her. After years of friendship with Kelly she owed her roommate her loyalty.

Reluctantly they broke apart, but his hands rested on either side of her neck as though he couldn't bear to let her go completely. "Thank you for the book," he said in a raw voice. "I'll treasure it always."

The sound of the front door opening caused Jo Marie's eyes to widen with a rush of guilt. Kelly would

take one look at her and realize what had happened.
Hot color blazed in her cheeks.

"Jo Marie!" Kelly's eager voice vibrated through the
apartment.

Andrew stepped out of the kitchen, granting Jo Marie
precious seconds to compose herself.

"Oh, heavens, you're here already, Drew. I'm sorry
I'm so late. But I've got so much to tell you."

With her hand covering her mouth to smother the
sound of her tears, Jo Marie leaned against the kitchen
counter, suddenly needing its support.

Five

"Are you all right?" Andrew stepped back into the kitchen and brushed his hand over his temples. He resembled a man driven to the end of his endurance, standing with one foot in heaven and the other in hell. His fingers were clenched at his side as if he couldn't decide if he should haul her back into his arms or leave her alone. But the tortured look in his eyes told Jo Marie how difficult it was not to hold and reassure her.

"I'm fine." Her voice was eggshell fragile. "Just leave. Please. I don't want Kelly to see me." Not like this, with tears streaming down her pale cheeks and her eyes full of confusion. One glance at Jo Marie and the astute Kelly would know exactly what had happened.

"I'll get her out of here as soon as she changes clothes," Andrew whispered urgently, his stormy gray eyes pleading with hers. "I didn't mean for this to happen."

"I know." With an agitated brush of her hand she dismissed him. "Please, just go."

"I'll talk to you tomorrow."

"No." Dark emotion flickered across her face. She didn't want to see him. Everything about today had been wrong. She should have avoided Andrew, feeling as she did. But in some ways, Jo Marie realized that the kiss had been inevitable. Those brief magical moments at the Mardi Gras demanded an exploration of the sensation they'd shared. Both had hoped to dismiss that February night as whimsy—a result of the craziness of the season. Instead, they had discovered how real it had been. From now on, Jo Marie vowed, she would shun Andrew. Her only defense was to avoid him completely.

"I'm sorry to keep you waiting." Kelly's happy voice drifted in from the other room. "Do I look okay?"

"You're lovely as always."

Jo Marie hoped that Kelly wouldn't catch the detached note in Andrew's gruff voice.

"You'll never guess who I spent the last hour talking to."

"Perhaps you could tell me on the way to mother's?" Andrew responded dryly.

"Drew." Some of the enthusiasm drained from Kelly's happy voice. "Are you feeling ill? You're quite pale."

"I'm fine."

"Maybe we should cancel this dinner. Really, I wouldn't mind."

"There's no reason to disappoint my mother."

"Drew?" Kelly seemed hesitant.

"Are you ready?" His firm voice brooked no disagreement.

"But I wanted to talk to Jo Marie."

"You can call her after dinner," Andrew responded

shortly, his voice fading as they moved toward the entryway.

The door clicked a minute later and Jo Marie's fingers loosened their death grip against the counter. Weakly, she wiped a hand over her face and eyes. Andrew and Kelly were engaged to be married. Tonight was his birthday and he was taking Kelly to dine with his family. And Jo Marie had been stealing a kiss from him in the kitchen. Self-reproach grew in her breast with every breath until she wanted to scream and lash out with it.

Maybe she could have justified her actions if Kelly hadn't been so excited and happy. Her roommate had come into the apartment bursting with enthusiasm for life, eager to see and talk to Andrew.

The evening seemed interminable and Jo Marie had a terrible time falling asleep, tossing and turning long past the time Kelly returned. Finally at the darkest part of the night, she flipped on the bedside lamp and threw aside the blankets. Pouring herself a glass of milk, Jo Marie leaned against the kitchen counter and drank it with small sips, her thoughts deep and dark. She couldn't ask Kelly to forgive her for what had happened without hurting her roommate and perhaps ruining their friendship. The only person there was to confront and condemn was herself.

Once she returned to bed, Jo Marie lay on her back, her head clasped in her hands. Moon shadows fluttered against the bare walls like the flickering scenes of a silent movie.

Unhappy beyond words, Jo Marie avoided her roommate, kept busy and occupied her time with other friends. But she was never at peace and always conscious that her thoughts never strayed from Kelly and Andrew. The episode with Andrew wouldn't happen again. She had to be strong.

Jo Marie didn't see her roommate until the following Monday morning. They met in the kitchen where Jo Marie was pouring herself a small glass of grapefruit juice.

"Morning." Jo Marie's stiff smile was only slightly forced.

"Howdy, stranger. I've missed you the past couple of days."

Jo Marie's hand tightened around the juice glass as she silently prayed Kelly wouldn't ask her about Saturday night. Her roommate must have known Jo Marie was in the apartment, otherwise Andrew wouldn't have been inside.

"I've missed you," Kelly continued. "It seems we hardly have time to talk anymore. And now that you're going to be doing volunteer work for the foundation, we'll have even less time together. You're spreading yourself too thin."

"There's always something going on this time of year." A chill seemed to settle around the area of Jo Marie's heart and she avoided her friend's look.

"I know, that's why I'm looking forward to this weekend and the party for Drew's company. By the way, he suggested that both of us stay the night on Saturday."

"Spend the night?" Jo Marie repeated like a recording and inhaled a shaky breath. That was the last thing she wanted.

"It makes sense, don't you think? We can lay awake

until dawn the way we used to and talk all night." A distant look came over Kelly as she buttered the hot toast and poured herself a cup of coffee. "Drew's going to have enough to worry about without dragging us back and forth. From what I understand, he goes all out for his company's Christmas party."

Hoping to hide her discomfort, Jo Marie rinsed out her glass and deposited it in the dishwasher, but a gnawing sensation attacked the pit of her stomach. Although she'd promised Kelly she would attend the lavish affair, she had to find a way of excusing herself without arousing suspicion. "I've been thinking about Andrew's party and honestly feel I shouldn't go—"

"Don't say it. You're going!" Kelly interrupted hastily. "There's no way I'd go without you. You're my best friend, Jo Marie Early, and as such I want you with me. Besides, you know how I hate these things."

"But as Drew's wife you'll be expected to attend a lot of these functions. I won't always be around."

A secret smile stole over her friend's pert face. "I know, that's why it's so important that you're there now."

"You didn't seem to need me Friday night."

Round blue eyes flashed Jo Marie a look of disbelief. "Are you crazy? I would have been embarrassingly uncomfortable without you."

It seemed to Jo Marie that Mark had spent nearly as much time with Kelly as she had. In fact, her brother had spent most of the evening with Kelly at his side. It was Mark whom Kelly really wanted, not her. But convincing her roommate of that was a different matter. Jo Marie doubted that Kelly had even admitted as much to herself.

"I'll think about going," Jo Marie promised. "But I can't honestly see that my being there or not would do any good."

"You've got to come," Kelly muttered, looking around unhappily. "I'd be miserable meeting and talking to all those people on my own." Silently, Kelly's bottomless blue eyes pleaded with Jo Marie. "I promise never to ask anything from you again. Say you'll come. Oh, please, Jo Marie, do this one last thing for me."

An awkward silence stretched between them and a feeling of dread settled over Jo Marie. Kelly seemed so genuinely distraught that it wasn't in Jo Marie's heart to refuse her. As Kelly had pointedly reminded her, she was Kelly's best friend. "All right, all right," she agreed reluctantly. "But I don't like it."

"You won't be sorry, I promise." A mischievous gleam lightened Kelly's features.

Jo Marie mumbled disdainfully under her breath as she moved out of the kitchen. Pausing at the closet, she took her trusted cardigan from the hanger. "Say, Kell, don't forget this is the week I'm flying to Mazatlán." Jo Marie was scheduled to take a familiarization tour of the Mexican resort town. She'd be flying with ten other travel agents from the city and staying at the Riviera Del Sol's expense. The luxury hotel was sponsoring the group in hopes of having the agents book their facilities for their clients. Jo Marie usually took the "fam" tours only once or twice a year. This one had been planned months before and she mused that it couldn't have come at a better time. Escaping from Andrew and Kelly was just the thing she needed. By the time she returned, she prayed, her life could be back to normal.

"This is the week?" Kelly stuck her head around the kitchen doorway. "Already?"

"You can still drive me to the airport, can't you?"

"Sure," Kelly answered absently. "But if I can't, Drew will."

Jo Marie's heart throbbed painfully. "No," she returned forcefully.

"He doesn't mind."

But I do, Jo Marie's heart cried as she fumbled with the buttons of her sweater. If Kelly wasn't home when it came time to leave for the airport, she would either call Mark or take a cab.

"I'm sure Drew wouldn't mind," Kelly repeated.

"I'll be late tonight," she answered, ignoring her friend's offer. She couldn't understand why Kelly would want her to spend time with Andrew. But so many things didn't make sense lately. Without a backward glance, Jo Marie went out the front door.

Joining several others at the bus stop outside the apartment building en route to the office, Jo Marie fought down feelings of guilt. She'd honestly thought she could get out of attending the party with Kelly. But there was little to be done, short of offending her friend. These constant recriminations regarding Kelly and Andrew were disrupting her neatly ordered life, and Jo Marie hated it.

Two of the other girls were in the office by the time Jo Marie arrived.

"There's a message for you," Paula announced. "I think it was the same guy who stopped in Saturday morning. You know, I'm beginning to think you've been holding out on me. Where'd you ever meet a hunk like that?"

"He's engaged," she quipped, seeking a light tone.

"He is?" Paula rolled her office chair over to Jo Marie's desk and handed her the pink slip. "You could have fooled me. He looked on the prowl, if you want my opinion. In fact, he was eyeing you like a starving man looking at a cream puff."

"Paula!" Jo Marie tried to toss off her co-worker's observation with a forced laugh. "He's engaged to my roommate."

Paula lifted one shoulder in a half shrug and scooted the chair back to her desk. "If you say so." But both her tone and her look were disbelieving.

Jo Marie read the message, which listed Andrew's office number and asked that she call him at her earliest convenience. Crumbling up the pink slip, she tossed it in the green metal wastebasket beside her desk. She might be attending this party, but it was under duress. And as far as Andrew was concerned, she had every intention of avoiding him.

Rather than rush back to the apartment after work, Jo Marie had dinner in a small café near her office. From there she walked to the Land For The Future headquarters.

She was embarrassingly early when she arrived outside of the office door. The foundation's headquarters were on the second floor of an older brick building in a bad part of town. Jo Marie decided to arrive earlier than she'd planned rather than kill time by walking around outside. From the time she'd left the travel agency, she'd wandered around with little else to do. Her greatest fear was that Andrew would be waiting for her at the apartment. She hadn't returned his call and he'd want to know why.

Jim Rowden, the office manager and spokesman, was busy on the telephone when Jo Marie arrived. Quietly she slipped into the chair at the desk opposite him and glanced over the letters and other notices that needed to be typed. As she pulled the cover from the top of the typewriter, Jo Marie noticed a shadowy movement from the other side of the milky white glass inset of the office door.

She stood to investigate and found a dark-haired man with a worn felt hat that fit loosely on top of his head. His clothes were ragged and the faint odor of cheap wine permeated the air. He was curling up in the doorway of an office nearest theirs.

His eyes met hers briefly and he tugged his thin sweater around his shoulders. "Are you going to throw me out of here?" The words were issued in subtle challenge.

Jo Marie teetered with indecision. If she did tell him to leave he'd either spend the night shivering in the cold or find another open building. On the other hand if she were to give him money, she was confident it wouldn't be a bed he'd spend it on.

"Well?" he challenged again.

"I won't say anything," she answered finally. "Just go down to the end of the hall so no one else will find you."

He gave her a look of mild surprise, stood and gathered his coat before turning and ambling down the long hall in an uneven gait. Jo Marie waited until he was curled up in another doorway. It was difficult to see that he was there without looking for him. A soft smile of satisfaction stole across her face as she closed the door and returned to her desk.

Jim replaced the receiver and smiled a welcome at Jo Marie. "How'd you like to attend a lecture with me tonight?"

"I'd like it fine," she agreed eagerly.

Jim's lecture was to a group of concerned city businessmen. He relayed the facts about the dangers of thoughtless and haphazard land development. He presented his case in a simple, straightforward fashion without emotionalism or sensationalism. In addition, he confidently answered their questions, defining the difference between building for the future and preserving a link with the past. Jo Marie was impressed and from the looks on the faces of his audience, the businessmen had been equally affected.

"I'll walk you to the bus stop," Jim told her hours later after they'd returned from the meeting. "I don't like the idea of you waiting at the bus stop alone. I'll go with you."

Jo Marie hadn't been that thrilled with the prospect herself. "Thanks, I'd appreciate that."

Jim's hand cupped her elbow as they leisurely strolled down the narrow street, chatting as they went. Jim's voice was drawling and smooth and Jo Marie mused that she could listen to him all night. The lamplight illuminated little in the descending fog and would have created an eerie feeling if Jim hadn't been at her side. But walking with him, she barely noticed the weather and instead found herself laughing at his subtle humor.

"How'd you ever get into this business?" she queried. Jim Rowden was an intelligent, warm human being who would be a success in any field he chose to pursue. He could be making twice and three times the money in the business world that he collected from the foundation.

At first introduction, Jim wasn't the kind of man who would bowl women over with his striking good looks or his suave manners. But he was a rare, dedicated man of conscience. Jo Marie had never known anyone like him and admired him greatly.

"I'm fairly new with the foundation," he admitted, "and it certainly wasn't what I'd been expecting to do with my life, especially since I struggled through college for a degree in biology. Afterward I went to work for the state, but this job gives me the opportunity to work first hand with saving some of the—well, you heard my speech."

"Yes, I did, and it was wonderful."

"You're good for my ego, Jo Marie. I hope you'll stick around."

Jo Marie's eyes glanced up the street, wondering how long they'd have to wait for a bus. She didn't want their discussion to end. As she did, a flash of midnight blue captured her attention and her heart dropped to her knees as the Mercedes pulled to a stop alongside the curb in front of them.

Andrew practically leaped from the driver's side. "Just what do you think you're doing?" The harsh anger in his voice shocked her.

"I beg your pardon?" Jim answered on Jo Marie's behalf, taking a step forward.

Andrew ignored Jim, his eyes cold and piercing as he

glanced over her. "I've spent the good part of an hour looking for you."

"Why?" Jo Marie demanded, tilting her chin in an act of defiance. "What business is it of yours where I am or who I'm with?"

"I'm making it my business."

"Is there a problem here, Jo Marie?" Jim questioned as he stepped forward.

"None whatsoever," she responded dryly and crossed her arms in front of her.

"Kelly's worried sick," Andrew hissed. "Now I suggest you get in the car and let me take you home before…" He let the rest of what he was saying die. He paused for several tense moments and exhaled a sharp breath. "I apologize, I had no right to come at you like that." He closed the car door and moved around the front of the Mercedes. "I'm Andrew Beaumont," he introduced himself and extended his hand to Jim.

"From Delta Development?" Jim's eyes widened appreciatively. "Jim Rowden. I've been wanting to meet you so that I could thank you personally for what you did for Rose's Hotel."

"I'm pleased I could help."

When Andrew decided to put on the charm it was like falling into a jar of pure honey, Jo Marie thought. She didn't know of a man, woman or child who couldn't be swayed by his beguiling showmanship. Having been under his spell in the past made it all the more recognizable now. But somehow, she realized, this was different. Andrew hadn't been acting the night of the Mardi Gras, she was convinced of that.

"Jo Marie was late coming home and luckily I remembered her saying something about volunteering for the foundation. Kelly asked that I come and get her. We were understandably worried about her taking the bus alone at this time of night."

"I'll admit I was a bit concerned myself," Jim returned, taking a step closer to Jo Marie. "That's why I'm here."

As Andrew opened the passenger's side of the car, Jo Marie turned her head to meet his gaze, her eyes fiery as she slid into the plush velvet seat.

"I'll see you Friday," she said to Jim.

"Enjoy Mexico," he responded and waved before turning and walking back toward the office building. A fine mist filled the evening air and Jim pulled up his collar as he hurried along the sidewalk.

Andrew didn't say a word as he turned the key in the ignition, checked the rearview mirror and pulled back onto the street.

"You didn't return my call." He stopped at a red light and the full force of his magnetic gray eyes was turned on her.

"No," she answered in a whisper, struggling not to reveal how easily he could affect her.

"Can't you see how important it is that we talk?"

"No." She wanted to shout the word. When their eyes met, Jo Marie was startled to find that only a few inches separated them. Andrew's look was centered on her mouth and with a determined effort she averted her gaze and stared out the side window. "I don't want to talk to you." Her fingers fumbled with the clasp of her purse in nervous agitation. "There's nothing more

we can say." She hated the husky emotion-filled way
her voice sounded.

"Jo Marie." He said her name so softly that she wasn't
entirely sure he'd spoken.

She turned back to him, knowing she should pull
away from the hypnotic darkness of his eyes, but doing
so was impossible.

"You'll come to my party?"

She wanted to explain her decision to attend—she
hadn't wanted to go—but one glance at Andrew said
that he understood. Words were unnecessary.

"It's going to be difficult for us both for a while."

He seemed to imply things would grow easier with
time. Jo Marie sincerely doubted that they ever would.

"You'll come?" he prompted softly.

Slowly she nodded. Jo Marie hadn't realized how
tense she was until she exhaled and felt some of the
coiled tightness leave her body. "Yes, I'll…be at the
party." Her breathy stammer spoke volumes.

"And wear the dress I gave you?"

She ended up nodding again, her tongue unable to
form words.

"I've dreamed of you walking into my arms wearing
that dress," he added on a husky tremor, then shook his
head as if he regretted having spoken.

Being alone with him in the close confines of the car
was torture. Her once restless fingers lay limp in her
lap. Jo Marie didn't know how she was going to avoid
Andrew when Kelly seemed to be constantly throwing them together. But she must for her own peace of
mind…she must.

* * *

All too quickly the brief respite of her trip to Mazatlán was over. Saturday arrived and Kelly and Jo Marie were brought to Andrew's home, which was a faithful reproduction of an antebellum mansion.

The dress he'd purchased was hanging in the closet of the bedroom she was to share with Kelly. Her friend threw herself across the canopy bed and exhaled on a happy sigh.

"Isn't this place something?"

Jo Marie didn't answer for a moment, her gaze falling on the dress that hung alone in the closet. "It's magnificent." There was little else that would describe this palace. The house was a three-story structure with huge white pillars and dark shutters. It faced the Mississippi River and had a huge garden in the back. Jo Marie learned that it was his mother who took an avid interest in the wide variety of flowers that grew in abundance there.

The rooms were large, their walls adorned with paintings and works of art. If Jo Marie was ever to doubt Andrew's wealth and position, his home would prove to be a constant reminder.

"Drew built it himself," Kelly explained with a proud lilt to her voice. "I don't mean he pounded in every nail, but he was here every day while it was being constructed. It took months."

"I can imagine." And no expense had been spared from the look of things.

"I suppose we should think about getting ready," Kelly continued. "I don't mind telling you that I've had a queasy stomach all day dreading this thing."

Kelly had! Jo Marie nearly laughed aloud. This party had haunted her all week. Even Mazatlán hadn't been far enough away to dispel the feeling of dread.

Jo Marie could hear the music drifting in from the reception hall by the time she had put on the finishing touches of her makeup. Kelly had already joined Andrew. A quick survey in the full-length mirror assured her that the beautiful gown was the most elegant thing she would ever own. The reflection that came back to her of a tall, regal woman was barely recognizable as herself. The dark crown of curls was styled on top of her head with a few stray tendrils curling about her ears. A lone strand of pearls graced her neck.

Self-consciously she moved from the room, closing the door. From the top of the winding stairway, she looked down on a milling crowd of arriving guests. Holding in her breath, she placed her gloved hand on the polished bannister, exhaled, and made her descent. Keeping her eyes on her feet for fear of tripping, Jo Marie was surprised when she glanced down to find Andrew waiting for her at the bottom of the staircase.

As he gave her his hand, their eyes met and held in a tender exchange. "You're beautiful."

The deep husky tone in his voice took her breath away and Jo Marie could do nothing more than smile in return.

Taking her hand, Andrew tucked it securely in the crook of his elbow and led her into the room where the other guests were mingling. Everyone was meeting for drinks in the huge living room and once the party was complete they would be moving up to the ballroom on the third floor. The evening was to culminate in a midnight buffet.

With Andrew holding her close by his side, Jo Marie had little option but to follow where he led. Moving from one end of the room to the other, he introduced her to so many people that her head swam trying to remember their names. Fortunately, Kelly and Andrew's engagement hadn't been officially announced and Jo Marie wasn't forced to make repeated explanations. Nonetheless, she was uncomfortable with the way he was linking the two of them together.

"Where's Kelly?" Jo Marie asked under her breath. "She should be the one with you. Not me."

"Kelly's with Mark on the other side of the room."

Jo Marie faltered in midstep and Andrew's hold tightened as he dropped his arm and slipped it around her slim waist. "With Mark?" She couldn't imagine her brother attending this party. Not feeling the way he did about Andrew.

Not until they were upstairs and the music was playing did Jo Marie have an opportunity to talk to her brother. He was sitting against the wall in a high-backed mahogany chair with a velvet cushion. Kelly was at his side. Jo Marie couldn't recall a time she'd seen her brother dress so formally or look more handsome. He'd had his hair trimmed and was clean shaven. She'd never dreamed she'd see Mark in a tuxedo.

"Hello, Mark."

Her brother looked up, guilt etched on his face. "Jo Marie." Briefly he exchanged looks with Kelly and stood, offering Jo Marie his seat.

"Thanks," she said as she sat and slipped the high-heeled sandals from her toes. "My feet could use a few moments' rest."

"You certainly haven't lacked for partners," Kelly observed happily. "You're a hit, Jo Marie. Even Mark was saying he couldn't believe you were his sister."

"I've never seen you look more attractive," Mark added. "But then I bet you didn't buy that dress out of petty cash either."

If there was a note of censure in her brother's voice, Jo Marie didn't hear it. "No." Absently her hand smoothed the silk skirt. "It was a gift from Andrew... and Kelly." Hastily she added her roommate's name. "I must admit though, I'm surprised to see you here."

"Andrew extended the invitation personally," Mark replied, holding his back ramrod stiff as he stared straight ahead.

Not understanding, Jo Marie glanced at her roommate. "Mark came for me," Kelly explained, her voice soft and vulnerable. "Because I...because I wanted him here."

"We're both here for you, Kelly," Jo Marie reminded her and punctuated her comment by arching her brows.

"I know, and I love you both for it."

"Would you care to dance?" Mark held out his hand to Kelly, taking her into his arms when they reached the boundary of the dance floor as if he never wanted to let her go.

Confused, Jo Marie watched their progress. Kelly was engaged to be married to Andrew, yet she was gazing into Mark's eyes as if he were her knight in shining armor who had come to slay dragons on her behalf.

When she'd come upon them, they'd acted as if she had intruded on their very private party.

Jo Marie saw Andrew approach her, his brows lowered as if something had displeased him. His strides were quick and decisive as he wove his way through the throng of guests.

"I've been looking for you. In fact, I was beginning to wonder if I'd ever get a chance to dance with you." The pitch of his voice suggested that she'd been deliberately avoiding him. And she had.

Jo Marie couldn't bring herself to meet his gaze, afraid of what he could read in her eyes. All night she'd been pretending it was Andrew who was holding her and yet she'd known she wouldn't be satisfied until he did.

"I believe this dance is mine," he said, presenting her with his hand.

Peering up at him, a smile came and she paused to slip the strap of her high heel over her ankle before standing.

Once on the dance floor, his arms tightened around her waist, bringing her so close that there wasn't a hair's space between them. He held her securely as if challenging her to move. Jo Marie discovered that she couldn't. This inexplicable feeling was beyond argument. With her hands resting on his muscular shoulders, she leaned her head against his broad chest and sighed her contentment.

She spoke first. "It's a wonderful party."

"You're more comfortable now, aren't you?" His fingers moved up and down her back in a leisurely exercise, drugging her with his firm caress against her bare skin.

"What do you mean?" She wasn't sure she understood his question and slowly lifted her gaze.

"Last week, you stayed on the outskirts of the crowd afraid of joining in or being yourself."

"Last week I was terrified that someone would recognize me as the one who had once demonstrated against you. I didn't want to do anything that would embarrass you," she explained dryly. Her cheek was pressed against his starched shirt and she thrilled to the uneven thump of his heart.

"And this week?"

"Tonight anyone who looked at us would know that we've long since resolved our differences."

She sensed more than felt Andrew's soft touch. The moment was quickly becoming too intimate. Using her hands for leverage, Jo Marie straightened, creating a space between them. "Does it bother you to have my brother dance with Kelly?"

Andrew looked back at her blankly. "No. Should it?"

"She's your fiancée." To the best of Jo Marie's knowledge, Andrew hadn't said more than a few words to Kelly all evening.

A cloud of emotion darkened his face. "She's wearing my ring."

"And...and you care for her."

Andrew's hold tightened painfully around her waist. "Yes, I care for Kelly. We've always been close." His eyes darkened to the color of burnt silver. "Perhaps too close."

The applause was polite when the dance number finished.

Jo Marie couldn't escape fast enough. She made an excuse and headed for the powder room. Andrew wasn't pleased and it showed in the grim set of his mouth, but he didn't try to stop her. Things weren't right. Mark shouldn't be sitting like an avenging angel at Kelly's side and Andrew should at least show some sign of jealousy.

When she returned to the ballroom, Andrew was busy and Jo Marie decided to sort through her thoughts in the fresh night air. A curtained glass door that led to the balcony was open, and unnoticed she slipped silently into the dark. A flash of white captured her attention and Jo Marie realized she wasn't alone. Inadvertently, she had invaded the private world of two young lovers. With their arms wrapped around each other they were locked in a passionate embrace. Smiling softly to herself, she turned to escape as silently as she'd come. But something stopped her. A sickening knot tightened her stomach.

The couple so passionately embracing were Kelly and Mark.

Six

Jo Marie woke just as dawn broke over a cloudless horizon. Standing at the bedroom window, she pressed her palms against the sill and surveyed the beauty of the landscape before her. Turning, she glanced at Kelly's sleeping figure. Her hands fell limply to her side as her face darkened with uncertainty. Last night while they'd prepared for bed, Jo Marie had been determined to confront her friend with the kiss she'd unintentionally witnessed. But when they'd turned out the lights, Kelly had chatted happily about the success of the party and what a good time she'd had. And Jo Marie had lost her nerve. What Mark and Kelly did wasn't any of her business, she mused. In addition, she had no right to judge her brother and her friend when she and Andrew had done the same thing.

The memory of Andrew's kiss produced a breathlessness, and surrendering to the feeling, Jo Marie closed her eyes. The infinitely sweet touch of his mouth seemed to have branded her. Her fingers shook as she raised them to the gentle curve of her lips. Jo Marie doubted that she would ever feel the same overpowering rush of sensation at another man's touch. Andrew was special, her dream man. Whole lifetimes could pass and she'd never find anyone she'd love more. The powerful ache in her heart drove her to the closet where a change of clothes were hanging.

Dawn's light was creeping up the stairs, awaking a sleeping world, when Jo Marie softly clicked the bedroom door closed. Her overnight bag was clenched tightly in her hand. She hated to sneak out, but the thought of facing everyone over the breakfast table was more than she could bear. Andrew and Kelly needed to be alone. Time together was something they hadn't had much of lately. This morning would be the perfect opportunity for them to sit down and discuss their coming marriage. Jo Marie would only be an intruder.

Moving so softly that no one was likely to hear her, Jo Marie crept down the stairs to the wide entry hall. She was tiptoeing toward the front door when a voice behind her interrupted her quiet departure.

"What do you think you're doing?"

Releasing a tiny, startled cry, Jo Marie dropped the suitcase and held her hand to her breast.

"Andrew, you've frightened me to death."

"Just what are you up to?"

"I'm… I'm leaving."

"That's fairly easy to ascertain. What I want to know is why." His angry gaze locked with hers, refusing to allow her to turn away.

"I thought you and Kelly should spend some time together and…and I wanted to be gone this morning before everyone woke." Regret crept into her voice.

Maybe sneaking out like this wasn't such a fabulous idea, after all.

He stared at her in the dim light as if he could examine her soul with his penetrating gaze. When he spoke again, his tone was lighter. "And just how did you expect to get to town. Walk?"

"Exactly."

"But it's miles."

"All the more reason to get an early start," she reasoned.

Andrew studied her as though he couldn't believe what he was hearing. "Is running away so important that you would sneak out of here like a cat burglar and not tell anyone where you're headed?"

How quickly her plan had backfired. By trying to leave unobtrusively she'd only managed to offend Andrew when she had every reason to thank him. "I didn't mean to be rude, although I can see now that I have been. I suppose this makes me look like an ungrateful house guest."

His answer was to narrow his eyes fractionally.

"I want you to know I left a note that explained where I was going to both you and Kelly. It's on the nightstand."

"And what did you say?"

"That I enjoyed the party immensely and that I've never felt more beautiful in any dress."

A brief troubled look stole over Andrew's face. "Once," he murmured absently. "Only once have you been more lovely." There was an unexpectedly gentle quality to his voice.

Her eyelashes fluttered closed. Andrew was reminding her of that February night. He too hadn't been able to forget the Mardi Gras. After all this time, after everything that had transpired since, neither of them could forget. The spell was as potent today as it had been those many months ago.

"Is that coffee I smell?" The question sought an invitation to linger with Andrew. Her original intent had been to escape so that Kelly could have the opportunity to spend this time alone with him. Instead, Jo Marie was seeking it herself. To sit in the early light of dawn and savor a few solitary minutes alone with Andrew was too tempting to ignore.

"Come and I'll get you a cup." Andrew led her toward the back of the house and his den. The room held a faint scent of leather and tobacco that mingled with the aroma of musk and spice.

Three walls were lined with leather-bound books that reached from the floor to the ceiling. Two wing chairs were angled in front of a large fireplace.

"Go ahead and sit down. I'll be back in a moment with the coffee."

A contented smile brightened Jo Marie's eyes as she sat and noticed the leather volume she'd given him lying open on the ottoman. Apparently he'd been reading it when he heard the noise at the front of the house and had left to investigate.

Andrew returned and carefully handed her the steaming earthenware mug. His eyes followed her gaze which rested on the open book. "I've been reading it. This is a wonderful book. Where did you ever find something like this?"

"I've known about it for a long time, but there were

only a few volumes available. I located this one about three months ago in a used-book store."

"It's very special to me because of the woman who bought it for me."

"No." Jo Marie's eyes widened as she lightly tossed her head from side to side. "Don't let that be the reason. Appreciate the book for all the interesting details it gives of New Orleans' colorful past. Or admire the pictures of the city architects' skill. But don't treasure it because of me."

Andrew looked for a moment as if he wanted to argue, but she spoke again.

"When you read this book ten, maybe twenty, years from now, I'll only be someone who briefly passed through your life. I imagine you'll have trouble remembering what I looked like."

"You'll never be anyone who flits in and out of my life."

He said it with such intensity that Jo Marie's fingers tightened around the thick handle of the mug. "All right," she agreed with a shaky laugh. "I'll admit I barged into your peaceful existence long before Kelly introduced us but—"

"But," Andrew interrupted on a short laugh, "it seems we were destined to meet. Do you honestly believe that either of us will ever forget that night?" A faint smile touched his eyes as he regarded her steadily.

Jo Marie knew that she never would. Andrew was her dream man. It had been far more than mere fate that had brought them together, something almost spiritual.

"No," she answered softly. "I'll never forget."

Regret moved across his features, creasing his wide

brow and pinching his mouth. "Nor will I forget," he murmured in a husky voice that sounded very much like a vow.

The air between them was electric. For months she'd thought of Andrew as the dream man. But coming to know him these past weeks had proven that he wasn't an apparition, but real. Human, vulnerable, proud, intelligent, generous—and everything that she had ever hoped to find in a man. She lowered her gaze and studied the dark depths of the steaming coffee. Andrew might be everything she had ever wanted in a man, but Kelly wore his ring and her roommate's stake on him was far more tangible than her own romantic dreams.

Taking an exaggerated drink of her coffee, Jo Marie carefully set aside the rose-colored mug and stood. "I really should be leaving."

"Please stay," Andrew requested. "Just sit with me a few minutes longer. It's been in this room that I've sat and thought about you so often. I'd always hoped that someday you would join me here."

Jo Marie dipped her head, her heart singing with the beauty of his words. She'd fantasized about him too. Since their meeting, her mind had conjured up his image so often that it wouldn't hurt to steal a few more moments of innocent happiness. Kelly would have him for a lifetime. Jo Marie had only today.

"I'll stay," she agreed and her voice throbbed with the excited beat of her heart.

"And when the times comes, I'll drive you back to the city."

She nodded her acceptance and finished her coffee.

"It's so peaceful in here. It feels like all I need to do is lean my head back, close my eyes and I'll be asleep."

"Go ahead," he urged in a whispered tone.

A smile touched her radiant features. She didn't want to fall asleep and miss these precious moments alone with him. "No." She shook her head. "Tell me about yourself. I want to know everything."

His returning smile was wry. "I'd hate to bore you."

"Bore me!" Her small laugh was incredulous. "There's no chance of that."

"All right, but lay back and close your eyes and let me start by telling you that I had a good childhood with parents who deeply loved each other."

As he requested, Jo Marie rested her head against the cushion and closed her eyes. "My parents are wonderful too."

"But being raised in an ideal family has its drawbacks," Andrew continued in a low, soothing voice. "When it came time for me to think about a wife and starting a family there was always a fear in the back of my mind that I would never find the happiness my parents shared. My father wasn't an easy man to love. And I won't be either."

In her mind, Jo Marie took exception to that, but she said nothing. The room was warm, and slipping off her shoes, she tucked her nylon-covered feet under her. Andrew continued speaking, his voice droning on as she tilted her head back.

"When I reached thirty without finding a wife, I became skeptical about the women I was meeting. There were some who never saw past the dollar signs and others who were interested only in themselves. I wanted a woman who could be soft and yielding, but one who wasn't afraid to fight for what she believes, even if it meant standing up against tough opposition. I wanted someone who would share my joys and divide my worries. A woman as beautiful on the inside as any outward beauty she may possess."

"Kelly's like that." The words nearly stuck in Jo Marie's throat. Kelly was everything Andrew was describing and more. As painful as it was to admit, Jo Marie understood why Andrew had asked her roommate to marry him. In addition to her fine personal qualities, Kelly had money of her own and Andrew need never think that she was marrying him for any financial gains.

"Yes, Kelly's like that." There was a doleful timbre to his voice that caused Jo Marie to open her eyes.

Fleetingly she wondered if Andrew had seen Mark and Kelly kissing on the terrace last night. If he had created the picture of a perfect woman in his mind, then finding Kelly in Mark's arms could destroy him. No matter how uncomfortable it became, Jo Marie realized she was going to have to confront Mark about his behavior. Having thoughtfully analyzed the situation, Jo Marie believed it would be far better for her to talk to her brother. She could speak more freely with him. It may be the hardest thing she'd ever do, but after listening to Andrew, Jo Marie realized that she must talk to Mark. The happiness of too many people was at stake.

Deciding to change the subject, Jo Marie shifted her position in the supple leather chair and looked to Andrew. "Kelly told me that you built the house yourself."

Grim amusement was carved in his features. "Yes, the work began on it this spring."

"Then you've only been living in it a few months?"

"Yes. The construction on the house kept me from going insane." He held her look, revealing nothing of his thoughts.

"Going insane?" Jo Marie didn't understand.

"You see, for a short time last February, only a matter of moments really, I felt my search for the right woman was over. And in those few, scant moments I thought I had met that special someone I could love for all time."

Jo Marie's heart was pounding so fast and loud that she wondered why it didn't burst right out of her chest. The thickening in her throat made swallowing painful. Each breath became labored as she turned her face away, unable to meet Andrew's gaze.

"But after those few minutes, I lost her," Andrew continued. "Ironically, I'd searched a lifetime for that special woman, and within a matter of minutes, she was gone. God knows I tried to find her again. For a month I went back to the spot where I'd last seen her and waited. When it seemed that all was lost I discovered I couldn't get the memory of her out of my mind. I even hired a detective to find her for me. For months he checked every hospital in the city, searching for her. But you see, at the time I thought she was a nurse."

Jo Marie felt moisture gathering in the corner of her eyes. Never had she believed that Andrew had looked for her to the extent that he hired someone.

"For a time I was convinced I was going insane. This woman, whose name I didn't even know, filled my every waking moment and haunted my sleep. Building the house was something I've always wanted to do. It helped fill the time until I could find her again. Every room was constructed with her in mind."

Andrew was explaining that he'd built the house for her. Jo Marie had thought she'd be uncomfortable in such a magnificent home. But she'd immediately felt the welcome in the walls. Little had she dreamed the reason why.

"Sometimes," Jo Marie began awkwardly, "people build things up in their minds and when they're confronted with reality they're inevitably disappointed." Andrew was making her out to be wearing angel's wings. So much time had passed that he no longer saw her as flesh and bone, but a wonderful fantasy his mind had created.

"Not this time," he countered smoothly.

"I wondered where I'd find the two of you." A sleepy-eyed Kelly stood poised in the doorway of the den. There wasn't any censure in her voice, only her usual morning brightness. "Isn't it a marvelous morning? The sun's up and there's a bright new day just waiting for us."

Self-consciously, Jo Marie unwound her feet from beneath her and reached for her shoes. "What time is it?"

"A quarter to eight." Andrew supplied the information.

Jo Marie was amazed to realize that she'd spent the better part of two hours talking to him. But it would be time she'd treasure all her life.

"If you have no objections," Kelly murmured and paused to take a wide yawn, "I thought I'd go to the hospital this morning. There's a special…patient I'd like to stop in and visit."

A patient or Mark, Jo Marie wanted to ask. Her brother had mentioned last night that he was going to be on duty in the morning. Jo Marie turned to Andrew, waiting for a reaction from him. Surely he would say or do something to stop her. Kelly was his fiancée and both of them seemed to be regarding their commitment to each other lightly.

"No problem." Andrew spoke at last. "In fact I thought I'd go into the city myself this morning. It is a beautiful day and there's no better way to spend a portion of it than in the most beautiful city in the world. You don't mind if I tag along with you, do you, Jo Marie?"

Half of her wanted to cry out in exaltation. If there was anything she wished to give of herself to Andrew it was her love of New Orleans. But at the same time she wanted to shake both Andrew and Kelly for the careless attitude they had toward their relationship.

"I'd like you to come." Jo Marie spoke finally, answering Andrew.

It didn't take Kelly more than a few moments to pack her things and be ready to leave. In her rush, she'd obviously missed the two sealed envelopes Jo Marie had left propped against the lamp on Kelly's nightstand. Or if she had discovered them, Kelly chose not to mention it. Not that it mattered, Jo Marie decided as Andrew started the car. But Kelly's actions revealed what a rush she was in to see Mark. If it was Mark that she was indeed seeing. Confused emotions flooded Jo Marie's face, pinching lines around her nose and mouth.

She could feel Andrew's caressing gaze as they drove toward the hospital.

"Is something troubling you?" Andrew questioned after they'd dropped Kelly off in front of Tulane Hospital. Amid protests from Jo Marie, Kelly had assured them that she would find her own way home. Standing on the sidewalk, she'd given Jo Marie a happy wave, before turning and walking toward the double glass doors that led to the lobby of the hospital.

"I think Kelly's going to see Mark," Jo Marie ventured in a short, rueful voice.

"I think she is too."

Jo Marie sat up sharply. "And that doesn't bother you?"

"Should it?" Andrew gave her a bemused look.

"Yes," she said and nodded emphatically. She would never have believed that Andrew could be so blind. "Yes, it should make you furious."

He turned and smiled briefly. "But it doesn't. Now tell me where you'd like to eat breakfast. Brennan's?"

Jo Marie felt trapped in a labyrinth in which no route made sense and from which she could see no escape. She was thoroughly confused by the actions of the three people she loved.

"I don't understand any of this," she cried in frustration. "You should be livid that Kelly and Mark are together."

A furrow of absent concentration darkened Andrew's brow as he drove. Briefly he glanced in her direction. "The time will come when you do understand," he explained cryptically.

Rubbing the side of her neck in agitation, Jo Marie

studied Andrew as he drove. His answer made no sense, but little about anyone's behavior this last month had made sense. She hadn't pictured herself as being obtuse, but obviously she was.

Breakfast at Brennan's was a treat known throughout the south. The restaurant was built in the classic Vieux Carre style complete with courtyard. Because they didn't have a reservation, they were put on a waiting list and told it would be another hour before there would be a table available. Andrew eyed Jo Marie, who nodded eagerly. For all she'd heard, the breakfast was worth the wait.

Taking her hand in his, they strolled down the quiet streets that comprised the French Quarter. Most of the stores were closed, the streets deserted.

"I was reading just this morning that the French established New Orleans in 1718. The Spanish took over the 3,000 French inhabitants in 1762, although there were so few Spaniards that barely anyone noticed until 1768. The French Quarter is like a city within a city."

Jo Marie smiled contentedly and looped her hand through his arm. "You mean to tell me that it takes a birthday present for you to know about your own fair city?"

Andrew chuckled and drew her closer by circling his arm around her shoulders. "Are you always snobbish or is this act for my benefit?"

They strolled for what seemed far longer than a mere hour, visiting Jackson Square and feeding the pigeons. Strolling back, with Andrew at her side, Jo Marie felt she would never be closer to heaven. Never would she want for anything more than today, this minute, with this man. Jo Marie felt tears mist her dusty eyes. A tremulous smile touched her mouth. Andrew was here with her. Within a short time he would be married to Kelly and she must accept that, but for now, he was hers.

The meal was everything they'd been promised. Ham, soft breads fresh from the bakery, eggs and a fabulous chicory coffee. A couple of times Jo Marie found herself glancing at Andrew. His expression revealed little and she wondered if he regretted having decided to spend this time with her. She prayed that wasn't the case.

When they stood to leave, Andrew reached for her hand and smiled down on her with shining gray eyes.

Jo Marie's heart throbbed with love. The radiant light of her happiness shone through when Andrew's arm slipped naturally around her shoulder as if branding her with his seal of protection.

"I enjoy being with you," he said and she couldn't doubt the sincerity in his voice. "You're the kind of woman who would be as much at ease at a formal ball as you would fishing from the riverside with rolled-up jeans."

"I'm not Huck Finn," she teased.

"No," he smiled, joining in her game. "Just my Florence Nightingale, the woman who has haunted me for the last nine months."

Self-consciously, Jo Marie eased the strap of her leather purse over her shoulder. "It's always been my belief that dreams have a way of fading, especially when faced with the bright light of the sun and reality."

"Normally, I'd agree with you," Andrew responded thoughtfully, "but not this time. There are moments so rare in one's life that recognizing what they are can sometimes be doubted. Of you, of that night, of us, I have no doubts."

"None?" Jo Marie barely recognized her own voice.

"None," he confirmed.

If that were so, then why did Kelly continue to wear his ring? How could he look at her with so much emotion and then ask another woman to share his life?

The ride to Jo Marie's apartment was accomplished in a companionable silence. Andrew pulled into the parking space and turned off the ignition. Jo Marie's gaze centered on the dashboard. Silently she'd hoped that he wouldn't come inside with her. The atmosphere when they were alone was volatile. And with everything that Andrew had told her this morning, Jo Marie doubted that she'd have the strength to stay out of his arms if he reached for her.

"I can see myself inside." Gallantly, she made an effort to avoid temptation.

"Nonsense," Andrew returned, and opening the car door, he removed her overnight case from the back seat.

Jo Marie opened her side and climbed out, not waiting for him to come around. A feeling of doom settled around her heart.

Her hand was steady as she inserted the key into the apartment lock, but that was the only thing that was. Her knees felt like rubber as the door swung open and she stepped inside the room, standing in the entryway. The drapes were pulled, blocking out the sunlight, making the apartment's surroundings all the more intimate.

"I have so much to thank you for," she began and nervously tugged a strand of dark hair behind her ear.

"A simple thank you seems like so little." She hoped Andrew understood that she didn't want him to come any farther into the apartment.

The door clicked closed and her heart sank. "Where would you like me to put your suitcase?"

Determined not to make this situation any worse for them, Jo Marie didn't move. "Just leave it here."

A smoldering light of amused anger burned in his eyes as he set the suitcase down. "There's no help for this," he whispered as his hand slid slowly, almost unwillingly along the back of her waist. "Be angry with me later."

Any protests died the moment his mouth met hers in a demanding kiss. An immediate answering hunger seared through her veins, melting all resistance until she was molded against the solid wall of his chest. His caressing fingers explored the curve of her neck and shoulders and his mouth followed, blazing a trail that led back to her waiting lips.

Jo Marie rotated her head, giving him access to any part of her face that his hungry mouth desired. She offered no protest when his hands sought the fullness of her breast, then sighed with the way her body responded to the gentleness of his fingers. He kissed her expertly, his mobile mouth moving insistently over hers, teasing her with light, biting nips that made her yearn for more and more. Then he'd change his tactics and kiss her with a hungry demand. Lost in a mindless haze, she clung to him as the tears filled her eyes and ran unheeded down her cheeks. Everything she feared was happening. And worse, she was powerless to stop him. Her throat felt dry and scratchy and she uttered a soft sob in effort to abate the flow of emotion.

Andrew went still. He cupped her face in his hands and examined her tear-streaked cheeks. His troubled expression swam in and out of her vision.

"Jo Marie," he whispered, his voice tortured. "Don't cry, darling, please don't cry." With an infinite tenderness he kissed away each tear and when he reached her trembling mouth, the taste of salt was on his lips. A series of long, drugging kisses only confused her more. It didn't seem possible she could want him so much and yet that it should be so wrong.

"Please." With every ounce of strength she possessed Jo Marie broke from his embrace. "I promised myself this wouldn't happen again," she whispered feeling miserable. Standing with her back to him, her hands cradled her waist to ward off a sudden chill.

Gently he pressed his hand to her shoulder and Jo Marie couldn't bring herself to brush it away. Even his touch had the power to disarm her.

"Jo Marie." His husky tone betrayed the depths of his turmoil. "Listen to me."

"No, what good would it do?" she asked on a quavering sob. "You're engaged to be married to my best friend. I can't help the way I feel about you. What I feel, what you feel, is wrong as long as Kelly's wearing your ring." With a determined effort she turned to face him, tears blurring her sad eyes. "It would be better if we didn't see each other again…at least until you're sure of what you want…or who you want."

Andrew jerked his hand through his hair. "You're right. I've got to get this mess straightened out."

"Promise me, Andrew, please promise me that you won't make an effort to see me until you know in your own mind what you want. I can't take much more of this." She wiped the moisture from her cheekbones with the tips of her fingers. "When I get up in the morning I want to look at myself in the mirror. I don't want to hate myself."

Andrew's mouth tightened with grim displeasure. He looked as if he wanted to argue. Tense moments passed before he slowly shook his head. "You deserve to be treated so much better than this. Someday, my love, you'll understand. Just trust me for now."

"I'm only asking one thing of you," she said unable to meet his gaze. "Don't touch me or make an effort to see me as long as Kelly's wearing your ring. It's not fair to any one of us." Her lashes fell to veil the hurt in her eyes. Andrew couldn't help but know that she was in love with him. She would have staked her life that her feelings were returned full measure. Fresh tears misted her eyes.

"I don't want to leave you like this."

"I'll be all right," she murmured miserably. "There's nothing that I can do. Everything rests with you, Andrew. Everything."

Dejected, he nodded and added a promise. "I'll take care of it today."

Again Jo Marie wiped the wetness from her face and forced a smile, but the effort was almost more than she could bear.

The door clicked, indicating that Andrew had gone and Jo Marie released a long sigh of pent-up emotion. Her reflection in the bathroom mirror showed that her lips were parted and trembling from the hungry possession of his mouth. Her eyes had darkened from the strength of her physical response.

Andrew had asked that she trust him and she would, with all her heart. He loved her, she was sure of it. He wouldn't have hired a detective to find her or built a huge home with her in mind if he didn't feel something strong toward her. Nor could he have held her and kissed her the way he had today without loving and needing her.

While she unpacked the small overnight bag a sense of peace came over her. Andrew would explain everything to Kelly, and she needn't worry. Kelly's interests seemed to be centered more on Mark lately, and maybe…just maybe, she wouldn't be hurt or upset and would accept that neither Andrew nor Jo Marie had planned for this to happen.

Time hung heavily on her hands and Jo Marie toyed with the idea of visiting her parents. But her mother knew her so well that she'd take one look at Jo Marie and want to know what was bothering her daughter. And today Jo Marie wasn't up to explanations.

A flip of the radio dial and Christmas music drifted into the room, surrounding her with its message of peace and love. Humming the words softly to herself, Jo Marie felt infinitely better. Everything was going to be fine, she felt confident.

A thick Sunday paper held her attention for the better part of an hour, but at the slightest noise, Jo Marie's attention wandered from the printed page and she glanced up expecting Kelly. One look at her friend would be enough to tell Jo Marie everything she needed to know.

Setting the paper aside, Jo Marie felt her nerves tingle with expectancy. She felt weighted with a terrible guilt. Kelly obviously loved Andrew enough to agree to be his wife, but she showed all the signs of falling in love with Mark. Kelly wasn't the kind of girl who would purposely hurt or lead a man on. She was too sensitive for that. And to add to the complications were Andrew and Jo Marie who had discovered each other again just when they had given up all hope. Jo Marie loved Andrew, but she wouldn't find her own happiness at her friend's expense. But Andrew was going to ask for his ring back, Jo Marie was sure of it. He'd said he'd clear things up today.

The door opened and inhaling a calming breath, Jo Marie stood.

Kelly came into the apartment, her face lowered as her gaze avoided her friend's.

"Hi," Jo Marie ventured hesitantly.

Kelly's face was red and blotchy; tears glistened in her eyes.

"Is something wrong?" Her voice faltered slightly.

"Drew and I had a fight, that's all." Kelly raised her hand to push back her hair and as she did so the engagement ring Andrew had given her sparkled in the sunlight.

Jo Marie felt the knot tighten in her stomach. Andrew had made his decision.

Seven

Somehow Jo Marie made it through the following days.
She didn't see Andrew and made excuses to avoid Kelly.
Her efforts consisted of trying to get through each day.
Once she left the office, she often went to the LFTF
headquarters, spending long hours helping Jim. Their
friendship had grown. Jim helped her laugh when it
would have been so easy to cry. A couple of times they
had coffee together and talked. But Jim did most of
the talking. This pain was so all-consuming that Jo
Marie felt like a newly fallen leaf tossed at will by a
fickle wind.

Jim asked her to accompany him on another speaking engagement which Jo Marie did willingly. The talk
was on a stretch of wetlands Jim wanted preserved and
it had been well received. Silently, Jo Marie mocked
herself for not being attracted to someone as wonderful as Jim Rowden. He was everything a woman could
want. In addition, she was convinced that he was interested in her. But it was Andrew who continued to fill

her thoughts, Andrew who haunted her dreams, Andrew whose soft whisper she heard in the wind.

Lost in the meandering trail of her musing, Jo Marie didn't hear Jim's words as they sauntered into the empty office. Her blank look prompted him to repeat himself. "I thought it went rather well tonight, didn't you?" he asked, grinning boyishly. He brushed the hair from his forehead and pulled out the chair opposite hers.

"Yes," Jo Marie agreed with an absent shake of her head. "It did go well. You're a wonderful speaker." She could feel Jim's gaze watching her and in an effort to avoid any questions, she stood and reached for her purse. "I'd better think about getting home."

"Want some company while you walk to the bus stop?"

"I brought the car tonight." She almost wished she was taking the bus. Jim was a friendly face in a world that had taken on ragged, pain-filled edges.

Kelly had been somber and sullen all week. Half the time she looked as if she were ready to burst into tears at the slightest provocation. Until this last week, Jo Marie had always viewed her roommate as an emotionally strong woman, but recently Jo Marie wondered if she really knew Kelly. Although her friend didn't enjoy large parties, she'd never known Kelly to be intimidated by them. Lately, Kelly had been playing the role of a damsel in distress to the hilt.

Mark had stopped by the apartment only once and he'd resembled a volcano about to explode. He'd left after fifteen minutes of pacing the living-room carpet when Kelly didn't show.

And Andrew—yes, Andrew—by heaven's grace she'd been able to avoid a confrontation with him. She'd seen him only once in the last five days and the look in his eyes had seared her heart. He desperately wanted to talk to her. The tormented message was clear in his eyes, but she'd gently shaken her head, indicating that she intended to hold him to his word.

"Something's bothering you, Jo Marie. Do you want to talk about it?" Dimples edged into Jim's round face. Funny how she'd never noticed them before tonight.

Sadness touched the depths of her eyes and she gently shook her head. "Thanks, but no. Not tonight."

"Venturing a guess, I'd say it had something to do with Mr. Delta Development."

"Oh?" Clenching her purse under her arm, Jo Marie feigned ignorance. "What makes you say that?"

Jim shook his head. "A number of things." He rose and tucked both hands in his pants pockets. "Let me walk you to your car. The least I can do is see that you get safely outside."

"The weather's been exceptionally cold lately, hasn't it?"

Jim's smile was inviting as he turned the lock in the office door. "Avoiding my questions, aren't you?"

"Yes." Jo Marie couldn't see any reason to lie.

"When you're ready to talk, I'll be happy to listen." Tucking the keys in his pocket, Jim reached for Jo Marie's hand, placing it at his elbow and patting it gently.

"Thanks, I'll remember that."

"Tell me something more about you," Jo Marie queried in a blatant effort to change the subject. Briefly Jim looked at her, his expression thoughtful.

They ventured onto the sidewalk. The full moon was

out, its silver rays clearing a path in the night as they strolled toward her car.

"I'm afraid I'd bore you. Most everything you already know. I've only been with the foundation a month."

"LFTF needs people like you, dedicated, passionate, caring."

"I wasn't the one who gave permission for a transient to sleep in a doorway."

Jo Marie softly sucked in her breath. "How'd you know?"

"He came back the second night looking for a hand-out. The guy knew a soft touch when he saw one."

"What happened?"

Jim shrugged his shoulder and Jo Marie stopped walking in mid-stride. "You gave him some money!" she declared righteously. "And you call me a soft touch."

"As a matter of fact, I didn't. We both knew what he'd spend it on."

"So what did you do?"

"Took him to dinner."

A gentle smile stole across her features at the picture that must have made. Jim dressed impeccably in his business suit and the alcoholic in tattered, ragged clothes.

"It's sad to think about." Slowly, Jo Marie shook her head.

"I got in touch with a friend of mine from a mission. He came for him afterward so that he'll have a place to sleep at least. To witness, close at hand like that, a man wasting his life is far worse to me than..." he paused and held her gaze for a long moment, looking deep into her brown eyes. Then he smiled faintly and shook his head. "Sorry, I didn't mean to get so serious."

"You weren't," Jo Marie replied, taking the car keys from her purse. "I'll be back Monday and maybe we could have a cup of coffee."

The deep blue eyes brightened perceptively. "I'd like that and listen, maybe we could have dinner one night soon."

Jo Marie nodded, revealing that she'd enjoy that as well. Jim was her friend and she doubted that her feelings would ever go beyond that, but the way she felt lately, she needed someone to lift her from the doldrums of self-pity.

The drive home was accomplished in a matter of minutes. Standing outside her apartment building, Jo Marie heaved a steadying breath. She dreaded walking into her own home—what a sad commentary on her life! Tonight, she promised herself, she'd make an effort to clear the air between herself and Kelly. Not knowing what Andrew had said to her roommate about his feelings for her, if anything, or the details of the argument, had put Jo Marie in a precarious position. The air between Jo Marie and her best friend was like the stillness before an electrical storm. The problem was that Jo Marie didn't know what to say to Kelly or how to go about making things right.

She made a quick survey of the cars in the parking lot to assure herself that Andrew wasn't inside. Relieved, she tucked her hands inside the pockets of her cardigan and hoped to give a nonchalant appearance when she walked through the front door.

Kelly glanced up from the book she was reading

when Jo Marie walked inside. The red, puffy eyes were a testimony of tears, but Kelly didn't explain and Jo Marie didn't pry.

"I hope there's something left over from dinner," she began on a forced note of cheerfulness. "I'm starved."

"I didn't fix anything," Kelly explained in an ominously quiet voice. "In fact I think I'm coming down with something. I've got a terrible stomachache."

Jo Marie had to bite her lip to keep from shouting that she knew what was wrong with the both of them. Their lives were beginning to resemble a three-ring circus. Where once Jo Marie and Kelly had been best friends, now they rarely spoke.

"What I think I'll do is take a long, leisurely bath and go to bed."

Jo Marie nodded, thinking Kelly's sudden urge for a hot soak was just an excuse to leave the room and avoid the problems that faced them.

While Kelly ran her bathwater, Jo Marie searched through the fridge looking for something appetizing. Normally this was the time of the year that she had to watch her weight. This Christmas she'd probably end up losing a few pounds.

The radio was playing a series of spirited Christmas carols and Jo Marie started humming along. She took out bread and cheese slices from the fridge. The cupboard offered a can of tomato soup.

By the time Kelly came out of the bathroom, Jo Marie had set two places at the table and was pouring hot soup into deep bowls.

"Dinner is served," she called.

Kelly surveyed the table and gave her friend a weak,

trembling smile. "I appreciate the effort, but I'm really not up to eating."

Exhaling a dejected sigh, Jo Marie turned to her friend. "How long are we going to continue pretending like this? We need to talk, Kell."

"Not tonight, please, not tonight."

The doorbell rang and a stricken look came over Kelly's pale features. "I don't want to see anyone," she announced and hurried into the bedroom, leaving Jo Marie to deal with whoever was calling.

Resentment burned in her dark eyes as Jo Marie crossed the room. If it was Andrew, she would simply explain that Kelly was ill and not invite him inside.

"Merry Christmas." A tired-looking Mark greeted Jo Marie sarcastically from the other side of the door.

"Hi." Jo Marie watched him carefully. Her brother looked terrible. Tiny lines etched about his eyes revealed lack of sleep. He looked as though he was suffering from both mental and physical exhaustion.

"Is Kelly around?" He walked into the living room, sat on the sofa and leaned forward, roughly rubbing his hands across his face as if that would keep him awake.

"No, she's gone to bed. I don't think she's feeling well."

Briefly, Mark stared at the closed bedroom door and as he did, his shoulder hunched in a gesture of defeat.

"How about something to eat? You look like you haven't had a decent meal in days."

"I haven't." He moved lackadaisically to the kitchen and pulled out a chair.

Lifting the steaming bowls of soup from the counter, Jo Marie brought them to the table and sat opposite her brother.

As Mark took the soup spoon, his tired eyes held a distant, unhappy look. Kelly's eyes had revealed the same light of despair. "We had an argument," he murmured.

"You and Kell?"

"I said some terrible things to her." He braced his elbow against the table and pinched the bridge of his nose. "I don't know what made me do it. The whole time I was shouting at her I felt as if it was some stranger doing this. I know it sounds crazy but it was almost as if I were standing outside myself watching, and hating myself for what I was doing."

"Was the fight over something important?"

Defensively, Mark straightened. "Yeah, but that's between Kelly and me." He attacked the toasted cheese sandwich with a vengeance.

"You're in love with Kelly, aren't you?" Jo Marie had yet to touch her meal, more concerned about what was happening between her brother and her best friend than about her soup and sandwich.

Mark hesitated thoughtfully and a faint grimness closed off his expression. "In love with Kelly? I am?"

"You obviously care for her."

"I care for my cat, too," he returned coldly and his expression hardened. "She's got what she wants—money. Just look at who she's marrying. It isn't enough that she's wealthy in her own right. No, she sets her sights on J. Paul Getty."

Jo Marie's chin trembled in a supreme effort not to reveal her reaction to his words. "You know Kelly better than that." Averting her gaze, Jo Marie struggled to hold back the emotion that tightly constricted her throat.

"Does either one of us really know Kelly?" Mark's voice was taut as a hunter's bow. Cyncism drove deep grooved lines around his nose and mouth. "Did she tell you that she and Drew have set their wedding date?" Mark's voice dipped with contempt.

A pain seared all the way through Jo Marie's soul. "No, she didn't say." With her gaze lowered, she struggled to keep her hands from shaking.

"Apparently they're going to make it official after the first of the year. They're planning on a spring wedding."

"How...nice." Jo Marie nearly choked on the words.

"Well, all I can say is that those two deserve each other." He tossed the melted cheese sandwich back on the plate and stood. "I guess I'm not very hungry, after all."

Jo Marie rose with him and glanced at the table. Neither one of them had done more than shred their sandwiches and stir their soup. "Neither am I," she said, and swallowed at the tightness gripping her throat.

Standing in the living room, Mark stared for a second time at the closed bedroom door.

"I'll tell Kelly you were by." For a second it seemed that Mark hadn't heard.

"No," he murmured after a long moment. "Maybe it's best to leave things as they are. Good night, sis, thanks for dinner." Resembling a man carrying the weight of the world on his shoulders, Mark left.

Leaning against the front door, Jo Marie released a bitter, pain-filled sigh and turned the dead bolt. Tears burned for release. So Andrew and Kelly were going to make a public announcement of their engagement after Christmas. It shouldn't shock her. Kelly had told her from the beginning that they were. The wedding plans were already in the making. Wiping the salty dampness from her cheek, Jo Marie bit into the tender skin inside her cheek to hold back a sob.

"There's a call for you on line one," Paula called to Jo Marie from her desk.

"Thanks." With an efficiency born of years of experience, Jo Marie punched in the telephone tab and lifted the receiver to her ear. "This is Jo Marie Early, may I help you?"

"Jo Marie, this is Jim. I hope you don't mind me calling you at work."

"No problem."

"Good. Listen, you, ah, mentioned something the other night about us having coffee together and I said something about having dinner."

If she hadn't known any better, Jo Marie would have guessed that Jim was uneasy. He was a gentle man with enough sensitivity to campaign for the future. His hesitancy surprised her now. "I remember."

"How would you feel about this Wednesday?" he continued. "We could make a night of it."

Jo Marie didn't need to think it over. "I'd like that very much." After Mark's revelation, she'd realized the best thing to do was to put the past and Andrew behind her and build a new life for herself.

"Good." Jim sounded pleased. "We can go Wednesday night…or would you prefer Friday?"

"Wednesday's fine." Jo Marie doubted that she could

ever feel again the deep, passionate attraction she'd experienced with Andrew, but Jim's appeal wasn't built on fantasy.

"I'll see you then. Goodbye, Jo Marie."

"Goodbye Jim, and thanks."

The mental uplifting of their short conversation was enough to see Jo Marie through a hectic afternoon. An airline lost her customer's reservations and the tickets didn't arrive in time. In addition the phone rang repeatedly.

By the time she walked into the apartment, her feet hurt and there was a nagging ache in the small of her back.

"I thought I heard you." Kelly sauntered into the kitchen and stood in the doorway dressed in a robe and slippers.

"How are you feeling?"

She lifted one shoulder in a weak shrug. "Better."

"You stayed home?" Kelly had still been in bed when Jo Marie left for work. Apparently her friend had phoned in sick.

"Yeah." She moved into the living room and sat on the sofa.

"Mark was by last night." Jo Marie mentioned the fact casually, waiting for a response from her roommate. Kelly didn't give her one. "He said that the two of you had a big fight," she continued.

"That's all we do anymore—argue."

"I don't know what he said to you, but he felt bad about it afterward."

A sad glimmer touched Kelly's eyes and her mouth formed a brittle line that Jo Marie supposed was meant to be a smile. "I know he didn't mean it. He's exhausted. I swear he's trying to work himself to death."

Now that her friend mentioned it, Jo Marie realized that she hadn't seen much of her brother lately. It used to be that he had an excuse to show up two or three times a week. Except for last night, he had been to the apartment only twice since Thanksgiving.

"I don't think he's eaten a decent meal in days," Kelly continued. "He's such a good doctor, Jo Marie, because he cares so much about his patients. Even the ones he knows he's going to lose. I'm a nurse, I've seen the way the other doctors close themselves off from any emotional involvement. But Mark's there, always giving." Her voice shook uncontrollably and she paused to bite into her lip until she regained her composure. "I wanted to talk to him the other night, and do you know where I found him? In pediatrics holding a little boy who's suffering with terminal cancer. He was rocking this child, holding him in his arms and telling him the pain wouldn't last too much longer. From the hallway, I heard Mark talk about heaven and how there wouldn't be any pain for him there. Mark's a wonderful man and wonderful doctor."

And he loves you so much it's tearing him apart, Jo Marie added silently.

"Yesterday he was frustrated and angry and he took it out on me. I'm not going to lie and say it didn't hurt. For a time I was devastated, but I'm over that now."

"But you didn't go to work today." They both knew why she'd chosen to stay home.

"No, I felt Mark and I needed a day away from each other."

"That's probably a good idea." There was so much she wanted to say to Kelly, but everything sounded so inadequate. At least they were talking, which was a major improvement over the previous five days.

The teakettle whistled sharply and Jo Marie returned to the kitchen bringing them both back a steaming cup of hot coffee.

"Thanks." Kelly's eyes brightened.

"Would you like me to talk to Mark?" Jo Marie's offer was sincere, but she wasn't exactly sure what she'd say. And in some ways it could make matters worse.

"No. We'll sort this out on our own."

The doorbell chimed and the two exchanged glances. "I'm not expecting anyone," Kelly murmured and glanced down self-consciously at her attire. "In fact I'd rather not be seen, so if you don't mind I'll vanish inside my room."

The last person Jo Marie expected to find on the other side of the door was Andrew. The welcome died in her eyes as their gazes met and clashed. Jo Marie quickly lowered hers. Her throat went dry and a rush of emotion brought a flood of color to her suddenly pale cheeks. A tense air of silence surrounded them. Andrew raised his hand as though he wanted to reach out and touch her. Instead he clenched his fist and lowered it to his side, apparently having changed his mind.

"Is Kelly ready?" he asked after a breathless moment. Jo Marie didn't move, her body blocking the front door, refusing him admittance.

She stared up at him blankly. "Ready?" she repeated.

"Yes, we're attending the opera tonight. Bizet's *Carmen*," he added as if in an afterthought.

"Oh, dear." Jo Marie's eyes widened. Kelly had obviously forgotten their date. The tickets for the elaborate opera had been sold out for weeks. Her roommate would have to go. "Come in, I'll check with Kelly."

"Andrew's here," Jo Marie announced and leaned against the wooden door inside the bedroom, her hands folded behind her.

"Drew?"

"Andrew to me, Drew to you," she responded cattily. "You have a date to see *Carmen*."

Kelly's hand flew to her forehead. "Oh, my goodness, I completely forgot."

"What are you going to do?"

"Explain, what else is there to do?" she snapped.

Jo Marie followed her friend into the living room. Andrew's gray eyes widened at the sight of Kelly dressed in her robe and slippers.

"You're ill?"

"Actually, I'm feeling better. Drew, I apologize, I completely forgot about tonight."

As Andrew glanced at his gold wristwatch, a frown marred his handsome face.

"Kelly can shower and dress in a matter of a few minutes," Jo Marie said sharply, guessing what Kelly was about to suggest.

"I couldn't possibly be ready in forty-five minutes," she denied. "There's only one thing to do. Jo Marie, you'll have to go in my place."

Andrew's level gaze crossed the width of the room to capture Jo Marie's. Little emotion was revealed in the impassive male features, but his gray eyes glinted with challenge.

"I can't." Her voice was level with hard determination.

"Why not?" Two sets of eyes studied her.

"I'm…" Her mind searched wildly for an excuse. "I'm baking cookies for the Science Club. We're meeting Saturday and this will be our last time before Christmas."

"I thought you worked Saturdays," Andrew cut in sharply.

"Every other Saturday." Calmly she met his gaze. Over the past couple of weeks, Kelly had purposely brought Jo Marie and Andrew together, but Jo Marie wouldn't fall prey to that game any longer. She'd made an agreement with him and refused to back down. As long as he was engaged to another woman she wouldn't…couldn't be with him. "I won't go," she explained in a steady voice which belied the inner turmoil that churned her stomach.

"There's plenty of time before the opening curtain if you'd care to change your mind."

Kelly tossed Jo Marie an odd look. "It looks like I'll have to go," she said with an exaggerated sigh. "I'll be as fast as I can." Kelly rushed back inside the bedroom leaving Jo Marie and Andrew separated by only a few feet.

"How have you been?" he asked, his eyes devouring her.

"Fine," she responded on a stiff note. The lie was only a little one. The width of the room stood between them, but it might as well have been whole light-years.

Bowing her head, she stared at the pattern in the carpet. When she suggested Kelly hurry and dress, she hadn't counted on being left alone with Andrew. "If you'll excuse me, I'll get started on those cookies."

To her dismay Andrew followed her into the kitchen.

"What are my chances of getting a cup of coffee?" He sounded pleased with himself, his smile was smug.

Wordlessly Jo Marie stood on her tiptoes and brought down a mug from the cupboard. She poured in the dark granules, stirred in hot water and walked past him to carry the mug into the living room. All the while her mind was screaming with him to leave her alone.

Andrew picked up the mug and followed her back into the kitchen. "I've wanted to talk to you for days."

"You agreed."

"Jo Marie, believe me, talking to Kelly isn't as easy as it seems. There are some things I'm not at liberty to explain that would resolve this whole mess."

"I'll just bet there are." The bitter taste of anger filled her mouth.

"Can't you trust me?" The words were barely audible and for an instant Jo Marie wasn't certain he'd spoken.

Everything within her yearned to reach out to him and be assured that the glorious times they'd shared had been as real for him as they'd been for her. Desperately she wanted to turn and tell him that she would trust him with her life, but not her heart. She couldn't, not when Kelly was wearing his engagement ring.

"Jo Marie." A faint pleading quality entered his voice. "I know how all this looks. At least give me a chance to explain. Have dinner with me tomorrow. I swear I won't so much as touch you. I'll leave everything up to you. Place. Time. You name it."

"No." Frantically she shook her head, her voice throbbing with the desire to do as he asked. "I can't."

"Jo Marie." He took a step toward her, then another, until he was so close his husky voice breathed against her dark hair.

Forcing herself into action, Jo Marie whirled around and backed out of the kitchen. "Don't talk to me like that. I realized last week that whatever you feel for Kelly is stronger than any love you have for me. I've tried to accept that as best I can."

Andrew's knuckles were clenched so tightly that they went white. He looked like an innocent man facing a firing squad, his eyes resigned, the line of his jaw tense, anger and disbelief etched in every rugged mark of his face.

"Just be patient, that's all I'm asking. In due time you'll understand everything."

"Will you stop?" she demanded angrily. "You're talking in puzzles and I've always hated those. All I know is that there are four people who—"

"I guess this will have to do," Kelly interrupted as she walked into the room. She had showered, dressed and dried her hair in record time.

Jo Marie swallowed the taste of jealousy as she watched the dark, troubled look dissolve from Andrew's eyes. "You look great," was all she could manage.

"We won't be too late," Kelly said on her way out.

"Don't worry," Jo Marie murmured and breathed in a sharp breath. "I won't be up; I'm exhausted."

Who was she trying to kid? Not until the key turned in the front door lock five hours later did Jo Marie so much as yawn. As much as she hated herself for being so weak, the entire time Kelly had been with Andrew, Jo Marie had been utterly miserable.

The dinner date with Jim the next evening was the only bright spot in a day that stretched out like an empty void. She dressed carefully and applied her makeup with extra care, hoping to camouflage the effects of a sleepless night.

"Don't fix dinner for me, I've got a date," was all she said to Kelly on her way out the door to the office.

As she knew it would, being with Jim was like stumbling upon an oasis in the middle of a sand-tossed desert. He made her laugh, teasing her affectionately. His humor was subtle and light and just the antidote for a broken heart. She'd known from the moment they'd met that she was going to like Jim Rowden. With him she could relax and be herself. And not once did she have to look over her shoulder.

"Are you going to tell me what's been troubling you?" he probed gently over their dessert.

"What? And cry all over my lime-chiffon pie?"

Jim's returning smile was one of understanding and encouragement. Again she noted the twin dimples that formed in his cheeks. "Whenever you're ready, I'm available to listen."

"Thanks." She shook her head, fighting back an unexpected swell of emotion. "Now what's this surprise you've been taunting me with most of the evening?" she questioned, averting the subject from herself.

"It's about the wetlands we've been crusading for during the last month. Well, I talked to a state senator today and he's going to introduce a bill that would make the land into a state park." Lacing his hands together,

Jim leaned toward the linen-covered table. "From everything he's heard, George claims from there it should be a piece of cake."

"Jim, that's wonderful." This was his first success and he beamed with pride over the accomplishment.

"Of course, nothing's definite yet, and I'm not even sure I should have told you, but you've heard me give two speeches on the wetlands and I wanted you to know."

"I'm honored that you did."

He acknowledged her statement with a short nod. "I should know better than to get my hopes up like this, but George—my friend—sounded so confident."

"Then you should be too. We both should."

Jim reached for her hand and squeezed it gently. "It would be very easy to share things with you, Jo Marie. You're quite a woman."

Flattery had always made her uncomfortable, but Jim sounded so sincere. It cost her a great deal of effort to simply smile and murmur her thanks.

Jim's arm rested across her shoulder as they walked back toward the office. He held open her car door for her and paused before lightly brushing his mouth over hers. The kiss was both gentle and reassuring. But it wasn't Andrew's kiss and Jim hadn't the power to evoke the same passionate response Andrew seemed to draw so easily from her.

On the ride home, Jo Marie silently berated herself for continuing to compare the two men. It was unfair to them both to even think in that mode.

The apartment was unlocked when Jo Marie let herself inside. She was hanging up her sweater-coat when she noticed Andrew. He was standing in the middle of the living room carpet, regarding her with stone cold eyes.

One glance and Jo Marie realized that she'd never seen a man look so angry.

"It's about time you got home." His eyes were flashing gray fire.

"What right is it of yours to demand what time I get in?"

"I have every right." His voice was like a whip lashing out at her. "I suppose you think you're playing a game. Every time I go out with Kelly, you'll pay me back by dating Jim?"

Stunned into speechlessness, Jo Marie felt her voice die in her throat.

"And if you insist on letting him kiss you the least you can do is look for someplace more private than the street." The white line about his mouth became more pronounced as his eyes filled with bitter contempt. "You surprise me, Jo Marie, I thought you had more class than that."

Eight

"How dare you…how dare you say such things to me!" Jo Marie's quavering voice became breathless with rage. Her eyes were dark and stormy as she turned around and jerked the front door open.

"What do you expect me to believe?" Andrew rammed his hand through his hair, ruffling the dark hair that grew at his temple.

"I expected a lot of things from you, but not that you'd follow me or spy on me. And then…then to have the audacity to confront and insult me." The fury in her faded to be replaced with a deep, emotional pain that pierced her heart.

Andrew's face was bloodless as he walked past her and out the door. As soon as he was through the portal, she slammed it closed with a sweeping arc of her hand.

Jo Marie was so furious that the room wasn't large enough to contain her anger. Her shoulders rose and sagged with her every breath. At one time Andrew had been her dream man. Quickly she was learning to separate the fantasy from the reality.

Pacing the carpet helped relieve some of the terrible tension building within her. Andrew's behavior was nothing short of odious. She should hate him for saying those kinds of things to her. Tears burned for release, but deep, concentrated breaths held them at bay. Andrew Beaumont wasn't worth the emotion. Staring sightlessly at the ceiling, her damp lashes pressed against her cheek.

The sound of the doorbell caused her to whirl around. Andrew. She'd stake a week's salary on the fact. In an act of defiance, she folded her arms across her waist and stared determinedly at the closed door. He could rot in the rain before she'd open that door.

Again the chimes rang in short, staccato raps. "Come on, Jo Marie, answer the damn door."

"No," she shouted from the other side.

"Fine, we'll carry on a conversation by shouting at each other. That should amuse your neighbors."

"Go away." Jo Marie was too upset to talk things out. Andrew had hurt her with his actions and words.

"Jo Marie." The appealing quality in his voice couldn't be ignored. "Please, open the door. All I want is to apologize."

Hating herself for being so weak, Jo Marie turned the lock and threw open the solid wood door. "You have one minute."

"I think I went a little crazy when I saw Jim kiss you," he said pacing the area in front of the door. "Jo Marie, promise me that you won't see him again. I don't think I can stand the thought of any man touching you."

"This is supposed to be an apology?" she asked sarcastically. "Get this, Mr. Beaumont," she said, fighting to keep from shouting at him as her finger punctuated the air. "You have no right to dictate anything to me."

His tight features darkened. "I can make your life miserable."

"And you think you haven't already?" she cried. "Just leave me alone. I don't need your threats. I don't want to see you again. Ever." To her horror, her voice cracked. Shaking her head, unable to talk any longer, she shut the door and clicked the lock.

Almost immediately the doorbell chimed, followed by continued knocking. Neither of them were in any mood to discuss things rationally. And perhaps it was better all the way around to simply leave things as they were. It hurt, more than Jo Marie wanted to admit, but she'd recover. She'd go on with her life and put Andrew, the dream man and all of it behind her.

Without glancing over her shoulder, she ignored the sound and moved into her bedroom.

The restaurant was crowded, the luncheon crowd filling it to capacity. With Christmas only a few days away the rush of last-minute shoppers filled the downtown area and flowed into the restaurants at lunch time.

Seeing Mark come through the doors, Jo Marie raised her hand and waved in an effort to attract her brother's attention. He looked less fatigued than the last time she'd seen him. A brief smile momentarily brightened his eyes, but faded quickly.

"I must admit this is a surprise," Jo Marie said as her brother slid into the upholstered booth opposite her. "I can't remember the last time we met for lunch."

"I can't remember either." Mark picked up the menu, decided and closed it after only a minute.

"That was quick."

"I haven't got a lot of time."

Same old Mark, always in a rush, hurrying from one place to another. "You called me, remember?" she taunted softly.

"Yeah, I remember." His gaze was focused on the paper napkin which he proceeded to fold into an intricate pattern. "This is going to sound a little crazy so promise me you won't laugh."

The edge of her mouth was already twitching. "I promise."

"I want you to attend the hospital Christmas party with me Saturday night."

"Me?"

"I don't have time to go out looking for a date and I don't think I can get out of it without offending half the staff."

In the past three weeks, Jo Marie had endured enough parties to last her a lifetime. "I guess I could go."

"Don't sound so enthusiastic."

"I'm beginning to feel the same way about parties as you do."

"I doubt that," he said forcefully and shredded the napkin in half.

The waitress came for their order and delivered steaming mugs of coffee almost immediately afterward.

Jo Marie lifted her own napkin, toying with the pressed paper edge. "Will Kelly and… Drew be there?"

"I doubt it. Why should they? There won't be any

ballroom dancing or a midnight buffet. It's a pot luck. Can you picture old 'money bags' sitting on a folding chair and balancing a paper plate on her lap? No. Kelly goes more for the two-hundred-dollar-a-place-setting affairs."

Jo Marie opened her mouth to argue, but decided it would do little good. Discussing Andrew—Drew, her mind corrected—or Kelly with Mark would be pointless.

"I suppose Kelly's told you?"

"Told me what?" Jo Marie glanced up curious and half-afraid. The last time Mark had relayed any information about Drew and Kelly it had been that they were going to publicly announce their engagement.

"She's given her two-week notice."

"No," Jo Marie gasped. "She wouldn't do that. Kelly loves nursing; she's a natural." Even more surprising was the fact that Kelly hadn't said a word to Jo Marie about leaving Tulane Hospital.

"I imagine with the wedding plans and all that she's decided to take any early retirement. Who can blame her, right?"

But it sounded very much like Mark was doing exactly that. His mouth was tight and his dark eyes were filled with something akin to pain. What a mess this Christmas was turning out to be.

"Let's not talk about Kelly or Drew or anyone for the moment, okay. It's Christmas next week." She forced a bit of yuletide cheer into her voice.

"Right," Mark returned with a short sigh. "It's almost Christmas." But for all the enthusiasm in his voice he could have been discussing German measles.

Their soup and sandwiches arrived and they ate in strained silence. "Well, are you coming or not?" Mark asked, pushing his empty plate aside.

"I guess." No need to force any enthusiasm into her voice. They both felt the same way about the party.

"Thanks, sis."

"Just consider it your Christmas present."

Mark reached for the white slip the waitress had placed on their table, examining it. "And consider this lunch yours," he announced and scooted from his seat. "See you Saturday night."

"Mark said you've given the hospital your two-week notice?" Jo Marie confronted her roommate first thing that evening.

"Yes," Kelly replied lifelessly.

"I suppose the wedding will fill your time from now on."

"The wedding?" Kelly gave her an absent look. "No," she shook her head and an aura of dejected defeat hung over her, dulling her responses. "I've got my application in at a couple of other hospitals."

"So you're going to continue working after you're married."

For a moment it didn't look as if Kelly had heard her. "Kell?" Jo Marie prompted.

"I'd hoped to."

Berating herself for caring how Kelly and Andrew lived their lives, Jo Marie picked up the evening paper and pretended an interest in the front page. But if Kelly had asked her so much as what the headline read she couldn't have answered.

Saturday night Jo Marie dressed in the blue dress that she'd sewn after Thanksgiving. It fit her well and revealed a subtle grace in her movements. Although she took extra time with her hair and cosmetics, her heart wasn't up to attending the party.

Jo Marie had casually draped a lace shawl over her shoulder when the front door opened and Kelly entered with Andrew at her side.

"You're going out," Kelly announced, stopping abruptly inside the living room. "You...you didn't say anything."

Jo Marie could feel Andrew's gaze scorching her in a slow, heated perusal, but she didn't look his way. "Yes, I'm going out; don't wait up for me."

"Drew and I have plans too."

Reaching for her evening bag, Jo Marie's mouth curved slightly upward in a poor imitation of a smile. "Have a good time."

Kelly said something more, but Jo Marie was already out the door, grateful to have escaped without another confrontation with Andrew.

Mark had given her the address of the party and asked that she meet him there. He didn't give any particular reason he couldn't pick her up. He didn't need an excuse. It was obvious he wanted to avoid Kelly.

She located the house without a problem and was greeted by loud music and a smoke-filled room. Making her way between the dancing couples, Jo Marie delivered the salad she had prepared on her brother's behalf to the kitchen. After exchanging pleasantries with the guests in the kitchen, Jo Marie went back to the main room to search for Mark.

For all the noisy commotion the party was an orderly one and Jo Marie spotted her brother almost immediately. He was sitting on the opposite side of the room talking to a group of other young men, who she assumed were fellow doctors. Making her way across the carpet, she was waylaid once by a nurse friend of Kelly's that she'd met a couple of times. They chatted for a few minutes about the weather.

"I suppose you've heard that Kelly's given her notice," Julie Frazier said with a hint of impatience. "It's a shame, if you ask me."

"I agree," Jo Marie murmured.

"Sometimes I'd like to knock those two over the head." Julie motioned toward Mark with the slight tilt of her head. "Your brother's one stubborn male."

"You don't need to tell me. I'm his sister."

"You know," Julie said and glanced down at the cold drink she was holding in her hand. "After Kelly had her tonsils out I could have sworn those two were headed for the altar. No one was more surprised than me when Kell turns up engaged to this mystery character."

"What do you mean about Kelly and Mark?" Kelly's tonsils had come out months ago during the Mardi Gras. No matter how much time passed, it wasn't likely that Jo Marie would forget that.

"Kelly was miserable—adult tonsillectomies are seldom painless—anyway, Kelly didn't want anyone around, not even her family. Mark was the only one who could get close to her. He spent hours with her, coaxing her to eat, spoon-feeding her. He even read her to sleep and then curled up in the chair beside her bed so he'd be there when she woke."

Jo Marie stared back in open disbelief. "Mark did that?" All these months Mark had been in love with Kelly and he hadn't said a word. Her gaze sought him now and she groaned inwardly at her own stupidity. For months she'd been so caught up in the fantasy of those few precious moments with Andrew that she'd been blind to what was right in front of her own eyes.

"Well, speaking of our friend, look who's just arrived."

Jo Marie's gaze turned toward the front door just as Kelly and Andrew came inside. From across the length of the room, her eyes clashed with Andrew's. She watched as the hard line of his mouth relaxed and he smiled. The effect on her was devastating; her heart somersaulted and color rushed up her neck, invading her face. These were all the emotions she had struggled against from the beginning. She hated herself for being so vulnerable when it came to this one man. She didn't want to feel any of these emotions toward him.

"Excuse me—" Julie interrupted Jo Marie's musings "—there's someone I wanted to see."

"Sure." Mentally, Jo Marie shook herself and joined Mark, knowing she would be safe at his side.

"Did you see who just arrived?" Jo Marie whispered in her brother's ear.

Mark's dusty dark eyes studied Kelly's arrival and Jo Marie witnessed an unconscious softening in his gaze. Kelly did look lovely tonight, and begrudgingly Jo Marie admitted that Andrew and Kelly were the most striking couple in the room. They belonged together— both were people of wealth and position. Two of a kind.

"I'm surprised that she came," Mark admitted slowly

and turned his back to the pair. "But she's got as much right to be here as anyone."

"Of course she does."

One of Mark's friends appointed himself as disc jockey and put on another series of records for slow dancing. Jo Marie and Mark stood against the wall and watched as several couples began dancing on the makeshift dance floor. When Andrew turned Kelly into his arms, Jo Marie diverted her gaze to another section of the room, unable to look at them without being affected.

"You don't want to dance, do you?" Mark mumbled indifferently.

"With you?"

"No, I'd get one of my friends to do the honors. It's bad enough having to invite my sister to a party. I'm not about to dance with you, too."

Jo Marie couldn't prevent a short laugh. "You really know how to sweet talk a woman don't you, brother dearest?"

"I try," he murmured and his eyes narrowed on Kelly whose arms were draped around Andrew's neck as she whispered in his ear. "But obviously not hard enough," he finished.

Standing on the outskirts of the dancing couples made Jo Marie uncomfortable. "I think I'll see what I can do to help in the kitchen," she said as an excuse to leave.

Julie Frazier was there, placing cold cuts on a round platter with the precision of a mathematician.

"Can I help?" Jo Marie offered, looking around for something that needed to be done.

Julie turned and smiled her appreciation. "Sure.

Would you put the serving spoons in the salads and set them out on the dining room table?"

"Glad to." She located the spoons in the silverware drawer and carried out a large glass bowl of potato salad. The Formica table was covered with a vinyl cloth decorated with green holly and red berries.

"And now ladies and gentlemen—" the disc jockey demanded the attention of the room "—this next number is a ladies' choice."

With her back to the table, Jo Marie watched as Kelly whispered something to Andrew. To her surprise, he nodded and stepped aside as Kelly made her way to the other side of the room. Her destination was clear—Kelly was heading directly to Mark. Jo Marie's pulse fluttered wildly. If Mark said or did anything cruel to her friend, Jo Marie would never forgive him.

Her heart was in her eyes as Kelly tentatively tapped Mark on the shoulder. Engrossed in a conversation, Mark apparently wasn't aware he was being touched. Kelly tried again and Mark turned, surprise rounding his eyes when he saw her roommate.

Jo Marie was far enough to the side so that she couldn't be seen by Mark and Kelly, but close enough to hear their conversation.

"May I have this dance?" Kelly questioned, her voice firm and low.

"I thought it was the man's prerogative to ask." The edge of Mark's mouth curled up sarcastically. "And if you've noticed, I haven't asked."

"This number is ladies' choice."

Mark tensed visibly as he glared across the room,

eyeing Andrew. "And what about Rockefeller over there?"

Slowly, Kelly shook her head, her inviting gaze resting on Mark. "I'm asking you. Don't turn me down, Mark, not tonight. I'll be leaving the hospital in a little while and then you'll never be bothered with me again."

Jo Marie doubted that her brother could have refused Kelly anything in that moment. Wordlessly he approached the dance floor and took Kelly in his arms. A slow ballad was playing and the soft, melodic sounds of Billy Joel filled the room. Kelly fit her body to Mark's. Her arms slid around his neck as she pressed her temple against his jaw. Mark reacted to the contact by closing his eyes and inhaling as his eyes drifted closed. His hold, which had been loose, tightened as he knotted his hands at the small of Kelly's back, arching her body closer.

For the first time that night, her brother looked completely at ease. Kelly belonged with Mark. Jo Marie had been wrong to think that Andrew and Kelly were meant for each other. They weren't, and their engagement didn't make sense.

Her eyes sought out the subject of her thoughts. Andrew was leaning against the wall only a few feet from her. His eyes locked with hers, refusing to release her. He wanted her to come to him. She couldn't. His gaze seemed to drink her in as it had the night of the Mardi Gras. She could almost feel him reaching out to her, imploring her to come, urging her to cross the room so he could take her in his arms.

With unconscious thought Jo Marie took one step forward and stopped. No. Being with Andrew would only cause her more pain. With a determined effort she lightly shook her head, effectively breaking the spell. Her heart was beating so hard that breathing was difficult. Her steps were marked with decision as she returned to the kitchen.

A sliding glass door led to a lighted patio. A need to escape for a few moments overtook her and silently she slipped past the others and escaped into the darkness of the night.

A chill ran up her arms and she rubbed her hands over her forearms in an effort to warm her blood. The stars were out in a dazzling display and Jo Marie tilted her face toward the heavens, gazing at the lovely sight.

Jo Marie stiffened as she felt more than heard someone join her. She didn't need to turn around to realize that it was Andrew.

He came and stood beside her, but he made no effort to speak, instead focusing his attention on the dark sky.

Whole eternities seemed to pass before Andrew spoke. "I came to ask your forgiveness."

All the pain of his accusation burned in her breast. "You hurt me," she said on a breathless note after a long pause.

"I know, my love, I know." Slowly he removed his suit jacket and with extraordinary concern, draped it over her shoulders, taking care not to touch her.

"I'd give anything to have those thoughtless words back. Seeing Jim take you in his arms was like waving a red flag in front of an angry bull. I lashed out at you, when it was circumstances that were at fault."

Something about the way he spoke, the emotion that coated his words, the regret that filled his voice made her feel that her heart was ready to burst right out of her breast. She didn't want to look at him, but somehow it was impossible to keep her eyes away. With an infinite tenderness, he brushed a stray curl from her cheek.

"Can you forgive me?"

"Oh, Andrew." She felt herself weakening.

"I'd go on my knees if it would help."

The tears felt locked in her throat. "No, that isn't necessary."

He relaxed as if a great burden had been lifted from his shoulders. "Thank you."

Neither moved, wanting to prolong this tender moment. When Andrew spoke it was like the whisper of a gentle breeze and she had to strain to hear him.

"When I first came out here you looked like a blue sapphire silhouetted in the moonlight. And I was thinking that if it were in my power, I'd weave golden moonbeams into your hair."

"Have you always been so poetic?"

His mouth curved upward in a slow, sensuous smile. "No." His eyes were filled with an undisguised hunger as he studied her. Ever so slowly, he raised his hand and placed it at the side of her neck.

The tender touch of his fingers against her soft skin caused a tingling sensation to race down her spine. The feeling was akin to pain. Jo Marie loved this man as she would never love again and he was promised to another woman.

"Jo Marie," he whispered and his warm breath fanned her mouth. "There's mistletoe here. Let me kiss you."

There wasn't, of course, but Jo Marie was unable

to pull away. She nodded her acquiescence. "One last time." She hadn't meant to verbalize her thoughts.

He brought her into his arms and she moistened her lips anticipating the hungry exploration of his mouth over hers. But she was to be disappointed. Andrew's lips lightly moved over hers like the gentle brush of the spring sun on a hungry earth. Gradually the kiss deepened as he worked his way from one corner of her mouth to another—again like the earth long starved from summer's absence.

"I always knew it would be like this for us, Florence Nightingale," he whispered against her hair. "Even when I couldn't find you, I felt a part of myself would never be the same."

"I did too. I nearly gave up dating."

"I thought I'd go crazy. You were so close all these months and yet I couldn't find you."

"But you did." Pressing her hands against the strong cushion of his chest she created a space between them. "And now it's too late."

Andrew's eyes darkened as he seemed to struggle within himself. "Jo Marie." A thick frown marred his face.

"Shh." She pressed her fingertips against his lips. "Don't try to explain. I understand and I've accepted it. For a long time it hurt so much that I didn't think I'd be able to bear it. But I can and I will."

His hand circled her wrist and he closed his eyes before kissing the tips of her fingers. "There's so much I want to explain and can't."

"I know." With his arm holding her close, Jo Marie felt a deep sense of peace surround her. "I'd never be the kind of wife you need. Your position demands a woman with culture and class. I'm proud to be an Early and proud of my family, but I'm not right for you."

The grip on her wrist tightened. "Is that what you think?" The frustrated anger in his voice was barely suppressed. "Do you honestly believe that?"

"Yes," she answered him boldly. "I'm at peace within myself. I have no regrets. You've touched my heart and a part of me will never be the same. How can I regret having loved you? It's not within me."

He dropped her hand and turned from her, his look a mixture of angry torment. "You honestly think I should marry Kelly."

It would devastate Mark, but her brother would need to find his own peace. "Or someone like her." She removed his suit jacket from her shoulders and handed it back to him, taking care to avoid touching him. "Thank you," she whispered with a small catch to her soft voice. Unable to resist any longer, she raised her hand and traced his jaw. Very lightly, she brushed her mouth over his. "Goodbye, Andrew."

He reached out his hand in an effort to stop her, but she slipped past him. It took her only a moment to collect her shawl. Within a matter of minutes, she was out the front door and on her way back to the apartment. Mark would never miss her.

Jo Marie spent Sunday with her family, returning late that evening when she was assured Kelly was asleep. Lying in bed, studying the darkness around her, Jo Marie realized that she'd said her final goodbye to Andrew. Continuing to see him would only make it difficult for them both. Avoiding him had never succeeded, not when she yearned for every opportunity to be with him. The best solution would be to leave completely. Kelly would be moving out soon and Jo Marie couldn't afford to pay the rent on her own. The excuse would be a convenient one although Kelly was sure to recognize it for what it was.

After work Monday afternoon, before she headed for the LFTF office, Jo Marie stopped off at the hospital, hoping to talk to Mark. With luck, she might be able to convince her brother to let her move in with him. But only until she could find another apartment and another roommate.

Julie Frazier, the nurse who worked with both Kelly and Mark, was at the nurses' station on the surgical floor when Jo Marie arrived.

"Hi," she greeted cheerfully. "I don't suppose you know where Mark is?"

Julie glanced up from a chart she was reading. "He's in the doctors' lounge having a cup of coffee."

"Great. I'll talk to you later." With her shoes making clicking sounds against the polished floor, Jo Marie mused that her timing couldn't have been more perfect. Now all she needed was to find her brother in a good mood.

The doctors' lounge was at the end of the hall and was divided into two sections. The front part contained a sofa and a couple of chairs. A small kitchen area was behind that. The sound of Mark's and Kelly's voices stopped Jo Marie just inside the lounge.

"You can leave," Mark was saying in a tight, pained

voice. "Believe me I have no intention of crying on your shoulder."

"I didn't come here for that," Kelly argued softly.

Jo Marie hesitated, unsure of what she should do. She didn't want to interrupt their conversation which seemed intense, nor did she wish to intentionally stay and listen in either.

"That case with the Randolph girl is still bothering you, isn't it?" Kelly demanded.

"No, I did everything I could. You know that."

"But it wasn't enough, was it?"

Jo Marie had to bite her tongue not to interrupt Kelly. It wasn't like her roommate to be unnecessarily cruel. Jo Marie vividly recalled her brother's doubts after the young child's death. It had been just before Thanksgiving and Mark had agonized that he had lost her.

"No," Mark shouted, "it wasn't enough."

"And now you're going to lose the Rickard boy." Kelly's voice softened perceptively.

Fleetingly Jo Marie wondered if this child was the one Kelly had mentioned who was dying of cancer.

"I've known that from the first." Mark's tone contained the steel edge of anger.

"Yes, but it hasn't gotten any easier, has it?"

"Listen, Kelly, I know what you're trying to do, but it isn't going to work."

"Mark," Kelly murmured his name on a sigh, "sometimes you are so blind."

"Maybe it's because I feel so inadequate. Maybe it's because I'm haunted with the fact that there might have been something more I could have done."

"But there isn't, don't you see?" Kelly's voice had

softened as if her pain was Mark's. "Now won't you tell me what's really bothering you?"

"Maybe it's because I don't like the odds with Tommy. His endless struggle against pain. The deck was stacked against him from the beginning and now he hasn't got a bettor's edge. In the end, death will win."

"And you'll have lost, and every loss is a personal one."

Jo Marie didn't feel that she could eavesdrop any longer. Silently she slipped from the room.

The conversation between Mark and Kelly played back in her mind as she drove toward the office and Jim. Mark would have serious problems as a doctor unless he came to terms with these feelings. Kelly had recognized that and had set personal relationships aside to help Mark settle these doubts within himself. He'd been angry with her and would probably continue to be until he fully understood what she was doing.

Luckily Jo Marie found a parking space within sight of the office. With Christmas just a few days away the area had become more crowded and finding parking was almost impossible.

Her thoughts were heavy as she climbed from the passenger's side and locked her door. Just as she turned to look both ways before crossing the street she caught a glimpse of the dark blue Mercedes. A cold chill raced up her spine. Andrew was inside talking to Jim.

Nine

"Is everything all right?" Wearily Jo Marie eyed Jim, looking for a telltale mannerism that would reveal the reason for Andrew's visit. She'd avoided bumping into him by waiting in a small antique shop across the street from the foundation. After he'd gone, she sauntered around for several additional minutes to be certain he was out of the neighborhood. Once assured it was safe, she crossed the street to the foundation's office.

"Should anything be wrong?" Jim lifted two thick brows in question.

"You tell me. I saw Andrew Beaumont's car parked outside."

"Ah, yes." Jim paused and smiled fleetingly. "And that concerns you?"

"No." She shook her head determinedly. "All right, yes!" She wasn't going to be able to fool Jim, who was an excellent judge of human nature.

A smile worked its way across his round face. "He came to meet the rest of the staff at my invitation. The LFTF Foundation is deeply indebted to your friend."

"My friend?"

Jim chuckled. "Neither one of you has been successful at hiding your feelings. Yes, my dear, sweet, Jo Marie, *your* friend."

Any argument died on her tongue.

"Would you care for a cup of coffee?" Jim asked, walking across the room and filling a Styrofoam cup for her.

Jo Marie smiled her appreciation as he handed it to her and sat on the edge of her desk, crossing his arms. "Beaumont and I had quite a discussion."

"And?" Jo Marie didn't bother to disguise her curiosity.

The phone rang before Jim could answer her. Jim reached for it and spent the next ten minutes in conversation. Jo Marie did her best to keep occupied, but her thoughts were doing a crazy tailspin. Andrew was here on business. She wouldn't believe it.

"Well?" Jo Marie questioned the minute Jim replaced the receiver.

His expression was empty for a moment. "Are we back to Beaumont again?"

"I don't mean to pry," Jo Marie said with a rueful smile, "but I'd really like to know why he was here."

Jim was just as straightforward. "Are you in love with him?"

Miserably, Jo Marie nodded. "A lot of good it's done either of us. Did he mention me?"

A wry grin twisted Jim's mouth. "Not directly, but he wanted to know my intentions."

"He didn't!" Jo Marie was aghast at such audacity.

Chuckling, Jim shook his head. "No, he came to ask

me about the foundation and pick up some of our literature. He's a good man, Jo Marie."

She studied the top of the desk and typewriter keys. "I know."

"He didn't mention you directly, but I think he would have liked to. I had the feeling he was frustrated and concerned about you working here so many nights, especially in this neighborhood."

"He needn't worry, you escort me to my car or wait at the bus stop until the bus arrives."

Jim made busy work with his hands. "I had the impression that Beaumont is deeply in love with you. If anything happened to you while under my protection, he wouldn't take it lightly."

Even hours later when Jo Marie stepped into the apartment the echo of Jim's words hadn't faded. Andrew was concerned for her safety and was deeply in love with her. But it was all so useless that she refused to be comforted.

Kelly was sitting up, a blanket wrapped around her legs and torso as she paid close attention to a television Christmas special.

"Hi, how'd it go tonight?" Kelly greeted, briefly glancing from the screen.

Her roommate looked pale and slightly drawn, but Jo Marie attributed that to the conversation she'd overheard between her brother and her roommate. She wanted to ask how everything was at the hospital, but doubted that she could adequately disguise her interest.

"Tonight…oh, everything went as it usually does… fine."

"Good." Kelly's answer was absentminded, her look pinched.

"Are you feeling all right, Kell?"

Softly, she shook her head. "I've got another stomachache."

"Fever?"

"None to speak of. I think I might be coming down with the flu."

Tilting her head to one side, Jo Marie mused that Kelly had been unnaturally pale lately. But again she had attributed that to painfully tense times they'd all been through in the past few weeks.

"You know, one advantage of having a brother in the medical profession is that he's willing to make house calls."

Kelly glanced her way, then turned back to the television. "No, it's nothing to call Mark about."

But Kelly didn't sound as convincing as Jo Marie would have liked. With a shrug, she went into the kitchen and poured herself a glass of milk.

"Want one?" She raised her glass to Kelly for inspection.

"No thanks," Kelly murmured and unsuccessfully tried to disguise a wince. "In fact, I think I'll head for bed. I'll be fine in the morning, so don't worry about me."

But Jo Marie couldn't help doing just that. Little things about Kelly hadn't made sense in a long time— like staying home because of an argument with Mark. Kelly wasn't a shy, fledgling nurse. She'd stood her ground with Mark more than once. Even her behavior at the Christmas parties had been peculiar. Nor was Kelly a shrinking violet, yet she'd behaved like one. Obviously it was all an act. But her reasons remained unclear.

In the morning, Kelly announced that she was going to take a day of sick leave. Jo Marie studied her friend with worried eyes. Twice during the morning she phoned to see how Kelly was doing.

"Fine," Kelly answered impatiently the second time. "Listen, I'd probably be able to get some decent rest if I didn't have to get up and answer the phone every fifteen minutes."

In spite of her friend's testiness, Jo Marie chuckled. "I'll try to restrain myself for the rest of the day."

"That would be greatly appreciated."

"Do you want me to bring you something back for dinner?"

"No," she answered emphatically. "Food sounds awful."

Mark breezed into the office around noon, surprising Jo Marie. Sitting on the corner of her desk, he dangled one foot as she finished a telephone conversation.

"Business must be slow if you've got time to be dropping in here," she said, replacing the receiver.

"I come to take you to lunch and you're complaining?"

"You've come to ask about Kelly?" She wouldn't hedge. The time for playing games had long passed.

"Oh?" Briefly he arched a brow in question. "Is that so?"

"She's got the flu. There, I just saved you the price of lunch." Jo Marie couldn't disguise her irritation.

"You didn't save me the price of anything," Mark returned lazily. "I was going to let you treat."

Unable to remain angry with her brother for long, Jo Marie joined him in a nearby café a few minutes later, but neither of them mentioned Kelly again. By unspoken agreement, Kelly, Andrew, and Kelly's unexpected resignation were never mentioned.

Jo Marie's minestrone soup and turkey sandwich arrived and she unwrapped the silverware from the paper napkin. "How would you feel about a roommate for a while?" Jo Marie broached the subject tentatively.

"Male or female?" Dusky dark eyes so like her own twinkled with mischief.

"This may surprise you—female."

Mark laid his sandwich aside. "I'll admit my interest has been piqued."

"You may not be as keen once you find out that it's me."

"You?"

"Well I'm going to have to find someplace else to move sooner or later and—"

"And you're interested in the sooner," he interrupted.

"Yes." She wouldn't mention her reasons, but Mark was astute enough to figure it out for himself.

Peeling open his sandwich, Mark removed a thin slice of tomato and set it on the beige plate. "As long as you do the laundry, clean, and do all the cooking I won't object."

A smile hovered at the edges of her mouth. "Your generosity overwhelms me, brother dearest."

"Let me know when you're ready and I'll help you cart your things over."

"Thanks, Mark."

Briefly he looked up from his meal and grinned. "What are big brothers for?"

Andrew's car was in the apartment parking lot when Jo Marie stepped off the bus that evening after work. The darkening sky convinced her that waiting outside for him to leave would likely result in a drenching. Putting aside her fears, she squared her shoulders and tucked her hands deep within her pockets. When Kelly was home she usually didn't keep the door locked so Jo Marie was surprised to discover that it was. While digging through her purse, she was even more surprised to hear loud voices from the other side of the door.

"This has to stop," Andrew was arguing. "And soon."

"I know," Kelly cried softly. "And I agree. I don't want to ruin anyone's life."

"Three days."

"All right—just until Friday."

Jo Marie made unnecessary noise as she came through the door. "I'm home," she announced as she stepped into the living room. Kelly was dressed in her robe and slippers, slouched on the sofa. Andrew had apparently been pacing the carpet. She could feel his gaze seek her out. But she managed to avoid it, diverting her attention instead to the picture on the wall behind him. "If you'll excuse me I think I'll take a hot shower."

"Friday," Andrew repeated in a low, impatient tone.

"Thank you, Drew," Kelly murmured and sighed softly.

Kelly was in the same position on the sofa when Jo Marie returned, having showered and changed clothes. "How are you feeling?"

"Not good."

For Kelly to admit to as much meant that she'd had a miserable day. "Is there anything I can do?"

Limply, Kelly laid her head back against the back of the couch and closed her eyes. "No, I'm fine. But this is the worst case of stomach flu I can ever remember?"

"You're sure it's the flu?"

Slowly Kelly opened her eyes. "I'm the nurse here."

"Yes, your majesty." With a dramatic twist to her chin, Jo Marie bowed in mock servitude. "Now would you like me to fix you something for dinner?"

"No."

"How about something cool to drink?"

Kelly nodded, but her look wasn't enthusiastic. "Fine."

As the evening progressed, Jo Marie studied her friend carefully. It could be just a bad case of the stomach flu, but Jo Marie couldn't help but be concerned. Kelly had always been so healthy and full of life. When a long series of cramps doubled Kelly over in pain, Jo Marie reached for the phone.

"Mark, can you come over?" She tried to keep the urgency from her voice.

"What's up?"

"It's Kelly. She's sick." Jo Marie attempted to keep her voice low enough so her roommate wouldn't hear. "She keeps insisting it's the flu, but I don't know. She's in a lot of pain for a simple intestinal virus."

Mark didn't hesitate. "I'll be right there."

Ten minutes later he was at the door. He didn't bother to knock, letting himself in. "Where's the patient?"

"Jo Marie." Kelly's round eyes tossed her a look of burning resentment. "You called Mark?"

"Guilty as charged, but I wouldn't have if I didn't think it was necessary."

Tears blurred the blue gaze. "I wish you hadn't," she murmured dejectedly. "It's just the flu."

"Let me be the judge of that." Mark spoke in a crisp professional tone, kneeling at her side. He opened the small black bag and took out the stethoscope.

Not knowing what else to do, Jo Marie hovered at his side for instructions. "Should I boil water or something?"

"Call Drew," Kelly insisted. "He at least won't overreact to a simple case of the flu."

Mark's mouth went taut, but he didn't rise to the intended gibe.

Reluctantly Jo Marie did as she was asked. Andrew answered on the third ring. "Beaumont here."

"Andrew, this is—"

"Jo Marie," he finished for her, his voice carrying a soft rush of pleasure.

"Hi," she began awkwardly and bit into the corner of her bottom lip. "Mark's here. Kelly's not feeling well and I think she may have something serious. She wanted to know if you could come over."

"I'll be there in ten minutes." He didn't take a breath's hesitation.

As it was, he arrived in eight and probably set several speed records in the process. Jo Marie answered his hard knock. "What's wrong with Kelly? She seemed fine this afternoon." He directed his question to Mark.

"I'd like to take Kelly over to the hospital for a couple of tests."

Jo Marie noted the way her brother's jaw had tightened as if being in the same room with Andrew was a test of his endurance. Dislike exuded from every pore.

"No," Kelly protested emphatically. "It's just the stomach flu."

"With the amount of tenderness in the cecum?" Mark argued, shaking his head slowly from side to side in a mocking gesture.

"Mark's the doctor," Andrew inserted and Jo Marie could have kissed him for being the voice of reason in a room where little evidence of it existed.

"You think it's my appendix?" Kelly said with shocked disbelief.

"It isn't going to hurt to run a couple of tests," Mark countered, again avoiding answering a direct question.

"Why should you care?" Kelly's soft voice wavered uncontrollably. "After yesterday I would have thought…"

"After yesterday," Mark cut in sharply, "I realized that you were right and that I owe you an apology." His eyes looked directly into Kelly's and the softness Jo Marie had witnessed in his gaze at the hospital Christmas party returned. He reached for Kelly's hand, folding it in his own. "Will you accept my apology? What you said yesterday made a lot of sense, but at the time I was angry at the world and took it out on you. Forgive me?"

With a trembling smile, Kelly nodded. "Yes, of course I do."

The look they shared was both poignant and tender, causing Jo Marie to feel like an intruder. Briefly, she wondered what Andrew was thinking.

"If it does turn out that I need surgery would you be the one to do it for me?"

Immediately Mark lowered his gaze. "No."

His stark response was cutting and Kelly flinched. "There's no one else I'd trust as much as you."

"I said I wouldn't." Mark pulled the stethoscope from his neck and placed it inside his bag.

"Instead of fighting about it now, why don't we see what happens?" Jo Marie attempted to reason. "There's no need to argue."

"There's every reason," Andrew intervened. "Tell us, Mark, why wouldn't you be Kelly's surgeon if she needed one?"

Jo Marie stared at Andrew, her dark eyes filled with irritation. Backing Mark into a corner wouldn't help the situation. She wanted to step forward and defend her brother, but Andrew stopped her with an abrupt motion of his hand, apparently having read her intent.

"Who I choose as my patients is my business." Mark's tone was dipped in acid.

"Isn't Kelly one of your patients?" Andrew questioned calmly. "You did hurry over here when you heard she was sick."

Coming to a standing position, Mark ignored the question and the man. "Maybe you'd like to change clothes." He directed his comment to Kelly.

Shaking her head she said, "No, I'm not going anywhere."

"Those tests are important." Mark's control on his anger was a fragile thread. "You're going to the hospital."

Again, Kelly shook her head. "No, I'm not."

"You're being unreasonable." Standing with his feet braced apart, Mark looked as if he was willing to take her to the hospital by force if necessary.

"Why not make an agreement," Andrew suggested with cool-headed resolve. "Kelly will agree to the tests, if you agree to be her doctor."

Tiredly, Mark rubbed a hand over his jaw and chin. "I can't do that."

"Why not?" Kelly implored.

"Yes, Mark, why not?" Andrew taunted.

Her brother's mouth thinned grimly as he turned aside and clenched his fists. "Because it isn't good practice to work on the people you're involved with emotionally."

The corners of Kelly's mouth lifted in a sad smile. "We're not emotionally involved. You've gone out of your way to prove that to me. If you have any emotion for me it would be hate."

Mark's face went white and it looked for an instant as if Kelly had physically struck him. "Hate you?" he repeated incredulously. "Maybe," he replied in brutal honesty. "You're able to bring out every other emotion in me. I've taken out a lot of anger on you recently. Most of which you didn't deserve and I apologize for that." He paused and ran a hand through his hair, mussing it. "No, Kelly," he corrected, "I can't hate you. It would be impossible when I love you so much," he announced with an impassive expression and pivoted sharply.

A tense silence engulfed the room until Kelly let out a small cry. "You love me? All these months you've put me through this torment and you love me?" She threw back the blanket and stood, placing her hands defiantly on her hips.

"A lot of good it did me." Mark's angry gaze crossed the width of the room to hold hers. "You're engaged to

Daddy Warbucks over there so what good would it do to let you know?"

Jo Marie couldn't believe what she was hearing and gave a nervous glance to Andrew. Casually standing to the side of the room, he didn't look the least disturbed by what was happening. If anything, his features were relaxed as if he were greatly relieved.

"And if you cared for me then why didn't you say something before now?" Kelly challenged.

Calmly he met her fiery gaze. "Because he's got money, you've got money. Tell me what can I offer you that could even come close to the things he can give you."

"And you relate love and happiness with things?" Her low words were scathing. "Let me tell you exactly what you can offer me, Mark Jubal Early. You have it in your power to give me the things that matter most in my life: your love, your friendship, your respect. And…and… if you turn around and walk out that door, by heaven I'll never forgive you."

"I have no intention of leaving," Mark snapped in return. "But I can't very well ask you to marry me when you're wearing another man's ring."

"Fine." Without hesitating Kelly slipped Andrew's diamond from her ring finger and handed it back to him. Lightly she brushed her mouth over his cheeks. "Thanks, Drew."

His hands cupped her shoulders as he kissed her back. "Much happiness, Kelly," he whispered.

Brother and sister observed the scene with open-mouthed astonishment.

Turning, Kelly moved to Mark's side. "Now," she breathed in happily, "if that was a proposal, I accept."

Mark was apparently too stunned to answer.

"Don't tell me you've already changed your mind?" Kelly muttered.

"No, I haven't changed my mind. What about the hospital tests?" he managed finally, his voice slightly raw as his eyes devoured her.

"Give me a minute to change." Kelly left the room and the three were left standing, Jo Marie and Mark staring blankly at each other. Everything was happening so fast that it was like a dream with dark shades of unreality.

Kelly reappeared and Mark tucked her arm in his. "We should be back in an hour," Mark murmured, but he only had eyes for the pert-faced woman on his arm. Kelly's gaze was filled with a happy radiance that brought tears of shared happiness to Jo Marie's eyes.

"Take your time and call if you need us," Andrew said as the happy couple walked toward the door.

Jo Marie doubted that either Kelly or Mark heard him. When she turned her attention to Andrew she discovered that he was already walking toward her. With eager strides he eliminated the distance separating them.

"As I recall, our agreement was that I wouldn't try to see you or contact you again while Kelly wore my engagement ring."

Her dark eyes smiled happily into his. "That's right."

"Then let's be rid of this thing once and for all." He led her into the kitchen where he carelessly tossed the diamond ring into the garbage.

Jo Marie gasped. Andrew was literally throwing

away thousands of dollars. The diamond was the largest she had ever seen.

"The ring is as phony as the engagement."

Still unable to comprehend what he was saying, she shook her head to clear her thoughts. "What?"

"The engagement isn't any more real than that so-called diamond."

"Why?" Reason had escaped her completely.

His hands brought Jo Marie into the loving circle of his arms. "By Thanksgiving I'd given up every hope of ever finding you again. I'd convinced myself that those golden moments were just a figment of my imagination and that some quirk of fate had brought us together, only to pull us apart."

It seemed the most natural thing in the world to have his arms around her. Her eyes had filled with moisture so that his features swam in and out of her vision. "I'd given up hope of finding you, too," she admitted in an achingly soft voice. "But I couldn't stop thinking about you."

Tenderly he kissed her, briefly tasting the sweetness of her lips. As if it was difficult to stop, he drew in an uneven breath and rubbed his jaw over the top of her head, mussing her hair. "I saw Kelly at her parents' house over the Thanksgiving holiday and she was miserable. We've always been close for second cousins and we had a long talk. She told me that she'd been in love with Mark for months. The worst part was that she was convinced that he shared her feelings, but his pride was holding him back. Apparently your brother has some strange ideas about wealth and position."

"He's learning," Jo Marie murmured, still caught

in the rapture of being in Andrew's arms. "Give him time." She said this knowing that Kelly was willing to devote the rest of her life to Mark.

"I told Kelly she should give him a little competition and if someone showed an interested in her, then Mark would step forward. But apparently she'd already tried that."

"My brother can be as stubborn as ten men."

"I'm afraid I walked into this phony engagement with my eyes wide open. I said that if Mark was worth his salt, he wouldn't stand by and let her marry another man. If he loved her, really loved her, he'd step in."

"But he nearly didn't."

"No," Andrew admitted. "I was wrong. Mark loved Kelly enough to sacrifice his own desires to give her what he thought she needed. I realized that the night of my Christmas party. By that time I was getting desperate. I'd found you and every minute of this engagement was agony. In desperation, I tried to talk to Mark. But that didn't work. He assumed I was warning him off Kelly and told me to make her happy or I'd pay the consequences."

The irony of the situation was almost comical. "You were already suffering the consequences. Why didn't you say something? Why didn't you explain?"

"Oh, love, if you'd been anyone but Mark's sister I would have." Again his mouth sought hers as if he couldn't get enough of her kisses. "Here I was trapped in the worst set of circumstances I've ever imagined. The woman who had haunted me for months was within my grasp and I was caught in a steel web."

"I love you, Andrew. I've loved you from the moment you held me all those months ago. I knew then that you were meant to be someone special in my life."

"This has taught me the most valuable lesson of my life." He arched her close. So close it was impossible to breath normally. "I'll never let you out of my arms again. I'm yours for life, Jo Marie, whether you want me or not. I've had to trust again every instinct that you would wait for me. Dear Lord, I had visions of you falling in love with Jim Rowden, and the worst part was I couldn't blame you if you did. I can only imagine what kind of man you thought me."

Lovingly, Jo Marie spread kisses over his face. "It's going to take me a lifetime to tell you."

"Oh, love." His grip tightened against the back of her waist, arching her closer until it was almost painful to breathe. Not that Jo Marie cared. Andrew was holding her and had promised never to let her go again.

"I knew something was wrong with you and Kelly from the beginning," she murmured between soft, exploring kisses. Jo Marie couldn't have helped but notice.

"I've learned so much from this," Andrew confessed. "I think I was going slowly mad. I want more than to share my life with you, Jo Marie. I want to see our children in your arms. I want to grow old with you at my side."

"Oh, Andrew." Her arms locked around his neck and the tears of happiness streamed down her face.

"I love you, Florence Nightingale."

"And you, Andrew Beaumont, will always be my dream man."

"Forever?" His look was skeptical.

She lifted her mouth to his. "For all eternity," she whispered in promise.

* * *

"An ulcer?" Jo Marie shook her head slowly.

"Well, with all the stress I was under in the past few weeks, it's little wonder," Kelly defended herself.

The four sat in the living room sipping hot cocoa. Kelly was obediently drinking plain heated milk and hating it. But her eyes were warm and happy as they rested on Mark who was beside her with an arm draped over her shoulders.

"I've felt terrible about all this, Jo Marie," Kelly continued. "Guilt is a horrible companion. I didn't know exactly what was going on with you and Andrew. But he let it be known that he was in love with you and wanted this masquerade over quickly."

"You felt guilty?" Mark snorted. "How do you think I felt kissing another man's fiancée?"

"About the same way Jo Marie and I felt," Andrew returned with a chuckle.

"You know, Beaumont. Now that you're marrying my sister, I don't think you're such a bad character after all."

"That's encouraging."

"I certainly hope you get along since you're both going to be standing at the altar at the same time."

Three pairs of blank eyes stared at Kelly. "Double wedding, silly. It makes sense, doesn't it? The four of us have been through a lot together. It's only fitting we start our new lives at the same time."

"But soon," Mark said emphatically. "Sometime in January."

Everything was moving so fast, Jo Marie barely had

time to assimilate the fact that Andrew loved her and she was going to share his life.

"Why not?" she agreed with a small laugh. "We've yet to do anything else conventionally."

Her eyes met Andrew's. They'd come a long way, all four of them, but they'd stuck it out through the doubts and the hurts. Now their whole lives stretched before them filled with promise.

* * * * *